Dear Reader,

I'm delighted to welcome you to a very special Bestselling Author Collection for 2024! In celebration of Harlequin's 75 years in publishing, this collection features fan-favorite stories from some of our readers' most cherished authors. Each book also includes a free full-length story by an exciting writer from one of our current programs.

Our company has grown and changed since its inception 75 years ago. Today, Harlequin publishes more than 100 titles a month in 30 countries and 15 languages, with stories for a diverse readership across a range of genres and formats, including hardcover, trade paperback, mass-market paperback, ebook and audiobook.

But our commitment to you, our romance reader, remains the same: in every Harlequin romance, a guaranteed happily-ever-after!

Thank you for coming on this journey with us. And happy reading as we embark on the next 75 years of bringing joy to readers around the world!

Dianne Moggy

Vice-President, Editorial

Harlequin

T0197854

Susan Mallery is the #1 *New York Times* bestselling author of novels about the relationships that shape women's lives—family, friendship and romance. Her warm, humorous stories make the world a happier place to live. Readers seem to agree—forty million copies of her books have been sold worldwide. A California native, Susan lives in Seattle with her husband and their much-loved pets, a ragdoll cat and an adorable poodle. Visit Susan online at susanmallery.com.

Jill Kemerer writes novels with love, humor and faith. Besides spoiling her mini dachshund and keeping up with her busy kids, Jill reads stacks of books, lives for her morning coffee and gushes over fluffy animals. She resides in Ohio with her husband and two children. Jill loves connecting with readers, so please visit her website, jillkemerer.com, or contact her at PO Box 2802, Whitehouse, OH 43571.

STILL THE ONE

#1 *NEW YORK TIMES* BESTSELLING AUTHOR
SUSAN MALLERY

Previously published as *Good Husband Material*

Harlequin

BESTSELLING AUTHOR COLLECTION

 **Harlequin®**
BESTSELLING
AUTHOR
COLLECTION

Recycling programs
for this product may
not exist in your area.

ISBN-13: 978-1-335-14758-5

Still the One
First published as Good Husband Material in 2002.
This edition published in 2024.
Copyright © 2002 by Susan Mallery, Inc.

Hometown Hero's Redemption
First published in 2017.
This edition published in 2024.
Copyright © 2017 by Jill Kemerer

 Harlequin Enterprises ULC
22 Adelaide St. West, 41st Floor
Toronto, Ontario M5H 4E3, Canada
www.Harlequin.com

Printed in U.S.A.

CONTENTS

STILL THE ONE

Susan Mallery

Chapter One

Kari Asbury fully expected to have trouble cashing her out-of-state check, she just didn't think she would have to put her life on the line to do it.

It wasn't just that the check was drawn from a bank in big, bad New York City; it was that her driver's license was also from that East Coast state. Ida Mae Montel would want to know why a girl born and raised in Possum Landing, Texas, would willingly run off to a place like that...a place with *Yankees*. And if a girl had to do such a thing, why on earth would she give up her Texas driver's license? Didn't everyone want to be from the Lone Star State?

No doubt Sue Ellen Boudine, the bank manager, would mosey on over to examine the check, all the while holding it like it was attached to a poisonous snake. They'd make a few calls (probably to friends, letting them know that Kari was back in town and with a New York driver's license, of all things), they'd hem and haw, and sigh heavily. Then they'd give Kari the money. Oh, but first they'd try to talk her into opening an account right there at the First Bank of Possum Landing.

Kari hesitated in front of the double glass doors, trying to figure out if she really needed the cash that badly. Maybe it would be better to pay the service fee and get the money out of the ATM machine. Then she reminded herself that the quicker everyone realized she'd returned to town for a very *temporary* visit, the quicker all the questions would be asked and answered. Then maybe she could have a little peace. Maybe.

There was the added thrill of finding out if Ida Mae still wore her hair in a beehive. How much hair spray did that upswept style require? Kari knew for a fact that Ida Mae only had her hair done once a week, yet it looked exactly the same on day seven as it did on day one.

Still smiling at the memory of Ida Mae's coiffure, she pulled open the door and stepped inside. She paused just past the threshold and waited for the shrieks of welcome and the group hug that would follow.

Nothing happened.

Kari frowned. She glanced around at the bank established in 1892—taking in the tall, narrow windows, the real wood counters and stylish paneling. Ida Mae was in her regular spot—the first position on the left—as befitted the head teller. But the older woman wasn't talking. She wasn't even smiling. Her small eyes widened with something that looked like panic, and she made an odd gesture with her hand.

Before Kari could figure out what it meant, something hard and cold pressed against her cheek.

"Well, lookee here. We got us another customer, boys. At least this one's young and pretty. What my mama used to call a tall drink of water. That's something."

Kari's heart stopped. It might be nearly ninety in

the shade outside, but here in the bank it felt closer to absolute zero.

Slowly, very slowly, she turned toward the man, who was holding a gun. He was short, stocky and wearing a ski mask. What on earth was going on?

"We're robbin' the bank," the man said, as if he could read her mind.

His astuteness startled her, until she realized his deduction wasn't much of a stretch.

She quickly glanced around. There were four of them, counting the man holding a gun on her. Two kept all the customers and most of the employees together at the far end of the bank, while the last one was behind the counter, putting money that Ida Mae handed him into a bag.

"You go ahead and set your purse on the floor," the man in front of her said. "Then start walking toward the other ladies. Do what you're told and no one will get hurt."

Kari flexed her hands slightly. Her chest tightened, and it was nearly impossible to speak. "I, uh, I don't have a purse."

She didn't. She'd come into the bank with a check and her driver's license. Both were in the back pocket of her shorts.

The robber stared at her for a couple of seconds, then nodded. "Seems you don't. Now head on over there."

This couldn't be happening, Kari thought, even as she headed for the cluster of other customers huddled by the far end of the counter.

She was halfway to the safety of that crowd when the rear door of the bank opened.

"Well, hell," a low voice drawled. "One of us has bad timing, boys. You think it's you or me?"

Several women screamed. One of the masked men by the crowd grabbed an older woman and held the gun to her head. "Stay back," he yelled. "Stay back or the old lady dies."

Kari didn't have time to react. The man who had first held a gun to her jerked her arm to drag her back to him. She felt the pressure of the pistol against her cheek again. He wrapped one wiry arm around her neck, keeping her securely in place.

"Seems to me we've got a problem," the man holding her said. "So, Sheriff, why don't you just back out real slow and no one will get hurt."

The sheriff in question gave a sigh of the long-suffering. "I wish I could do that. But I can't. Want to know why?"

Kari felt as if she'd slipped into an alternative universe. This couldn't be happening to her. One second she'd been too scared to breathe, and the next, Gage Reynolds had walked back into her life. Right in the middle of a holdup.

Eight years ago he'd been a young deputy, tall and handsome in his khaki uniform. He was still good-looking enough to make an angel want to sin. He was also the sheriff, if the gleaming badge on his shirt pocket was to be believed. But for a man of the law, he didn't seem all that interested in the robbery going on right in front of him.

He took off his dust-colored cowboy hat and slapped it against his thigh. His dark hair gleamed, as did the interest in his eyes.

"Don't make me kill her," the gunman said, his tone low and controlled.

"You know who you've got there, son?" Gage asked

casually, almost as if he hadn't figured out what was going on in the bank. "That's Kari Asbury."

"Back off, Sheriff."

The robber pressed the gun in a little deeper. Kari winced. Gage didn't seem to notice.

"She's the one who got away."

Kari could smell the criminal's sweat. She was willing to bet he hadn't planned on a hostage situation, and the fact he might be in over his head didn't make her breathe any easier. What on earth was Gage going on about?

"That's right," Gage continued, setting his hat on a table and stretching. "Eight years ago, that pretty lady there left me standing at the altar."

Despite the gun jammed into her cheek, Kari spluttered with indignation. "I did *not* leave you standing at the altar. We weren't even engaged."

"Maybe. But you knew I was gonna ask, and you took off. That's practically the same thing. Don't you think?"

He asked the last question of the robber, who actually considered before replying.

"If you hadn't really proposed, then she didn't leave you at the altar."

"Fair enough, but she *did* stand me up for the prom."

Kari couldn't believe it. Except for her grandmother's funeral seven years ago, she hadn't seen Gage since the afternoon of her high school prom. While she'd known that Possum Landing was small enough that they would eventually run into each other again, this wasn't exactly what she'd had in mind.

"It was complicated," she said, unable to believe she was being forced to defend herself in front of bank robbers.

"Did you or did you not skip town without warning? You left nothing but a note, Kari. You played with my heart like it was a football."

The bank robber glared at her. "That wasn't very nice."

She glared right back. "I was eighteen years old, okay? I apologized in the note."

"I've never gotten over it," Gage said, emotional pain oozing from every pore. He reached into his breast pocket and pulled out a package of gum. "You see before you a broken man."

Kari resisted the urge to roll her eyes. She didn't know what Gage's game was, but she wished he would play it with someone else.

Her confusion turned to outrage when Gage took a stick of gum for himself, then offered the pack to the bank robber. Next they would be going out for a beer together.

Gage watched the anger flash in Kari's eyes. If she could have spit fire, he would be a scorched stick figure right about now. In different circumstances, Gage might have worried the issue, but not now.

The gunman shook off the gum, but that wasn't important. The gesture had been made and well received. Gage had established rapport.

"She went on up to New York City," Gage continued, tucking the gum package back into his breast pocket. "Wanted to be a fashion model."

The robber studied Kari, then shrugged. "She's pretty enough, but if she's back, then she didn't make it."

Gage sighed heavily again. "I guess not. All that pain and suffering for nothing."

Kari stiffened at his words, but didn't try to break away. Gage willed her to cooperate for just a few more seconds. While every instinct in his body screamed at him to jerk her free of the gunman, he forced himself to stay relaxed and focused. There were more people to protect than just Kari. Between the bank employees and the customers there were fifteen innocent citizens within the old walls. Fifteen unprepared folk and four men with guns. Gage didn't like the odds.

Using his peripheral vision, he checked on the progress of the tactical team circling around the building. Just another minute or two and they would be in place.

"You want me to shoot her?" the gunman asked. Kari gasped. Her big blue eyes widened even more, and the color drained from her face.

Gage chewed his gum for a second, then shrugged. "You know, that's mighty neighborly of you, but I think I'd rather deal with her in my own way, in my own time."

The team was nearly in place. Gage's heart was about to jump out of his chest, but he gave no outward sign. Another few seconds, he thought. Another—

"Hey, look!" One of the robbers near the back turned suddenly. Everyone looked. A tactical team member dropped out of sight a moment too late. The gunman holding Kari snarled in rage.

"Dammit all to hell and back." But that's all he got to say.

Gage lunged forward. He jerked Kari free, yelled at her to get down on the floor, then planted a booted foot firmly in the robber's midsection.

The bad guy gave a yelp of dismay as all the air rushed out of his lungs and he fell flat on his ass. He scooted a couple of feet backward, but by the time he sucked in a breath, two armed tactical team members had guns on him.

But they weren't as quick to capture the man by Ida Mae. A gunshot exploded.

Gage reacted without thinking. He turned and threw himself over Kari, covering her body with his.

A half-dozen or so rounds were fired. He pulled out his sidearm, looking for targets, and kept his free arm over Kari's face.

"Don't move," he growled in her ear. "I can't," she gasped back.

After what felt like a lifetime, but was probably just seconds, a man called out. "I give, I give. You shot me."

There were muffled sounds, then a steady voice yelled, "Clear."

Five more "clear"s followed. Gage rolled off Kari and glanced around to check on the town folk. Everyone was fine—even Ida Mae, who had kicked the wounded gunman after she climbed to her feet. The leader of the tactical team walked over and stared down at Gage. He was covered in black from head to toe, with a visor over his face and enough firepower to take Cuba.

"I can't figure out if you were a damn fool or especially brave for walking in on a bank robbery in progress," the man said.

Gage sat up and grinned. "Someone had to do it, and I figured none of your boys was going to volunteer. Plus we know these were small-town criminals. They're used to seeing someone like me around. One of you all dressed in the Darth Vader clothes would have scared 'em into acting like fools. Someone could have gotten killed."

The man nodded. "If you ever get tired of small-town life, you'd be a fine addition to our team."

Gage didn't even consider his offer. "I'm flattered," he said easily, "but I'm right where I want to be."

The man nodded and walked off. "You knew they were there."

He turned and saw Kari staring at him. She still lay on the ground. Her once long blond hair had been cut short and stylish. Makeup accentuated her already big, beautiful blue eyes. Time had sculpted her face into something even more lovely than he remembered.

"The tactical team?" he asked. "Sure. They were circling the building."

"So I wasn't in danger?"

"Kari, a criminal was holding a gun to your head. I wouldn't say that ever qualifies as safe."

She smiled then. A slow, sexy smile that he still remembered. Lordy but she'd been a looker back then. Time hadn't changed that.

He suddenly became aware of the adrenaline pouring through his body. And the fact that he hadn't had sex in far too long. Eight years ago, he and Kari had never gotten around to that particular pleasure. He wondered if she would be more open to the experience now.

He got to his feet. If she was back in Possum Landing for any length of time, he would be sure to find out.

"Welcome back," he said, and held out his hand to help her up.

She placed her fingers against his palm. "Jeez, Gage, if you wanted to find a unique way to welcome me home, couldn't you just have held a parade?"

* * *

"You can go now, Ms. Asbury," the wiry detective said nearly four hours later.

Kari sighed in relief. She'd given her statement, been questioned, been fed and watered, and now she was finally free to head home. As far as she could tell, there were only a couple of problems. The first was that her heart refused to return to normal. Every time she thought about what had happened in the bank, her chest felt as if it were filled with thundering horse hooves. The second problem was that she had walked to the bank, a scant mile or so from her house, but the sheriff's station was clear on the other side of town. It was summer in the middle of Texas, which meant billion-degree heat and humidity to match.

"Do you think I could have a ride home?" she asked. "Or is Willy still running a cab around these parts?"

The detective gave her a once-over, then grinned. "Wish I could take you home myself. Unfortunately I have more work to do. I'll get one of the deputies to take you."

Kari smiled her thanks. When she was alone, she glanced out of the glass-enclosed office. Just looking around, she told herself. She wasn't actually looking for someone specific. Certainly not Gage.

But like a bee heading for the sweetest flower, she found herself settling her gaze on him. He was across the large office, still in a glass room of his own, chatting with some members of the federal tactical team. Were they trying to talk him into leaving Possum Landing to join them? Kari shook her head. She might have been gone for eight years, but some things never changed. Gage Reynolds would no more leave Possum Landing than NASA would send Ida Mae up in the next space shuttle.

She watched as Gage spoke and the other men laughed. Time had honed him into a hard man, she thought. Hard in a good way—with thick muscles and a steady set to his face. Despite the fact that she'd been there when it happened, she couldn't believe that he'd actually walked into a bank robbery. On purpose! He'd been calm and cool and he'd about made her crazy.

The detective strolled back into the office. "Ms. Asbury, if you'll wait by the front desk, the deputy will be with you in a couple of minutes."

She smiled her thanks and followed him out to the waiting area. Ida Mae sat there, her hands folded primly on her lap. When she saw Kari, her wrinkled face broke out into a welcoming smile. "Kari."

The older woman rose and held out her arms. Kari moved forward and accepted the hug. Everything about it was familiar—Ida Mae's bony arms, her beehive hairdo with not a hair out of place, the scent of the gardenia perfume she always wore.

"You're looking fine, child," Ida Mae said as she released Kari and sank back onto the bench.

Kari settled next to her. "You haven't changed a bit," she said, then patted her hand. "Are you all right?"

Ida Mae touched her chest. "I thought I was gonna have a heart attack right there in the middle of the bank. I couldn't believe my own eyes when those boys pulled guns on us. Then you walked in and it was like seeing a ghost. And then Gage strolled in. Wasn't he brave?"

"Absolutely," Kari agreed. She wasn't sure she could have knowingly walked in on a bank robbery, regardless of who was at risk. But Gage had always believed in doing what was right.

Ida Mae gave her a knowing look. "He's still a handsome devil, too, don't you think? Is he taller than when you left?"

Kari wanted to roll her eyes, but figured she was getting a little old for that particular response. Fortunately, Ida Mae was on a tear and didn't require an answer.

"No one knew you were coming back," the older woman said. "Of course, we knew you'd have to eventually, what with you still owning your grandma's house and all. I can tell you, tongues wagged when you left town all those years ago. Poor Gage. You about broke his heart. Of course, you were young and you had to follow your dreams. It's just too bad that your dreams didn't include him."

Kari didn't know what to say. Her heart had been broken, too, but she didn't want to get into that. The past was the past. At least, that's what she told herself, even though she didn't actually believe it.

Ida Mae smiled. "It's good that you're back."

Kari sighed softly. "Ida Mae, I'm not back. I'm just here for the summer." Then she was going to shake the dust from this small town off her shoes and never look back.

"Uh-huh." Ida Mae didn't look convinced. Fortunately the deputy arrived just then. Kari asked Ida Mae if she needed a ride home, as well.

"No, no. My Nelson is probably waiting out front for me. I called him just before you walked out."

Led by the deputy, they headed out the front door and down the three steps to the sidewalk. By the time she saw that Nelson was indeed waiting for his wife,

Kari had broken out into a sweat and was having trouble breathing in the heat.

"Little Kari Asbury," Nelson said as he approached. He grinned at her as he mopped his forehead with a handkerchief. "You're all grown up."

Kari smiled.

"Didn't she turn out pretty?" Ida Mae said fondly. "But then, you were always a lovely girl. You should have entered the Miss Texas pageant. You could have gone far with a title like that."

Kari smiled weakly. "It was very nice to see you both," she said politely, then headed toward the squad car that the deputy had pulled around.

"Gage has had a couple of close calls," Nelson called after her, "but no one's gotten him down the aisle."

Kari waved by way of response. She wasn't going to touch that particular topic.

"Good to have you back," Nelson yelled louder.

This one Kari couldn't resist. She turned toward the older man and shook her head. "I'm not back."

Nelson only waved.

"Just perfect," she muttered as she climbed into the car with the deputy. He'd told her his name, but she'd already forgotten it. Probably because he looked so impossibly young. She was only twenty-six, but next to this guy she felt ancient.

She gave him her address and leaned back against the seat, breathing in the air-conditioned coolness. There were a thousand and one details to occupy her mind, yet instead of dealing with them, she found herself remembering the first time she'd met Gage. She'd been all of seventeen and he'd been twenty-three. At the time, he'd seemed so much older and more mature.

"I know this is a crazy question," she said, glancing at the young man next to her. "But how old are you?"

He was blond, with blue eyes and pale cheeks. He gave her a startled glance. "Twenty-three."

"Oh."

The same age Gage had been eight years ago. That didn't seem possible. If Gage had been as young as this guy, Kari shouldn't have had any trouble standing up to him. Why had she found it so incredibly difficult to share her feelings while they'd been dating? Why had the thought of telling him the truth terrified her?

There wasn't an easy answer to the question, and before she could come up with a hard one, they arrived at her house.

Kari thanked the deputy and stepped out into the late afternoon. In front of her stood the old house where she'd grown up. It had been built in the forties, and had a wide porch and gabled windows. Different colored versions of the same house sat all along the street, including the home next door. She glanced at it, wondering when she would have her next run-in with her neighbor. As if returning to Possum Landing for the summer wasn't complicated enough, Gage Reynolds now lived next door.

Kari walked inside her grandmother's house and stood in the main parlor. Never a living room, she thought with a smile. It was a parlor, where people "set" when it wasn't nice enough to settle on the front porch. She remembered countless hours spent listening to her grandmother's friends talking about everything from who was pregnant to who was cheating on whom.

She'd arrived after dark last night. She hadn't turned on many lights after she'd come in, and somehow she'd convinced herself that the house was different. Only now, she saw it wasn't.

The old sofas were the same, as was the horsehair chair her grandmother had inherited from *her* grandmother. Kari had always hated that piece—it was both slick and uncomfortable. Now she touched the antique and felt the memories wash over her.

Maybe it was the result of all the emotions from the robbery, maybe it was just the reality of being home. Either way, she suddenly sensed the ghosts in the house. At least they were friendly, she told herself as she moved into the old kitchen. Her grandmother had always loved her.

Kari looked at the pecan cabinets and the stove and oven unit that had to be at least thirty years old. If she expected to get a decent price for the old place, she would have to do some serious updating. That was the reason she'd come home for the summer, after all.

A restlessness filled her. She hurried upstairs and changed out of her clothes. After showering, she slipped on a cotton dress and padded back downstairs barefoot. She toured the house, almost as if she were waiting for something to happen.

And then it did.

There was a knock on the door. She didn't have to answer it to know who had come calling. Her stomach lurched and her heart took up that thundering hoof dance again. She drew in a deep breath and reached for the handle.

Chapter Two

Gage stood on Kari's front porch. She didn't bother pretending to be surprised. Her time with him in the bank had been too rushed and too emotionally charged for her to notice much about his appearance…and how he might have changed. But now that they were in a more normal situation, she could take the time to appreciate how he'd filled out in the years she'd been away.

He looked taller than she remembered. Or maybe he was just bigger. Regardless, he was very much a man now. Still too good-looking for her peace of mind. He appealed to her, but, then, he always had.

"If you're inviting me to attend another bank robbery," she said with a smile, "I'm going to have to pass."

Gage grinned and held up both hands. "No more crime…not if I can prevent it." He leaned against the door frame. "The reason I stopped by was to make sure that you were all right after all the excitement today. Plus, I knew you'd want to thank me for saving your life by inviting me to dinner."

She tilted her head as she considered him. "What if my husband objects?"

He didn't even have the grace to look the least bit worried. "You're not married. Ida Mae keeps track of these things, and she would have told me."

"Figures." She stepped back to allow him inside. Gage moved into the front room while she closed the door behind him. "What makes you think I've had time to go to the grocery store?" she asked.

"If you haven't, I have a couple of steaks in the freezer. I could get those out."

She shook her head. "Actually, I did my shopping this morning. That's the reason I ran out of cash and had to go get more at the bank." She frowned. "Come to think of it, I never did cash that check."

"You can do it tomorrow."

"I guess I'll have to."

She led the way into the kitchen. Having him here was strange, she thought. An odd blending of past and present. How many times had he come over for dinner eight years ago? Her grandmother had always welcomed him at their table. Kari had been so in love that she'd been thrilled he'd wanted to spend mealtimes with her. Of course, she'd been young enough to be excited even if all he wanted was for her to keep him company while he washed his car. All she'd needed to be happy was a few hours in Gage's presence. Life had been a whole lot simpler in those days.

He leaned against a counter and sniffed. "That smells mighty good. And familiar."

"Grandmother's sauce recipe. I put it in the slow cooker this morning, right after I got back from the grocery store. I also got out the old bread maker, but as it's been gathering dust forever, I can't promise it'll all work."

His dark gaze settled on her. "It works just fine." His words made her break out in goose bumps, which was crazy. He was a smooth-talking good-ol' boy from Possum Landing. She lived in New York City. No way Gage Reynolds should be able to get to her. And he didn't. Not really.

"Did you get all the paperwork wrapped up, or whatever it was you had to do after the robbery?" she asked as she checked on the pasta sauce.

"Everything is tied up in a neat package." He crossed to the kitchen table and picked up the bottle of wine she'd left there.

"Kari Asbury, is this liquor? Have you brought the devil's brew into our saintly dry county?"

She glanced up and chuckled. "You know it. I remembered there weren't any liquor sales allowed around here and figured I had better bring my own. I stopped on my way over from the airport."

"I'm shocked. Completely shocked."

She grinned. "So you probably don't want to know that there's beer in the refrigerator."

"Not at all." He opened the door and pulled out a bottle. When he offered it to her, she shook her head.

"I'll wait for wine with dinner."

He opened the drawer with the bottle opener in it on the first try. Gage moved around with the ease of someone familiar with the place. But then, he *had* been. He'd moved in next door, the spring before her senior year. She remembered watching him carry in boxes and pieces of furniture. Her grandmother had told her who he was—the new deputy. Gage Reynolds. He'd been in the army and had traveled the world. To her seventeen-year-old eyes, a young man of twenty-three had seemed impossibly grown-up and mature. When they'd started dating that fall, he'd seemed a man of the world and she'd been— "Are we still neighbors?" she asked, turning back to face him.

"I'm still next door."

She thought of Ida Mae's comment that Gage had never made it to the altar. Somehow he'd managed to not get caught. Looking at him now, his khaki uniform emphasizing the breadth of his shoulders and the muscles in his legs, she wondered how the lovely ladies of Possum Landing had managed to keep from trapping him.

Not her business, she reminded herself. She checked the timer on the bread machine and saw there was still fifteen minutes to go, plus cooling time.

"Let's go into the parlor," she said. "We'll be more comfortable."

He nodded and led the way.

As she followed him, she found her gaze drifting lower, to his rear. She nearly stumbled in shock. What on earth was wrong with her? She didn't ever stare at men's butts. Nothing about them had ever seemed overly interesting. Until now.

She sighed. Obviously, living next door to Gage was going to be more complicated than she'd realized.

He settled into a wing chair, while she took the sofa. Gage drank some of his beer, then put the bottle on a crocheted coaster and leaned back. He should have looked awkward and out of place in this fussy, feminine room, but he didn't. Perhaps because he'd always been comfortable anywhere.

"What are you thinking?" he asked.

"That you look at home in my grandmother's house."

"I spent a lot of time here," he reminded her. "Even after you left, she and I stayed close."

She didn't want to think about that…about the confidences that might have been shared.

Gage studied her face. "You've changed."

She wasn't sure if he meant the comment in a good way or a bad way. "It's been a long time."

"I never thought you'd come back."

It was the second time in less than three hours that someone had mentioned her being back. "I'm not back," she clarified. "At least, not for anything permanent."

Gage didn't look surprised by her statement, nor did he seem to take issue with her defensive tone. "So why are you suddenly here? It's been seven years since your grandmother died."

Her temper faded as quickly as it had flared. She sighed. "I want to fix up the house so I can sell it. I'm just here for the summer while I do that."

He nodded without saying anything. She had the uncomfortable sense of having been judged and found wanting. Which wasn't fair. Gage wasn't the type of man to judge people without just cause. So her need to squirm in her seat had nothing to do with him and everything to do with her own state of mind.

Rather than deal with personal inadequacies that were probably better left unexplored in public, she changed the subject. "I can't believe there was a bank robbery right here in Possum Landing. It's going to be the talk of the town for weeks."

"Probably. But it wasn't that much of a surprise."

"I can't believe that. Things couldn't have changed that much."

He nodded. "We're still just a bump in the road, with

plenty of small-town problems, but nothing even close to big-city crime. These boys were working their way across the state, robbing hometown banks. I'd been keeping track of their progress, figuring they'd get here sooner or later. Four days ago, the feds came calling. They wanted to set up a sting. I didn't have a problem with that. We talked to everyone at the bank, marked a drawer full of money, then waited for the hit to take place."

Kari couldn't believe it. "All that excitement right here, and I was in the thick of it."

Gage narrowed his eyes. "As you saw, things got out of hand. I don't know if those robbers got lazy or cocky, but this time, they decided to hold up the bank while there were still customers inside. Previ— ously they'd waited until just before the doors were locked for the day, to go in."

"So you weren't expecting to deal with a hostage situation?"

"No one was. The feds wanted to wait it out, but those were my people inside. Someone had to do something."

She turned that thought over in her mind. "So you just waltzed inside to distract them?"

"It seemed like the easiest way to get the job done. Plus, I wanted to be there to make sure no one went crazy and got shot. At least, no one from here. I don't much care about the criminals."

Of course. In Gage's mind, they had brought the situation upon themselves. He wouldn't take responsibility for their coming to Possum Landing to hold up a bank in the first place.

"I have to agree with the federal officer," she said. "I don't know if you were brave or stupid."

He smiled. "You could probably make a case for either point of view." He took another drink of his beer. "You know that I wasn't really mad at you. I was trying to distract that one guy so he didn't take you hostage."

She shivered at the memory of the gun held to her head. "It took me a few minutes to catch on to what you were doing."

But that didn't stop her from wondering how much of what he had said was true. Did Gage really think she was the one who got away?

Did she want to be?

Once she easily would have said yes. Back before she'd left town, Gage had been her entire world. She would have thrown herself in front of a moving train if he'd asked. She'd loved him with all the crazy devotion a teenager was capable of. That had been the trouble—she'd loved him too much. When she'd figured out there were problems, she hadn't known how to deal with them. So she'd run. When he hadn't come after her, he'd confirmed her greatest fear in the world…that he hadn't loved her at all.

They spent all of dinner talking about mutual friends. Gage brought her up to date on various weddings, divorces and births.

"I can't believe Sally has twins," Kari said, as they moved to the porch and sat on the wooden swing.

"Two girls. I told Bob he has his work cut out for him once they become teenagers."

"Fortunately that's a long way off."

Kari set her glass of wine on the dusty, peeling table beside the swing and leaned back to look up at the sky. It might be after dark, but it was still plenty hot and humid. She could feel her dress sticking to her skin. Her head felt funny—fuzzy, heavy and more than a little out of sync. No doubt it was due to the combination of the fear she'd experienced earlier in the day and a little too much wine with dinner. She didn't normally allow herself more than half a glass on special occasions, but tonight she and Gage had nearly split the bottle.

Gage stretched out his long legs. He didn't seem bothered by the wine. No doubt his additional body mass helped, not to mention the fact that he wouldn't have spent the past several years trying to maintain an unnaturally thin body.

"Tell me about life in New York," he said.

"There isn't much to tell," she admitted, wondering if she should be pleased or worried that he'd finally asked her a vaguely personal question. "When I arrived, I found out that small-town girls who had been told they were pretty enough to be a model were spilling out of every modeling agency within a thirty-mile radius. The competition was tough and the odds of making it into the big time were close to zero."

"You did okay."

She glanced at him, not sure if he was assuming or if he actually knew. "After the first year or so, I got work. Eventually I made enough to support myself and pay for college. As of last month, I have teaching credentials, which is what I always wanted."

Gage glanced at her. "You're still too skinny to be a PE teacher."

She laughed. "I know. I sure won't miss all those years of dieting. I'm proud to tell you that I've worked my way up from a size two to a six. My goal is to be a size ten and even eat chocolate now and then."

He swept his gaze over her. She half expected a comment on her body, but instead he only asked, "So what kind of teacher are you?"

"Math at the middle-school level," she said.

"A lot of those boys are going to have a crush on you."

"They'll get over it."

"I don't know. I still get a hankering for Ms. Rosens. She taught eighth grade social studies. I don't think I'd bothered to notice girls before. Then she walked into the room and I was a goner. She married the high school football coach. It took me a year to get over it."

She laughed.

They rocked in silence for a few minutes. Life was so normal here, Kari thought, enjoying the quiet of the evening. Instead of sirens and tire screeches, there were only the calls of the night critters. All around Possum Landing people would be out on their porches, enjoying the stars and visiting with neighbors. No one would worry about half a glass of wine causing facial puffiness, or being too bloated for a lingerie shoot. No one would lose a job for gaining three pounds.

This was normal, she reminded herself. She'd nearly been gone long enough to forget what that was like.

"Why teaching?" Gage asked unexpectedly.

"It's what I always wanted."

"After the modeling."

"Right."

She didn't want to go there—not now. Maybe later they would rehash their past and hurl accusations at each other, but not tonight.

"Where are you applying?"

"To schools around Texas. There are a couple of

openings in the Dallas area and in Abilene. I have some interviews scheduled. That's why this seemed like the perfect time to come back and fix up the house. Then I can move on."

She paused, expecting him to respond. But he didn't.

Which was just as well, because she suddenly found that sitting next to him on the old swing where he'd kissed her for the first time was more difficult than she would have thought. Her chest felt tight and her skin tingled all over.

It was just the wine, she told herself. Or it was the old memories, swimming around them like so many ghosts. The past was a powerful influence. No doubt she would need a little time to get used to being back in Possum Landing.

"Did you apply locally?" Gage asked.

"No."

She waited, but he didn't ask why.

"Enough about me," she said, shifting in her seat and angling toward him. "What about your life? Last I heard, you were still a deputy. When did you run for sheriff?"

"Last year. I wasn't sure I'd make it my first time out, but I did."

She wasn't surprised. Gage had always been good at his job and well liked by the community. "So you got what you always wanted."

"Uh-huh." He glanced at her. "I was always real clear about my goals. I grew up here. I'm a fifth-generation resident of Possum Landing. I knew I wanted to see the world, then come back home and make my life here. So I did."

She admired his ability to know what he wanted and go after it. She had never been quite that focused.

There had been the occasional powerful distraction. One of them was sitting right next to her.

"I'm glad you're where you want to be," she said. Then, because she wasn't always as bright as she looked, she said, "But you never married."

Gage smiled. "There have been a few close calls."

"You always were a favorite with the ladies."

His smile faded. "I never gave you cause to worry when we were together. I didn't fool around on you, Kari."

"I never thought you did." She shrugged. "But there were plenty of women eager to see if they could capture your attention. The fact that you and I were going out didn't seem to impress them."

"It impressed me."

His voice seemed to scrape along her skin like a rough caress. She shivered slightly.

"Yes, well, I..." Her voice trailed off. So much for being sophisticated, she thought wryly. Yup, her time in the big city had sure polished her.

"It's getting late," Gage said.

He rose, and she wasn't sure if she was sad or relieved that he was going. Part of her didn't want the evening to end, but another part of her was grateful that she wouldn't have another chance to say something stupid. As much as she'd grown and matured, she'd never quite been able to kick that particular habit.

She stood as well, noticing again how tall he was. Especially in his worn cowboy boots. Barefoot, he only had four inches on her. Now she had to tilt her head slightly to meet his gaze.

The look in his eyes nearly took her breath away. There was a combination of confidence and fire that made her insides sort of melt and her breathing turn ragged.

What on earth was wrong with her? She couldn't possibly be feeling anything like anticipation. That would be crazy. That would be—

"You're still the prettiest girl in Possum Landing," he said as he took a step toward her.

She suddenly felt overwhelmed by the Texas heat. "I, um, I'm not really a girl anymore."

He smiled a slow, easy, "I'm in charge here and don't you forget it" kind of smile that didn't do anything positive for her equilibrium. She seemed to have forgotten how to breathe.

"I know," he murmured as he put his hand on the back of her neck and drew her close. "Did I mention I like your hair short?"

She opened her mouth to answer. Big mistake. Or not, depending on one's point of view.

Because just at that moment, he lowered his mouth to hers. She didn't have time to prepare…which was probably a good thing. Because the second his lips touched hers, protesting seemed like a really silly idea—when Gage could kiss this good.

Kari wasn't exactly sure what he was doing that was so special. Sure there was soft, firm pressure and plenty of passion. As if the night wasn't warm enough, they were generating enough heat between them to boil water on contact. But there was something else, some chemistry that left her desperate and longing. Something that urged her to wrap her arms around him so that when he pulled her close, they were touching everywhere it mattered.

He moved his mouth against hers, then lightly licked her lower lip. Pleasure shot through her like lightning. She clutched at his strong shoulders, savoring the hardness of his body against hers, liking the feel of his hands on her hips and his chest flattening her breasts.

Her head tilted slightly, as did his, in preparation for the kiss to deepen. Because there wasn't a doubt in her mind that they were taking this to the next level.

So when he stroked her lower lip again, she parted her mouth for him. And when he slowly eased his tongue inside, she was ready and very willing to dance this particular dance.

He tasted sweet and sexy. He was a man who enjoyed women and knew enough to make sure they enjoyed him. Kari had a hazy recollection of her first kiss with Gage, when he'd been so sure and she'd felt like a dolt. Right up until he'd touched his tongue to hers and she'd melted like butter on a hot griddle.

Now that same trickling sensation started deep inside. Her body was more than ready for a trip down memory lane. She wasn't so sure the rest of her could play catch-up that fast...even if the passion threatened to overwhelm her.

He moved his hand up from her hips to her sides, then around to her back, moving higher and higher until he cupped her head. He slid his fingers into her short hair and softly whispered her name.

She continued to hold on to him because the alternative was to fall on her rear end right there on the porch. When he broke the kiss and began to nibble along the line of her jaw, she didn't care where she fell as long as he caught her. And when he sucked on her earlobe, every cell in her body screamed out that sex with Gage Reynolds would be a perfect homecoming.

Fortunately, the choice wasn't hers. Just when she was starting to think they were wearing too many layers, he stepped back. His eyes were bright, his mouth damp with their kisses. She was pleased to see that his breathing was a tad too fast and that parts of him were not as…modest as they had been a few moments before.

They stared at each other. Kari didn't know what to say. Finding out that Gage kissed better than she remembered meant one of three things: her memory was faulty, he'd been practicing while she'd been gone, or the chemistry between them was more powerful than it had been eight years ago. She wasn't sure which she wanted it to be.

He didn't speak, either. Instead, he leaned close, gave her one last hot, hard kiss, and walked down the porch steps, into the night.

Kari was left staring after him. Restlessness seized her, making her want to follow him and…and…

She sucked in a breath before slowly turning and heading back into the house. Obviously, coming back to Possum Landing was going to be a whole lot more complicated than she'd first realized.

Chapter Three

Gage ambled toward the offices of the *Possum Landing Gazette* the following morning. Under normal circumstances, he would have put off this meeting for as long as possible. But ever since the previous evening, he hadn't been able to concentrate on his work, so he figured this was a better use of his time than staring out the window and remembering.

He'd always known that Kari would come back to Possum Landing one day. He'd felt it in his bones. From time to time he'd considered what his reaction to that event would be, assuming he would be little more than mildly interested in how she'd changed and only slightly curious as to her future plans. He hadn't thought there would still be any chemistry between them. He wasn't sure if that made him a fool, or an optimist.

The chemistry was there in spades. As were a lot of old feelings he didn't want to acknowledge. Being around her made him remember what it was like to want her…and not just in bed. There had been a time when he'd longed to spend his whole life with her, making babies and creating a past they could both be proud of.

Instead, she'd gone away and he'd found contentment in his present life. While the kiss the previous evening had shown him that parts of him were still very interested in the woman she'd become, the rest of him couldn't afford to be.

Kari was a beautiful woman. Wanting her in bed made sense. Expecting anything else would take him down a road he refused to travel. He'd been there once and he hadn't liked the destination.

So, for however long she stayed in Possum Landing, he would be a good neighbor and enjoy her company. If that led to something between the sheets, that was just fine with him. He hadn't had much interest in the fairer sex these past few months. Instead, a restlessness had seized him, making him want something he couldn't define. If nothing else, Kari could prove to be a welcome distraction.

Gage entered the newspaper office and nodded at the receptionist. "I know my way," he called as he headed down a long corridor. "I'd be obliged if you'd tell Daisy I'm here."

The woman picked up the phone to call back to the reporter. Gage pulled off his cowboy hat and slapped it against his thigh.

He didn't much want to be here, but experience had taught him that it was safer to show up for interviews than to allow Daisy to come to him. This way, he was in charge and could head out when he felt the need to escape. He'd figured out that by leaning against the conference room chairs just so, he could activate the test button on his pager. It went off, and he could glance down at the screen and pretend something had come up, forcing him to leave. He was also sure to seem real regretful about having to head out unexpectedly. He was just as sure to ignore Daisy's not-so-subtle hints that they should get together sometime soon.

Daisy was a fine figure of a woman. A petite redhead with big green eyes and a mouth that promised three kinds of heaven if a man were only to ask. They'd been in the same class in high school but had never dated. Newly divorced, Daisy was more than willing to reacquaint herself with Gage. He appreciated the compliment and couldn't for the life of him figure out why he wasn't interested. But he wasn't. As he'd yet to decide on an easy way to let her down, he did the next best thing and avoided anything personal.

He wove his way through the half dozen or so desks in the main room of the newspaper office. Daisy was in the back, by a window. She looked up and smiled as Gage approached. Her long, red hair had been piled on her head in a mass of sexy curls. The sleeveless blouse she wore dipped low enough to prove that her cleavage was God-given and not the result of padding. Her smile more than welcomed…it offered. Gage smiled in return, all the while monitoring parts south. Over the years he'd found that part of him was a fairly good judge of his interest in a woman. As had occurred every other time he'd been in Daisy's company, there wasn't even a hint of a stirring. No matter how much Daisy might wish the contrary, as far as he was concerned, there wasn't any future for them.

"Gage," she murmured as he approached. "You're looking fine this morning. Being a hero seems to agree with you."

"Daisy," he said with a smile. "If you're going to write anything about me being a hero in your article, I'm not going to cooperate. I was doing my job—nothing more."

She sighed and tilted her head. "Brave *and* modest. Two of my favorite qualities in a man." She batted her long lashes at him. "I have a call to make. Why don't you wait for me in the conference room, and I'll join you there."

"Sure thing."

He spoke easily, even though the last place he wanted Daisy to send him was that back room with no windows and only one door. Yesterday, facing four armed bank robbers hadn't done much but increase his heart rate. But the thought of being trapped in a small place with Daisy on the hunt made his insides shrivel up and play dead.

Still, there was no escaping the inevitable. And he always had his handy-dandy test button escape route. He walked down the hallway that led to the conference room and stepped inside. But instead of finding it empty, he saw someone else waiting. A tall, slender someone with short blond hair and the prettiest blue eyes this side of the Mississippi.

"Morning, Kari," he said as he stepped into the room.

She glanced up from the list she'd been making, frowned in confusion, then smiled. "Gage. What are you doing here?"

"Waiting on Daisy. She's going to interview me about yesterday's bank robbery." He hesitated before taking a seat.

Some decisions were harder than others and this was one of them. Did he want to sit next to her so he could catch the occasional whiff of her soft perfume, or sit across from her so he could look at her lovely face? He decided to enjoy the view, and pulled out the chair directly opposite hers.

"What brings you to the newspaper this morning?" he asked as he set his hat on the table.

Kari's mouth twisted slightly. "Daisy called and asked to interview me about the bank robbery. I wonder why she wanted us to come at the same time."

Gage had a couple of ideas, but figured this wasn't the time to go into them. Instead he studied Kari, who seemed to be trying *not* to look at him. Was that because of last night? Their kiss? The heat they'd ignited had kept him up half the night. He might not have much of a reaction to Daisy, but being around Kari proved that he could be intrigued in about a tenth of a second under the right circumstances.

This morning she wore a white summery dress that emphasized her slender shape. He eyed her short hair, which fluttered around her ears.

"What?" she said, watching him watch her. She touched her hair. "I know—it's short."

"I said I liked it."

"I wasn't sure if you were lying," she admitted with a smile. "I always figured you were more of a long hair kind of a guy."

He leaned back in his chair. "Actually, I try to be flexible. If it looks nice, I like it."

He continued to take in her features, noting changes and similarities.

"What are you thinking?" she asked.

He grinned. He was thinking that he would very much like to take her to bed. Once they'd shared several hours of one of life's greatest pleasures, he would like to get to know the woman she'd become while she'd been gone. Not that he was going to say that to her. From time to time, circumstances forced a man to tell little white lies.

"I was wondering how much work you're planning on doing at your grandmother's house."

Kari blinked at Gage. She'd expected him to say a lot of things, but not that. He'd been looking at her as if he were the big bad wolf and she were lunch. But in the kind of way that made her body heat up and her heart rate slip into overdrive.

So, she'd been thinking about last night's kiss and he'd been mulling over paint chips and siding. Obviously her ability to read Gage and handle herself with grace and style hadn't improved at all in the time she'd been gone.

"I'm still figuring that out," she said. "The biweekly cleaning service kept the house livable, but it's still old and out of date. I could redo the whole place, but that doesn't make sense. I have a limit to both my time and money, so I'm going to have to prioritize."

He nodded thoughtfully.

My, oh my, but he still looked good, she thought, as she had yesterday. And the pleasure she took in seeing him hadn't worn off yet. She wondered if it would. By the end of summer, would he be little more than just some good-looking guy who happened to live next door? Could she possibly get that lucky?

Before she could answer her own question, Daisy breezed into the conference room. From her low-cut blouse to the red lipstick emphasizing her full lips, she was a walking, breathing pinup girl. Kari felt bony and string-bean-like in comparison.

"Thanks so much for coming," she said as she closed

the door, then took the seat next to Gage. "I'm writing a follow-up article for the paper and I thought it would be fun to interview you both together. I hope you don't mind."

Kari shook her head and tried not to notice how close Daisy sat to Gage. The other woman brushed her arm against his and smiled at him in a way that had Kari thinking they were way more than friends.

But that didn't make sense. Gage wasn't the kind of man to be involved with one woman and kiss another. Which meant Gage and Daisy had once been a couple or that they were still in the flirting stage. Either concept gave her the willies.

Daisy set her notebook on the table in front of her but didn't open it. She leaned toward Kari. "Wasn't that something? I mean, a bank robbery right here in PL."

Kari blinked. "PL?"

"Possum Landing. Nothing exciting ever happens here." She smiled at Gage. "At least, nothing in public. I thought it was so amazing. And, Gage, throwing yourself in front of the bullets. That was amazing, too. And brave."

He grunted.

With a speed that left Kari scrambling, Daisy turned to her and changed the subject. "So, you're back. After all those years in New York. What was it like there?"

"Interesting," Kari said cautiously, not sure what this had to do with the holdup the previous day. "Different from here."

"Isn't everywhere," Daisy said with a laugh. "I've spent time in the city, but I have to tell you, I'm a small-town girl at heart. PL is an amazing place and has everything I could ever want."

She spoke earnestly, focusing all her attention on Gage for several seconds before swinging it back on Kari.

"What's it like seeing Gage again after all these years?"

Kari blinked. "I'm, uh, not sure what that has to do with the bank robbery."

"I would have thought it was obvious. Your former fiancé risks his life for you. He protects you from the hail of gunfire. You can't tell me you didn't think it was romantic. Don't you think it was the perfect homecoming? I mean, now that you're back."

Kari risked a glance at Gage, but he looked as confused as she felt. What on earth was Daisy's point with all this? As Kari didn't want anything she said taken out of context and printed for the whole town to see, she tried to think before she spoke.

"First of all," she said slowly, "Gage and I were never engaged. We dated. Second, I'm not back. Not permanently."

"Uh-huh." Daisy opened her notebook and scribbled a few lines. "Gage, what were you thinking when you walked into the bank?"

"That I should have followed my mama's advice and studied to be an engineer."

Kari smiled slightly and felt herself relax. Trust Gage to ease the tension in the room. But before she could savor her newfound peace, Daisy broke into peals of laughter, tossing her pen on the table and clutching Gage's arm.

"Aren't you a hoot?" she said, beaming at him. "I've always enjoyed your humor."

The expression on her face said she had enjoyed other

things, as well, but Kari didn't want to dwell on that. She tried to ignore the couple across the table. Daisy wasn't having any of that. She turned her attention back to Kari and gave her a look of friendly concern.

"I'm so pleased to hear you say that you're not staying for the long haul. You and Gage had something special once, but I've found that old flames never light up as brightly the second time around. They seem to fizzle and just fade away."

Kari smiled through clenched teeth. "Well, bless your heart for being so concerned."

Daisy beamed back.

They completed the interview fairly quickly, now that Daisy had gotten her message across. Obviously she'd called Kari and Gage in together to see them in the same room, and to warn Kari off. Like Kari was interested in starting up something with an ex-boyfriend.

Small-town life, Kari thought grimly. How could she have forgotten the downside of everyone knowing everyone else?

Daisy continued to coo over Gage and he continued to ignore her advances. Despite being incredibly uncomfortable, Kari couldn't help wondering about the state of their real relationship and vowed to ask Gage the next time she felt brave. In the meantime, she would do her best to avoid Daisy.

People in big cities thought nothing happened in small towns, she thought as she finally made her escape. People in big cities were wrong.

"You spoil me, Mama," Gage said a few nights later as he cleared the table at his mother's house.

Edie Reynolds, an attractive, dark-haired woman in

her late fifties, smiled. "I'm not sure cooking dinner for you once a week constitutes spoiling, Gage. Besides, I need to be sure you're getting a balanced meal at least once in a while."

He began scraping plates and loading the dishwasher. "I'm a little too old to be eating pizza every night," he teased. "Just last week I had a vegetable with my steak."

"Good for you."

He winked at her as he worked. His mother shook her head, then picked up her glass of wine. "I'm still very angry with you. What were you thinking when you burst in on those bank robbers?" She held up her free hand. "Don't bother telling me you weren't thinking. I've already figured that out."

"I was doing my job. Several citizens were in danger and I had to protect them."

She set her glass down, her mouth twisting. "I guess this means your father and I did too good a job teaching you about responsibility."

"You wouldn't have it any other way."

"Probably not," she admitted.

The phone rang. His mother sighed. "Betty Sue from the hospital auxiliary has been calling me every twenty minutes about our fund-raiser. I'm amazed we got through dinner without her interrupting. This will just take a second." She picked up the receiver on the counter and spoke in a cheerful tone.

"Hello? Why, Betty Sue, what a surprise. No, no, we'd just finished eating. Uh-huh. Sure."

Edie headed for the living room. "If you want to rearrange the placement of the booths, you're going to have to clear it with the committee. I know they told you to run things, but..."

Gage grinned as he tuned out the conversation. His mother's charity work was as much a part of her as her White Diamonds perfume.

He finished with the dishes and rinsed the dishcloth before wiping down the counters. Every now and then his mother protested that he didn't need to help after dinner, but he never listened. He figured she'd done more than her share of work while he and his brother Quinn were growing up. Loading the dishwasher hardly began to pay her back.

He finished with his chores and leaned against the counter, waiting for her to finish her conversation with Betty Sue. The kitchen had been remodeled about seven years ago, but the basic structure was still the same. The old house was crammed full of memories. Gage had lived here from the time he was born until he'd left to join the army.

Of course, every part of Possum Landing had memories. It was one of the things he liked about the town— he belonged here. He could trace his family back five generations on his father's side. There were dozens of old pictures in the main hallway—photos of Reynolds at the turn of the previous century, when Possum Landing had been just a brash, new cow town.

His mother returned to the kitchen and set the phone back on its base. "That woman is doing her best to make me insane. I can't tell you how sorry I am that I actually voted for her to run the fund-raiser. I must have been experiencing a black out or something."

He laughed. "You'll survive. How's the bathroom sink?"

"The leak is fixed. Don't fret, Gage. There aren't any chores for you this week."

She led the way back into the living room, where they sat on opposite ends of the recovered sofa. Edie had replaced the ugly floral pattern with narrow-striped fabric.

"I don't invite you over just to get free labor," she said.

"I know, Mama, but I'm happy to help."

She nodded. "Will you be all right when John takes over that sort of chore?"

His mother had never been one to walk around a problem—if she saw trouble, she headed right for it. He leaned forward and lightly touched the back of her hand.

"I've told you before, I'm pleased about John. Daddy's been gone five years. You're getting a second chance to be happy."

She didn't look convinced. "I'm telling the truth."

He was. The loss of his father had been a blow to both of them. Edie had spent the first year in a daze. Finally she'd pulled herself together and had tried to get on with her life. A part-time job she'd taken for something to do rather than because she needed the money had helped. As had her friends. Nearly a year before, she'd met John, a retired contractor.

Gage was willing to admit that he'd been a bit put off by the thought of his mother dating, but he'd quickly come around. John was a solid man who treated Edie as if she were a princess. Gage couldn't have picked better for his mother himself.

"You'll still come to dinner, won't you? Once we're married?"

"I promise."

He'd been coming to dinner once a week ever since he'd returned to Possum Landing after being in the army. Like many things in his life, it was a tradition. His mother's dark gaze sharpened a little and he braced himself. Sure enough, she went right for the most interesting topic.

"I heard Kari Asbury is back in town."

"Subtle, Mama." He grinned. "According to Kari, she's not back, she's here for a short period of time while she fixes up her grandmother's house and sells it."

Edie frowned. "And then what? Is she going back to New York? She's a lovely girl, but isn't she getting a little old to be a fashion model?"

"She's going to be a teacher. She has her credentials and is applying for jobs in different parts of Texas."

"Not Possum Landing?"

"Not as far as I can tell."

"Are you all right with that?"

"Sure."

"If you're lying to me, I'm not averse to getting out the old switch."

He grinned. "You'd have to catch me first. I'm still a fast runner, Mama."

Her face softened with affection. "Just be careful, Gage. There was a time when she broke your heart. I would hate to see that happen again."

"It won't," he said confidently. A man was allowed to be a fool for a woman once in a lifetime, but not twice. "We'll always be friends. We have too much past between us to avoid that. We're neighbors, so I'll be seeing her, but it won't amount to anything significant."

It was only a white lie, he thought cheerfully. Because getting Kari into bed was definitely his goal. And if things were as hot between them as he guessed they would be, the event would certainly qualify as "significant." But that wasn't something he wanted to share with his mother.

"You heard from Quinn lately?" he asked, changing the subject.

"Not since that one letter a month ago." She sighed. "I worry about that boy."

Gage didn't think there was any point in mentioning that Quinn was thirty and a trained military operative. "Boy" hadn't described him in years.

"He should be getting leave in the next few months."

"I'm hoping he'll make time to come to the wedding. I don't know if he will, though."

Gage wasn't sure, either. He and Quinn had once been close, but time and circumstances had changed things. They'd both headed into the military after high school, but unlike Gage, Quinn had stayed in. He'd gone into Special Forces, then joined a secret group that worked around the world wherever there was trouble.

Despite being from the same family as Gage, Quinn had never fit in. Mostly because their father had made his life a living hell.

As always, the thought made Gage uncomfortable. He'd never understood why he'd been the golden boy of the family and Quinn had been the unwelcome stranger. He also didn't know why he was thinking so much about the past lately.

Maybe it was Kari returning and stirring it up. Maybe now was a good time to ask a question that should have been asked long ago.

"Why didn't Daddy like Quinn?"

Edie stiffened slightly. "What are you saying, Gage? Your father loved you two boys equally. He was a good father."

Gage stared at her, wondering why she was lying. Why avoid the obvious?

"The old farmer's market opened last week. I'm going to head over there this weekend and see if I can get some berries. Maybe I'll bake a pie for next time."

The change of subject was both obvious and awkward. Gage hesitated a second before giving in and saying that he always enjoyed her pies.

But as they chatted about the summer heat and who was vacationing where, he couldn't shake the feeling that there were secrets hiding just below the surface. Had they always been there and he had never noticed? Twenty minutes later, he hugged his mother goodbye, then picked up the trash bag from the kitchen and carried it out as he did every time he left. He put it in the large container by the garage and waved before stepping into his truck.

His mother waved back, then returned to the house. Gage watched the closed back door for a while before starting the truck and heading home. What had happened tonight? Was something different, or was he making something out of nothing?

He slowly drove the familiar streets of Possum Landing. The signal by the railroad tracks had already started its slow flashing for the night. Those downtown would stay on until midnight, but on the outskirts of town they went to flashing at eight.

Unease settled at the base of his spine, making him want to turn around and demand answers from his mother. The problem was, he wasn't sure what the questions were supposed to be.

Maybe instead of answers, he needed a woman. It had been a long time and his need hadn't gone away. There were, he supposed, several women he could call on. They would invite him inside for dessert…and breakfast. He paused at the stop sign. No doubt Daisy would do the happy dance if he turned his attention in her direction. Of course, she would want a whole lot more than breakfast. Daisy was a woman in search of a happy ending. Gage was sure it was possible—just not with him.

He drummed his fingers on the steering wheel, then swore and headed home. None of those welcoming beds appealed to him tonight. They hadn't in a long time. He'd reached that place in his life where the idea of variety only made him tired. He wanted the familiar. He wanted to settle down, get married and have a half-dozen kids. So why couldn't he make it happen? Why hadn't he fallen in love and popped the question? Why hadn't he— He turned into his driveway, his headlights sweeping the front of the house next door. Someone sat on the top step, shielding her eyes from the flash of light.

A familiar someone who made parts of him stand up at attention without even trying.

Been there, done that, he told himself as he killed the engine and stepped out into the quiet of the night. But that didn't stop him from heading toward her, crossing his lawn and then hers.

Anticipation filled him. He wondered how she liked her eggs.

Chapter Four

Kari watched as Gage approached. He moved with the liquid grace of a man comfortable in his own skin. He was what people called "a man's man," which made the most female part of her flutter. How ironic. She'd spent nearly eight years surrounded by some of the most handsome, appealing male models New York had to offer—a good percentage of whom had *not* been gay—and she'd never once felt herself melt just by watching them move. What was it about Gage that got to her? Was she just a sucker for a man in uniform, or was it something specific about him?

"So, how was your date?" she asked to distract herself from the liquid heat easing through her belly. "You're back early, so I'm going to guess the ever-delightful Daisy is playing hard to get."

She thought about mentioning her surprise that Daisy would let Gage leave without visiting the promised land, but was afraid the comment would come out sounding catty.

He settled next to her on the front step and rested his forearms on his knees. "You always were a nosy thing back when you were in high school. I see that hasn't changed."

"Not for a second." She grinned.

He glanced at her and gave her an answering smile that made her heart do a triple flip.

"I had dinner with my mother," he said. "I do it every week."

"Oh."

She tried to think of a witty comeback but couldn't. The admission didn't surprise her. Gage had always been good to the women in his life…his mother, her grandmother. She remembered reading an article somewhere, something about paying attention to how a man treats his mother because it's a good indication of how he'll treat his wife. Not that she was planning on marrying Gage Reynolds. Still, it was nice to reconfirm that he was one of the good guys.

"How *is* your mom?" she asked.

"Good. She had a rough time after my dad died. They'd been together for so long, I'm not sure she thought she could make it without him. Eventually she got it together. Last year she started dating again. She met a guy named John. They're engaged."

Kari straightened. "Wow. That's great." Then she remembered how close Gage had been to his father. "Are you okay with it?"

He nodded. "Sure. John is one of the good guys."

Takes one to know one, Kari thought. "When's the wedding?"

"This fall. He's a retired contractor. He has a lot of family up in Dallas. That's where he is this week. One of his granddaughters is having a birthday, and he wanted to be there for the party."

"They say people who have one successful marriage can have another."

Gage stared up at the night. "I believe that's true. My folks loved each other. There were plenty of fights and difficult times, but on the whole, they were in love. From what John has said about his late wife, they had a strong marriage, too. I figure the two of them are going to do just fine."

"I'd like to see your mother again. I always liked her."

"She's working up at the hardware store. It's a part-time job to get her out of the house. You should head on up and say hi."

"I will."

When Kari and Gage had been dating, Edie had welcomed her with open arms. Kari didn't know if the woman had done that with all Gage's girlfriends, but she liked to think she and Edie had been especially close. Of course, Edie wouldn't have been thrilled about her dumping Gage via a note and running away.

"Is she still mad at me for what I did?"

He glanced at her, laughter lurking in his dark eyes. "She seems to have recovered."

"Okay. Then, I'll pop over and congratulate her on the upcoming nuptials. I think it's great that she's found someone. No one should be alone."

As soon as the words fell from her mouth, she wanted to call them back. Obviously, both she and Gage were alone. She knew her circumstances—but what were his? He was the kind of man who had always attracted women, so the choice to be single must have been his. Why?

She was about to ask, when he beat her to the punch.

"So, why aren't you married, Kari?"

Before she could answer, he shrugged. "Never mind.

I forgot. You weren't interested in home and hearth. You had things to do and places to be."

She bristled. "That's not true. Of course I want to get married and have kids. I've always wanted that."

"Just not with me?"

He didn't look at her as he spoke, and she didn't know what he was thinking.

"Just not on your timetable," she told him. She sighed. "Eight years ago, you were right on track with your life. You had seen the world and were ready to settle down. I was a senior in high school with a lot of unrealized dreams. I was young and hopeful, and as much as I cared about you, I was terrified by your life plan. You seemed so much older—so sure of yourself. Everything you said was reasonable, yet it felt wrong for me at the time. I didn't want to be like my mother and grandmother, marrying out of high school, having kids right away. I wanted *my* chance to see the world and live my dreams."

"I thought I was one of your dreams."

"You were. Just not right then. When I heard you were going to propose, I panicked, which is why I ran away. I thought…" She hesitated. "You were so clear on the way everything would be. I was afraid I'd get lost in that."

He sat close enough for her to feel the heat of his body and inhale the scent of him. She was torn between wanting to lean against him and heading for the hills. Confessions in the night were frequently dangerous. What would be the outcome of this one?

Gage surprised her by saying "You're right." She blinked at him. "I didn't expect that."

He shrugged. "I thought I knew everything back then.

You were what I wanted in a wife, we were in love—why wouldn't we get married and settle down? You talked about going to New York and being a model, but I didn't think you were serious." He glanced at her and shrugged again. "That was pretty arrogant of me. I'm sorry, Kari. I should have listened to you. Instead I focused on what I wanted and tried to steamroll my way to the finish line."

His confession caught her off guard. "Thanks," she murmured. "I wish we'd had this conversation eight years ago."

"Me, too. Maybe we would have found a way to make it work."

She nodded but didn't say anything. Privately, she doubted that would have happened. Even after all this time, the truth still hurt her. Gage might have wanted to marry her, but he hadn't loved her enough to come after her and ask her to return home with him. He hadn't loved her enough to get in touch with her and say he would wait while she followed her dreams. She took off, and he seemed to simply get on with his life.

"So I went into the army when I wanted to see the world and you went off to New York," he said lightly, as if trying to shift the tone of their conversation. "I'm guessing you had a better time."

She tamped her sadness and laughed. "Oh, I don't know. At least you got regular meals."

"Was money that tight?"

"A little. At first. But I got some part-time jobs and eventually modeling work. The food thing is more about being the American ideal of a working model. I didn't eat because I had to lose weight. I was young and determined, which meant I wasn't sensible. It wasn't a very healthy lifestyle."

"Aside from the lack of food, is it what you thought it would be?"

"I don't know. I think young women want to be models because it's glamorous. Where else can an eighteen-year-old girl make that kind of money and travel all over the world? There are lots of invitations. Men want to date models. Being a model is an instant identity."

She pulled her knees close to her chest and wrapped her arms around her legs. "But the reality can be difficult. Thousands of girls come to New York, and only a tiny percentage make it to supermodel status. A few more are successful. I was a little below that—a working model who earned enough to pay the bills and put myself through college, with a bit of a nest egg left over. The truth is, I never fit in. I found some of the parties were scary places. I wasn't allowed to eat, I never was one to drink. And men who only date models have expectations I wasn't comfortable with."

She smiled at him. "I guess you can take the girl out of Possum Landing, but you can't take Possum Landing out of the girl."

"I'm glad."

As he studied her, she wondered what he was thinking. Had her experiences shocked him? Compared with most of her friends, she'd practically been a nun, but she wasn't going to tell Gage that. It would sound too much like making excuses.

"You were talking about finding a teaching job near Dallas," he said. "Will you miss New York?"

"Some things, but I'm ready for a change. I was born and bred in Texas. This is where I belong."

He rubbed the cracked paint on the handrail. "What are your plans for the old house?"

Kari considered the question. "I'm still debating."
She suddenly remembered. "Oh, I went around and
did an inventory of furniture…mostly the antiques."

Gage looked interested but didn't say anything.

She sighed. "I loved my grandmother, but she was a
bit of a pack rat. Anyway, I have a list. There are some I
want to keep for myself…mostly those with sentimental
value. I checked and my parents don't want anything.
So I'm going to sell the others, except for the ones you'd
like."

He raised his eyebrows. "What do you mean?"

"I didn't know if you were interested in antiques. If
you are, I'd like you to have first pick at what she had."

"Why?"

Wasn't it obvious? "Come on, Gage, we both know
how much you helped her. You were always willing to
run over and fix whatever was broken. After I left, you
kept her company and helped her out, even though you
had to have been really angry with me."

"I wouldn't have let that affect my relationship with
her."

She noticed he didn't deny the anger, which made
her uncomfortable. Funny how after all this time Gage's
disapproval still had the power to make her cringe.

"That's my point," she said, staying on topic. "You
could have been difficult and you weren't. After she
died, you contacted the real estate management company whenever there was a problem with the house. I
owe you. I figured you'd be deeply insulted if I offered
money, so this seemed like a good compromise."

He stared at her. Despite the fact that the sun had
gone down a while ago, the Texas summer night was
still warm. As his intense gaze settled on her face, she

had the feeling that the temperature had climbed a couple of degrees. Despite the fact that she was wearing shorts and a cotton sleeveless shirt, she felt confined... restricted...and far too *dressed*.

Kari couldn't help smiling. Boy, he was good. If he could make her writhe just by looking at her, what would happen if he ever kissed her again?

Too late, she remembered she'd promised herself she wasn't going to think of the kiss again. Not when she'd spent most of two days reliving it. She'd firmly put it out of her mind...almost.

"All right," he said slowly. "I'll consider taking one of the antiques as payment. If you haven't kept it for yourself, I wouldn't say no to the sideboard in the dining room."

It took her a second to figure out what on earth he was talking about. As far as her mind was concerned, the previous conversation hadn't even taken place. Then all her synapses clicked into place.

"No, I haven't claimed that one. Consider it yours."

"I'm much obliged."

His eyes held hers for a couple more heartbeats, then he finally looked away. She felt as if she'd been released from a force field. If she hadn't been sitting already, she would have collapsed.

She struggled to pick up the thread of their conversation. Oh, yeah. They'd been talking about her fixing up the house. "I'm going to paint the whole place," she said. "Inside and out. I'm doing the inside myself and hiring someone to do the outside."

Gage glanced up at the tall eaves and nodded. "Good idea. I'd hate to see you falling off a ladder."

"Me, too." She stretched out her legs in front of her.

"There are a couple of windows that need replacing, and the whole kitchen is a 1950s disaster. I'll strip the cabinets and refinish them. I've already ordered new appliances and carpeting. I think that's about it."

"Sounds like you'll be busy."

"That's the plan. I'm going to start slow with the painting. Just do one room at a time. Everything needs a primer coat—it's been years between paint jobs."

He seemed to consider the night sky, then he turned to her. "I have a couple of days off coming up. I could offer you some brawn for moving things around and reaching the high places."

She shivered slightly at the thought of his "brawn."

"I'm five-ten—I can reach the high places on my own. But I will say yes to whatever help you're willing to offer."

"Then, I'll be here."

She found herself leaning toward him as he spoke, as if what he said had great significance and she wanted to be close enough to breathe in every word. She sighed. Whatever was wrong with her was more serious than she'd thought. After all this time, she couldn't possibly still be crazy about Gage. Not when they'd both gone in such different directions.

He rose suddenly. "It's getting late," he said, moving off the stairs. "I should be getting back home." She waited—more breathless than she wanted to admit—until he gave her a slight nod and headed toward his place.

"'Night, Gage," she called after him, as if his leaving was a good thing. As if she wasn't thinking about what it would be like if he kissed her again. Not that he was going to, obviously. Apparently, that one kiss had been enough for him. It had been enough for her, too. More than enough. In fact, she was really glad that he didn't plan to try anything. She would have to say no and it would get really embarrassing for both of them.

She *hated* that he hadn't kissed her.

By the next afternoon, Kari still hadn't figured out why. Why he hadn't and why it bugged her. Didn't Gage find her attractive? Hadn't he enjoyed their previous kiss? She *really* hated that his not kissing her had kept her up in the night nearly as much as his kissing her had.

It was the past, she told herself as she stood in her grandmother's bedroom and slowly opened dresser drawers. But after all this time, she was finding herself being sucked back into what had once been.

Kari shook her head to chase away the ghosts, then plopped on the floor to study the contents of the bottom drawer. There were several sweaters wrapped in lengths of cotton and protected by cedar chips. She held up a pale blue sweater, admiring the workmanship and the old-fashioned style. This particular sweater had been a favorite. Kari could see her grandmother in it as clearly as if the woman stood in front of her.

"Oh, Grammy, I miss you," she whispered into the silence of the morning. "I know you've been gone a long time, but I still think about you every day. And I love you."

Kari paused, then smiled slightly as she imagined her grandmother whispering back that she loved her favorite girl, too. More than ever. Despite everything, her grandmother had been the one constant in her life.

Kari slowly put the sweater back. She realized she needed a few boxes so she could sort those items that were going with her from those that were not. She touched the sweater before closing the drawer. That she would keep. It would be a talisman—her way to connect to some of her happiest memories.

The middle drawer yielded scarves and gloves, while the top drawer held her grandmother's costume jewelry. There were plenty of real pieces, Kari remembered as she touched a pin in the shape of a dragonfly. They were in a jewelry chest on the top of the dresser. A string of pearls and matching earrings, a few gold chains. Perhaps her grandmother had worn them, too, but all of Kari's memories of the woman who had raised her were much more connected with the costume pieces.

There were the gaudy necklaces that Kari had dressed up in when she was little and the fake pearl choker her grandmother had worn to church every Sunday. The bangle bracelets and the butterfly earrings and the tiny enameled rose pin Kari had been allowed to wear on her first date with Gage.

She shifted on the floor so that she leaned against the old bed. The rose pin didn't look the worse for wear. She rubbed her fingers across the smooth petals, remembering how her grandmother had pinned it on Kari's blouse five minutes before Gage had arrived to pick her up.

"For luck," her grandmother had said with a smile. Kari smiled, too, now, even as she fought tears. Back then she'd wanted every bit of luck available. She hadn't been able to believe that someone as grown up and handsome as Gage Reynolds had asked her out. When he'd issued the invitation, it had been all she could do not to ask him why he'd bothered.

But she hadn't. And when she'd gotten nervous on that date, she'd touched the rose pin for luck. It had happened so many times, Gage had finally commented on the tiny piece of jewelry.

They'd been walking out back, Kari remembered, her mouth trembling slightly as she battled with tears. After a dinner at which she'd barely managed to swallow two bites, he'd taken her for a walk in the pecan grove.

She could still smell the earth and hear the crunch of the fallen pecans under their feet. She'd thought then that he might kiss her, but he hadn't. Instead, he'd taken her hand in his. She'd almost died right there on the spot.

It wasn't that no one had held her hand before. Other boys had. But that was the difference…they were boys. Gage was a man. Still, despite the age difference and her complete lack of subtlety, he'd laced his fingers with hers as they'd walked along. Kari had relived the moment for days.

They'd been out exactly five times before he finally kissed her. She touched the pin again, smiling as she remembered pinning it on her sweater that October evening. Once again, Gage had taken her to dinner and she'd only managed to eat a third of her entrée. She hadn't been dieting—that didn't come until her move to New York. Instead, she'd been too nervous to eat. Too worried about putting a foot wrong or appearing immature. After only five dates, she was well on her way to being in love with Gage. Her fate had been sealed that evening, as she leaned against the pecan tree, her heart beating so fast it practically took flight.

She closed her eyes, still able to feel the tree pressing into her back. She'd been scared and hopeful and apprehensive and excited, all at the same time. Gage had been talking and talking and she'd been wishing he would just *do it*. But what if he didn't want to kiss her? What if…

And then he had. He'd lightly touched the pin, telling her how pretty it was. But not as pretty as her. Then, while she was still swooning over the compliment, he'd bent low and brushed his mouth to hers.

Kari sighed softly. As first-kiss memories went, she would bet that hers was one of the best. Before then, she'd dated some, and kissed some, but never anyone like him. In fact, she couldn't remember any of her first kisses with other boys. But she remembered Gage. Everything from the way he'd put his hand on her shoulder to how he'd stroked her cheek with his warm fingers.

A shiver caught her unaware as it lazily drifted down her back. The restless feeling returned, and with it all the questions as to why he hadn't bothered to kiss her again the previous night.

Impulsively, she fastened the rose pin to her T-shirt. Maybe she was still floundering around in her love life, but she had some fabulous memories. However it might have ended, Gage had treated her incredibly well when they were together. There weren't many men like him.

She had the brief thought that it would be wonderful to be meeting him now, for the first time. She had a feeling that without all their past baggage to trip over, they could make something wonderful happen between them.

The daydream sustained her for a second or two, until she reminded herself that it didn't matter what would or would not be happening if she and Gage had just met. Possum Landing was his world, and she was most definitely not back to stay.

Chapter Five

After walking through the upstairs and deciding on paint colors, Kari made a list and headed for the hardware store. Since she'd last been in Possum Landing, one of those new home improvement superstores had opened up on the main highway about ten miles away. She was sure their selection was bigger, their prices were lower and that she probably wouldn't run into one person she knew. But starting a refurbishing project without stopping by Greene's Hardware Center would probably cause someone from the city council to stop by with a written complaint. Her grandmother had always taught her the importance of supporting the local community. And old Ed Greene had owned the store since before Kari was born.

New York was a big city made up of small neighborhoods. Over time, Kari had come to know the people who worked at the Chinese place where she ate once a week, and she and the lady at the dry cleaner had been on speaking terms. But those relationships hadn't had the same history that existed here in Possum Landing.

So she drove across town to Greene's, then pulled

into the parking lot that had last been repaved in the 1980s. The metal sign was still there, as was an old advertisement for a certain brand of exterior paint. Advertising slogans, long out of date, covered most of the front windows.

Kari smiled in anticipation, knowing there would be a jumble of merchandise inside. If she wasn't careful she would come out with more than just paint. She still remembered the old rooster weather vane her grandmother had come home with one afternoon. For the life of her, she couldn't figure out how Ed had talked her into buying it.

Kari pulled her list out of her purse, determined to be strong. She walked up the creaking steps of the building's front porch and stepped into the past.

Old file cabinets stood by the front door. They contained everything from stencils to paint chips, instruction on lawn care and packets of exotic grass seeds. To the right was a long wooden counter with PegBoard behind it. Dozens of small tools hung in a seemingly unorganized array. The place smelled of dust and cut wood and varnish. For a moment Kari felt as if she were eight again. She could almost hear her grandmother calling for her to stay out of trouble.

"Kari?"

The female voice was familiar. Kari turned and saw Edie Reynolds walking in from the back room. Gage's mother was a tall, dark-haired woman, still attractive and vibrant. She smiled broadly as she approached and pulled Kari into a welcoming hug.

"I'd heard you were back in town," Edie said when she released her. "How are you? You look great."

"You, too," Kari managed to say, too surprised by

the friendly greeting to protest that she wasn't back for any length of time. She knew that Gage's mother would have known about her son's plans to propose and that she, Kari, had broken off the relationship in a less than honorable way. Apparently, Edie had decided to forgive and forget.

Edie pulled out one of the stools in front of the counter and took a seat, then motioned for Kari to do the same.

"Tell me everything," the older woman said. "You're staying at your grandmother's house, right?" She smiled. "Actually, I suppose it's your house now."

"I still think of it as hers," Kari admitted. "I want to fix it up and sell it. That's why I'm here. I need supplies."

"We have plenty." Edie laughed. "So you were in New York. Did you like it? Gage showed me some of your pictures. You were in some pretty big magazines."

"I managed to make a living. But it wasn't the career I thought I wanted. I went to college and just received my teaching credentials."

"Good for you." Edie glanced around the store. "As you can see, nothing's changed."

Kari didn't know if she agreed or not. Some things seemed different, while others—like her reaction to Gage—didn't seem to have evolved at all.

"You working here is different," Kari said. "I only remember seeing Ed behind the counter."

"That old coot," Edie said affectionately. "I took a part-time job a year or so after Ralph died. I didn't need the money, but I desperately needed to get out of the house. The walls were starting to close in on me."

"I'm sorry about Ralph," Kari said.

Edie sighed. "He was a good man. One of the best. I still miss him, of course. I'll always miss him." She smiled again. "Which probably makes the news of my engagement a little hard to understand."

"Not at all. I think it's wonderful you found someone."

"We met right here," Edie said, her eyes twinkling. "He's retired now, but he was still working then. A contractor on a job. He ran out of nails and popped in to buy some. It was just one of those things. I had started dating a few months before and really hated the whole process, but with John…everything felt right. Somehow I knew."

Kari envied Edie her certainty. She'd dated from time to time, and no man had ever felt right. Well, Gage had, but that had been years ago.

"When's the wedding?" Kari asked.

"This fall. We're still planning the honeymoon. I can't wait."

"It sounds wonderful."

"I'm hoping it will be. Now, enough about me, tell me about yourself. I'll bet you never expected a bank robbery to welcome you back."

Kari nodded. "I managed to avoid crime the whole time I was in New York, but after less than twenty-four hours in Possum Landing I had a man holding a gun to my head." She touched Edie's arm. "Gage was very brave."

"I know. I hate that he put himself in danger, but as he pointed out to me, it's his job. I tell myself that the good news is he doesn't have to do it very often. Possum Landing is hardly a center of criminal activity."

They chatted for a few more minutes, then Edie

helped Kari buy primer and paint, brushes, rollers, tarps and all the other supplies she would need for her painting project.

She left the hardware store with her trunk full and her spirits light. There was something to be said for a place where everyone knew her name.

"You'd better be awake or there's going to be hell to pay," Gage called as he strolled in through the back door without knocking.

Kari didn't bother looking up at him. Instead, she grabbed another mug from the cupboard and filled it with hot coffee.

"Good morning to you, too," she said, turning to face him as she handed him the mug.

Whatever else she'd started to say fled her brain as she took in the worn jeans and tattered T-shirt he wore. She'd only seen him in his uniform since she'd returned to Possum Landing, and while the khaki shirt and pants emphasized the strength of his body, they had nothing on worn denim.

What was it about a sexy man in blue jeans? Kari wondered as her chest tightened slightly. Was it the movement of strong thigh muscles under fabric made soft by dozens of washings? The slight fading by the crotch, or the low-slung settling on narrow hips? She barely noticed the cooler he set on her kitchen table.

"I have a list of demands," he said after taking a sip.

She blinked. "Demands for what?"

"Work. I might work for free, but I don't come cheap. I expect a break every two hours and I expect to be well fed. Before we start, I want to know what's for breakfast and lunch."

She burst out laughing, but Gage didn't even crack a smile.

"Okay, big guy," she said. "Here's the deal. Take a break whenever you want—I don't care how often or how long. Seeing as I'm not paying you, I can't really complain. There's cold cereal for breakfast and I have sandwich fixings for lunch. Oh, and you'll be making your own sandwich."

Gage muttered something about Kari not being a Southern flower of motherhood, then started opening cupboards. "Cereal," he complained. "Aren't you even going to offer me pancakes?"

"Nope."

He muttered some more. "I'm just glad I stopped by my mama's place. She made potato salad and macaroni salad. I'll share, but that means you have to make my sandwich."

"Blackmail."

"Whatever works."

She poured herself more coffee and sighed. "All right. It's a deal."

He poked through her cereal collection, which consisted of several single-serving boxes.

"You turned into a Yankee while you were gone. I'll bet you can't even make grits anymore."

"I couldn't make them when I lived here, so you're right. I can't make them now."

He pretended outrage. "I could arrest you for that, you know. This is Possum Landing. We have standards."

She topped off his coffee mug, then started for the stairs. "If you're done complaining, let's get to work."

"Oh, great. No pancakes, you won't make my sandwich and now you're turning into a slave driver. Don't that just beat all?"

Kari chuckled as she reached the second floor. Gage's teasing had managed to divert her attention from his jeans and what they did to her imagination...not to mention her libido. Far better to play word games than dream about other kinds of games. That would only get her into trouble.

"I thought we'd start in here," she said, walking into one of the small spare bedrooms. "I haven't painted in years and I doubt I did a very good job when I was twelve. So I'm trying to gear up."

He looked around. She'd taken out the smaller pieces of furniture and had pushed the rest into the center of the room.

After setting his mug on a windowsill, Gage grabbed a four-drawer dresser and picked it up. "Let's get rid of a little more so we have room to work," he said. "Where can I put this?"

She stared at him. Last night she'd practically pulled a muscle just trying to move the dresser across the floor. Gage picked it up as if it weighed as much as a cat. Figures.

"In my grandmother's room."

He followed her down the hall. "Are you sleeping in there? Isn't it the biggest bedroom?"

"No and yes. I'm in my old room. I just felt better being in there."

He put down the dresser and turned. "She wouldn't mind," he said seriously. "She loved you."

"I know. I just..." How to explain? "I want to keep the memories as they are."

"Okay."

He put his arm around her as they walked back to the spare room. Kari tried not to react. Gage's gesture was friendly, nothing more. Nothing romantic...or sexual. Her imagination was working overtime and she was going to make it stop right this minute.

So why did she feel each of his fingertips where they touched her bare arm? And why did the hairs on the back of her neck suddenly stand at attention?

"I, uh, did some patching yesterday," she said, slipping free of his embrace. Casual or not, his touch made her breathing ragged. "There were some nail holes and a few cracks. I guess we sand it next."

He stepped around her and studied her supplies. "I'll sand. It's man's work."

"*Man's* work?"

"Sure."

"What will I be doing while you're dragging home the woolly mammoth?"

"You can clean up your putty knife and take off the baseboards."

She eyed the strips of wood encircling the room just above the carpeting. "Why isn't that man's work?"

He sighed. "If I have to explain everything, we'll never get the painting started, let alone finished."

"Uh-huh. Why do I know this is more about you doing what you want to do than defining tasks by gender?"

Gage looked up blankly. "I'm sorry. Did you say something?"

Kari thought about throwing something at him, but laughed, instead. While he went to work with sandpaper, she knelt on the opposite side of the room and gently began to pull the baseboards free of the wall.

They worked in silence for nearly half an hour. "You do good work," Gage said finally.

'Thanks. I can read directions. Plus, I've learned to be good at odd jobs."

"Why is that?"

"The need to eat and pay rent," she said easily. "I told you, I didn't get any modeling work for over a year. New York isn't exactly cheap. So I worked different places to support myself. Some months it was tough."

He finished sanding and picked up a screwdriver. In a matter of seconds, he'd popped the pins out of the hinges and removed the door.

"You didn't call home and ask for money."

It was a statement, not a question. Obviously, he and Grammy had talked about her after she'd left.

"Nope. It had been my decision to leave, so it was my responsibility to make it on my own. I didn't want to get complacent, thinking that I always had someone waiting to send me money. The only thing I allowed myself was the promise my grandmother had made to send me a ticket home should I ever want it."

"Were you tempted?"

"A couple of times. But I held on and then things began to turn around. I got my first well-paying modeling job right before she died. She didn't get to see the magazine spread, but she knew about it, so that was something."

Kari pulled off the last piece of baseboard and dragged it out into the hallway.

Gage reached for the can of primer. "You know she was proud of you," he said.

She nodded. "I know. She never made me feel bad for leaving, and she always said I was going to make it."

"And you did."

"Sort of. But in the meantime, there were all those other lovely jobs."

He poured primer into two small buckets, then took a brush and handed her another. "Any painting?" he asked.

"No. I think there's a union. I did more conventional things. Worked in retail, walked dogs, delivered packages."

"Waited on tables?"

She shook her head. "I didn't eat much, and being around food was torture. I tried to avoid restaurants whenever possible. My favorite gig was house-sitting. I stayed in some amazing places. Great views, soft beds, and not a cockroach in sight."

"Were you ever scared?" Gage asked.

"Sometimes. At first. I'd never been on my own. It was a trial by fire."

While Gage enjoyed hearing about her previous life, he didn't ask the one question he wanted to. Had she missed him? Had she thought about him after she left, or had she shaken off his memory like so much unwanted dust?

"It was quiet after you left," he said instead as he brushed primer on the wall by the window.

Kari crouched by the door frame. She half turned and glanced at him over her shoulder. "I'm sorry if…" Her voice trailed off. "I never asked because I was afraid of what I'd hear. I'm sorry if it was bad for you after…"

He knew what she meant. After she left. After she stood him up and walked out of his life. Word spreads fast in a small town and by prom night nearly everyone knew that he'd bought an engagement ring for Kari. It was months before well-meaning folk stopped asking "No, how are you *really?*"

"It wasn't so bad," he said, because it was true. The blow to his pride was nothing compared with the pain in his heart. He'd never been in love before. Having Kari walk away so easily had taught him a hard lesson—that being in love didn't guarantee being loved in return.

Until Kari had left him, he'd assumed they would spend the rest of their lives together. He'd planned a future that had included only one woman. Finding out she didn't share his dreams...or want to marry him... had shattered his hopes and broken his heart.

"I used to look for your pictures in women's magazines," he admitted.

She stood up and laughed. "I can't believe you bought them."

"Some. I went to the next town, though."

"I should hope so. We can't have one of Possum Landing's finest checking out fashion magazines." Her laughter faded. "I'm guessing you gave up long before you found me on one of the pages."

"Nope. I told you I saw that hair ad."

There had been others. It was nearly five years before he'd been able to let Kari go.

"That was my first big break," she said.

"I liked the lingerie spread," he teased. "You looked good in the black stuff, but the teal was my favorite."

The brush fell out of Kari's hand. Fortunately it tumbled onto the tarp rather than the carpet. She blinked at him as a flush climbed up her cheeks.

"You saw that?" she asked in a strangled voice.

"Uh-huh."

She cleared her throat, then realized she'd dropped

her brush and picked it up. "Yes, well, I don't know
how the regular lingerie models stand it. I hated wearing so little and how everyone stared at me. Plus, I was
starving. I hadn't eaten for three days beforehand so I
wouldn't be bloated. I started to get light-headed, so
I worried that I was going to have a really spacey expression on my face and the client wouldn't like it."
She shivered slightly. "I never looked at those pictures
when they came out. They were a part of my portfolio,
but I avoided them."

"You were beautiful," he said sincerely. "I had no
idea what was under all those clothes you used to wear."

"Just the usual body parts."

"It's all in the details, darlin'."

Kari laughed.

They worked in silence for a few minutes. Gage
didn't mind that they weren't talking. Being around
Kari took some getting used to. At one time she'd been
everything, then she'd been gone and he'd had to figure
out how to make her not matter. Having her back confused him. While his body was very clear on what it
wanted from her, the rest of him wasn't so sure.

Not that it was going to be an issue. She was moving on. Which meant anything other than sex would
make him a fool for love twice. No way was he going
to let that happen.

"I always wanted to thank you," Kari said as she
poured primer into roller trays.

He noticed she was careful not to look at him. "For
what you did…or didn't do, when we were going out."

He had no idea what she was talking about. "What
didn't I do?"

She shrugged. "You know."

"Actually, I don't."

She turned to him. "You never pushed me. Now the age difference between us is nothing, but back then it was a big deal. You had been in the military and traveled the world. You'd seen and done things and you never…" Her voice trailed off.

Gage stared at her. "Are you talking about sex?"

For the second time in a half hour, she blushed. "Yes. You never pushed me. I didn't think it was a big deal back then, but now, I know that it was. You wanted things from me, but you never made me feel that I had to give in to keep you."

"You didn't. Kari, I wanted to marry you. I wasn't going to dump you because you were young and innocent."

"I know. I just want to thank you for that."

He wondered what kind of guys she'd met that would make her think his behavior was anything but normal.

She picked up a roller. "I thought you were a knight in shining armor that first night we met."

He frowned. "I was doing my job and you were damn lucky I came along."

"I know." She smiled sadly. "I was so excited to be invited to that party with real college boys. I'd never been to one before. One of my friends, Sally, had beer at her seventeenth birthday party, but that was a girls-only sleepover, and while it was exciting for us, it didn't have the same thrill as a boy-girl party with hard liquor."

He shook his head. "Unless you've changed, you're not much of a drinker at all."

She laughed. "Oh, I didn't want to drink any, I just wanted to be in with the cool kids. I never was all that popular."

That surprised Gage. He remembered her having
lots of friends in high school. But he knew that she'd
never belonged to any one social group. Part of the reason was that Kari hadn't fit any label, part of it was that
she had been so pretty. She'd intimidated the boys and
alienated the girls.

"I was so scared," she said with a sigh. "Walking
down that back road by myself."

"You should have been scared."

He remembered their first official meeting. He'd
moved back to Possum Landing after getting out of
the service and had taken a job as a deputy. He'd bought
his house a year later, right beside Kari's grandmother's
place. While in the process of moving in, he'd noticed
the pretty young woman next door. He hadn't thought
anything of her at the time. Not until he'd been called
out to a loud party on the edge of town.

Gage had given a warning and had known he would
be called back in less than an hour. The second time he
would get tough, but he always figured everyone deserved one chance to screw up. On his way back to the
station he'd seen an old Caddy crawling along at about
five miles an hour. The top was down and there were
four very drunk college guys in the vehicle. Gage had
hit his lights. A flash of movement on the side of the
road had caught his attention. It was only then that he
saw a teenage girl looking scared and out of place.

He'd sized up the situation in less than a minute.
Girl goes to wild party, tries to escape and has no ride
home, so she walks. Drunk boys follow, looking for
trouble. He told her to climb into his squad car before
telling the guys to walk back to the party or risk being
arrested for drunk driving. They'd protested, but finally

agreed. Gage had taken the keys, saying they could get them back the following day...as long as they were accompanied by a parent. Then he'd returned to his car to find a trembling teenager fighting tears.

He'd prayed she wouldn't break down before he got her home. It was only when she whispered her address that he realized she was his neighbor.

Now, all these years later, he remembered how concerned he'd felt. Kari was only a kid. But kid or not, she'd been drinking.

"You nearly threw up in my car," he complained, speaking his thoughts out loud.

Kari glared at him. "I did not. I got out of the car before I threw up."

"You looked awful."

"Gee, thanks. I felt awful. But you were really nice. You gave me your handkerchief afterward."

"You notice I didn't ask for it back."

She laughed. "Yes, I did notice that." She rolled on more primer. "I haven't thought about that night for a long time. I was in over my head. Everyone at the party was drunk. I drank some, but not enough to forget myself. Some of the boys wanted to have sex and I didn't."

"So you started walking home."

"And you saved me."

"I gave you a ride."

"Yes, and then you lectured me on being stupid."

Gage remembered that. He hadn't let her out of the car until he'd given her a stern talking to. Her blue eyes had widened as he talked about the dangers of parties that could get out of hand.

He'd given the lecture several times before, but never

had he been distracted by a passenger. He found himself having thoughts that didn't go with the job.

"Then you asked me how old I was," Kari continued. "I couldn't figure out why. I thought maybe it had something to do with arresting me."

"Not exactly."

"I know that, now."

"You'd been eighteen for two days," he said in disgust. "I was twenty-three, almost twenty-four. Six years seemed like a big gap back then."

"But you asked me out, anyway."

"I couldn't help myself."

He was telling the truth. Gage had tried to talk himself out of his attraction for nearly a month. Finally he'd gone to Kari's grandmother and sought her opinion.

"Grammy said it was fine," Kari said softly. "I think she really hoped I would marry you and live next door."

She turned away suddenly, but not before Gage thought he saw tears in her eyes.

"She would have liked that," he said quietly, "but more than anything, she wanted your happiness."

"I know," she said with a nod. "It's just…" She glanced around the room. "Being back here makes me miss her. Silly, huh?"

"No. You loved her. That's never silly."

She gave him a grateful smile. He felt a tightening low in his gut. Being back might make her miss her grandmother, but it made Gage miss other things. Oddly enough, they were things that had never happened. He didn't have memories of making love with Kari, yet he knew exactly what the experience would be. He knew the taste of her and how she would feel. He knew the sounds she would make and the magic that would flare between them. Despite the years and the miles, he still wanted her.

"You always understand," she said.

"Not even close."

"You understood me before and you still understand me."

"Maybe you're just simple."

She chuckled. "That must be it."

He didn't want it to be anything else—he didn't want to have any kind of connection to Kari Asbury. Sex was easy, but anything else would be complicated…and potentially dangerous.

"You're probably just really good with women," she said. "I mean, I was gone on you in thirty seconds, and now Daisy obviously has the hots for you."

"I don't want to talk about either of you."

"You want to talk about me," she teased. "Don't you? Don't you want to take a long walk down memory lane?"

"Isn't that what we've been doing?"

"I guess." She stared at him. "Have you slept with her?"

He stared back. "No."

"You didn't sleep with me, either. You do have sex with some of them, don't you, Gage?"

He saw the twinkle in her eyes. He kept his face sober as he continued to paint. "Sure. But I'm sort of a go-all-night kind of lover and that cuts into my sleep. I can't take on any new women until I get rested again."

She groaned. "Oh, please."

"Right now? You want to do it on the tarp?"

She laughed, then her humor faded. "I'm sorry *you*

weren't my first time," she said, not looking at him, then shrugged. "You probably didn't want to know that."

He was stunned by the confession, probably because he had so many regrets about the same thing. "I wanted that, too," he admitted. "I'd thought about it a lot, but I wanted to wait…"

"And then I was gone," she said, finishing the sentence. "I'm sorry. For a lot of things."

"Me, too."

They didn't speak for a while, but he didn't mind the silence. He'd always felt comfortable around Kari. He hadn't thought they needed to make peace with the past, but a little closure never hurt anyone.

Finally he put down his brush and stretched. "Hey, I've been working way longer than two hours. It's time for a break. I think you should make my sandwich now."

"Excuse me, I believe I told you I wasn't making anything. That you were on your own."

She straightened, and he wrapped an arm around her shoulders. "Naw. You *want* to wait on me. It's a chick thing."

"I'm tall and wiry, Gage. I could take you right now."

He grinned. "Not even on a bet, kid."

Chapter Six

"What do you mean you're not going to help me clean up?" Kari asked in pretended outrage after they'd finished lunch.

Gage leaned back in his chair, looking full and satisfied and very sexy.

"I made my own sandwich," he said, ticking off items on his fingers. "Despite protests. I brought the potato and macaroni salads."

"But you didn't make them. Your mom did."

"I carried them, and it's damn far from my house to yours." He held up another finger. "I'm providing free labor and charming company, so it seems to me that cleaning would clearly be your responsibility."

She shook her head, more charmed than irritated. "You need to get married so some woman can whip you into shape."

He glanced down at his midsection. "Don't you like my shape? I've never had complaints before."

She didn't want to think about how he looked in his worn jeans and T-shirt. Just a quick glance at his muscles and the way he moved was enough to make her squirm. Not that she was going to admit it.

"You're passable," she said, going for a bored tone.

"You're just used to those sissy boys in New York."

She laughed. "Some of them are pretty nice looking."

"Real men are born in Texas."

"Like you?"

He leaned toward her. "Exactly like me."

They were flirting, she realized. It wasn't something she did very often, mostly because she was afraid of messing up. But with Gage that didn't seem to matter. If she put a step wrong, he wouldn't say anything to make her feel bad. He was, as he had always been, safe.

The thought surprised her. Why would she still think of Gage as safe? What did she know about him? He could have changed. He probably had, she thought, but not in any ways that affected his character.

"Maybe I'll take a nap," he said.

She glared at him. "You will not. I'm practically paying you to help me, so you'll get your butt back upstairs and keep working."

He grinned. "Make me."

Something hot and sensual flared to life inside her. Something that made her wish for a witty comeback or the physical courage to walk over there and—

The phone rang.

"Talk about being saved by the bell," Kari muttered as she crossed the kitchen.

"I'll go start work," he said, rising. "But don't you take too long. I'm keeping track of hours, and if I work more than you, there will be hell to pay."

She dismissed him with a wave and reached for the phone. "Hello?"

"Hello, darling. How are you doing?"

Her humor faded as if it had never been. Tension instantly filled her. "Hi, Mom. I'm great. What's up with you?" Kari hoped her mother didn't hear the tension in her voice.

"Your father and I are planning a trip soon. You know, the usual."

Kari did know. She hated the fact that twenty-plus years after the fact, the information still had the power to make her feel angry and bitter.

"I received your letter," Aurora Asbury continued. "I never understand why you write instead of calling. Although, I always enjoy hearing from you."

"Thanks," Kari said. She wasn't about to admit that she wrote because it was one-way communication and a whole lot easier than picking up the phone.

"How's the house?" Aurora asked. "It's so old. Are you really going to be able to fix it up?"

"Sure. It won't be too much work, and I'll enjoy the challenge." Kari pressed her lips together. She felt both startled to hear from her mother and guilty about the house. Her grandmother, Aurora's mother, had left it to her, not her mother. Of course, her mother had never been around. She and Kari's father had been traveling the world.

"I think your plan to sell it is a good one," her mother said. "I *had* thought you might want to keep it for old time's sake."

"I don't want to do that." Kari drew in a breath. "So, um, how's Houston?"

"Hot and humid." Aurora sighed. "I can't wait for your father's next assignment. We should be heading overseas soon. I'm hoping for something in the Far East, but you know the company. We never know for sure until he gets his assignment."

There was a pause and then, "Are you sure you'll be all right there in Possum Landing, darling? It's such a small, stifling town. You could always hire someone to update the house, and stay with us for a few weeks."

Kari felt a surge of irritation. The invitation was coming a few years too late. "I'll be fine here," she said. "I'm enjoying reminiscing."

"I don't understand why you would want to stay in Texas after living in New York, but it's your choice." She paused, then said, "I was thinking of coming up for a quick visit in the next few weeks."

Kari stiffened. "Sure. That would be great." What she really wanted to ask was "why?" but she didn't.

Aurora had many faults, but since being cruel wasn't one of them, Kari refused to be cruel herself.

"I'm not sure. I'll let you know."

"Okay. Well, I need to get back to work. I'm starting the painting."

"All right, darling. You take care of yourself."

"You, too, Mom."

Kari said goodbye, then hung up. She stood in the kitchen for several minutes, trying to recapture her good mood. When it didn't happen, she figured Gage was the best antidote for a burst emotional bubble and headed up the stairs.

"You're late," he complained, the second she walked into the room. "I'm going to have to—" He broke off and stared at her. "What happened? Bad news?"

"No. Just my mom calling."

"And?"

"And nothing. She might come to visit."

Gage didn't say anything. He clearly remembered that her relationship with Aurora had always been difficult.

She shrugged and moved toward the tray of primer he'd set up for her. "I know I should let it go."

"No one is saying you have to."

"I guess." She walked to the last bare wall. "It's just that I can't get past what she did. I mean, why have a kid if you're just going to abandon it?"

She hunched her shoulders, anticipating that he would defend Aurora's decision, but he didn't.

Kari was grateful. Sometimes she was okay with the past—mostly when she was happy in her life and her mother didn't call. But sometimes she felt the same sense of loss and confusion she had when she was young.

Her parents had married when her mother was barely eighteen. Her father was a petrochemical engineer working for a large oil company. Kari had come along sixteen months after the wedding, and four months later, her father had received his first overseas assignment. Somehow the decision was made to leave Kari with her grandmother. It was supposed to be a temporary arrangement—there had been some concern about taking such a small child so far away. But somehow, Aurora had never returned to claim her daughter.

"I spent my whole life waiting for her to come back for me," Kari said as she rolled primer on the wall. "Don't get me wrong. I loved being with Grammy and, after a while, it would have been weird to leave everything and go live with them. But even though I was happy, it hurt."

Gage lightly touched her arm. She smiled at him

gratefully. "The thing is," she continued, "they always used the excuse that they didn't want to take a baby with them overseas. But my brothers were born there and never sent back here."

"It's their loss," he said gently.

She attempted a smile. "I tell myself that, from time to time. Sometimes I even believe it."

She tried to shake off the emotional edginess, along with the pain. Her life was great—she didn't need her family messing things up.

"I'm okay," she said. "Really. Those of us who weren't raised in the perfect family have to learn to adjust."

Gage grinned. "We weren't perfect."

"Sure you were. Parents who loved each other. A home, a brother you actually got to know and spend time with. What more could you ask for?"

"I guess when you put it like that." He shrugged. "It wasn't always good for Quinn, though. He and Dad never got along."

Kari had never met Gage's younger brother. Quinn had left to join the military before Kari met Gage.

"What was the problem?" Kari asked.

"I never knew. Quinn was a bit of a rebel, but the trouble started long before that. It's almost as if…" His voice trailed off.

Kari didn't want to pry, so she changed the subject. "What's he doing now?"

"Still in the service."

"Really? Doing what?"

"I have no idea. He's in some special secret group. They travel around the world and take care of…things. Quinn eliminates people."

Kari nearly dropped her roller. "He kills them?"

Gage nodded.

"For a living?"

"Yeah."

She couldn't imagine such a thing. Killing people for any reason was outside of her realm of imagination. She wanted to ask more questions, but had a feeling Gage didn't want to talk about it further.

"Okay, then," she said. "I guess the fact that one of my brothers is an accountant and the other is a zoologist is really boring by comparison."

"It sure is."

She stuck her tongue out at him.

"Childish," he muttered. "I see you haven't changed at all."

"Of course I have. I'm even more charming than when I left."

"That wouldn't have taken much. Besides, I'm the charming one in this relationship." He grinned as he spoke, and she couldn't help laughing.

"What is it with you?" she asked.

"I think it's something in the water," he said with mock seriousness. "After all, the Reynolds family has been in Possum Landing for five generations. That makes us very special."

"Do you ever wonder what made them stop here in the first place?"

"Good sense."

"Right. Because everyone in America wants to live in a place called Possum Landing."

"You bet."

She continued to paint the wall, while he put a coat of primer on the closet door. They didn't talk for a time.

When they finished the room and started to leave, she touched his hand.

"Thanks," she said. "For coming over and making me laugh."

His dark eyes flared slightly. "I'm glad I can help. No matter what, Kari, we were always friends." Friends. Was that what she wanted, too?

They spent the rest of the afternoon moving furniture out of the second small bedroom, patching the walls and waiting for the primer to dry. By three, they'd put on the first coat of paint.

"It's such a girl color," Gage teased as he rolled yellow paint over the walls.

Kari looked up from the door frame, where she was painting trim. "It is not. Pink is a girl color. Yellow is neutral. I wanted something bright and cheerful that would open up the room."

"What about a skylight?"

She turned away to hide her grin. "I'm ignoring you."

"Your loss. Are you doing all the bedrooms up here in yellow?"

"I haven't decided." There were a total of four on this floor. Hers, her grandmother's and the two they were working on. "I want to do Grammy's room next, which means moving her furniture into here."

"Are you giving it away?"

"I'd like to keep the dresser, but, yes, the rest of it will go." She hesitated, feeling faintly guilty. "I *want* to keep all of it...or even if I don't, I think I should."

"Why?"

"Because it was hers. Because of the memories."

"I doubt she'll mind if you only keep what you like.

Her purpose in leaving you the house wasn't to make you unhappy."

"I guess."

Sometimes Gage annoyed her by being sensible, but sometimes he got it just right.

They worked well together, she thought as she moved to paint around the window. The banter made her laugh, the companionship lightened her spirits. Being around Gage made her happy.

She shook her head slightly. *Happy.* When was the last time she'd enjoyed that particular emotion? She'd been content, even pleased with the direction of her life. But happy?

"I'm done in here," he said a few minutes later. "I'm going out back to start cleaning up the brushes and rollers."

"Okay. I'll just be a little longer."

He grabbed the equipment and headed for the stairs. Kari finished painting and followed him. She went out the back door and around to the side of the house—a spray of cold water caught her full in the face.

She screamed. "What on earth—?"

But that's as much as she got out before another blast of freezing water hit her in the chest. She shrieked and jumped back to safety. Okay, she thought as she brushed off her face and arms, if that's how he wanted to play it.

She ran to the other side of the house. Sure enough, she found a coiled hose, which she unscrewed from the tap and dragged around to the back door tap. A few quick twists had it connected. She turned the water on full, then went on the attack.

Gage obviously thought she'd headed into the house, because he stood bent over, cleaning brushes in a bucket and chuckling to himself. She caught him square in the backside.

He jumped and growled, then turned on her. The battle was on.

Kari raced to the safety of the far side of the yard. Her hose stretched that far, but his didn't. While she was able to attack directly, he was forced to arc water toward her. She danced easily out of its reach.

"Big, bad sheriff can't catch me," she teased as she blasted him. "Big, bad sheriff is all wet."

"Dammit, Kari!" He muttered something, then disappeared around the side of the house. Seconds later he appeared without the hose. He walked toward the tap by the back door and turned it off, then put his hands on his wet hips and stared at her. He looked unamused.

She dropped the hose and took off toward the far end of the yard. It had been about nine years since she'd tried to take the fence, but she was willing to give it a try. The alternative was getting caught.

"Don't you dare!" she yelled as she ran, not sure what she was telling him not to do.

"I dare just fine," he said, sounding way too close.

But she was nearly there. Just a few more feet of grass and then she would be— He caught her around the waist, pulling her hard against him and knocking most of the air out of her. She struggled, gasping and laughing the whole time, but it was pointless. Gage's arm was like a steel band. A very wet, steel band.

"Let go of me," she demanded.

"Not until I teach you a lesson."

"You and what army?"

"I can do it just fine myself, little girl."

"I'm not a little girl."

"No. You're an all grown-up Yankee."

"Who are you calling a Yankee?"

He carried her like a sack to the center of the lawn, then released her. She took off instantly—and didn't get more than one step before he grabbed her again. This time when he pulled her against him, they were facing each other.

Her hair dripped in her face, as did his. They were both breathing hard and very, very close.

"Troublemaker," he murmured, staring into her eyes.

His were dark and unreadable, but that was okay. While she couldn't tell what was going on in his brain, there was enough action in his body to keep her occupied. He seemed to be pressing against her in a way that made her think of games more adult than a water fight. The expression of his face had changed as well. His features tightened with something that looked very much like passion. Which was okay with her—sometime in the past three seconds she'd gone from shivering to being filled with anticipation.

"Maybe you need a little trouble in your life," she said softly.

"Maybe I do. Maybe you do, too."

She didn't have an answer for that, which was a good thing, because there wasn't any time to speak. His mouth settled on hers and all rational thought fled. His lips were still damp from the water, but not the least bit cool. The arm around her waist tightened, pulling her even closer. They connected everywhere that was possible, with her hands touching his shoulders and his tongue brushing against her bottom lip.

She parted for him instantly, wanting, *needing* to taste him. The second he stroked the inside of her lower lip, shivers began low in her belly and radiated out in all directions. Her breasts swelled within the confines of her damp bra. Her thighs pressed together tightly. A light breeze cooled her wet skin, but parts of her were getting plenty hot.

He cupped her face as he deepened the kiss. She clung to him, wanting him to claim her, mark her, do with her whatever he wanted. She longed to be possessed by him.

Her fingers curled into his shoulders. Then she moved her hands to his back where she could feel the hard breadth of his muscles. His tongue circled hers, teasing, touching, seducing. She answered in kind, straining toward him. Every part of her melted against him.

Her breasts ached where they flattened against his hard chest. Her nipples tightened unbearably. When his hands moved to her waist, her breath caught.

His fingers moved higher and hers moved lower. While he inched his way up her damp T-shirt along her rib cage, she slipped down to his waist. Her heart thundered loud and fast until it was all she could hear. Her body trembled. Her thoughts circled, almost frenzied, unable to figure out what to concentrate on. The fabulous kiss? The slow ascent to her chest? The brush of damp jeans against her palms as she moved lower still?

He reached her breasts at the same instant she cupped his tight, high rear. Which was remarkable timing, because when his hands brushed against her, fire ripped through her body, making her gasp and nearly lose her balance. She grabbed on to him and squeezed, which caused him to arch against her. As his thumbs swept over her hypersensitive nipples, his hips bumped hers and she felt his need.

Pleasure shot through her. From their kiss, from the gentle stroking on her sensitive, aroused flesh, from the ridged maleness pressing into her belly. It was too much. It was amazing.

Gage pulled back just enough to put a little space between them. Before she could protest, he cupped her breasts fully, and she saw the wisdom in his actions. He explored her curves, brushing slightly, smoothing and inciting. Want filled her until she couldn't think about anything else…then he broke their kiss and began nibbling along her jaw and by her ear.

His hot breath tickled, his tongue teased, his teeth delighted. She clung to him as her world began to spin. There was only this moment, she thought hazily. The feel of Gage next to her, and what he did to her body.

She gasped when he nipped at her earlobe. Either he'd learned a whole lot while she'd been gone, or he'd been even more gentle back when they'd been going out because she didn't remember anything like this. Not ever. Back then, he'd kissed her and left her breathless, but he'd never—

She gasped as he walked behind her, licking her neck and sucking on her skin. He cupped her breasts at the same time and played with her nipples. Involuntarily, she opened her eyes and saw his large, strong hands moving against her. The combination of feeling and sight nearly made her collapse.

That was why the alarm bell caught her by surprise. The alarm began as a distant, indistinct noise that grew louder with each beat of her heart, until it filled her head and made it impossible to concentrate on the delights Gage offered. It twisted her mind, clearing the sensual fog that surrounded her and forcing her to think sensibly.

What on earth was she doing? Did she really want to start something now? Like this? What would happen if she and Gage made love? Would it just be a quick trip down memory lane or would it be more? She hated that her brain insisted on being mature right now. Why couldn't she simply give in and then have recriminations later like everyone else?

Unfortunately the mood had been broken. She stepped away and sucked in a deep breath. It took more courage than she would have thought to turn and face him.

"I can't," she said, not quite looking him in the face. "I mean, I've never done the sex only thing. I'm not sure I could start now. So if anything were to happen— physically, I mean—it would lead to trouble. At least, for me."

She risked a glance and saw that he was looking at her with an intensity that made her take another step back. Not that she could read a single thought, which left her in the position of stumbling on with what she was trying to say.

"I'm leaving at the end of the summer. I would like us to be friends, but anything else…" She cleared her throat. "I just don't want to get my heart broken again. I mean, you already did that once."

Gage stared at Kari. He could accept that she wanted to call a temporary halt to their afternoon activities. Even he was willing to admit they'd gone a little too far, too fast. But that she had the guts to stand there and go on about *him* breaking *her* heart? His temper flared.

"What the hell are you talking about?" he demanded.

She blinked. "Excuse me?"

"I didn't break your heart. You're the one who left. You walked away without a backward glance. No warning, nothing. I was going to propose to you, Kari. I had planned to spend the rest of my life with you. You changed your mind and dumped me. So don't go telling me about *your* heart. You trampled mine pretty damn good."

Color rose to her cheeks. "That's not fair. I didn't deliberately set out to be mean. I wanted to talk to you but I couldn't. You didn't want to listen. You only wanted things your way, on your schedule."

He refused to be deflected from the point. "You dumped me without a word."

"I left a note."

He glared at her. "Yeah, a note. That's so great. I was about to propose and you left a lousy note. You're right. That makes everything fine."

"I'm not saying it makes things fine." She planted her hands on her hips. Her wet hair hung in her eyes; her mouth trembled as she spoke. "I couldn't risk speaking with you. I knew you'd do everything you could to change my mind. You would never understand why I had to leave."

"I loved you. Of course I wouldn't want you to go away. Why is that so horrible?"

"It's not." She took a deep breath. "You're deliberately misunderstanding me. My point is, I deserved to have a life, too. I deserved to have my dreams and the opportunity to make them come true. But you didn't care about that. You weren't willing to listen. Besides, it's not as if you even missed me."

Her words stunned him. He could still remember what it had been like when he found out she'd left. It was as if the world would never be right again. "What the hell are you talking about? I was destroyed."

"Right. And that's why you raced after me and begged me to come home. Admit it, Gage. You never really loved me. You loved the idea of getting married and starting a family. You certainly never cared enough to come after me and make sure I was all right."

She ducked her head as she spoke, and for a second, he thought he saw tears in her eyes. He swore. "Is that what this is about?" he demanded. "Some stupid teenage girl test? If you really love me, you'll race after me to the ends of the earth?"

She raised her head. There *were* tears in her eyes, but he didn't care. He couldn't believe she was making him the bad guy in this.

"Yes, it was a test. And guess what? You failed."

Fury overwhelmed him. He thought of all that had happened after she'd disappeared. How he'd raged and ached and thought he would never get over losing her. He thought about all the times he had gotten in his car to go after her, only to stop himself, because, dammit, letting her go had been the right thing to do. He thought about how he had looked for her in all those magazines, how he'd touched the glossy photo when he'd finally found her picture, still needing her as much as he needed to breathe.

He remembered that despite trying like hell to fall

for someone else, he'd never been able to love anyone but Kari.

He thought about telling her all that—but why bother? She believed what she wanted to believe. So without saying anything, he turned on his heel and walked away.

Chapter Seven

"The nerve of that man" and other variations on the theme occupied all Kari's thoughts through the evening and well into the next day. She still couldn't believe what Gage had said to her. And how he'd acted! Like she'd said something so terrible.

Was it wrong of her to want to make decisions about her life? Of course not. But he'd refused to see that, just like he'd refused to understand what she'd been trying to say. Okay, maybe running away from a man she knew wanted to marry her, without explaining why and leaving only a note, wasn't very mature, but she'd been barely eighteen years old. Certainly not old enough to be getting engaged, let alone getting married and having kids! Which was what Gage had wanted. He'd planned it all out, from the date of their wedding to how long they would wait before starting a family to how many children were going to make up that family.

She'd gotten scared. She'd panicked and run.

She flopped down on the sofa in the parlor and stared out the front window. Upstairs there was plenty of work to be done, but she couldn't seem to motivate herself to do it.

Not only was she uncomfortable about arguing with Gage, but she hated all the memories that fight had stirred up. She'd been so in love with him, so crazy for him, that leaving had been incredibly hard. She'd cried the whole way to New York, and then some. She'd wanted to return home, and a thousand times she'd nearly done that. She'd picked up the phone to call him twice that many times. But, in the end, she hadn't. Because she'd known that coming back to Possum Landing would mean giving in to what Gage wanted for her life. It wasn't only the loss of her dreams that she feared… it was the loss of herself.

But he hadn't seen it that way back then, or yesterday. They'd both said things they didn't mean—at least, she hoped they didn't—and now they weren't speaking.

Kari stirred restlessly on the sofa and frowned. She didn't want to be *not* speaking to Gage. He was an important part of her past and about her only real friend in town. He was a good man and she really liked him. Obviously, her body thought he was a deity—but what did her body know? Avoiding each other didn't make any sense.

That decided, she headed for the kitchen where a batch of peanut butter cookies were cooling. After transferring all but a half dozen onto a plate, she went upstairs and changed into a bright blue sleeveless dress and a pair of tan sandals. She fluffed her hair, touched up her lipstick and practiced her best smile. She would make the first move to show good faith and get things right between them. Once they were speaking again, she would do her best to avoid conversations about the past, because that only seemed to get them in trouble. Oh, and kissing. They would have to avoid that, too, because it led to other kinds of trouble.

She walked downstairs, covered the cookies with plastic wrap, then grabbed her purse and headed for the front door. Seven minutes later she pulled up in front of the sheriff's station. Two minutes after that, she was escorted back to Gage's office.

As she walked down the long corridor, she found her heart fluttering a bit inside her chest. The odd sensation made her feel nervous and just a little out of breath.

Emotional reaction to their fight, she told herself. She was simply nervous that Gage might still be angry with her. She certainly wasn't *anticipating* seeing him again.

He was on the phone when she paused in the doorway to his office. Rather than focus on how good he looked in his khaki uniform, she glanced around at her surroundings.

Gage looked up and saw her. His expression stayed unreadable—something that seemed to happen a lot— although she thought she might have caught the hint of a smile tugging at the corner of his mouth. He hesitated briefly before motioning her in.

She moved to a straight-backed chair in front of his desk, and perched on the edge. Gage wrapped up his conversation and set down the receiver. She swallowed. Now that she was here, she didn't know exactly what to say. Her situation wasn't helped by the continued fluttering of her heart, not to mention a noticeable weakness in her arms and legs. It was as if she'd just had a very large, very stiff shot of something alcoholic.

What on earth was wrong with her? Then, unbidden, the memory of the passion she and Gage had shared rose in her mind, filling her body with sensations and her imagination with possibilities.

She silently screamed at herself to get down to business. Namely, apologizing. There would be no sexual fantasies about Gage. Not now. Not ever! And she really meant it.

"Kari," he said, his voice low and sexy. *Really* sexy.

She shivered. "I, um, brought a peace offering." She pushed the plate of cookies across the desk toward him. "I figure we both overreacted, but I'm willing to be mature about it."

She was teasing, and hoped he would get the joke. Instead of saying anything, though, he peeled back the plastic wrap and pulled out a cookie. After taking a bite, he chewed.

"I can be mature," he said as he leaned back in his chair and smiled at her. "With motivation."

She relaxed in her seat. "Are these enough motivation?"

"Maybe. It might take another dozen or so."

"I'll see what I can do." The rapid beating of her heart continued, but the tension fled. "I'm sorry," she said seriously.

"Me, too. Like you said, I overreacted."

"I said a lot of things…" She paused. "I'm sorry about saying I tested you and you failed. I didn't mean it like that. I was a kid back then and completely unprepared for a grown-up relationship. I ran away because I was scared and couldn't face you. I thought you'd be mad and try to get me to change my mind." She shrugged. "Like I said, not really mature. But I didn't plan to hurt you. I thought you'd come after me, and when you didn't, I decided you didn't really love me.

I thought I was a placeholder. That any woman would have done as long as she fulfilled your need for a wife and mother for your kids."

Gage picked up a pen and turned it over in his hands. "It wasn't like that, Kari. Any of it. I wanted to go after you. Hell, I thought about it a hundred times a day. I missed you more than I can ever explain, but that didn't mean I couldn't see your side of things. I didn't want to understand why you'd run off, but in my heart I knew. I didn't think I had the right to drag you back. You needed to follow your dreams. I'd just hoped they would be the same as mine."

"They were…just not then. I needed time."

He nodded. They looked at each other, then away.

Kari pressed her lips together. "Maybe we could start over. Be friends?"

"I'd like that. We can hardly be strangers if you're dragging me over to work on your house every other minute."

"I did *not* drag you. You volunteered."

"That's your story."

She smiled. "You make me crazy."

"In the best way possible."

That was true. And speaking of being made crazy… She cleared her throat. "About the kissing."

He waved a hand. "You don't have to thank me. I didn't mind doing it."

"Gee, thanks. Actually, what I was going to say was that I think we need to avoid it. Kissing can lead to other things and those other things would provide a complication neither of us needs."

"Fine by me. I can control myself."

"So can I."

She was almost *sure* she was telling the truth. She should have been able to without a problem. It's just that she sort of wanted to know what it would be like to make love with Gage. In every other area of her life, he'd always been the best man she'd ever known. No doubt he would shine at lovemaking, too.

She knew he would be sensitive and considerate, two things that really mattered to her—what with her never actually having done, well, *that* before. Someone, somewhere was going to have to be her first time, and she'd always thought Gage would be really good at that. Right up until he freaked out when she told him that she was still a virgin.

Rather than tread on dangerous ground, she changed the subject. "I don't remember the sheriff's station being this big."

He grinned. "How many times were you in it before?"

She laughed. "Okay. Never."

"We have a contract to patrol state-owned land. Several of the small towns hire us to take care of them, as well. The department has more than doubled since you left. I have some other plans for expansion. More territory and more officers means a bigger budget. We can qualify for some federal grants and upgrade equipment, stay ahead of the bad guys."

He looked so strong and sure sitting in his chair.

A man in charge of his kingdom.

"You're good at what you do, aren't you," she said.

"If I'm not, I won't get reelected."

"I doubt that's going to happen. Something tells me that you'll be sheriff of Possum Landing for a very long time."

"It's what I want."

She envied how he'd always known that. She'd had to search for what she wanted. "Speaking of wants and dreams, I'm heading up to Dallas in the morning. I have an interview."

"Good luck with that."

"Thanks."

She waited, kind of hoping he might express a little regret that she was leaving, but of course he didn't. Which made sense. After all, he knew her stay in town was temporary. He wasn't about to forget that, or start acting surprised when she had interviews in other places. Expecting anything else was really foolish and he knew better than to be that.

"I'll be back on Saturday," she said, rising.

Obviously, with her mental state, she had better head home fast. Before she said or did something she would regret. Like throw herself at him. What if he rejected her? She glanced around at the glass walls and everyone who could see in. Actually she would be in more trouble if he didn't reject her.

"I'll see you then," he said. "You'll dazzle them, Kari."

"Thanks. I'll do my best. 'Bye."

She waved and left his office, then returned to the entrance. The young deputy who had driven her home walked by. He nodded politely and called her ma'am, which made her feel old.

Once outside, she breathed in the afternoon heat and was grateful she'd driven. Any walk longer than ten feet would cause her to sweat through her clothes in about forty seconds. Now, if only she could hire a little elf to go turn on her car and start the air-conditioning. That would be heavenly.

No elf appeared, but just as Kari was about to open her car door, she heard someone call her name. Not Gage, unfortunately. This was a female someone. Kari's body tensed and her shoulders hunched up. Great. Just what she needed.

Still, she forced herself to smile pleasantly as she turned and saw Daisy walking toward her.

The pretty reporter wore a skirt tight enough to cut off the circulation to her shapely legs. An equally snug shirt emphasized large breasts that instantly made Kari feel like a thirteen-year-old still waiting for puberty. Okay, yes, she was tall and slender and she'd been a model, but that didn't change the fact that she was a scant 34B, with hips as wide as a twelve-year-old boy's.

Still, Kari had posture on her side, so she squared her shoulders and forced herself to think tall, elegant, I've-been-in-a-national-magazine type thoughts.

"Hi, Daisy," she said with a big ol' Texas-size smile. "Nice to see you again."

"You, too."

The curvaceous bombshell paused on the sidewalk by the front of Kari's car and gave her a look that could only be called pitying. "This must be so hard for you," she said.

Kari had a feeling Daisy didn't mean the heat, although that was plenty difficult to adjust to. "I'm not sure what you're talking about," she said when she couldn't think of anything else.

Daisy sighed heavily. "Gage, of course. You're still sweet on him. I saw the plate of cookies you took in to the sheriff's office just now. I was across the street getting my nails done."

Kari nodded without turning. She could feel herself flushing, even though she knew she had nothing to be embarrassed about.

Daisy blinked her long lashes. "The thing is, Kari, Gage doesn't go back. He never has. He stays friends with his old girlfriends, but nothing more. And believe you me, more than one girl has tried to get that horse back in the barn." She lowered her voice conspiratorially. "Can you blame them? Gage Reynolds is a catch with a capital *C*. But once things are over, they stay over. What with you being gone and all, I didn't think you knew. I just don't want to see you get hurt."

Kari doubted Daisy's motivation, if not her information. Somehow, she couldn't see the other woman staying up nights worrying about Kari's pain or lack thereof.

"I appreciate the tip," she said, dying to make a move toward her car but not wanting to be rude. She wondered how the very passionate kisses she and Gage had shared fit in with Daisy's revelation. At the same time, she couldn't help smiling at the mental image of him as a runaway horse to be recaptured.

A thought suddenly occurred to her. She glanced at the petite beauty standing on the sidewalk. Something twisted in her stomach and made her swallow hard.

"I didn't know," she said slowly, finally putting all the pieces together.

And she hadn't. Daisy's interest in Gage, her warning Kari away. The fact that Daisy was divorced.

"Didn't know what?" Daisy asked.

Kari felt trapped. "That you're interested in him."

What she was thinking was "in love," but she didn't want to say that.

Daisy shrugged. "I am. I won't deny it. He's a good man and there aren't many of those around. I know. I was married to a real jerk, which explains my divorce."

Kari shifted uncomfortably. She didn't want Daisy saying too much. Somehow it felt wrong. Guilt blossomed inside her. Here she'd been playing fast and loose with an ex-boyfriend, while Daisy had been… What? She didn't know Daisy's position on Gage.

"Are you in love with him?" she asked before she could stop herself.

Oddly enough, Daisy laughed. "Love? I don't think so. I've been in love and it was nothing but trouble. I like Gage a lot. I think we could have a successful marriage, and that's what matters to me. I'm thinking with my head and not any other body part. Not this time. I want a steady man who'll come home when he says and be a decent father to our kids. That man is Gage."

Kari couldn't disagree with her assessment of Gage, but Daisy's plan sounded so cold-blooded, which wasn't Gage's style.

"Does Gage share your feelings on the subject?" she asked.

"No. Like most men, he thinks falling in love makes everything hunky-dory. Which is fine with me. He can love me all he wants. I'll be the sensible one in the relationship." Daisy's eyes narrowed. "So don't for a moment think you can waltz back in here and pick up where you left off."

"It never crossed my mind," Kari said honestly.

"Good. I intend to win him. I just need a little time."

"I'm sure things will work out perfectly." Kari itched

to get back in her car and drive away. More than that, she wished this conversation had never taken place.

The other woman sighed. "Don't take this personally, but I wish you'd never come back."

Kari was starting to have the same wish. She wasn't sure if she felt sorry for Gage or not. He was a big, strong guy—he should be able to handle Daisy. She also felt unsettled, but couldn't say why. Nor did she know what to say to end the conversation.

Finally she opened her car door. "For what it's worth," she said, tossing her purse onto the passenger seat, "I'm not back. Not permanently. So you don't have to worry about me."

"Oh, I didn't plan to."

Daisy waggled her fingers, then turned and headed for the sheriff's office. Kari considered calling out "good luck," but she knew in her heart that she would be lying.

"I don't know. Australia." Edie fingered the glossy travel brochure in front of her. "It's very far."

John, her fiancé, smiled indulgently. "Travel does tend to take one away from one's regular world. That's the point."

Edie rolled her eyes. "I know that. I just never thought…" Her voice trailed off. "Australia," she repeated softly.

Gage watched her from his place on the opposite side of the kitchen table. He'd joined his mother and John for dinner. Once the plates had been cleared, John had pulled out several brochures for trips to exotic places. He and Edie had yet to pick a honeymoon destination.

As Gage sipped his coffee, he couldn't help being pleased with his mother's happiness. His father's death had nearly destroyed her. For a while he'd worried that he was going to lose her, as well. Eventually, she'd started to heal. But she hadn't returned to anything close to normal until she'd met John.

Physically, John wasn't anything like Gage's father, Ralph. The retired contractor was several inches shorter, stocky to Ralph's lean build, and blond with blue eyes to Ralph's dark coloring. But he was a good man with a generous nature and a loving heart. He'd wanted to sweep Edie off her feet and marry her that first month. Instead, he'd courted her slowly, giving her all the time she'd needed. It had taken over a year for her to agree to marry him, but since she'd admitted her feelings, they'd been inseparable.

While their budding romance had been strange to Gage, he'd tried to stay open to the idea. He'd quickly come to see that John wasn't trying to take anyone's place. And his mother deserved a chance at happiness. "After touring Australia, we board the cruise ship. There are stops in Singapore, Hong Kong and other parts of China before heading to Japan. We'll fly back from there."

Edie shook her head. "Of course it sounds lovely." She glanced at her fiancé and smiled lovingly. "I won't even mention that it will be very expensive."

John gave a playful growl. "Good."

"I've always wanted to see that part of the world," she said wistfully.

"Then, you should say thank you, give your fiancé a big kiss and start making plans," Gage said easily. "Go for it, Mama."

They could both afford the time the long trip would take, and John had retired a millionaire. Even after settling money on his daughters and grandchildren, there was still plenty to keep him and his new wife in style.

Edie glanced from him to John, then nodded tentatively.

John grinned. "Where's that kiss your son suggested you give me?"

She brushed his mouth with hers.

Gage sipped at his coffee again. There had always been good times around this table. Years before, when his father was still alive, they'd often talked long into the night. Ralph had been devoted to his wife in many ways, but he'd been a stubborn man who didn't bend on many things. He hadn't liked to travel, and Edie's pleas to see if not the world, then parts of the country, went ignored.

Ralph had been born and bred in Possum Landing, and as far as he was concerned, a man couldn't do better. Gage knew he had a little of his father in him. He loved the town where he'd been born, and he never wanted to live anywhere else. Unlike his father, though, he hadn't made Possum Landing his whole world. He enjoyed going to different places. He supposed that was because he was also his mother's son. Edie opened the brochure and spread it over the kitchen table. "I can't believe we're going to do this. Gage, look. We can take a trip to the Australian outback. Oh! There's snorkeling on the Great Barrier Reef."

"Watch out for sharks," he teased.

She gave him a loving smile and returned her attention to the pictures.

While his mother and John planned their trip, Gage stared out the open window into the night. He hadn't been very good company tonight, probably because he felt distracted. He didn't want to admit the cause of the problem, but he knew exactly what it was. Or rather who.

Kari.

She was back from her interview. Her trip had taken her away for three days, but she'd returned that morning. He'd seen her car. While he'd told himself that her comings and goings didn't matter to him, he'd acknowledged an inner relief at knowing she was once again in the house next door.

Trouble, he told himself grimly. Way too much trouble.

He knew at some point he was going to see her. No doubt he would continue to help her with the work she was doing on her grandmother's house. But something had changed between them. He didn't know if it was the fight or what had happened right before the fight. Passion had ignited and they'd both nearly gone up in flames. After all this time, he wouldn't have thought that was possible.

He finished his coffee, then stood and stretched. "It seems to me you lovebirds need to be alone," he teased.

Edie looked up. "Oh, Gage. Don't go. Are we ignoring you?"

He circled around the table, bent down and kissed her cheek. "You're planning your honeymoon, Mama. I don't think you need your grown son hanging around while you do that." He shook John's hand. "Don't let her talk you into a dark cabin in the ship's hold. She'll try."

John grinned. "Don't I know it. But I'm going to insist on a suite."

"Oh, John. That would be *so* expensive."

The men shared a quick look that spoke of their mutual affection for Edie.

Before leaving, Gage headed for the trash container under the sink.

"You don't have to do that," John told him. "I'll take it out later."

Gage shook his head. "Don't sweat it. I have years of practice. Besides, once you two are married, I plan to let you take over all the chores."

"It's a deal."

Gage called out a good-night and walked out the back door. The porch light illuminated his way. He whistled tunelessly as he went to the trash can and pulled off the lid. He was about to set the plastic bag inside when he saw a beautiful cloth box resting on several paper bags. While the floral print made him want to gag, he recognized the container. His mother kept pictures and other treasures inside. She'd had it for as long as he could remember. Why would she be throwing it out now?

Must be a mistake, he thought as he took it out of the trash can and put the kitchen bag in its place. He set the lid down and turned toward the house. But at the bottom porch step, he stumbled slightly. The cloth box went flying out of his hands, hit the next step up and tipped open. Dozens and dozens of pictures spilled out onto the concrete.

Gage swore under his breath. As he bent to retrieve them, he recognized old photos of his mother, back when she was young. So damn beautiful, he thought as he started to pick them up. He saw her with Ralph and with her family. There were several—Gage frowned as he shuffled through the pictures. There was his mother with a man he didn't recognize. At first he dismissed the pictures as taken before she'd married, but there was a wedding ring on her finger. Yet the man had his arm around her in a way that implied they were more than just friends. Gage stared at him. He was a stranger, yet there was something familiar about him. Gage picked up more pictures and flipped through them. The man appeared in several different shots. Always close to Gage's mother. Always looking pleased about something.

And then he got it. The man looked like Quinn, Gage's brother. Now that Gage looked closer, he saw a lot of himself in the man, too. So he *must* be a relative. But who?

The back door opened. "I didn't hear your truck start," his mother said. "Is there—" She gasped.

He glanced up and saw the color drain from her face. She pressed a hand to her mouth. Her eyes widened, and for a second he thought she was going to faint.

"Mama?"

She shook her head. "Dear God," she whispered. "I threw those out."

"I know. I saw the box. You always kept your treasures in it. I thought it was a mistake." But looking at her stricken expression he realized it hadn't been anything of the sort.

Something went cold inside him. Suddenly he wished he'd never picked up the box. He could be home by now. But instead of backing away, he held up a picture of the stranger with his mother.

"Who is this guy?"

She stared at him as if he held a gun. "S-someone I used to know." Her low voice was barely audible. Gage had the sensation of walking through a minefield.

"Who is he? He looks a lot like Quinn, and I guess a little like me. Is he a relative? An uncle?"

He kept asking even though she didn't answer. He asked because if he didn't, if he allowed himself to think anything, he might figure out something he didn't want to know.

John stepped outside. He took one look at the pictures, then pulled Edie close. "It's all right," he murmured to her.

Gage's gut tightened. John knew. Whatever the secret was, the other man knew. Suddenly Gage had to know, too.

"Who is he?" he repeated.

Tears spilled from her eyes. She turned to her fiancé and clung to him, her entire body shaking with her sobs. Gage hadn't felt afraid in a long time, but he felt a cold uncertainty now.

"John?"

"We should all go inside," the older man said quietly. "Let's talk about this inside."

"No. Tell me now."

John stroked Edie's hair. "Gage, there are things…" He broke off and sighed. "Edie, what do you want me to do?"

His mother looked at John. Whatever the man saw in her eyes caused him to nod. He turned to Gage. "Please come inside, Gage. I don't want to tell you like this."

"I'm not going anywhere until you answer the question. Who is this man?"

John took a deep breath. "He's your father."

Chapter Eight

Kari paced the length of the parlor, pausing every trip to glance out the front window to see if Gage had returned yet. She knew that he was having dinner at his mom's tonight and that she could stop pacing because as long as she stayed at the front of the house, she would hear his truck approach. But logic didn't seem to eliminate her need to keep walking.

She wanted to see him, she admitted to herself. She wanted to talk to him and joke with him and just plain be in the same room with him. She'd only been gone three days, but it felt longer than that. Somehow, reconnecting with Gage would make her homecoming more complete.

Well, not a homecoming, she told herself firmly. This wasn't home and she wasn't back. It's just that she was in Possum Landing temporarily and he was a part of that. Or something.

She crossed to the window again and stared out into the night. She had so much she wanted to tell him. Her interview had gone really well. She'd met with the principal and several of the teachers. The following day she'd met with a small committee from the board of education. On her second interview with the principal, the woman had hinted that an offer more than likely would be forthcoming. So things were going really great. That's why she wanted to see Gage. She wanted him to help her celebrate. Or something.

"Where are you?" she muttered aloud, dropping the curtain and resuming her circuit of the parlor. The restlessness had returned and with it a longing for something she couldn't define or name. It filled her until she wanted to jump out of her skin.

Just when she knew she couldn't stand it one more second, she heard his truck pull into the driveway next door. Kari ran to the front door and pulled it open, then hurried across the porch and down the front steps. Her heart quickened, as did her footsteps. As he stepped down from the cab, she crossed the last few feet between them. They had agreed to no more kissing, but was it permissible to throw herself in his arms? Because that's what she felt like doing. Just launching herself in his general direction and— He turned toward her. Light from the house spilled into the night, illuminating a bit of the driveway and part of his face. She came to a stop as if she'd hit a brick wall. Something had happened— she saw it in his eyes. Something bad.

"Gage?"

He stared at her, his expression bleak, his mouth set. Instead of speaking, he shook his head, then walked toward his house.

Kari hesitated, not sure what to do. Finally she followed him up the steps, so much like those at her grandmother's, into a house that mirrored hers.

Same front room, same hallway, same stairs—only

reversed and modernized. Several floor lamps provided light. She had a quick impression of hardwood floors, overstuffed furniture and freshly painted walls, before Gage captured her attention by crossing to a cabinet at the end of the parlor. He opened it, pulled out a bottle of scotch and poured himself a drink. He downed it in two gulps, poured another and moved to the sofa, where he sank down.

"Help yourself," he said, his voice low and hoarse. She watched him take another gulp, then set the half-full glass on the wooden coffee table, leaned back and closed his eyes.

Fear flickered inside her. Instead of claiming the drink he'd offered, she headed for the sofa and settled next to him. She was close enough to study him, but far enough away that she didn't crowd him.

After a few minutes of silence, she lightly touched his arm. "Want to talk about it?"

He shrugged. "I don't know what to say."

"Is everyone all right? Your mom? Quinn? Did you hear from the government?"

He turned toward her and opened his eyes. Anguish darkened the brown irises. He looked like a man who had been to hell and faced the devil.

"No one's dead," he said flatly. "At least, no one who wasn't dead before."

She didn't know what to say to that. But without knowing the problem, how could she help? Or could she? He hadn't told her to go away, which relieved her, but she had a bad feeling that if he did finally spill the beans, she wasn't going to be any happier for knowing.

He rubbed his temples, then reached for his drink. After finishing it, he set the glass back on the table.

"I've only been really furious once before in my life," he said, his voice still lacking expression or emotion. "I've been mad and angry, just like everyone else. But I'm talking about that inner rage that burns hot and makes a man want to take on the world."

She stared at him. He didn't look angry. He didn't look anything.

"When was that?" she asked.

"When you left."

She winced.

He shrugged. "It's the truth. I read and reread your note about a hundred times, then I went and got skunk drunk. I decided to go after you. It's a little fuzzy now, but I think I had this plan to chase down your bus and drag you off. I was going to tell you exactly what I thought of you. I knew better, but I wanted to do it, anyway. I'd never been so angry in my life."

She swallowed. "What happened?"

"I got lucky. When I crashed, I only hurt myself. I totaled the car and walked away with a few scars." He glanced at her. "I learned my lesson. I may get drunk tonight, but I won't be driving."

"Okay."

She was no closer than she had been to getting at the problem. No one was dead and he didn't plan on getting drunk, then chasing someone down in a car.

"If you're keeping me company, it's going to be a long night," he said. "You might as well pour me another and get yourself one, too. You're going to need it."

Kari took his advice. She carried his glass back to the cabinet, got one for herself and poured for both of them. When she returned to the sofa, she said, "Tell me what happened."

Gage stared into his drink. What had happened? Nothing. Everything. How was he to explain that his entire world had shifted on its axis? Nothing he knew as true was as it had been before. Nothing was as it had been just an hour before. In a heartbeat—with less than half a dozen words—everything had changed.

"I was at my mom's for dinner," he began slowly, not looking at her, not wanting her to see inside of him, not wanting to know what she was thinking. "When I left, I took the trash out, like I always do. There was a box in the trash can outside. A cloth-covered one my mom had kept for years. She always stored important pictures and stuff in it, so I thought it must be a mistake. I started to carry it back inside, but I tripped on the steps and it went flying. Everything fell out. There were pictures inside."

He fell silent. His brain didn't seem to be working. He could speak the words, but he wasn't thinking them first. They simply came out on their own. He thought about what had happened, but it was as if he were viewing a movie. That man on the stairs wasn't him. The woman wasn't his mother. They hadn't had that conversation.

"A man." He continued before he could stop himself. "My mother with a man."

Kari leaned close and touched his arm again. He liked that. She was warm and steady in his cold, spinning world.

"She had an affair?"

He nodded.

Beside him, Kari sighed. "I know that's a tough one. You have this idea of your parents' marriage and it's one in which they both never mess up. You must have been really shocked."

She didn't understand. Probably because he hadn't told her all of it. The most important part. The part that had torpedoed his past and dropped land mines in his future.

"John knew," he said flatly. "He came out on the porch. She started to cry and couldn't speak, but he told me." Against his will he turned to look at Kari. "The man in the picture is my father."

She stared at him. Her eyes widened, her lips parted and color drained from her face. "Gage," she breathed.

He nodded slightly. "Yeah. I can't believe it, either. It can't be true. My dad—I mean Ralph." He shuddered. None of this made sense. It would never make sense. Anger filled him again. Anger and pain—a deadly combination. Only, this time he wasn't going to get drunk and go tearing down city streets. This time he was going to sit here and do nothing until it all went away.

"Your father," she said.

"Which one?"

"Your real one. Ralph. I don't understand. Your parents were so in love. Everyone knew it. They spent all their time together. They were always talking and laughing. I know your mom. She's not the kind of woman who would…" Her voice trailed off.

Gage knew what she meant. He would never have guessed his mother was the kind of woman who would have an affair and then pass her bastard off as her husband's kid. And he could never see his father allowing it.

"How did it happen?" she asked.

"I don't know. I didn't stick around long enough to ask questions." Instead, he'd walked out, the sound of his mother's sobs following him to his truck. "I don't want it to be true," he admitted quietly. "Not any of it. If I'm not my father's son…"

Who was he? Five generations of Reynolds living in Possum Landing. He'd always taken pride in that. He'd made his history a part of who he was. Except, that wasn't his history anymore. He didn't have one— just lies.

Kari shifted close and tucked her arm around his. She leaned her head on his shoulder. "Oh, Gage. I don't know what to say. I have so many questions, but no way to make you feel better. I'm sorry."

He didn't say anything, nor did he move away. Having Kari next to him felt right. Her touch and her words alone weren't enough to make him feel better, but that didn't mean he wanted her to move away. He needed the connection to her tonight more than he ever had.

They sat in silence for a long time.

"He's Quinn's father, too," Gage said finally. "I could see the resemblance in the pictures."

Kari raised her head. "Quinn's father? But then the affair was ongoing. For at least a couple of years. How is that possible?"

"I don't know. While the guy in the picture looked familiar because of Quinn looking so much like him, I've never seen him before. I'm guessing he's not from around here."

He couldn't comprehend his mother having a brief affair, let alone something that lasted long enough to produce two children. Where the hell had his father, Ralph, been in all this? Gage would have bet his life that his dad— He swore, *not* his father. He didn't know his father. Damn. He would have bet his life that Ralph wouldn't tolerate Edie being unfaithful, no matter how much he loved her. So what had happened?

The phone rang. He didn't move.

Kari turned her head toward the sound. "Aren't you going to get that?"

"No."

"It's probably your mom, or maybe John."

Gage shrugged. He didn't want to talk to either of them.

Kari started to say something, but the start of the message cut her off. The sound of his voice filled the room. "It's Gage. I'm not in. Leave a message at the tone."

"G-Gage—?" His mother's voice broke. "Are you there? I'm so s-sorry. I know you're upset and—" She began to cry.

Kari got up and walked to the phone. He didn't try to stop her because it didn't matter. She and his mother could talk all night and it wouldn't change anything.

Without Kari beside him, the anger burned hotter and brighter. He didn't like being afraid, so he sank into rage, instead. It was safer, easier. The sense of betrayal nearly overwhelmed him. He knew that whatever his mother had to say, whatever the excuses might be, they weren't going to be enough. He would never forgive her.

When Kari returned, she sat on the coffee table, her knees between his. She leaned toward him and took his hands in hers.

"Your mom wanted to know that you're okay," she told him. "I said you were still in shock."

Her blue eyes were steady as she looked at his face. Despite his pain and confusion, he thought she was one of the most beautiful women he'd ever known. Her wide eyes, her full mouth, her perfect skin.

She squeezed his fingers. "She wants to talk to you."

Rage returned. "No," he said flatly.

"You're going to have to do it sometime."

"Why?"

"To get your questions answered."

"I don't have any."

"Gage, of course you do. Too many questions. Edie said she has to explain. There are things you don't understand."

"You think?" he asked bitterly.

Kari continued to hold his hands. "Your relationship with your mother has always been extremely important to you. After all these years, you're not going to turn your back on her regardless of how angry you are right now."

"Want to bet?"

"Absolutely. I know you. You need to hear her out. You need to know and understand the truth. There are things you have to be told."

He jerked his hands free and glared at her. "Like the fact that the man I thought was my father isn't? I already know that one."

"Biology doesn't change the memories. Your father loved you very much."

"I don't know if my father even knows I'm alive."

"Ralph is your father in every sense of the word."

"Not anymore." Not ever.

Kari glared at Gage. She hated when he got stubborn. He was like a giant steer in the middle of the road. All the prodding in the world wasn't going to get him to move until he decided he was good and ready.

Only, being stubborn this time was going to hurt both him and Edie.

Kari didn't know what had happened thirty-plus years ago. Nor had Edie explained how she'd come to be pregnant by a man other than her husband. But Kari knew there had to be a darn good explanation, and if Gage would stop being angry for one second, he would figure it out, too.

But she couldn't bring herself to be upset with him. Not when he looked so broken. The big, strong man she'd always known still sat in front of her, but behind his eyes lurked something dark and lonely. Something that cried out to her.

Impulsively she leaned toward him, sliding to the edge of the coffee table. She could just stretch her hands far enough to reach his shoulders. When she touched the cloth of his shirt, she drew him toward her.

He didn't cooperate, which was just so like him.

How difficult could one man be?

"Work with me, here," she said in frustration, then moved to the sofa and knelt beside him.

She rested her hands on his shoulders and brushed his mouth with hers. The kiss came from a need to comfort and connect.

For a second he didn't respond. But just as she was about to move back, his arms came around her waist and he hauled her up against him. Her knee sank in between the cushions, causing her to almost lose her balance. But before she could fall, he turned her slightly, shifting her weight until she sat on his lap, her body angled toward his.

It wasn't exactly what she'd had in mind when she'd first kissed him, but now that she was here, she found that being cradled next to Gage was a really nice way to spend an evening. Especially when he slightly opened his mouth and swept his tongue across her lower lip.

Suddenly the tension in the room shifted. It was no longer about an external situation, but about what was growing between *them*. Hot tension. Sexual tension. Need. Desire.

Her hold on his shoulders changed from gentle to intense. The compassionate ache inside her became a very different kind of ache. She wanted to offer a whole lot more than just comfort.

She parted her lips to admit him, then stroked her tongue against his when he accepted the invitation. He wrapped his arms around her and pulled her even closer to his chest. Then his hands were everywherestroking her back, her hips, her legs. In turn she touched his face, feeling rough stubble, then the smooth silk of his hair. She tried to press herself against him, but in their current positions it was impossible.

Still, the deep, powerful, passionate kisses took some of the sting out of that. When he retreated, she followed, only to have him close his mouth around her tongue and suck. Shivers raced through her. Warm, liquid heat stirred between her legs. Her breasts swelled inside her bra as her nipples tightened. She thought he might have noticed because he moved his hand along the outside of her leg to her hips, then up her waist and rib cage to her breasts. Once there, he settled his palm over her curves. The delightful weight made her squirm. The shivering increased, as did her desire to have him touch her all over…without clothes as a barrier.

The concept should have shocked her, but it didn't. This was Gage—the man she'd always trusted. If he wanted to make love tonight, she would only encourage the idea. She'd never been sure with anyone else, but she was sure with him.

So she arched into his touch and moaned softly when he brushed his thumb against her tight nipple. Against her hip—the one nestling into his groin—she felt something hard pressing into her. She wiggled to get a little closer.

Suddenly he moved her, shifting her so she had to scramble to keep her balance. He set her on her feet, then rose, as well. Questions filled his eyes, but so did need and wanting.

"Kari?"

She leaned in to him and ran her hands up and down his strong chest. It seemed to be the answer he was looking for. He drew her close and kissed her again, this time plunging inside of her and taking what he wanted. She reveled in his desire. Heat filled her, melting her until it was difficult to remain standing.

He cupped her face, then slipped his fingers through her hair. He broke the kiss, started it again, then stopped.

When she looked at him, she saw the darkness was gone. Instead, humor brightened his expression.

"I'm trying to stop long enough to get us upstairs," he said. "I have a very comfortable bed, not to mention protection. But I can't keep my hands off you."

"Who says you have to?" she asked as she turned toward the stairs. "Last one upstairs has to strip for the winner."

Gage chuckled, then moved after her. Halfway up the stairs, he grabbed her by the waist and drew her to him. They were on different steps, and she shrieked when she almost lost her balance.

"It's okay," he whispered, picking her up and turning so that she dangled in front of him while he faced the bottom of the staircase.

"What on earth are you doing?" she demanded.

"Making sure I get there first." He spoke directly into her ear. "I like to watch."

She barely had time to absorb his words before he reached the landing.

"I win," he said, releasing her so that her feet touched solid flooring again. He clicked on a light.

She sidled away and glanced at him from under her lashes. *I like to watch.* His words made her both excited and a little uncomfortable.

"Gage, I don't know if I can—"

He captured her hand and raised it to his mouth, where he planted tiny, damp kisses on the inside of her wrist. "I know. It's okay. I was teasing."

"Are you sure?" She looked at him anxiously. "I want to do what—" She cleared her throat. "I just couldn't…"

This was probably the time to tell him that she was a virgin, although she had a bad feeling that if she did, he would stop. Which wasn't what she wanted.

And while she fit the technical description of someone who had never had actual penetration, she'd played around some. It's not as if she'd never seen a naked man before. She'd even climaxed once, although that sure hadn't been the experience she'd been hoping for.

"You don't have to strip for me," he said gently as he touched her cheek. "We can save that for next time."

Relief filled her. "I'm not sure I should commit to that, either. Maybe you should strip for me next time."

"It's a deal."

He stared at her, then bent down and kissed her. As his tongue slipped into her mouth, he cupped her breasts, angling his hands so he could rub her tight nipples. The combination of sensations made her knees nearly give way. She had to hold on to him to keep upright.

Then they were moving. As he kissed her and touched her, he urged her backward, heading them toward the large bedroom at the end of the hallway. But before they were halfway there, he broke the kiss long enough to pull off her T-shirt. Then she felt his hands on her breasts with one less layer between them.

His fingers touched the top of her breasts, his thumbs teasing the nipples while his palms supported her curves. He was warm, gentle and very sexy, she thought dreamily as they started to move again.

This time when they stopped, she kicked off her sandals. Gage had something else in mind. He reached for the fastening on her bra and undid it. The wisp of lace seemed to vanish into thin air. Then his hands were back, but on bare flesh this time.

She arched her head as he cupped her, stroked her, teased her. His skin was slightly rough—not enough to hurt her, but just enough to be…delicious. As he played with her breasts, he kissed along her jaw, then licked the sensitive skin just below her ear. She moaned in delight as pleasure swept through her body.

"I want to touch you everywhere," he whispered in her ear. "I want to touch you and taste you and listen to your breathing change. I want to take you to the edge and back, until you don't have any choice but to fall over. Then I want to catch you and make it happen again and again."

She shivered at his words and began to wonder how much farther it was to the bedroom. They began to move. When her bare feet felt the change from hardwood to carpet, she knew they were close. Gage moved away long enough to turn on a lamp on the nightstand and pull back the covers. Then he returned to her side. But he didn't touch her breasts. Instead, he knelt on the floor and went to work on her shorts. They came off easily, as did her panties. In a matter of seconds, she was naked. Before she could be embarrassed, he pressed a kiss to her belly and began to move lower.

Kari had an idea of his ultimate destination and it worried her. Someone else had done that to her once. All her friends raved about the glories of oral sex, while she had found it embarrassing and more than a little painful. All that sucking and biting had left her bruised and seeking escape. But how to say that without sounding like an idiot?

She put her hand on his head to get his attention, but before she could speak, he reached his goal. He used his fingers to part her slightly, then leaned in close and licked the most sensitive part of her.

Liquid fire shot through her. There was no other way to describe it, she thought, more than a little dazed. The slow, gentle movement of his tongue made her want to moan, or even scream. If he didn't do that again, she wouldn't be able to survive.

Fortunately he did do it again…and again. He licked and pressed and kissed so very lightly. She found herself wanting more. There was also the issue of her standing, which meant she couldn't part her legs enough. But she didn't want him to stop so that she could climb onto the mattress. It was a dilemma unlike any she'd ever faced.

Gage solved it for her by shifting her onto the edge of the bed. She fell back, legs spread shamelessly, her entire body begging him to do more and more until she got so lost in the pleasure that she couldn't find her way out.

He chuckled softly as he moved close, draping her legs over his shoulders. She was exposed and completely at his mercy. She couldn't remember ever being so vulnerable in her life. She felt wonderful.

Then he licked her again, and she felt even better than wonderful. He knew exactly how to touch her, how to make her breathing stop, how to make her scream. He moved faster, then slower, controlling the building passion, making her get so close she couldn't help but release, then he pulled her back at the last second and left her panting.

As he worked his magic between her legs, he reached up and touched her breasts. He cupped the curves and lightly pinched her nipples. The combination of sensations made it impossible for her to catch her breath. Then he was moving faster and faster, and she knew that this time if he stopped she would have a heart attack and die right there in his bed and—

She screamed. Her cry of pleasure filled the room as he took her to the edge and gently pushed her out into the warm, sensual darkness. Shudders raced through her body. Heat filled her as her release went on for a lifetime, rising and falling, but never, ever ending.

It was better than anything she'd ever read about. Obviously she'd been doing something very wrong until this point.

With a sigh of contentment, she floated back to reality and found herself lying on Gage's bed. He'd shifted her fully onto the mattress and was in the process of taking off his clothes. She looked at him as he undressed, taking in the firm muscles and, as he dropped his boxers, the size of him.

Kari searched her feelings and knew this was right for her. There wasn't a doubt in her mind that he would stop if she asked him to. But instead of questions or uncertainty, a little voice inside whispered only one thing—*It's about time!*

Gage watched Kari watching him. She seemed lost in thought, then gave a slow smile. "What's so funny?" he asked as he reached for the box of condoms in his nightstand.

"I was just thinking that we've waited a long time to do this. So far, I have to say the experience has been extraordinary."

"I'll do my best to make sure it continues to be so."

"I have every confidence."

He wasn't so sure. Pleasuring her had been easy. He liked everything about her body, from her slender curves to the way she tasted. But once he was on top of her and inside her it was going to be a different story. He had a bad feeling that he wasn't going to last all that long. He felt as if he could explode at any second.

He slipped onto the bed next to her and touched her flat stomach. "So this is where I tell you it's been a really long time since I've been with anyone. Add that to the fact that I used to spend hours fantasizing about making love with you, and we've got trouble. If you're hoping for a stellar performance, you may have to wait for round two."

She leaned on one elbow and kissed him. "You say the sweetest things. Did you really fantasize about me?"

He chuckled. "All those evenings spent kissing in

the front seat of my car. Kissing and kissing and very little else. Of course I fantasized. I was so hard, I could barely walk—so what else could I do?"

"Maybe you'd like to take one of those fantasies out for a test drive."

Her words were all the invitation he needed. He slipped on the condom and positioned himself between her legs. He glanced at her perfect body, then shifted his gaze to her face. Her blue eyes stared back just as intently. He began to slip inside her.

She was hot, wet and tight. The combination didn't bode well for his self-control. He gritted his teeth and thought about all the paperwork on his desk. Then he moved on to the city council meeting about adding a traffic light. He was—

He swore silently as he continued to fill her. It was impossible to think of anything but how good she felt. He wanted to lose control. Which would take about two seconds.

No. Better to go slow the first time. He wanted it to be good for her.

He stopped suddenly at an unexpected barrier.

What...?

But before he could think coherently enough to figure out what was wrong, Kari put her hands on his hips and drew him forward. At the same moment, she arched and made a request using a very bad word.

How was he supposed to refuse?

So he pushed into her, breaking through the barrier. At that second, she stiffened and gave a muffled cry. Only, it wasn't of pleasure. Her eyelids drifted closed. His heart sank.

Dammit all to hell. She'd been a virgin.

Chapter Nine

Gage started to withdraw, but before he could, Kari opened her eyes and clamped her hands on his hips. "Don't," she whispered fiercely. "There's no reason to stop."

He could think of about fifty…or at least one really good one. But she was moving beneath him, urging him on.

"It's already done," she pointed out. "There's no going back."

Not exactly words he wanted to hear. Unfortunately he'd reached the point of no return, and one way or the other, his body was going to make sure he finished what he'd started. He decided to pull out, to not make things worse, but parts of him had other ideas. He'd barely started his retreat when the powerful rush of his release exploded from him, temporarily making rational thought impossible.

He pushed deep inside her until the last of the shudders faded, then withdrew. As he did, he was damn grateful he'd taken care of birth control.

He rolled off her without saying anything and headed

for the bathroom. Once he settled next to her again, he closed his eyes and prayed fervently for no more surprises…at least not for the next twenty-four hours. He didn't think his heart would survive another one. But in the meantime there were the ramifications of the latest newsflash in his life.

He shifted until he could see Kari. She lay on her side of the bed, naked and studying him with a wary expression. As much as he wanted to remind her that she should have told him, that he should have been part of the decision-making process, he didn't want to turn her first time into something ugly. So he banked any lingering temper and remembered what it had felt like to make her climax. He recalled the taste of her skin and the soft sound of her cries. He smiled softly and touched her cheek.

"Want to tell me why?" he asked quietly.

"Why I'm a virgin? Why I chose you? Why now?"

"Any of those would be a good starting point." Color stained her cheeks, leftover proof of her pleasure. Or maybe she was embarrassed. Her mussed hair framed her face, her mouth was swollen, her eyes were heavy lidded. She looked like a woman who had been well loved. She didn't look anything like a virgin.

She lifted one bare shoulder in a shrug. "I didn't set out to have this happen. I never intended to stay a virgin this long. It's just one of those things."

"Go on," he said, when she stopped talking.

"There's not much to say. I did date while I was in New York, but not all that much. Men who were obsessed with models terrified me, so I avoided anyone who seemed like a groupie. I was selective, cautious, and I moved slow. Most of them gave up on me before I had a chance to give in."

"Their loss."

She smiled slowly. "That's what I always said. I played around some, heavy petting, that sort of thing. But somehow, I never really got around to...you know." She shrugged again.

He wasn't sure what to make of her brief explanation. While he had always regretted not being her first, it had never occurred to him there might be a second chance for them.

"That explains why you were still a virgin," he said slowly. "But why now? Why with me?"

She stared at the bed, tracing a pattern with her finger. "I wanted my first time to be with someone I liked and respected. That's a more difficult combination to find than I would have thought. I didn't come home thinking we'd do what we ended up doing together, but tonight, when I knew you wanted me—" She cleared her throat, then continued. "It just seemed like the right thing to do."

No woman had ever shocked him so much in bed. He still wasn't sure what he felt. No way Kari would have set him up. But he was sure confused.

"I wish you'd told me," he said. "I would have done things differently if I'd known."

"Yeah, you would have run."

He grinned. "Darlin', this is Texas. We don't have any hills."

"What about in the Hill Country?"

"Bumps. They're glorified bumps."

She laughed softly, then her humor faded. "I thought you'd be mad. Or you'd change your mind. Or both."

He considered the possibilities. Had he known, would he have wanted to take on the responsibility of being Kari's first?

"I didn't want to make it a big deal," she said as if she could read his mind. "Are you mad?"

"No. Startled maybe."

Her mouth curved up at the corners. "I'll bet. If you could have seen the look on your face."

He didn't smile back. Instead, he moved close and drew her to him. What was done was done. He might not have controlled how it started, but he would make sure it ended well.

"I'm sorry I hurt you," he said.

"That comes with the territory," she said, snuggling closer still. "The rest of it was great."

"Thank you."

If nothing else, she'd taken his mind off his troubles. Now, in his bed, with both of them naked after just having made love, he refused to think about the other surprise in his life. He focused on the feel of Kari's bare skin and the scent of her body.

"Do you want me to go?" she asked suddenly.

"Go where?"

"Back to my place?"

He rubbed her back, then slipped his hand to her hip. "I would like whatever you would like. Do you want to spend the night?"

"Here?"

"Right here in this bed. Unless you're a cover hog. Then, you'll have to sleep in the guest room."

"I don't really know what I am," she admitted. "Maybe it's time we found out."

She gave him a smile that could light up the sky. "Maybe it is."

He pulled up the covers and flicked out the light.

Kari rested her head on his shoulder. "Gage?" she said into the darkness. "Yeah."

"You made my first time terrific. Thank you."

"You're welcome."

He held her tightly against him and listened to the sound of her breathing. If he'd been in possession of all the facts, maybe he wouldn't have chosen to sleep with Kari tonight, but now that it had happened, he couldn't find it in himself to regret it. Not for a minute.

Kari awoke sometime in the middle of the night. A bit of street light filtered in through a crack in the drapes. Gage lay beside her, but she couldn't hear his breathing, so she didn't know if he was awake or not. Her body both tingled and ached. The remnants of amazing sexual pleasure lingered, but there was a faint soreness between her legs.

She turned toward Gage, studying the barely visible outline of his profile.

He could have been furious with her. After all, she hadn't warned him what he was getting into. In the end, he'd been sweet and funny and he'd made her feel really good. Not just about the sex, but about choosing him.

Her decision hadn't been conscious, she acknowledged. In light of what had been going on, it had seemed to be the logical thing to do. Being with him had felt right. She'd been afraid the actual act of making love would be awkward or embarrassing, but he'd made it all easy and exciting.

"Why aren't you asleep?" he asked unexpectedly.

She blinked. "How do you know I'm not?"

"I can hear you thinking."

She laughed. "Okay. Why aren't you sleeping?"

"Too much on my mind."

"Oh, Gage." She slid closer and placed her arm across his chest. "I wish I could help."

"Me, too. But I have to work things out for myself."

His tone indicated he didn't actually believe that was possible. She thought about telling him there wasn't anything to work out. He had to come to peace with his mother's revelation. However, she doubted he would appreciate the advice.

"Want to talk about it?" she asked.

"No. But thanks for offering."

"Want a massage?"

"No."

"Want me to talk dirty?"

He turned toward her. She thought she caught a glimpse of a smile. "I have another suggestion. Turn over so you're facing the other way."

She did as he requested, shifting until her back was to him. He moved behind her, spooning his body to hers. She felt his strong thighs pressing against hers and his chest heating her back. He wrapped an arm around her waist.

"Go to sleep, Kari," he whispered. "Dream good dreams."

"You, too."

She had more to say, but suddenly it was very difficult to talk. Everything felt heavy, then light, then she didn't remember anything at all.

* * *

Kari awoke just after dawn to an empty bed and the smell of coffee. She was also naked and in Gage's bed.

Several thoughts occurred to her at once. First, it was daylight. It was one thing to not mind being naked in a man's bed while it was still night, but in the morning everything looked different. Her second thought was that she'd come over without even closing her front door, let alone locking it. While this was not a big deal in Possum Landing, she'd been in New York long enough to realize she'd behaved like a blockhead. Third...

Gage walked into the bedroom with two cups of coffee, chasing the third thing completely from her mind. Probably because he'd pulled on jeans. Jeans and nothing else.

Kari sat up, pulling the sheet with her, and stared at his bare chest. Hair dusted the defined muscles, narrowing into a thin line that bisected his belly. He was tanned, strong and so masculine she would swear she could feel a swoon coming on.

The stubble darkening his jaw only added to his appeal. He looked dangerous and sexy, not to mention very yummy.

He smiled at her. "How did you sleep?"

"Good. Better than I would have thought. I was never one for spending the night."

His smile broadened. "That must be a virgin thing."

"Must be."

He handed her a mug of coffee and sat on the edge of the bed. "You okay?"

Suddenly shy, she studied the dark liquid before she sipped it. "Yes. Fine. Great."

"Kari?" His voice was a low growl.

She glanced up at him. "I'm fine," she repeated. "Are you okay with everything?"

"Yeah. Still dealing with the shock, but if you don't have any regrets, I don't either."

Relief filled her. "No regrets. I'll admit I should have told you. But I know you would have completely freaked, so I can't be sorry that I didn't."

"I'll give you that—but no more secrets, okay?"

She smiled. "That was my last big one."

He nodded. "Want to take a shower?"

"Sure." She put her mug on the nightstand. "I'll go first—or do you want to?"

He didn't answer. Instead he simply stared at her. Kari blinked. Then heat flared on her face. *Shower,* he'd said. *Do you want to take a shower?* She swallowed.

"Oh," she said in a tiny voice. "You mean together."

"Uh-huh. I have a big old-fashioned tub with a showerhead above it. Plenty of room for two."

"Oh." Oh my!

She had instant visions of them wet and naked and under a stream of hot water. Based on what had happened last night, she was sure whatever she imagined couldn't come close to the glories of reality. Any initial embarrassment would be worth the final result. After all, Gage was very good at what he did.

"Sure," she said, with more bravery than she actually felt. She threw back the covers and headed for the bathroom. "Give me five minutes to, uh, get ready."

"Sure."

She heard him chuckle behind her as she raced into the bathroom and closed the door. One minute to tinkle, one minute and thirty seconds to brush her teeth, one minute to wash the makeup off her face.

She turned on the hot water and let it run. As she'd hoped, Gage took the hint and entered the bathroom... sans clothing. Of course, all he'd had to pull off was jeans, but still, there he was naked and rather ready.

Were they going to— Could they actually do it in the shower? As she fretted logistics, he moved close enough to brush the hair off her forehead, then kissed her.

"You're thinking again. I can hear the gears creaking as they turn faster and faster."

"I can't help it. This is a new experience."

"You'll like it," he promised.

Somehow, she didn't doubt that.

He reached past her and adjusted the water, then stepped into the old-fashioned claw-foot tub. He held the curtain open for her as she stepped in beside him. The master bath, like much of the house, had been completely refurbished. She wasn't sure, but she thought he might have broken through to the bedroom next door and taken about five feet of floor space. In her grandmother's bathroom, there wasn't this much room.

She was working out the construction details in her mind, when Gage directed her to stand beneath the spray. As warm water ran down the front of her body, he went to work on the other side. He lathered soap in his hands, then rubbed them over her shoulders and down her arms. He lathered her back, her fanny and her legs. Then he turned her toward him so she could rinse off.

While the warm spray sluiced down her skin, he leaned close and kissed her. She parted instantly for him, welcoming him, teasing him, tasting that appealing combination of mint and coffee. As he kissed her, he poured shampoo into his hands, then began to wash her hair. The combination of his tongue in her mouth and his fingers massaging her scalp was a sensual delight. She found herself swaying slightly, needing to rest her hands on his chest to steady herself.

He broke the kiss and had her lean her head back to rinse out the shampoo.

Hands made slick from soap glided over her skin. He circled her breasts, then massaged her nipples until they were hard and she was panting. Desire filled her. When he moved lower, she parted her legs to allow him access.

He soaped her gently, then rubbed lightly, as if aware parts of her were still a little tender. Then he reached above her and unfastened the showerhead. She noticed for the first time that it was on a hose. He lowered it and adjusted the spray to a lighter misting, then applied the warm water to her chest, her breasts, then even lower—between her legs.

She gasped. The pulsing water not only washed away soap, it vibrated against her most sensitive places. Tension swept through her, making her hold on to him with both hands. When he bent down and kissed her mouth, she kissed him back hard.

Their tongues danced together. Between her legs the water flowed just enough to excite, but not enough to take her over the edge. When he finally moved the showerhead back into place, she found herself trembling in anticipation of the next round.

"Your turn," she said, reaching for the soap.

She explored his back, taking her time over rippling muscles and a high, tight rear end that deserved a good nibbling. She made a mental note to take care of that soon. After rinsing him off, she had him turn so she could do the front.

Washing his hair proved something of a challenge

as he was several inches taller than her, but she gave it her best shot, and he helped. Then she concentrated on the rest of him.

She massaged his chest, paying attention to his tight nipples. His breath caught when she brushed against them, so she did it several times. She moved lower and lower, dragging her soapy hands to his arousal jutting out toward her. Her fingers encircled him, moving lower, washing between his legs, rubbing back and forth. Just the act of touching him was enough to quicken her breathing. She still ached, but in a completely different way. She wanted him inside her. She wanted to make love with him again. She wanted—

He turned suddenly and rinsed off. "We'll be running out of hot water soon," he said. "I keep meaning to replace the old water heater, but so far I haven't been motivated. You might change that."

She stared at his back. That was it? They weren't going to… But he was hard. She was wet. They had time, means, opportunity and plenty of desire.

He turned off the water and she nearly screamed. Then Gage turned back around and caught a glimpse of her face. He chuckled.

"Stop looking so indignant."

"I'm not," she lied.

"Sure you are. But you're wrong."

With that he bent close, cupped her face and kissed her. She wrapped her arms around him as she surrendered to the need between them. He shifted his weight.

"Step out of the tub, Kari."

She broke the kiss long enough to see what she was doing, then did as he requested. When he'd moved out, as well, he dragged a towel off the rack and flung it on the tile counter, then opened a drawer by the sink and pulled out a condom.

Before she knew what was going on, he'd lifted her to the counter, then dropped to his knees between her spread legs. She knew instantly what he was going to do and found herself halfway to paradise before his tongue even touched her there.

Seconds after the first intimate kiss, every muscle in her body tensed. She felt herself spiraling out of control. He brought her close to the edge, but this time instead of letting her down gently, then building her again, he stopped and stood up.

"It'll be okay," he promised, slipping on the condom.

He moved between her legs and began to kiss her neck. Shivers rippled through her as he stroked her breasts and nipples. She felt a hard probing, and instinctively she parted for him, then reached to guide him in.

This time there wasn't any pain. He still stretched her, but it didn't seem as much as it had last night. She was wet and ready, and the combination of his kissing and his fingers on her breasts made it difficult for her to think about anything but surrender.

He began to move in and out of her. With each slow thrust, she felt her body molding itself around him a little more and a little more. When he moved to kiss her mouth, she welcomed him, pulling him close. His hand dropped from her breasts to between her legs, where he rubbed against her most sensitive place, moving in counterpoint to his thrusting, bringing her closer and closer until she had no choice but to scream his name as her release claimed her.

She couldn't believe what was happening. The orgasm filled her inside and out, while he continued to move, drawing out the pleasure until he, too, stiffened and exhaled her name. They climaxed together, her body rippling around him, his surging. As the last tendrils of release drifted away, Gage raised his head and looked into her eyes.

At that moment she could see down to his soul and didn't doubt he could do the same. The profound connection shook her to the core of her being, and she knew then that nothing would ever be the same.

Still tingling from their recent encounter, Kari dressed and followed Gage down to the kitchen for breakfast. Her emotions seemed to have stabilized, but the sensation of having experienced something profound didn't go away. Still, participating in the ordinary helped. He pulled out eggs and bacon, while she grabbed bread from the freezer for toast.

Every inch of her body felt contented. The occasional aftermath of pleasure shot through her, making her catch her breath as she had a sensual flashback. Gage sure knew how to have a good time both in and out of bed, she thought happily.

"Scrambled all right?" he asked, holding up several eggs.

"Perfect. And I like my bacon extra crisp."

"That's my girl."

While she set the table, he started cooking. Soon the scent of eggs and bacon filled the kitchen. Kari poured them more coffee, then put the toast on a plate she'd warmed in the oven. At the same time he carried two frying pans to the table and set them on the extra place mats.

They sat down across from each other, and Gage offered her the bacon. Kari liked that things were easy between them. No awkward moments, no bumping as they moved. She couldn't imagine the morning after being so comfortable with any of the other men she'd gone out with in the past few years. Of course, she doubted she would have spent the night with them, anyway.

She looked up, prepared to share her observation, when she caught Gage looking past her. The faraway look in his eyes told her that he was thinking about something other than their lovemaking. He'd remembered what he'd learned the night before. Her heart ached for him.

She sighed.

He glanced at her. "What?"

"I just wish I could find something magical to say so you'd feel better."

"Not possible."

"I know."

Everything had changed for him. In a single moment, he'd lost the anchor to his world—his past. He'd always prided himself on being one of the fifth generation of Reynolds to live in Possum Landing. He'd been his father's son. He'd—

She frowned. Why did that have to be different? "Gage, I understand that you no longer have the biological connection to Ralph Reynolds that you had before, but that doesn't mean he's not your father."

He glared at her. "He's not my father."

"That's just biology. What about the heart? He still loved you from the second you were born. He held you and taught you and supported you. He came to every football and baseball game you ever played in. He taught you to fish, and drive. All those dad things."

"How could he have loved me?" he asked bitterly.

"His wife had cheated on him. I was another man's bastard."

She didn't have all the answers, but she was very sure about one thing. "No one seeing the two of you together could doubt his feelings for you. I saw it every time we went over there. His love for you lit up his whole face. You can't doubt that."

He shrugged as if he wasn't sure he believed her. Kari didn't know how else to express her feelings. Maybe with time Gage would be able to look at the past and see his father's actions for what they were—a parent's love for his child.

But now wasn't the time to push, so she changed the subject and they discussed renovations on her grandmother's house as they finished breakfast. She'd just poured them a last cup of coffee when there was a knock on the front door.

When Gage didn't budge, she asked, "Want me to get that?"

They both knew who it was. Edie was familiar enough with her son's schedule to know what time he had to leave for work. A quick glance at the clock told Kari there was more than an hour until he had to head out to the station.

She put down the coffeepot and walked to the front door. She had the sudden thought that it didn't look good for her to be here this early. What would Edie think? Then she reminded herself that after what had happened the previous evening, Gage's sleeping arrangements would be the last thing on his mother's mind. She pulled open the door.

"Hi, Edie," she said gently as she took in the other woman's drawn face. Edie looked older than her years, and tired, as if all the life had been sucked out of her.

Edie swallowed, then nodded without speaking. She didn't seem surprised to see Kari as she stepped into the house, but she didn't move past the foyer.

"How is he?"

"Okay, considering. A little confused and angry."

"That makes sense."

Edie wore jeans and a loose T-shirt. The clothes seemed to hang on her. Worry drew her eyebrows together.

"He's in the kitchen," Kari said at last. "I was just about to make more coffee. Do you want some?"

"No coffee for me, thanks."

Edie didn't seem startled to find Kari making coffee in her son's house, either. No doubt she wasn't thinking about something as inconsequential as that.

Impulsively Kari touched her arm. "He'll get over it," she promised. "He needs time."

"I know."

Tears filled Edie's eyes. She blinked them back, then followed Kari to the kitchen.

Gage stood at the sink, scraping dishes and loading the dishwasher. He didn't turn at the sound of their footsteps.

Great. So he was going to make this as difficult as possible for everyone.

"Gage, your mom's here."

"G-Gage?" Edie's voice shook as she spoke.

He put the last plate in the dishwasher and turned to look at her. Kari caught her breath. His face was so set, it could have been carved from stone. He looked angry and unapproachable. She wanted to run for safety, and she wasn't even the one with the recent confession. She could only imagine how Edie felt.

"You two need to talk," she said gently. "As it's a private matter, I'll head home."

Gage spared her a quick glance. "You can stay if you'd like. You already know as much as I do."

Kari shifted uncomfortably. "I know, but your mom would probably be more comfortable to keep it just family."

Edie sighed. "No, Kari. If you're willing to stay, I think you should. Gage may need to have a friend."

Kari hesitated, then nodded slowly. She wasn't sure how she would describe her relationship with Gage. *Friend* was as good a word as any. She motioned to the now cleared table, then crossed to the counter and fixed a fresh pot of coffee. Gage finished with the dishes, then moved to the table. No one spoke until Kari returned to her seat.

Talk about awkward, she thought grimly as they sat in silence. She glanced from mother to son. Edie had pulled a tissue out of her pocket and was twisting it between her fingers.

"I know what you're thinking," she began, as the coffeemaker began to drip. "That I cheated on your father. I suppose that's technically true, but that's not the whole truth." She glanced up at her son. "I loved your father with all my heart. It started the day I met him and it's never faded. Not even once."

"Then, why the hell am I some other man's bastard?"

She flinched slightly but didn't look away. "The trouble began about a year after we married. We'd wanted a big family and had been trying from the very beginning. When nothing happened, we went to the doctor. We found out we couldn't have children."

Chapter Ten

Couldn't have children? "But you have two," Kari said before she could stop herself. She bit her lower lip. "Sorry."

Gage surprised her by reaching across the table and covering her hand with his. "It's okay."

She smiled gratefully as he turned his attention to his mother. "Are you saying Quinn and I are adopted?"

Edie shook her head. "No. We… It was difficult. Thirty years ago they couldn't do as much to help infertile couples. We each took tests and found out that Ralph was the one who couldn't have children. There was something wrong with his sperm."

"So you went out and had an affair?" Gage's rage was a tangible presence in the room.

Edie flinched slightly and turned away, but not before Kari saw the tears return to her eyes.

Kari squeezed his fingers. "You have to listen. If you want to be angry when she's done, that's your right, but let her talk."

His jaw tightened, but he didn't release her hand or disagree. He nodded slightly, indicating his mother should go on.

Edie glanced from Kari to Gage, then continued. "As I said, there weren't as many options back then. Your father… Ralph and I didn't have a lot of money. We explored different treatments, discussed adoption. I was comfortable with that, but he didn't want to go through the process. He was concerned that we wouldn't know where the child came from or who its parents were. You know how that sort of thing was important to him."

Gage nodded curtly.

Kari ached for them both. Nothing about this was easy—she could feel their pain, understand the distance between them. Family and heritage *had* been important to Gage's father, and to Gage. So where did that leave him now? Who *were* his people? Where *was* he from?

"He kept saying he wanted me to experience having my own child. We fought and argued and cried together. At one point he threatened to leave me. But I begged him not to go. In the end, he came up with a compromise. That I would find someone who looked like him and get pregnant."

Gage's head snapped up, and he glared at his mother. "You're telling me this was *his* idea?" His tone clearly stated he didn't believe her.

"I can't prove it," she murmured. "I can only tell you that except for this, I've never lied to you."

Kari held her breath. She believed Edie. There was too much anguish in the other woman's eyes for it to be anything but the truth. Yet Gage hesitated.

Without committing himself to accepting or not, he said, "Go on."

She hesitated a second, then continued. "We fought

about that, as well," Edie said. "In the end, I agreed. I went up to Dallas because we didn't want the scandal of me being with someone from around here. Word would get out, and we didn't want anyone to know the truth. There was a convention there. Ralph had read about it and he thought that would be the perfect place. We might not get to know much about the man, but we would know something."

She picked at the place mat in front of her. "They were all in law enforcement. It was some kind of sheriff's convention. Your biological father—Earl Haynes—was a sheriff."

Kari tried to keep her face blank but doubted she succeeded. Involuntarily her gaze flew to the star on Gage's chest. He'd wanted to be a sheriff all his life—at least, that's what he'd always told her.

His fingers tightened on hers.

"So that's where you met him?" he asked coldly.

"Yes. I met him the first day. He was tall and dark haired, and very charming. We got to know each other. At first I didn't think I could go through with it, but I felt I had to. After a few days, I found myself caring for Earl in a way I hadn't thought I would."

Gage glared at her. "You fell for him?"

"Maybe. I don't know. I'd never been with anyone but Ralph. Earl was like him, but different, too. Exciting. He'd seen a lot of the world, been with a lot of women. I didn't know how to be intimate without giving away a piece of my heart."

Tears trickled from the corners of her eyes. She brushed them away. "I was so confused, and ashamed. I wanted to go home and I didn't. Earl asked me to go back to California with him, but I couldn't. I knew I belonged with Ralph, so I came home."

Gage tore his hand free of Kari's light hold and sprang to his feet. "Who the hell are you? How dare you come in here and tell me you didn't just sleep with some man to get pregnant, but that you also fell for him. You said you loved my father. You said you never stopped loving him."

"I didn't," Edie said, pleading with her son. "I did love him. Earl distracted me from what was important. Do you think I'm proud of what happened or how I felt? I don't want to tell you this, Gage, but I have to. You need to understand the circumstances so you'll know why things were the way they were."

Gage crossed to the sink, where he stood with his back to the table. When he didn't say anything else, Edie went on.

"I came back home and we found out I was pregnant. Ralph never said anything about what had happened. He never asked or blamed me, and when you were born, he was as proud as any father could have been. He loved you with every fiber of his being."

Gage visibly stiffened, but didn't speak. Edie looked at Kari, who gave her a reassuring smile.

"You also looked like Ralph, which pleased him," Edie said, then swallowed. "Everything was perfect. We had you, we had each other. But I couldn't forget. What I didn't know then was that my feelings for Earl were just a girlish fantasy—the result of never having been on a date with a man other than Ralph. I mistook infatuation for love, and when you were three months old, I returned to Dallas."

Gage swore loudly. "You saw him again?"

Edie nodded. "I couldn't help myself. I didn't tell Ralph. I left the baby with my mother and drove to Dallas. I only went for one night." She sighed heavily. "Let's just say, I learned my lesson. I saw the difference between infatuation and real love, and I saw clearly who was the better man. I came home, but it was too late."

Kari was stunned. Ralph must have been furious with his young wife. The first time they'd agreed on a plan. But to return to Earl Haynes again…

Gage crossed to the table and braced his hands on the back of the chair. "Quinn," he breathed.

Kari stared at him. Of course. His younger brother. How could she have forgotten?

Edie nodded. "Ralph didn't understand. He was furious and so very hurt. We nearly divorced. I still loved him with all my heart and I begged him to forgive me for being such a fool. In the end, he did forgive me. Then we found out I was pregnant. He didn't take it well."

Gage straightened. "No wonder," he said slowly. "No wonder he hated Quinn. My brother was a constant reminder of your betrayal."

Tears filled Edie's eyes again. "I could never convince him differently. I tried to make things right for Quinn, but I couldn't make up for his father not loving him."

Gage stared at his mother. She'd been a part of his life for as long as he could remember, but suddenly he didn't know her. It was as if a stranger sat at the table telling him secrets from the past.

He wanted to scream out his anger. He wanted to throw something, break something, hurt something. He wanted to turn back time and forget all he'd been told so he wouldn't have to know. He wanted to put the cloth box back in the trash can and never open it. "You lied," he said wearily. "Both of you." Mother and father. Except Ralph wasn't his father.

He was no relation at all.

His mother, who had always known what he was thinking, stared at him. "Ralph *is* your father in every way that matters. Nothing can change that. You have a past with him and it will always be there."

Gage shook his head. He'd had enough for one day. "I need to get to work."

His mother wiped her face. "There's more, Gage. More things you need to hear."

He couldn't imagine what those things might be. Nor did he want to. "Not now."

"Then, when?"

"I don't know."

"It has to be soon."

He wanted to ask why. He wanted to refuse her request. Instead, he nodded.

She rose slowly; it seemed she'd become old overnight. After walking to the doorway, she paused as if she would say more. Then she turned and left.

Gage crossed to the window and stared out at the morning. The sky was a clear Texas blue, the temperature already in the eighties. The central air unit he'd replaced three years ago kept the house cool, as did several ceiling fans. He focused on those now, on their whisper-quiet sound and the faint brush of air against the back of his neck. He heard Kari walk up behind him. She placed a hand on the small of his back.

"Gage," she said gently.

He didn't move. "What else could she have to say?" he asked. "Think there's another bombshell?"

"I don't know."

"I don't want to hear anything else. I don't want to talk to her again."

Behind him, Kari sighed. He heard the exhale, felt her disapproval.

"I know this has been a shock, but in time you'll see—"

He spun to face her. "See what? That everything I've believed all my life is a lie? I don't want to see that. I don't want to see that my mother went off to get herself pregnant by a man she'd never met before. Or that she liked doing it with him so much, she went again the following year. I don't want to finally understand why my father always hated my brother. I don't want it to be real and not just something Quinn imagined. I don't have to know any of it."

She stood her ground. "There's more to it than that."

"Is there? Like what? Am I really a part of the Reynolds family? Is Ralph really my father?"

"Of course. Yes, to both. You're furious about something that happened over thirty years ago. You're just learning it now, so it has a big impact on you, but these are not new events. Nothing has changed but your perception. You love your mom—you always have. Despite everything, I know that's not going to change. All I'm saying is that you both need time, and that you have to be careful not to say things you'll regret."

"She's the one who should have regrets," he said bitterly.

"I'm sure she regrets hurting her husband, but I don't believe for a second she regrets either you or Quinn."

He couldn't disagree with that. However, he was not in the mood to be reasonable. "Interesting all this advice coming from you," he growled. "Last I heard, you weren't so quick to forgive your family for what they did to you."

Finally he had gotten what he'd thought he wanted. Kari dropped her gaze and took a step back. But instead of feeling vindicated, he only felt lousy.

"Sorry," he said quickly. "I shouldn't have said that."

"No, you're right. I want to say that my situation is different, and of course it is. Every situation is different. But your point is that I'm not in a place to throw stones. I can't argue with that."

He held out his arms and she stepped into his embrace. "I hate this," he murmured into her hair. "The information, the questions, how it's all changing."

"I know."

"It will never be the same again. I'm not who I was."

"You're exactly the same man you were at this time yesterday."

No, he wasn't. She couldn't see the changes, but he knew they were there. "I don't belong here anymore."

Kari raised her head and stared at him. "Possum Landing is still your home. I'm the one who wanted to get away and see the world, but you'd already done that. You wanted to come home."

"Is it home?" he asked. "There aren't five generations anymore. At least, not in my history."

"I'm sorry," she whispered.

"Yeah. Me, too."

He released her, then glanced at his watch. "I have to get to the station. Are you going to be around tonight?"

"Sure."

"Can I come by?"

"Absolutely."

* * *

Gage spent the morning dealing with the crisis of two teenage boys from a neighboring town taking a joy-ride through a field at four in the morning. They'd been drunk and damn lucky. When they'd plowed through a barbed-wire fence and jerked loose several fence posts, the one that had shot through their front window had missed them both.

The rancher was threatening charges, while one parent thought jail time would teach his wayward son a lesson and the other kept saying "Boys will be boys."

"They'll be dead boys if they keep this up," Gage said flatly to the four adults. "I'm booking them both. They have clean records, so I doubt they'll get more than a warning and some community service. Maybe it will be enough to teach them a lesson, maybe not." Then he stalked out before any of the parents could speak with him. Normally he didn't mind taking the time to deal individually with kids headed in the wrong direction. He liked to think that he'd steered more than one teenager back onto the straight and narrow. But not today. Today all he could think about was the lie that was his past, and his suddenly unclear future.

He stalked into his office and closed the door. Several staff members looked up at the sound. Gage couldn't remember the last time he'd shut himself off from what was going on in the station. Mostly he liked to be in the thick of things. Hell, maybe he should have just stayed home.

But instead of clocking out for the day, he reached for the phone and dialed a number from memory. He gave the appropriate name, number and password to the computer before a pleasant-sounding woman picked up the phone.

"Bailey," she said crisply.

"I'd like to get a message to my brother," he said. He heard her typing on a keyboard. "Yes, Sheriff Reynolds. I have authorization right here. What is the message?"

There was the rub, he thought grimly. What to say? "Tell him…" He cleared his throat. "Tell him to call me as soon as he can. It's a family matter. No one's sick or anything," he added quickly.

"Very well, sir. I'll see that he gets the message." Gage didn't bother asking when that might happen. He'd tried to contact Quinn enough to know it could be weeks before he heard back, maybe even a couple of months. Or it could be tomorrow. There was no way to be sure.

"Thanks," he said, and hung up.

He leaned back in his chair and stared into the office. Instead of seeing people working, talking and carrying files, he saw his past. The idyllic days of growing up in Possum Landing. He'd been so damn sure he belonged. Now he wasn't sure of anything. His identity had been ripped from him.

As far as he could tell, the only good thing to come out of all of this was an explanation for his brother. Not that an answer would be enough to make up for Quinn's particular hell while he'd been growing up.

Gage had never understood the problem between father and son. Gage could do no wrong and Quinn could do no right. Ralph hadn't cared about his younger son's good grades, ability at sports or school awards. The only time he'd bothered to attend a game of Quinn's was when Gage was on the same team.

He'd never said a word when Quinn made the varsity baseball team during his sophomore year. Quinn had been a ghost in the house, and now he lived his life like a demon. All the pain, and for what? A lie?

Gage turned in his chair and gazed at the computer. The blinking cursor seemed to taunt him. *Lies,* it blinked over and over. *Lies, lies, lies.*

So what was the truth?

There was only one way to find out. He clicked on a law-enforcement search engine, then typed in a single name: Earl Haynes.

The ancient, shuddering air-conditioning didn't come close to cooling the attic. Unable to face more painting because it reminded her of Gage, Kari had decided on cleaning out the attic, instead. She'd opened all the windows and had dragged up a floor fan that she'd set on high. It might be hot up here, but at least there was a breeze.

She sat on the dusty floor in front of several open boxes and trunks. Grammy had kept everything. Clothes, hats, shoes, pictures, newspapers, magazines, blankets, lamps. Kari shook her head as she gazed at the collection of about a dozen old, broken lamps. Some were lovely and probably worth repairing, but others were just plain old and ugly. They should have been thrown out years ago.

But that wasn't her grandmother's way, she thought as she dug into the next layer of the trunk in front of her. She encountered something soft, like fur, then something hard like—"Whoa!"

She jumped to her feet, prepared to flee. There was an animal in there.

An old umbrella lay by the door. She picked it up and cautiously approached the trunk. A couple of good, hard pokes didn't produce any movement. Kari used the umbrella to push aside several garments, then stared down at an unblinking black eye.

"Well, that's totally gross," she said, bending over and picking up a fox stole with the fox head and tail still attached. "All you need are your little feet, huh?"

While she wasn't one to turn down a nicely cooked steak, she drew the line at wearing an animal head across her shoulders. This poor creature was going right into the give-away pile.

The next box held more contemporary items, including some baby and toddler clothes that had probably belonged to her. She held up a ruffly dress, trying to remember when she'd ever been that small.

"Not possible," she murmured.

Below that was her uniform from her lone year as a cheerleader, back in middle school, and below that was something white and sparkly.

Her breath caught in her throat as she pulled out the long, flowing strapless gown. The fabric of the bodice twisted once in front, then wrapped around to the back. Clinging fabric fell all the way to the floor. She crossed to the old mirror in the corner and held the dress up in front of her.

She'd never actually worn it, but she'd tried it on about four hundred times. Her prom dress. Kari squeezed her eyes shut for a second, then stared at her reflection. If she squinted, she didn't look all that different. With a little pretending, it could be eight years ago, when she'd been so young and innocent and in love, and Gage had been the man of her dreams.

Gage. She sighed. She'd been trying *not* to think about him all day. That was the point of keeping busy, because if she wasn't, she worried and fretted, neither of which were productive. Unfortunately, the blast from the past in her arms had dissolved her mature resolve to keep an emotional distance from the situation.

Instead, she remembered her excitement at the thought of going to her prom with Gage. After all, the other girls were going with boys from school, or from one of the nearby colleges. But she had been going with a *man*.

Only, that hadn't happened. Instead of dancing the night away, she'd been on a bus heading to New York. Instead of laughing, she'd spent the night in tears. And while she couldn't regret the outcome—leaving had been the right thing to do—she was ashamed of how she'd handled the situation.

"Too young," she told her reflection. "Of course, if I was old enough to be in love with Gage, I was old enough to tell him I was leaving, right?"

Her reflection didn't answer.

She put the dress down and walked to the stairs. She wanted to call Gage and ask if he was all right. She wanted to go to the station and see him. But she couldn't. Not today. Yesterday all those things would have been fine because he wouldn't have misunderstood her motives, but now everything was different. Now he might think she was pressuring him because of last night and this morning. She didn't want him thinking she was one of those clingy women who gave their hearts every time they made love with a man. She wasn't like that at all. At least, she didn't think she was. Not that she had any experience in that particular arena.

No, the reason she wanted to talk to Gage had nothing to do with their intimacy and everything to do with what he'd just found out. She was being a good friend, nothing more.

The phone rang, interrupting her thoughts. She dashed down the narrow attic stairs and flew toward her grandmother's bedroom, where the upstairs phone was kept.

"Hello?" she said breathlessly. Gage had called. He'd called!

"Ms. Asbury?" a cool, female voice asked. Kari's heart sank.

"Yes."

"I'm Mrs. Wilson. I'm calling you about your résumé. Do you have a moment?"

"Sure." Kari sat on the bed and tried to catch her breath.

Fifteen minutes later she had an interview scheduled for the following week. At this rate she would have a job in no time, she told herself as she hung up. In Abilene or Dallas or some other Texas city.

Just not Possum Landing.

Kari didn't know where that thought had come from, but she didn't like it. She was back in town for a visit, she reminded herself. This time was about fixing up the house to sell it, not reconnecting with anyone. This wasn't about Gage.

She repeated that thought forcefully, as if the energy invoked would make it more convincing. Unfortunately, all the energy in the world didn't change the fact that she had a bad feeling she was lying to herself.

Chapter Eleven

Gage showed up at Kari's door at a little after six. Until he'd walked from his house to hers, he hadn't been sure he would come. He'd nearly canceled a dozen times, reaching for the phone to call and tell her that something had come up. Or that he needed to spend the night by himself to figure out what he was going to do next. This wasn't her problem; she didn't need to be involved.

But every time he picked up the phone, he put it back down again. Maybe he *should* spend the evening thinking by himself, but he couldn't. Not yet. In the past twenty-four hours, he'd come to need Kari. He needed to see her, to be with her, to hear her voice and hold her close. He didn't know what the needing meant and he wasn't sure he liked it. But he acknowledged it.

Kari was a part of his past. Expecting anything more than a few nostalgic conversations and maybe a couple of tumbles in bed was a mistake. *More* than a mistake— hadn't he already fallen for her once?

So here he stood on her front porch, needing to see her and hating the need. He reached out and knocked once. When she opened the front door and smiled at him, he felt as if things weren't as bad as he'd first thought. "I come bearing gifts," he said, handing her a bucket of fried chicken with all the fixings that he'd picked up on the way home. "The diner still makes the best anywhere."

Kari laughed and took the container. Her blond hair swayed slightly as she shook her head. "Do you know, I haven't had fried chicken since I left here eight years ago?"

"Then, I would say it's about time."

She inhaled deeply, then licked her lips. "I guess so."

Still smiling, she stepped back to let him in the house. He walked inside, a folder still tucked under one arm.

"What's that?" she asked.

"Information on my biological father," he said. "I did some research today. I'll fill you in over dinner." She led him into the kitchen. The small table by the window had been set for two. She offered wine or beer— he took the latter.

He watched her as she crossed to the refrigerator and pulled out a bottle. She wore a loose sundress that skimmed her curves before flaring out slightly at the hem. Her feet were bare. He could see that she'd painted her toenails a light pink. Gold hoops glinted at her ears, while makeup emphasized the perfect bone structure of her face.

When she was younger, he'd thought she was the prettiest girl he'd ever seen. Sometimes when they'd gone out he hadn't wanted to do anything more than sit across from her and gaze at her face.

Time had changed her. The twenty or so pounds she'd lost had angled her face and hollowed her cheeks. She'd been a pretty girl before and now she was a beau-

tiful woman. He could imagine her in twenty years…
still amazing.

She raised her eyebrows. "Is there a sudden wart
on my nose?"

"No. I was thinking how nice you look."

She glanced down at the dress. "I'd say something
like 'this old thing,' but it happens to be from an exclu-
sive designer's summer collection. He offered it to me
as a going-away present when I was in his show right
before I left."

"It's nice."

"It retails for about two thousand dollars."

Gage nearly spit. "You're kidding."

"Not even a little." She grinned. "Suddenly I look
a little better than nice, huh?"

"You always do, and it has nothing to do with the
dress."

She sighed. "Nice line. Perfect timing, very sincere.
You've gotten better, Gage, and I wouldn't have thought
that was possible."

He shrugged off the compliment. He hadn't meant
his comment as a line—he'd been telling the truth. But
explaining that would take them in a difficult direction.
Better to change the subject.

"Are you telling the truth when you say you haven't
had fried chicken since you left?"

"Of course." She carried the large bucket to the table
and pulled off the top. "I haven't had anything fried. It's
not easy staying as thin as I've been. No fried chicken,
no French fries, no burgers." She tilted her head. "I've
had ice cream a couple of times and chocolate. I let myself have one small piece once a month. Now that I'm a
normal person again, I can eat what I want."

"Then, let's get started," he said, putting his folder on the counter and joining her at the table.

Fifteen minutes later, they were up to their elbows in fried chicken, mashed potatoes and coleslaw. Kari licked her fingers and sighed. "I'd forgotten how good this is. Even Grammy couldn't come close to the recipe."

"It's been passed down for several generations. You have the same chance of getting the family recipe out of Mary Ellen as you have of stopping the rotation of the earth. Many folks have tried over the years. There was even a break-in once. Only the recipe book was taken."

"You're kidding."

"Nope. We never did find out who'd done it. Of course, Mary Ellen told everyone who would listen that the fried chicken recipe had been given to her by her mama and no one in the family was ever fool enough to write it down."

Kari laughed.

Gage smiled slightly, but his humor faded. Talk of things being passed down reminded him of his own situation.

She read his mind. "What did you find out today?" He wiped his hands on a napkin, then reached for the folder he'd left on the counter. After flipping it open, he read the computer printout.

"Earl Haynes is from a small town in Northern California. Like my mom said, he's a sheriff, or at least he was. He's down in Florida now. Retired and living with a woman young enough to be his daughter."

He flipped the page. "He had four sons by his first marriage, and a daughter by another woman. Apparently old Earl likes getting women pregnant, even if he doesn't like sticking around."

"Isn't it a little early to be judging him so harshly? You don't know all the circumstances."

He shrugged. There was no point in explaining that he had a knot in his gut warning him the information about his father wasn't going to be good.

"Let's just say the first reports aren't that impressive," he told her.

"It's interesting that he's a sheriff," she said. "You went into law enforcement and Quinn went into the military. I wonder if that's significant."

He didn't want it to be. The little he'd learned about Earl Haynes told him that he didn't want the man to matter at all.

"What about your brothers?" she asked when he didn't say anything.

He looked at her. "What do you mean?"

"You said Earl Haynes had four sons and a daughter. So you have five half siblings. Four of them are brothers."

Gage hadn't thought of that. He'd always regretted that both his parents were only children—there hadn't been any cousins. Now he suddenly had brothers and a sister.

"Well, hell," he muttered.

"Do you want to get in touch with them?"

"I don't know."

He hadn't thought that far ahead. He didn't want to have any part of Earl Haynes or his family. "Let's talk about something else," he said. "Tell me about your day."

Kari took a bite of mashed potatoes. When she swallowed, she glanced at him from under her lashes. "I didn't get any painting done," she admitted. "I was too restless. I went upstairs and started cleaning the attic."

"Must have been hot."

She grinned. "It was. Even with all the windows open and a fan going. I found some interesting stuff, though. Old clothes, some jewelry." She hesitated, then sighed. "Grammy kept a lot of my old clothes and toys. I was feeling very nostalgic."

"What did you see there?"

"My old prom dress. I can't remember how many times I tried it on. I used to put my hair in different styles, then try on the dress to see what looked the best. I wanted everything about that night to be perfect."

Only, it hadn't been, he thought sadly. She'd disappeared and he'd been left holding a diamond engagement ring.

"I'm sorry, Gage," she said softly. "Sorry for running off, sorry for not telling you what I was so afraid of. Mostly I'm sorry for hurting you and leaving you to clean up my mess."

The words had come years too late, but it was good to hear them. "You don't have to apologize. I know you didn't take off just to hurt me."

"I should have said something. I was just so scared."

"You had a right to be." For the first time he could admit the truth. "You were too young. Hell, I was too young. I'd been so sure about what I wanted that I didn't want to think there might be another side."

Kari leaned back in her chair and voiced the question she'd asked herself over the years. "I wonder if we would have made it."

"I don't know. I like to think we would have."

"Me, too."

Kari studied him—his dark eyes, the firm set of his jaw. Tonight his mouth was set...no smile teased at the corner. He participated in the conversation, but she could tell that he was distracted.

Seeing him like this was such a change. The Gage she remembered had always known his place in the world. While the man before her now was still capable and confident, his foundation had shifted. She wondered how he would be affected.

His pain and confusion were tangible. Impulsively, she stretched her hand across the small table and touched his arm. "Tell me what I can do to help," she said.

"Nothing." He shrugged. "I don't think I'm going to be good company tonight."

The statement surprised her. "I'm not expecting a comedy show," she said lightly. "I thought—"

She didn't want to say what she'd thought. That he would stay with her tonight. That they would make love in her small bed, then curl up together and sleep in a tangle of arms and legs. Even if they weren't intimate, she wanted to be physically close. But Gage was already getting to his feet.

"I'm sorry," he said. "I've got a lot to think about. Maybe we can try this in a couple of days if I can take a rain check?"

As he was already standing, she didn't seem to have much choice. "Sure. I understand."

And she did. The problem was, she was also disappointed.

He started to collect plates, but she shooed him away. "You brought dinner," she protested. "I can handle cleanup."

He nodded and headed for the door. She followed him.

He paused long enough to drop a quick kiss on her forehead and offer a promise to be in touch. Then he was gone. Kari was left standing by herself, wondering what had gone wrong.

Despite the warmth of the evening, a coldness crept through her. They'd made love the previous night and this morning, but tonight Gage hadn't wanted to stay. Their intimacy obviously hadn't touched him the same way it had touched her. He'd been able to withdraw and regroup, while she'd…

Kari wasn't sure what had happened to her. How much of what was happening was due to her personal insecurities and how much of it was Gage withdrawing? Was he really going to a place where she wouldn't be able to reach him?

She hated the anxiousness that filled her, and the restlessness. She wanted to be with him. Obviously, she'd connected more when they'd made love than she'd realized.

That's all it was, she told herself as she returned to the kitchen. An emotional reaction to a physical encounter. There was no way she was foolish enough to let her heart get engaged. She'd already fallen in love with Gage once. That had ended badly. She was smart enough not to make the same mistake again.

Wasn't she?

Kari had barely finished dressing the following morning when there was a loud knocking on her front door. Her heart jumped in her chest as she hurried down the stairs.

Gage, she thought happily, her bare feet moving swiftly as she unfastened the lock and turned the knob.

But the person standing in front of her wasn't a tall, handsome, dark-haired man. Instead, a stylishly dressed woman in her forties smiled at Kari.

"Hello, darling," her mother said. "I know I should have called and warned you I was stopping by, but the decision to come was an impulse. Your father and I are going to London in the morning. I wanted to come see my baby girl before we left."

"Hi, Mom," Kari said, trying to summon enthusiasm as she stepped back to let her mother into the house.

Aurora presented her cheek for a kiss. Kari responded dutifully, then offered coffee.

"I would love some," her mother said. "I was up before dawn so I could make the drive here."

"You drove?" Kari asked in some surprise.

"I thought about flying into Dallas and then driving down, but by the time I got to the airport, waited for my flight, then rented a car, it seemed to take as much time."

She smiled as she spoke. Aurora Reynolds was a beautiful woman. She'd made it to the final five of a state beauty pageant during her senior year of high school before abandoning her plans of fame and fortune to marry an up-and-coming engineer. Like her mother before her, and her mother's mother before that, she'd married at eighteen, had her first child by the time she was nineteen and had never worked outside the home a day in her life.

"I think I remember where everything is," Aurora said as she bustled around the kitchen. She spooned grounds into the coffeemaker, then retrieved bread from the freezer and pulled the toaster from its place under the counter.

As she worked, she chattered, bringing Kari up to date on the various events in everyone's life.

"I don't understand why he married her," she was saying. "Your brother is the most stubborn man. I said twenty-three was too young—but did he listen? Of course not."

Kari nodded without actually participating. She was used to fleeting visits during which her mother would drop in, talk for hours about people she didn't know, air-kiss and then take off for some exotic destination. The pattern had been repeating itself for as long as she could remember.

As to her mother's comment about her "knowing" anything about her brothers, Kari didn't. She saw them once every couple of years for a day or so. Theirs wasn't a close family. At least, not for her. She couldn't say what the four of them did when she wasn't around. For all she knew, they lived in each other's pockets.

"How are you progressing with the sorting?" her mother asked after she put bread in the toaster and there was nothing to do but wait.

"It's slow but interesting. Grammy kept so much. I found a fox stole yesterday. It nearly scared the life out of me."

Aurora laughed. "I remember that old thing. I used to play dress-up with it."

"Would you like to have it?" Kari had planned to give the thing away, but if her mother wanted it, she could have it.

"No, darling. I prefer the memory to the dusty reality."

She leaned against the counter, a tall, blond beauty who still turned heads. Looking fresh and stylish in cotton trousers and a crisp blouse, she seemed to defy the heat. Kari knew what small success she'd had as a model came from her mother's side of the family.

"There are some old dresses and other things," Kari persisted. "Do you want to look at any of them?"

"I don't think so. I didn't inherit my mother's desire to save everything. But if there are some photo albums, I'll take a look at them."

"Sure." Kari was eager to escape the kitchen. "Dozens. I have a few in the living room. Let me get them."

She hurried into the other room and grabbed an armful of photo albums covering events over the past fifty years.

"I think your high school pictures are in this one," Kari said, setting the stack on the counter and picking up the top album.

"Hmm." Her mother didn't sound very interested as she poured them each coffee and carried the mugs to the table. Several slices of toast already sat on a plate there.

Her mother put down the mugs, then sorted through the albums. She came across one filled with pictures of Kari from about age three to eight or nine.

"What a sweet girl you were," her mother said with a sigh. "You hair was so light, and look at that smile."

Aurora's expression softened as she slowly turned pages. Kari watched her in some surprise. Her mother hadn't bothered to keep her around all those years ago, so why was she going misty over a few pictures?

She didn't voice the question, but her mother must have known what she was thinking because she closed the album and stared at her daughter.

"You think I'm a fraud," her mother said flatly.

Kari took a step back. "No. Of course not."

"I suppose it's not a big stretch for you to assume that I never cared, but you're wrong."

Clutching the album to her chest, her mother crossed to the table and took a seat. "I remember when you left for New York. Mama was concerned because you had no one there to help you. She was afraid you'd be too stubborn to come home if things got bad, but I knew you'd be all right."

Her mother sighed, tracing her fingers along the top of the album. "I like to think you got your strength from me. That ability to do what's right even when it hurts. Leaving Gage behind wasn't easy, but it was the right thing to do, wasn't it?"

Kari sat in the chair across from her mother and nodded.

"I thought so. I've made tough decisions, too." Aurora looked past her daughter and stared out the kitchen window.

"You were such a tiny thing when you were born," she said quietly. "We had a big problem with colic and you had recurring ear infections. The doctor said you'd outgrow the problem and be fine, but in the meantime your father had been offered a job in Thailand. We talked about me staying with you because you couldn't possibly make the trip. I was terrified to be that far from a familiar doctor."

Kari tried to remember if she'd heard this story before. From her earliest memories, she'd been in Texas and her parents had been somewhere else. Once, she'd asked to go with them when they'd come to visit. Her mother had said that was fine, but Grammy was too old to travel that far and live in a foreign country. Given the choice between her beloved Grammy and parents who were strangers, she'd chosen to stay.

"I didn't know what to do. You needed me, your father needed me. Then Mama said she would keep you for a few weeks, until things settled down. The doctor was sure you would be ready by the time you were seven or eight months old. It broke my heart to leave you, but in the end, that's what I did."

Aurora sipped her coffee, then opened the album on the table. As she turned pages, she spoke. "Once we were settled in Thailand, we found out travel wasn't as simple as we had thought. Your ear infections continued longer than we expected they would. There wasn't a doctor nearby, so I waited to bring you to join us. Then I became pregnant with your brother." She glanced up and smiled sheepishly. "That wasn't planned, I can assure you." Her smile faded and suddenly she looked every one of her years. "I didn't want to travel the first few months. Then a wonderful doctor settled in our area. The timing was perfect, I thought. He would deliver my next child and then I could come and bring you home. I waited until your brother was three months old and then I returned here, to Possum Landing."

Her mother turned away and drew in a deep breath. "I'd been gone too long. When I finally arrived, you were nearly two and a half. I walked in the door and called your name. But you didn't remember me. You hid, and when I tried to pick you up, you cried and only Mama could calm you down."

Kari felt her throat getting a little tight. Nothing in her mother's story was familiar, yet she sensed every word was true. Against her will, she imagined her mother's pain and heartbreak at being a stranger to her first-born child.

"I didn't know what to do," Aurora said. "I stayed for two weeks, but the situation didn't improve. I think you somehow knew that my plan was to take you away. You wouldn't let Mama out of your sight and continued to run from me. Mama wanted to keep you. She loved you as if you were her own. I couldn't fight the two of you. In the end it seemed kinder to leave you here. So I went back to Thailand without you."

Kari nodded but found she couldn't speak. Not without tears threatening. She'd always felt she'd been abandoned by her parents, but maybe the truth wasn't so simple.

"Looking back, I can't help thinking I took the easy way out," her mother admitted. "I could have dragged you with me. In time you would have accepted me as your mother. Maybe that would have been better. But I didn't. I can't say Mama didn't love you with all her heart, or raise you perfectly, but I regret what I lost. I never should have left you behind in the first place. I should have found another way." She offered a sad smile. "I suppose that sounds selfish."

"No," Kari managed to reply. "I understand." She did…sort of. Her head spun. Too much had happened too quickly. She'd come back to Possum Landing expecting to spend a few weeks fixing up her late grandmother's house. Instead, she'd come face-toface with ghosts from her past. First Gage and now her mother.

"Now I suppose it's too late for things to be different between us," Aurora said casually, not quite meeting her daughter's eyes.

Kari hesitated. "I appreciate hearing about what re-

ally happened. It's different from what I imagined."
She grabbed her coffee mug but didn't pick it up. "Why
now?" she asked.

"The time was never right," her mother said. "At
first, I didn't want to take you away from Mama. I always hoped..." She shrugged. "I thought you might
come ask me on your own. Eventually, I realized you
thought I'd simply turned my back on you."

Kari didn't respond. That had been what she'd thought.
Apparently, she'd been wrong.

She thought about what she and Gage had spoken
about just yesterday, when she'd told him he would have
to forgive his parents if he wanted to make peace with
the past. Could she do any less?

"I need some time," Kari told her mother. "This is
a lot to absorb."

"That's fine." Her mother glanced at her watch. "Oh
dear. I have to head back. There are a thousand and
one things to do before we head to London tomorrow."

Aurora rose and Kari did the same. "Do you mind if
I keep this?" her mother asked, motioning to the photo
album.

"Take as many as you'd like. There are plenty."

Her mother smiled. "I just want this one of you."

Kari didn't know what to say, so she gave in to impulse and moved close for a hug. After Aurora disappeared in a cloud of perfume and a promise to "bring
you something wonderful from London," Kari returned
to the kitchen, where she poured out her now cold coffee.

Just two hours before, her world had been only mildly
confusing. Now it was like living inside a tornado where
everything was spinning too fast to allow her to hold on.

She didn't know what to make of her mother's story.

It shouldn't change anything but her perception of the past, yet somehow everything looked different. Now she had a more clear understanding of what Gage was going through, albeit on a smaller scale.

Nothing was ever simple, she thought, moving to the side window and staring at his house. So much had happened in such a short period of time.

Chapter Twelve

Kari decided the best antidote for feeling unsettled was hard work. She finished painting the second upstairs bedroom, then started on her grandmother's room. The old pieces of furniture slid away from the walls more easily than she had anticipated. She pushed everything toward the center of the room to give herself space to work. She took down drapes, picked up throw rugs and draped drop cloths over everything. By two-thirty she was sweaty, exhausted and in need of a break.

In an effort to get away from her own company, she decided on a trip to the grocery store. As much as she might want to see Gage that night, she figured it was unlikely. So she settled on "chick" food for dinner. A salad, yummy bread, with a pint of her favorite ice cream for dessert.

She'd just stopped by the tomato display to pick out a couple for her salad when something slammed into her grocery cart. One of the wheels rolled into her foot, making her jump. Kari turned in surprise—then wished she hadn't.

Daisy stood behind her own cart, glaring at Kari. "I

can't believe it," the petite redhead said, her eyes flashing with rage. "I told you about my plans for Gage, but you didn't care. Well, fine. Try for him if you want, but you're destined to fail. I might have felt sorry for you before, but now I figure you've earned it."

Kari had the urge to tilt her head and wiggle her earlobe. She couldn't have heard any of that correctly. "I have no idea what you're talking about," she said at last.

Daisy looked disbelieving. "Sure you don't. I told you I was interested in Gage, but you didn't care. You just waltzed into his bed without giving a damn about anyone else. I'll have you know, Gage doesn't like his women that easy. But I guess you already knew that."

Kari opened her mouth, but before she could speak, Daisy narrowed her gaze.

"Don't try to deny it. I saw you leaving his place a couple of mornings ago. I doubt you'd just dropped by to borrow some coffee."

The joys of small towns, Kari thought, trying to find the humor in the situation. She shook her head. "First of all, what I do or don't do with Gage isn't anyone's business but ours. Second, I don't know why you're so put out. You and I aren't friends. In fact, we've barely met. I don't owe you anything. If you were in love with him, I might give your feelings some consideration, but you've already admitted you're not. Your interest in Gage comes from the fact that you think he'll be a good husband and father. While I'm sure he'd appreciate the endorsement, I suspect if he does decide to marry, he's going to want his future wife to be madly in love with him."

Daisy's eyes flashed with temper. "I suspect what

he'll want is someone who doesn't take off at the first sign of trouble."

Kari acknowledged the direct hit with a slight wince, but didn't otherwise respond to that comment. "If Gage is interested in you," she said, instead, "no one else would matter to him, so I wouldn't be a threat to you. If he's not interested, then warning me off doesn't make any difference at all."

"You're judging me." Daisy was fuming. "But you're no better. You had him and you let him go. How smart was that?"

"I was young and foolish," Kari admitted. "I didn't realize how wonderful he was, but I do now."

"You're not going to get him back."

Kari grabbed a tomato and put it in her cart. "I don't think you get to decide that," she said coolly, then pulled her cart from Daisy's and stalked away.

As she walked, she kept her head high, but she was shaking inside. The encounter had rattled her more than she wanted to admit.

As she approached the checkout stand, she thought of half a dozen things she should have said to Daisy, including the fact that at least she'd been smart enough to fall in love with him eight years ago. If Kari thought for a second that she was going to stay around and that he was interested, she would— Kari cut that thought off before she could finish it. Being annoyed with Daisy was one thing, but acting foolishly was another. She didn't love Gage. She refused to believe she was the kind of woman who would still be in love with him after all this time. She wasn't. She hadn't secretly been waiting to come back to him. The idea was laughable.

No. She had left and she had gotten on with her life.

She was still getting on with it. Gage was just a memory. The past, not the future.

Gage pulled into the cemetery and parked by the curb. He waited a long time before getting out of his car. The rational side of him knew that there was no hope of getting answers here. His father had long since moved beyond speaking.

His father.

Just thinking the words propelled him from the car. Ralph Reynolds—the name on Gage's birth certificate. The man who had loved him and raised him and shown him right from wrong. Ralph? No, he thought as he crossed the freshly cut lawn. Not Ralph. *Dad.*

Kari was right. Biology be damned. This man he had loved and mourned was his real father. He might not share the blood that ran in Gage's veins, but he had influenced him and molded him.

He crossed to the simple marble marker. Ralph Emerson Reynolds. There were the dates of his birth and death, followed by "Beloved husband and father."

He *had* been beloved, Gage reminded himself. Ralph's unexpected death from a heart attack had devastated the family. Even Quinn had been caught by surprise.

Gage crouched by the marble marker. "Hey, Dad," he said, then stopped because talking to himself in the middle of a cemetery felt strange. Then he continued. "Mama told me. About my biological father." He swallowed. "I wish you'd told me the truth. It wouldn't have changed anything."

He stared at the marble. "Okay. It would have changed things. But hearing it from you would have been better than finding out the way I did. You could have explained things to me. You could have told Quinn why he was never good enough.''

Gage stood and paced on the grass. Quinn had deserved to know why his best had never mattered. Ralph Reynolds had been a great father to Gage, but he'd been a real bastard to Quinn.

''You shouldn't have done it,'' Gage said, spinning back to the tombstone. ''You should have treated us the same. If you could accept me—someone else's son— you should have accepted him.''

He wanted to rage against his father, but it was years too late. Maybe that's why he hadn't been told. Maybe Ralph had pretended; maybe he'd forgotten the truth. At least for Gage.

Damn. There weren't going to be any sudden illuminations that would set his world to rights.

His chest tightened, his throat burned. He looked up at the sky, then back at the grave. ''I still would have loved you, no matter what. Why didn't you believe that?''

There was only silence, punctuated by the background songs of the birds. There were no answers here, there was no peace. His father had long since left for another place. This problem was for the living. Which meant Gage had another stop to make.

In the way that mothers always seem to know what their sons are up to, Edie stood on the porch, watching for him as he drove up. She didn't walk down the stairs to greet him or smile. She stayed where she was, waiting to see his reaction.

He tried to remember how their last conversation

had ended, but it was all a blur. Too much emotion, he thought. Too many revelations.

"Hey," he said as he climbed the stairs. He saw the front door was open and that John hovered in the front room.

"Gage."

Edie pressed her hands together. All the energy seemed to have been drained out of her. Her eyes remained dull and flat.

Without saying anything, he crossed to her and pulled her into his arms. She collapsed against him, a sudden sob catching in her throat.

"It's okay, Mama," he said, as she started to cry. "I was really pissed off, but it's okay now."

"I'm sorry," she said shakily. "So sorry. I never meant to hurt you. There were so many times I wanted to tell you the truth."

"I know." He stroked her hair. "I believe you. Dad wouldn't have wanted you to say anything. If he couldn't fix the problem, he pretended it didn't exist. Didn't we used to joke about that?"

She raised her head and stared at him. Tears dampened her cheeks. "He *is* your father, Gage. No matter what, that hasn't changed."

"I know. I lost it for a while, but it's back."

John came out and joined him. He put an arm around Edie and held out his hand to Gage. They shook, then John nodded. "I told her you'd come around."

"Thanks."

His mother beamed at him. "Do you want to come in? We could talk. There are still some things—"

He cut her off with a quick smile. "I need some time, okay?"

He saw that she didn't want to put off the rest of whatever it was she had to share, but he didn't care if he never knew any more.

"Just a couple of days," he promised, and turned back to his car.

She and John stood on the porch, watching him as he pulled out. He waved and his mother smiled at him.

She thought everything was all right now. That it was all behind them, Gage thought as he headed back to the station. What she'd done...well, she'd had her reasons. Some he agreed with, some he didn't. It would take a long time for him to get over the fact that his mother had thought she was in love with someone else while she was still married to his father.

But what Edie and Ralph Reynolds had done...had survived...wasn't his business. He had to deal with what had had an impact on him.

The truth was that forgiving his mother and making peace with his father didn't change one fact: he was not the man he'd always thought he was.

Kari washed brushes in the sink in the utility room. It was after nine in the evening, and she focused on the task at hand in an effort to keep her brain from repeating the same thought over and over again.

It had been nearly a week since she'd seen Gage. A week! Six days and twenty-two hours.

Why? She knew that he'd been avoiding her, but couldn't quite pin down the reason. She wanted to believe it was all about his past, but she had a bad feeling that some of it was personal. With everything else going on in his life, the last thing he would want to worry about was her virginity, or how he'd made that disappear. No doubt he thought she would already be picking out china patterns, while he'd simply been interested in getting laid.

Kari turned off the water and sighed. Okay, that was a slight exaggeration. Gage wasn't the kind of guy to only want sex for sex's sake. If he was, he would never have been so careful while they were dating. He would have pushed her, and, as much as she'd been in love with him, she would have given in.

So Gage hadn't been looking for an easy score and she wasn't looking to get married to the first man she slept with. Reality lay somewhere in between.

She set the wet brushes on a rack, then washed her hands and dried them on a towel. Despite the pulsing urge inside her, she was *not* going to cross to the front window and stare out from an opening in the lace curtains. Spying on Gage, watching for when he got home, was way too pathetic. Besides, she'd been doing it too much lately. If she wanted to talk to him, she should simply call, like a normal person. Or go to his house, or even his office. If she didn't...

Kari walked into the kitchen and crossed to the refrigerator. She'd bought a pint of cookie-dough ice cream on her last visit to the grocery, and this seemed like a fine time to have it for dinner. Despite all her logical conversations with herself, the bottom line was that she was alone on a Saturday night, watching for the boy next door to come home and ask her out. This was worse than when she was in high school. She had managed to live in a big city for eight years, have different experiences, even have something close to a successful modeling career. Yet nothing had changed. The situation would be pretty funny if it were happening to someone else.

The phone rang, causing her to slam the freezer door. Her heart rate increased. There were only two types of calls in her current world—Gage, or not Gage. This increased the pathetic factor, but was completely true.

"Hello?" she said, trying not to sound breathless.

"Hi, Kari," Gage said. "What's going on?"

Over the past week, she'd planned her conversation with him dozens of times. She'd had witty lines and blasé lines and casual questions all lined up. Now, of course, she couldn't think of anything but "Not much. I've been working on the house. Just finished painting for the day."

"I've been meaning to get back there and help you."

The road to hell and all that, she thought. "My remodeling job isn't your responsibility," she said. "How are you doing?"

"Okay. Still trying to figure things out."

Silence. She sighed. Things had been so much easier before. Before they'd made love. Before he'd found out about his past.

He cleared his throat. "The reason I phoned is that there's a big dance up at the country club. I've had a few calls from worried parents. They're concerned that the kids might be renting hotel rooms for the night. I did some checking around and it looks like a group of them are planning to spend the night at the Possum Landing Lodge. I'm on my way over to break things up. I was hoping you'd come with me."

She frowned. "To break up a party?"

"Yeah, well, the odds are that some of these teenagers are going to be going at it in the room, and I don't want to have to deal with a bunch of half-dressed girls."

Not exactly the invitation she'd been waiting for, but it was better than nothing. "Sure, I'll help."

"Great. I'll be by in about ten minutes."

"Okay. 'Bye."

She hung up, then flew upstairs to replace her paint-spattered shorts and T-shirt with a crisp summer dress. There wasn't time for a shower or a fabulous hairstyle, so she ran a brush through her hair, fluffing up the ends while she worked. After racing into the bathroom, she brushed her teeth, applied mascara and lip gloss and slipped on some silver hoops. A pair of sandals completed her outfit. She hurried back downstairs and collected her house key, then walked to the front door. She'd just reached it when Gage knocked. She opened the door and tried not to smile at him.

Against her will, her mouth curved up and every cell in her body danced. Talk about betrayal.

Even more frustrating, he looked really, really good. There were shadows under his eyes as if he hadn't been sleeping much, and his uniform was a little rumpled—but none of that mattered. Not when she could see into his eyes and watch him smile back at her.

"Hi," he said. "Thanks for the help."

"No problem."

He didn't move back, so she couldn't step out of the house. They looked at each other. He reached out his hand and lightly touched her cheek. "I've been avoiding you."

The admission surprised her. She decided to offer one of her own. "I noticed."

"It wasn't because of…" He paused. "I've had a lot on my mind. I didn't want to dump it all on you."

"We're friends, Gage. I'm happy to listen."

"I may take you up on that. I've been doing a lot of thinking and I don't seem to be making any progress."

"Have you talked with your mom? Are things okay there?"

He nodded. "A couple of days ago I went to see her. She's still trying to tell me more stuff, and I don't want to hear it. I know that I have to listen eventually. But other than that, we're fine."

She wanted to ask if she and Gage were fine, too. If making love had changed things forever, or if they could go back to their easy, teasing, fun relationship. "I've missed you," she said before she could stop herself.

"I've missed you, too. More than I should."

Her heart skipped a beat and she felt positively giddy. Man, oh man, she had it bad.

"You ready?" he asked.

"Sure."

He stepped back, and she moved onto the porch, closing the door behind her. As they walked to the car, Gage rested his hand on the back of her neck. She liked the heat of him and the feel of his body close to hers. Unfortunately, there didn't seem to be much about Gage she didn't like.

They drove in silence to the motel. When they arrived, several parents were already pacing in the parking lot. Gage spoke to them, then went to the main office and collected keys from the night manager.

"Ready?" he asked Kari, as they walked up the stairs.

"No, but that's okay."

It was dark and quiet in the corridor. Voices from the

parking lot faded as they moved toward the rear of the motel. Up ahead, light spilled out of an open door. The sound of laughter and loud voices drifted toward them.

"Do you do this sort of thing often?" she asked, trailing behind him.

"When asked. I prefer to come out at the request of the parents and clear things up before they get out of hand. That way I can get everyone home with a warning. If I get a call from the motel management, then it's official and I have to get tough. Most of the kids are mortified to be caught by me and their folks. They don't need much more encouragement to stop."

"For those who need more?"

"They'll be in trouble soon enough," Gage said, glancing at her as he paused near an open door. "Ready?"

She nodded, then braced herself for plenty of shrieking and tears. Gage stepped past the threshold and stalked toward the center of the room.

"Evening," he said calmly, as if he'd been invited. Several teenagers screamed.

Kari followed him in. Kids were in various stages of undress. Two girls ducked into an adjoining room and quickly closed the door behind them. Two boys were brave enough, or drunk enough, to challenge Gage.

"We're not doing anything wrong, Sheriff," a skinny boy with dark hair said belligerently. "This is private property. You ain't got no right—"

Gage stood directly in front of the boy. "You talking to me, Jimmy?"

The teenager took a step back. His too-long hair hung in his eyes. He still wore a shirt and tie, although both were undone. The color faded from his face.

"Uh, yes, Sheriff. We've been quiet. We haven't made any trouble."

"That's good," Gage said evenly. "Your mama called me because she was real concerned. You're eighteen now, but your girlfriend is still only seventeen. Your mama was afraid you'd have a bit too much to drink and then things might get out of control."

Jimmy took another step back, which brought him in contact with the wall. "My mama called you?"

"Uh-huh. She's waiting downstairs in the parking lot."

One of the other boys snickered. Kari almost felt sorry for Jimmy.

Gage turned to those laughing. "Your mamas are here, too, boys. So let's all get dressed and head downstairs." He motioned to the adjoining room. "You want to see to the ladies?"

Kari nodded. She walked through the doorway and found herself in a living room. This must be the suite the Possum Landing Lodge was always advertising. The decorations were early tacky, with a gaudy red couch and fake oak coffee and end tables. Three velvet paintings decorated the walls.

"At least there's no Elvis," she said, passing a picture of dogs playing poker. She followed the sound of heated conversation.

"I can't believe this is happening," one girl said, as Kari entered the bedroom. "Tonight Jimmy and I were going to go all the way."

"Guess that will have to wait," Kari said, leaning against the door frame. "I realize you don't know me from a rock, but for what it's worth, my advice would be to make that very special occasion a little more private."

Two girls, both young, pretty and blond, glared at her. She could read their minds. What could an old lady like Kari possibly know about having fun?

As Kari waited, they scrambled into dresses and high heels. When they hurried past her, she went to check the bathroom, where another girl sat on the floor. Her pale cheeks told their own story.

"You done being sick?" Kari asked.

The girl nodded and slowly got to her feet.

"Want some help?"

The teenager shook her head, then ran out of the bathroom. Kari turned to leave, then stared at the ice-filled bathtub. There had to be at least a dozen bottles of cheap liquor and wine chilling there.

"Great," she muttered, and went to find Gage.

She found him lecturing the last of the boys. The teenager escaped with a grumbled promise to think before acting next time.

"At least we got here in time," Gage said with a sigh as he closed the door of the suite. "All the girls gone?"

"Yes. One had been throwing up. She's not going to feel too great in the morning. Apparently, a big party was planned. There's a bathtub full of liquor in there."

He headed for the restroom. "Let's dump it, then we can head out of here."

"You don't want to keep any for yourself?" she teased, as he bent down and grabbed a couple of bottles.

He glanced at the labels and shuddered. "My tastes have matured." His gaze slid to her. "In nearly everything."

She wasn't sure what he meant, but she liked that he finally seemed to have noticed she was there.

Gage poured while Kari handed him bottles. They

worked quickly and soon the bathroom reeked of cheap liquor. It was only when they finished and moved back into the bedroom that he realized where he was.

The honeymoon suite.

The big round bed dominated the floor space, leaving little room for much more than a small dresser and a TV on a stand. Thick drapes kept out the night. The wood paneling had seen better days, as had the carpet. But eight years ago, Gage had thought this was just the place to secure his future with the woman he loved.

"What are you thinking?" Kari asked. "You have the strangest expression on your face."

He shrugged. "Ghosts."

"Ah. You liked to bring your lady friends here for a big seduction scene?"

"Not exactly. But I had planned to bring you here. I was going to propose, and after you said yes, I was going to make love to you."

Kari's smile faded. Several emotions skittered across her face, but he couldn't read them. Or maybe he didn't want to. Maybe it was better not to know what she was thinking. After all, she'd skipped town rather than marry him.

"You had it all planned out," she murmured.

"Down to the smallest detail, including proposing *before* we made love so you wouldn't think it was just about sex."

"I wouldn't have thought that. Not about you. I know the kind of man you are."

"Yeah, well…" He suddenly felt awkward and stupid for mentioning anything and headed for the door. But before he got there, Kari spoke again.

"Daisy and I practically had a fistfight over you in the produce aisle."

That brought him up short. "What are you talking about?"

She smiled. "Your wannabe girlfriend tried to warn me off. She said you weren't interested in me and that I could never have you back."

"What did you say?"

"A lot of things."

Which told him precisely nothing. Before he could figure out if he wanted to continue the conversation, she crossed to the nightstand and flipped on the clock radio. Tinny music filled the room. She fiddled with the knob until an oldies station came in, then crossed to stand in front of him.

"Dance with me," she said.

Then she was in his arms, and he found he didn't want to refuse her. Not when she felt so right pressed against him. Whatever might have gone wrong emotionally between them, physically they'd always been right together.

They moved together, swaying in time to the old ballad. He thought about what should have happened in this room all those years ago.

"I'm sorry you never got to your prom," he said, resting his cheek against her soft hair.

"Me, too. I would have liked to have those memories." She sighed. "I'm sorry I ran away. You were so good to me. I should have realized I could talk to you about anything—even being scared."

Past and present blurred. Gage closed his eyes. "Nothing is easy," he told her. "If I didn't know it before, I'm learning it now."

"Because of your mom?"

"Yeah. She loved her husband. I know she did. Yet there was this other man. She loved him, too, and I never figured it out. I want to be angry, but if she hadn't gone back to him, Quinn wouldn't exist."

"Sometimes life isn't as tidy as we would like." He agreed with that. His life had changed forever.

What had once been taken for granted wasn't a part of him anymore. A single piece of information had changed him forever. Changed him in a way that made everything else different.

He pulled Kari closer, enjoying the familiar heat of her body, the way she felt and the scent of her skin. Being with her allowed him to forget the issue of his father, for at least a short time. He could get lost in the past, in remembering something much sweeter. How he'd loved Kari more than he'd ever thought he *could* love someone. How he'd loved her long after she'd left, when he should have let go. The things he'd loved about her hadn't changed—her spirit, her generosity, her determination. She was the same woman—more mature, more experienced, but fundamentally the same.

The information could have been dangerous. Under other circumstances it would have been. If things were different he might think the reason he'd never been able to fall for anyone else was that he was a one-woman man and Kari was that woman. He might have worried about falling in love with her again.

But not anymore. Seeing her now, having her back in town, reminded him of all that might have been, but couldn't be now. Even if she wasn't leaving, they couldn't possibly be together. Everything was different now. Himself most of all.

"I'm glad we didn't get married," he said.

She raised her head and looked at him. "What are you talking about?"

Wasn't it obvious? "What if we'd married and had kids together? Eventually, I would have found out about my father."

"So?"

"It changes everything."

"Not for me. I feel badly that you're in pain and I want you to get your questions answered, but aside from that, it has no impact on anything. You're still the same man I knew eight years ago. If we'd married, you'd still be my husband and the father to my children. I would still love you."

Her blue eyes held his gaze. He could read her sincerity. She believed what she was saying, even if she was wrong.

"It changes everything," he said.

"You are the most stubborn man. I can't decide what to do with you."

Then she raised herself up on her toes and kissed him.

Chapter Thirteen

The soft pressure on his lips stunned Gage into immediate arousal. Need pulsed through him in waves that threatened to drown him in desire. Without thinking, he pulled her close and deepened the kiss, plunging his tongue inside her mouth, tasting her, teasing her, stroking her, *wanting* her.

She responded in kind, her body pressing against his, her hips against his arousal. She rubbed against him, as if they weren't close enough. When she closed her lips and sucked, he thought he was going to lose it right there.

"Oh, Gage," she breathed, making it clear that the heat wasn't being generated all on one side.

He'd made love with her enough times to know the joining would be spectacular, but not enough to have expectations of a sure thing. Kari's obvious interest excited and pleased him. She'd been a virgin their first time and he'd worried later that things hadn't gone well for her. Clearly, she'd decided she very much liked the act of making love. He started to back her toward the bed.

The bed. He raised his head and stared at the round

mattress. How many times had he imagined them together here?

She turned and saw what had caught his attention. "Is it too weird to be here?"

"I don't know," he admitted.

"Do you want me to convince you, or just stop?"

He swung his gaze back to her. "Are you offering to seduce me?"

Color bloomed on her cheeks. She cleared her throat. "Yes, well, I'm not saying I could—just that if you were intrigued by the idea, I would be willing..." Her voice trailed off. "You did say you liked to watch."

Desire slammed into him like a truck going eighty. He didn't know why every single man in New York hadn't begged her to marry him, but somehow they'd missed the amazing jewel glittering in their midst. Somehow he, Gage, had gotten damn lucky.

Not only had Kari never been with another man before making love with him, but she was now offering to seduce him. As if he needed encouragement or persuasion.

He reached for her, determined to show her exactly what she did for him without even trying, when reality intruded.

"I don't have anything with me." He groaned. "Damn."

A slow smile teased her mouth. "Are we talking protection?"

He nodded.

Her smile broadened. "Our young friends might have been foolish about some things, but they were well prepared for others." She motioned to the television. "Exhibit A."

He turned and saw what he'd missed before. Sitting on top of the television was a jumbo box of condoms. There had to be at least a hundred inside.

"Somebody was planning on getting lucky in a big way," he said, pulling her back into his arms.

"Looks like it's going to be you."

"Looks like."

He lowered his head and kissed her. Despite the raging need inside him, he was determined to be gentle and take it slow. That mental promise lasted right up until Kari gently bit down on his tongue at the same time she slipped a hand between them and rubbed his arousal. He swore.

Kari shivered slightly at Gage's explicit language, but not out of shock. Instead she felt bone-melting need. She didn't know if it was the past intruding, or Gage's emotional vulnerability or her own emotional state, but something had happened tonight. Something that made her want to rip both their clothes off and make love to him.

She wanted to be taken. She wanted his body in hers, their hearts beating as one. She wanted the touching, the pleasure, the shared breath, the trembling aftermath. She wanted to bare her soul to him and stare down into the depths of his.

Her need made her bold in a way she'd never been before. When he jerked down the back zipper of her dress, she shrugged out of it as if she spent most of her day undressing in front of him. Before he could unfasten her bra, she did it for him. The scrap of lace slid to the floor. She brought his hands to her breasts, then gasped when she felt the heat of his touch. The ache between her thighs intensified as he cupped her curves while teasing her already tight nipples.

She reached for the buttons of his shirt while they kissed. Her fingers fumbled, but she kept at the task until she could rub her palms against the hair on his chest. From there she went to work on his belt, then his trousers. When she'd undone the zipper, she eased her hand inside his boxer shorts and wrapped her fingers around his hardness.

Such soft skin, she thought, deepening the kiss and beginning to move her hand. Soft skin around pulsing hardness. She eased back and forth, moving faster and faster until he caught her wrist and pulled her away.

"Not like that," he said with a smile.

She delighted in his confession—that she could have made him lose control with a simple touch.

While he stepped out of his shoes and pulled off his socks, she slipped off her panties. He continued to undress while she crossed to the condom box and removed one square packet. She turned to find Gage standing in the center of the room. He was naked.

She looked at him, from his dark eyes to his mouth, then to his chest, his flat belly and finally to his jutting maleness. He held out his hand for the condom. She handed it to him, then watched while he slipped it on. When he moved to the bed, she followed. He stretched out on his back. "I thought you might like being on top," he said, his expression faintly wicked. Kari thought about the position—her sliding up and down while he filled her. She thought about his hands on her body, touching, moving, stroking, delighting, and nearly stumbled in her eagerness.

She slid onto the bed, then stretched one leg over

him. He filled her completely as she eased onto him. He sucked in a breath, then instructed her not to move. "We need to get you caught up," he said, then proceeded to show her what he meant.

He touched her everywhere—from her ears to her breasts, down to her legs and between her thighs. He stroked the arc of curves, found secret places of delight and teased her into a frenzy. Tension filled her, making her want to ride him, but he held her back.

"Not yet," he whispered.

They kissed. He moved one hand to her nipples and tickled them until the pulsing inside her grew. Her thighs clenched and unclenched. Her breathing grew ragged. Finally, when she ached and perspiration dotted her back, he moved inside her.

She responded instantly, sliding up and down. On the first round trip, she felt herself falling off the edge. He made sure she went all the way by slipping his hand between her legs and rubbing her dampness until everything shattered.

Her climax overtook her, making her cry out. She leaned forward, bracing her hands on the bed, riding him faster and faster, each up and down movement sending new waves of pleasure through her. She lost herself and didn't care about anything but her passion and her need.

There was more and more until nothing existed but the feel of him inside her. Then his hands settled on her hips, steadying her movements. His thrusts deepened as he collected himself. Kari forced her eyes open so she could watch her lover's release, only to find him watching her.

Then as he stiffened and called out her name, she

saw down into his soul. For that one endless moment in time their hearts beat together. Then the pulsing of his climax carried her off on another mindless round of pleasure, and they lost themselves in the glory of their lovemaking.

When they finally disentangled, Kari expected Gage to roll away. He'd been distant from her ever since he found out about Ralph not being his biological father. But instead of sitting up or reaching for his clothes, he drew her close and wrapped his arms around her.

"Pretty amazing," he said quietly. "Even better than I'd imagined. And I'd imagined a lot."

"I know what you mean. I'm still trying to catch my breath."

He shifted so he was facing her, but kept an arm on her waist. "I haven't seen you in a few days."

She thought about explaining that it had actually been a whole week, but didn't. "I've been working on the house. And you?"

"Work. Other stuff," he said casually.

"Is that getting better or worse?"

"About the same."

She wasn't sure she agreed with him. Not when he'd made the ridiculous statement about being glad they hadn't married and had children, based on some secret from the past.

"My mom came by for a visit," she said.

"How was that?"

"Weird, as always." She touched the line of his jaw, rubbing her fingers against his stubble. "I always had a very clear view of what happened when I was little. My parents went away and forgot about me. The fact that they kept my brothers with them only seemed to prove my point. But after talking with my mother, I'm not so sure."

She filled him in on the details of how she came to be left behind. "I saw my parents as the bad guys, but what was black and white is now gray. I still think they were wrong to leave me, but I can understand why they did what they did. I want to tell myself it doesn't affect anything, but it does. Still, the fact that my interpretation of the past might be different doesn't change my feelings. Am I making any sense?"

"Yes."

She stared into his dark eyes. "I guess my point is, I understand your confusion a little more clearly. Nothing is different for you, yet everything is different. Information changes perception—but does it change emotion? Am I less angry with my mother now that I know the circumstances that contributed to her decisions? I'm not sure."

"Me, neither. About any of it."

She moved her hand to his mouth and traced his lips. "Don't you dare think you're anything but a wonderful man. You're the best man I've ever known."

"I doubt that."

"Don't. I'm telling the truth." She made an *X* above her left breast. "I swear."

"Thank you." He kissed her lightly.

Kari kissed him back. As she did, her words repeated themselves inside her head. Gage *was* the best man she'd ever known. He was everything any woman could want. He was...

Her chest tightened suddenly as she got it. The realization nearly made her laugh out loud. It also nearly made her cry.

She was in love with him. After all this time and all the miles she'd traveled, she was still in love with him.

Why hadn't she figured it out before? The clues had been there—her reaction to seeing him after all this time. Her willingness to make love with him after putting off other men. Her eagerness to spend time with him. The way she worried about him. Her ambivalence about looking for a teaching position in Dallas or Abilene.

"Kari? Are you okay?"

She nodded because speaking was impossible. Now what? What happened when one of her interviews led to a job offer? Did she hang around Possum Landing, hoping Gage would fall in love with her, too? He'd just said he was grateful they hadn't married. Hardly words to hang her dreams on.

The mature solution was to ask him about his feelings, to find out where things stood between them. She opened her mouth, then closed it. Not yet, she thought, burying her face in his shoulder. She needed a little time to get used to the idea of being in love with Gage.

"Hey," he said, stroking her back. "It's okay."

"I know," she lied, because she didn't know anything.

He kissed her head. "Want to come home with me and spend the night?"

She nodded. She loved him—there was nowhere else she would rather be.

Gage didn't have to work the next day, so they slept in late, then went over to her grandmother's house and set to work. They'd just started moving furniture out of the dining room, when there was a knock on the front door.

Kari went to answer it and found Edie waiting on the porch.

"Is Gage here?" his mother asked. "He wasn't home, but his truck is in the driveway, so I thought he might be helping you."

"Sure." Kari held open the front door, then called for Gage.

As she invited the older woman inside, she tried to quell the worry inside her. The past few hours had been magical. She and Gage had slept in each other's arms, only to awaken and make love again at dawn. Her feelings were still so new and tender that she didn't want anything to break the mood between them. Unfortunately, Edie's visit was bound to do just that.

Gage nodded at his mother. "What's going on?"

"You're avoiding me," Edie said bluntly. "I decided if you weren't going to come to me, I would chase you down myself. We need to talk."

Kari's throat went dry. "I'll go upstairs."

"No." Gage shot out a hand and grabbed her wrist. "You don't have to go." He gazed at her. "I'd prefer that you stay."

She nodded and led the way into the parlor. Edie perched on a chair, while Kari and Gage sat next to each other on the sofa.

"If you tell me that you're not really my mother, I'm going to be really pissed off," Gage said lightly.

Edie smiled slightly. "Sorry. You're stuck with me."

"I don't mind."

He reached for Kari's hand and laced their fingers

together. She looked from him to his mom and wished this would all just go away.

"So here's the thing," Edie began. "When I went to Dallas the second time, I didn't know what I wanted or what I was feeling. Everything confused me. I just knew I had to see Earl one more time. Which I did. Obviously. Quinn is proof of that. But that's not all that happened."

Kari felt Gage brace himself against more bad news.

"We spent the night together. The next morning there was a knock on the hotel room door. A young woman stood there. She was barely eighteen." Edie shook her head. "She didn't look a day over fifteen, and she had two little babies with her. The second I saw her face, I knew the truth. Earl had been with her, as well. She'd brought her boys to meet their father."

Kari's stomach did a flip. She hadn't thought things could get worse, but she'd been wrong.

"Another conquest," Edie said bitterly. "I realized in that moment, that was all I'd been to him. Any feelings were on my side. I don't know how much of what he told me was truth and how much was lies. It didn't matter. What I had thought was love was infatuation. Or maybe it was just a justification to myself. If I thought I loved him, then sleeping with him didn't make me such a horrible person."

Tears filled her eyes. She blinked them away. Kari tightened her hold on Gage's hand. She was afraid to look at him. For once, she didn't want to know what he was thinking.

"What happened?" Gage asked, his voice low.

"The girl showed him the babies. He didn't deny they were his. He didn't do anything but get dressed and tell her he wished her well. That was it. No offer to marry her or even help out with his sons. I felt so stupid. The girl took off in tears. I ran into her in the lobby and found out her parents had thrown her and her two babies out the day she turned eighteen.''

Gage wanted to run. He wanted to run so far and so fast that the words would be erased from his mind. He wanted to close his eyes and have the past disappear. But his mother kept talking, and he couldn't stop himself from listening.

But as she spoke an ugly thought appeared in his brain. This man—this Earl Haynes who used women and abandoned them—was an integral part of himself. Earl's biology was in Gage.

He thought of his own past, his inability to settle down with someone. How easily he moved from relationship to relationship. Was that because of his biological father? Was he a philanderer, too?

No! He didn't want that history, that blood, flowing through his veins. He didn't want to be a part of it.

But it was too late. The past had already occurred and he couldn't undo it. Not now.

Then, before he could make peace with any of it, his mother's words caught his attention.

"I couldn't leave her there alone," she was saying. "So I brought her home. We made up a dead husband and gave her a new last name."

Gage swore as the pieces all fell into place. Vivian Harmon was a close friend of the family. Her two sons, Kevin and Nash, were his age. Both tall, dark-haired, with dark eyes. And no father.

"Kevin and Nash?" he said.

She nodded. "Your half brothers. Vivian and I have talked about telling you four. We've gone back and forth a dozen times over the years. At first, I didn't want to say anything because of Ralph. He didn't want you to know. Vivian and I talked about it again after his death. At that point, I was too afraid to confess the truth. So I asked Vivian to keep quiet. She didn't mind. She'd married Howard years before and he'd been like a father to the boys. She never thought they were missing out."

Gage felt as if the room were spinning. He didn't just have faceless half siblings in California, he had two right here in Texas. Not that Nash and Kevin lived here now. Nash was a negotiator with the FBI and Kevin was a U.S. Marshal, but they came home on occasion. He and Quinn had played with the twins all their lives. They'd double-dated, been on the same football and baseball teams, worked on each other's cars and shared their dreams with each other. Never had they considered the fact that they might share a whole lot more.

"Vivian's going to tell the boys," Edie said. "Now that you're all going to know, it might help you four to talk about it."

Gage wasn't sure what they were supposed to say. "He has a family," he told her. "Earl Haynes. I looked him up on the Internet. He's retired now, but he was a sheriff in a small town in California."

His mother nodded slightly.

"There are other children. He has several sons from his first wife and a daughter by another woman."

Edie winced. "I suspected there was more family, but I wasn't sure."

"You never asked."

"I didn't want to know," she admitted.

At least she was being honest. "It's too much," he said.

"I'm sorry." She paused. "Do you have any other questions?"

"None that I can think of." He laughed humorlessly. "Just tell me that there aren't any other revelations."

"None that I'm aware of."

"Good."

He could live the rest of his life without any more secrets, he thought grimly.

Edie rose. "You haven't heard from Quinn yet, have you?"

"No. I'll let you know when he gets in touch."

Gage still didn't know how he was going to tell his brother the truth. Nor did he know how Quinn would react. It was a lot to take in.

He released Kari's hand, stood and walked his mother to the door. Tears filled her eyes.

"I'm sorry," she whispered.

He nodded and gave her a quick hug. When she'd left, he returned to the parlor.

Kari stood by the window. She turned to look at him. As they'd planned to work in the house, she wore a paint-spattered T-shirt and cutoffs. A scarf covered her hair, and she hadn't bothered with makeup. She still looked beautiful.

He wanted to go to her and hold her so tightly that he couldn't tell where one ended and the other began. He wanted to breathe in the scent of her and return to that place where he'd felt everything was going to be all right. Unfortunately, that time had passed.

"I know I said I'd help, but I need to head out and—" He broke off, not knowing what he had to do. He only knew that he needed to be by himself for a while.

"It's okay," she said. "I understand."

"I'll be in touch."

"You said that before."

Had he? "This time I mean it. I'll call you tonight."

He walked to the front door and let himself out. He crossed to his own yard and was about to climb the front porch steps, when he heard her calling his name. He turned.

"What's up?" he asked.

She crossed the driveway to stand next to him. "This is wrong," she said, determination blazing in her eyes. "I know you're going through a lot right now, but you can't let it destroy everything."

"What are you talking about?"

She swallowed. "Last time, I was the one to walk away. It looks like this time you're going to walk away. Do you think we'll ever get it right?"

Chapter Fourteen

Gage felt as if he'd been turned to stone. He couldn't move, couldn't speak. Then the sensation passed and he was able to draw in a breath.

Do you think we'll ever get it right?

"What the hell are you talking about?" he demanded.

Kari didn't back down from his obvious temper. Instead, she planted her hands on her hips and glared back at him.

"I'm talking about us. You and me. There's something here, Gage. I know you can feel it. Lord knows, it's keeping me up at night. Eight years ago I panicked. I was too young to tell you I needed time, so I ran. My fears and my desire to experience my dreams kept us apart. I've grown up and you've changed, too, yet whatever we had is still alive. But I'm afraid that this time your past is going to rip us apart."

He didn't know what to say. While he was willing to admit there was something between Kari and himself, he'd never thought past the moment. He knew about her plans, and they didn't include him. He'd been okay with that. Now she was suddenly changing the rules.

"Are you saying you're not leaving Possum Landing?" he asked, not sure how he felt about any of this.

"I'm saying I don't know. Last night you told me you were glad we'd never married and had children. You said the fact that Ralph isn't your biological father changes everything."

"It does." How could it not?

She dropped her hands to her sides and took a deep breath. "See, that's what I'm afraid of. I want you to see that it doesn't matter."

His temper erupted. "You're ignoring the obvious. I understand that Ralph Reynolds had a tremendous influence on my life. He raised me to believe certain things and to act a certain way, but those are only influences. What about my basic character? Were you listening to what my mother said about Earl Haynes? He got a seventeen-year-old girl pregnant. When he found out about her twins, he simply walked away. That is my heritage. That is the character of the man who fathered me. I have to live with that and make peace with it, if possible. I may not know much about him, but I know he was a cheating bastard who wouldn't take responsibility for his own children. I'm not willing to take a chance on passing those qualities on. Are you?"

Pain flashed through her blue eyes. Her mouth trembled. "You're not him," she said softly. "You're not him."

"Are you willing to bet your children's future on that?"

"Yes," she said with a confidence that stunned him. "I know you. I've known you for years. You're the kind of man who would put his life on the line for his town because he doesn't know another way to do things. You're the kind of man who looks after other people's grandmothers, and cares for his own mother when her husband dies. You're responsible, caring, gentle, loving and passionate. You're a good man.''

Her words hit him like arrows finding their way to his soul. ''You don't know what the hell you're talking about,'' he said, turning away.

She grabbed his arm and stepped in front of him. ''I know exactly what I'm saying. You are the same man you were last month and last year. Believing anything else is giving power to a ghost. I believe in you with all my heart.'' She stopped talking and pressed a hand to her mouth. Tears filled her eyes. ''Oh, Gage.''

He watched her warily.

She blinked the tears away. ''I just realized, it doesn't matter how much I believe in you. If you won't believe in yourself, there's no point in having this conversation. I can't convince you. I can't make you believe. And loving you won't matter because you won't let it.''

He froze. ''What did you say?''

She lowered her hand. ''I love you. I'm beginning to think I never stopped. You still have every quality I loved before, but you're even better now. How was I supposed to resist that?''

Her words stunned him. She loved him? Now? ''I don't believe you,'' he said flatly.

''I'm not surprised. Worse, I don't know how to convince you. I'm beginning to think I don't know anything.'' She sighed and took a step back, holding out her hands, palms up.

''I love you and I'm terrified you're going to let me walk away because of some ridiculous obsession with the past and what it means to you today. I'm afraid we're going to lose our second chance, and I'm willing to bet there won't be a third."

Kari's declaration had caught him off guard. Defenseless and confused, he wanted to retreat. *No more words,* he thought. *No more.*

But she wasn't finished. "It all comes down to making choices," she said. "Are you willing to trust yourself?" She gave a strangled laugh. "I guess that's *your* most significant question. Mine is different. Do you still love me? Are you interested in any of this? I've been going on, based on the assumption that my feelings matter to you—and they may not. But if they do, it's your choice. Are you willing to let the biology rule your life? You do have a choice in this."

She turned away and started for her house. When she reached the driveway, she glanced back at him.

"Let me know what you decide. I hope you have enough sense to see how lucky we are to have found each other again. I think we could be wonderful together. At one time I was set on leaving Possum Landing, but that's not an issue anymore. What I don't know is if you can get past everything you've learned recently. One way or the other, I have to make a decision. To stay or go. When you figure out what you want, let me know."

And then she was gone. Gage stared after her, watching her disappear into the house, feeling his lifeblood flow away.

She loved him.

After all these years, after all the waiting—he'd just realized that's what he'd been doing—she finally realized she loved him. She'd come to the same conclusion he had—that all they'd loved about each other was still in place, only better.

The information came a couple of weeks too late. He might want to be with Kari with all his heart, but did that matter? He had nothing to offer her. Without a past he could depend on, he had no future.

Kari walked into the house to find the phone ringing. At first she thought about ignoring it. There was no way that Gage could have run inside and called her. Besides, if he had something he wanted to say, he would simply come over and tell her.

So she let the machine get it. But when a woman identified herself as someone from the Abilene school where she'd interviewed, she grabbed the receiver.

"Hello?"

"Kari?"

"Yes."

"Hi! This is Margaret Cunningham. We spoke during your interview?"

"I remember. How are you?" Kari wiped the tears from her face.

"Great. I have wonderful news. We were all so impressed, and I'm delighted to be calling you with a job offer."

Kari wasn't even surprised. Of course this would happen moments after she made her declaration to Gage. Fate was nothing if not ironic.

She listened while the other woman gave details about the job, including a starting salary and when they would like her to start. Kari wrote it all down and promised to call back within forty-eight hours. When she'd hung up, she grabbed a pillow from a nearby chair and sent it sailing across the room.

"Dammit, Gage," she yelled into the silence. "Now what? You're not going to tell me what I want to hear, are you. And if you are, you'll take your time, and then what am I supposed to do? I told you I loved you. Doesn't that mean anything?"

She wanted to stomp her feet, as well, but figured that was immature and wouldn't help. She hurt inside. Probably because she'd done the right thing at last and declared her feelings, only to have Gage not respond to them. He'd listened and then had let her walk away. Not exactly the sign of a man overwhelmed by loving feelings.

She sank onto the chair and covered her face with her hands. That's what was really wrong, she thought sadly. She'd admitted she loved Gage and he hadn't offered her love in return. He hadn't offered her anything.

Over the next twenty-four hours, Kari alternately cried, ate ice cream, threw unbreakable objects and slept. She also hovered by the phone, willing it to ring.

When it did, she found herself being offered another job, this one in the Dallas area.

Sometime close to noon the next day, while she cried her way through a shower, she finally got it. It was as if the heavens had opened and God had spoken to her directly.

She couldn't force Gage to love her back and she couldn't insist he live on her timetable. The only control she had was over herself. Her feelings, her goals, her life. Gage was his own person. He had to make the decisions that were right for him.

The realization left her feeling very much alone. What did she do now? Did she keep her life on hold, hoping he would come to terms with everything and realize that they belonged together? Or did she move on, aware that he might never come around?

After her shower, she dressed and fussed with her hair. She applied makeup, then headed out the door. She found Gage at the sheriff's station. He was talking with one of the deputies, so Kari waited until they were finished. When Gage was alone in his office, she slipped inside and closed the door behind her.

He looked tired. Dark shadows stained the skin under his eyes. While she couldn't read his thoughts, she felt he looked a little wary. No doubt he feared her next confession.

"About yesterday," she said, settling into a chair across from his desk. She really wanted to pace, but figured if she stayed standing, he would, as well. Although the closed door gave them the illusion of privacy, in reality Gage's office walls were glass. Anyone could watch what was going on. Better to have things appear calm. At least no one could hear the thundering of her heart.

"Kari," Gage began, but she held up her hand to stop him.

"I'd like to go first," she said quickly. He hesitated, then nodded.

Every cell in her body screamed at her to run to him and beg him to say he loved her. She desperately wanted him to sweep her up in his arms, hold her close and swear he would never let her go. She wanted him to declare his love with a sincerity and passion that would keep her tingling for the rest of her life.

Instead, she was going to tell him it was okay for him to let her go.

"I was wrong yesterday," she said. "I shouldn't have confessed my feelings. Or if I did, I should have done it differently. Nothing about this situation is your fault. You have so much going on right now and I just added to your load. For me this is huge, but for you it's just one more piece of the puzzle."

She forced herself to smile and hoped it came out even borderline normal. "You need time to figure out what's going on. You have a lot to come to grips with. I'm not saying I don't love you. I do. I can't imagine life without you. But I'm not going to force myself on you. You need time, and I'm going to give you that."

Now came the tricky part. She swallowed and twisted her fingers together. "So, to that end, I'm accepting a job in Abilene. It's close enough that if you change your mind—" She cleared her throat. "It would be doable until my school year ended. And if you decide this is… I mean, if I'm not what you want, then I'll be getting on with my life."

He looked as if she'd sucker punched him. "Kari, don't."

"Don't what? Leave? Isn't it the right thing to do?"

He shook his head. She had a bad feeling he'd meant "Don't love me."

Pain gripped her. She forced herself to go on. "Just to keep things from being too awkward, I've hired someone to finish the work on the house. The property management company will take care of selling it. So I'm heading out in the morning. I wanted to tell you that, too. Goodbye, I mean."

"You don't have to leave because of me."

It hurt to breathe. He was saying he shouldn't be the reason she left—not "Don't go."

"There's nothing to keep me here," she said, forcing herself to breathe in and out. The pain would pass eventually. Life would go on. This wouldn't kill her, no matter how it felt right now.

"My family, such as it is, lives elsewhere. With my grandmother gone, Possum Landing isn't home anymore. She was always the one who mattered. My mother might have given birth to me, but my grandmother was the keeper of my heart while I was growing up." She stood slowly.

There was so much more she wanted to say—but what was the point? Obviously her love was one-sided. Not the haven she had wanted it to be. If only...

"Goodbye, Gage," she said finally.

Gathering every ounce of courage and strength, she turned and walked out of his office. She didn't look back, not even once. She'd done the right thing. When she'd begun to heal in, oh, fifty years or so, she could be proud of that. Right now, she just wanted to be anywhere but here.

Gage watched her go. With each step she took, he felt a piece of his soul crumble to dust.

She was leaving. She'd said as much and he believed her. Under the circumstances, it would be best for both of them. She would get on with her life and he would try to figure out who he was now that he was no longer one of five generations of Reynolds, born and bred in Possum Landing.

He turned to his computer screen, but the small characters there didn't make any sense. Instead of words, he saw Kari leaving. Again. He'd let her go the first time because she'd deserved to have a chance at her dreams. This time he was letting her go because...

Because it was the right thing to do. Because she deserved more than he had to offer. Because— He swore as her words echoed inside him. While Aurora was her mother, she wasn't the keeper of Kari's heart. Her grandmother had been that. For Kari, Aurora was nothing more than biology. No yesterdays bound them together. No shared laughter, no talks late at night, no Christmas mornings.

Gage curled his hands into fists as a kaleidoscope of memories rushed through his brain. His father teaching him to ride a bike, then, years later, to drive a car. His father taking him fishing. Just the two of them, leaving town several hours before dawn for a camping trip. Long walks, evenings by the fire building models. Frank conversations about women and sex—Ralph Reynolds had admitted knowing less about the former than the latter. His father had taught him to tell the truth, be polite, think of others. He'd taught Gage respect and courage.

Earl Haynes might have given Gage life, but Ralph Reynolds had made sure that life meant something.

Gage stood up with a force that sent his chair sailing across the room. He raced to the door and out toward the front of the building. He might not have all the answers, but he knew one thing for sure—he wasn't going to lose Kari a second time. Not if she was willing to take a chance on him.

He pushed open the front door and saw her on the sidewalk. "Kari," he called. "Wait."

She turned. He saw tears on her beautiful face. Tears and an expression so lost and empty that it nearly broke his heart. Then she saw him. And as he watched, hope struggled with pain.

"Don't go," he said when he reached her side. He wrapped his arms around her. "Please, don't go. I can't lose you again."

He cupped her face and stared into her eyes. "Kari, I love you. I've always loved you. I didn't want to admit it, even to myself, but I've been waiting for you to come back. Don't go."

A smile played around her mouth. It blossomed until she beamed at him.

"Really? You love me?"

"Always."

"What about what your mother told you?"

"I don't have all the answers."

Her smile never wavered as love filled her eyes, chasing away the tears. "You don't have to. We'll figure them out together. No matter what, I'll be here for you."

That was all he wanted to hear. He kissed her. "I love you. Stay. Please. I know you have to work in Abilene for a year. That's what you agreed to, right? We'll work it out. I want to be with you. I want to marry you and have babies with you."

She laughed. "I haven't accepted the job yet. I was going to go home and call right now. I guess I'll have to tell them no."

He couldn't believe she would do that for him. He pulled her close again and pressed his face into her soft hair. "I never want to lose you again."

"You won't. I'll marry you, Gage. And we'll have those babies. When you figure out what you want to do about your half siblings in California, we'll deal with that, as well."

He raised his head and looked at her. Love filled him, banishing the shadows and making everything right. "How did I get so lucky?"

"I could ask the same thing. My answer is that I love you. After all this time, you're still the one."

* * * * *

Also by Jill Kemerer

Love Inspired

Wyoming Legacies

The Cowboy's Christmas Compromise
United by the Twins
Training the K-9 Companion

Wyoming Ranchers

The Prodigal's Holiday Hope
A Cowboy to Rely On
Guarding His Secret
The Mistletoe Favor
Depending on the Cowboy
The Cowboy's Little Secret

Visit her Author Profile page at LoveInspired.com
or jillkemerer.com for more titles!

HOMETOWN HERO'S REDEMPTION

Jill Kemerer

Thank you to the Waterville Fire Department for your bravery and sacrifice. We are blessed by your heroism. Special thanks to Steven Brubaker for answering my endless list of questions so patiently. Any errors in the book are mine!

Finally, thank you to all the men and women who dedicate their lives to keeping us safe. Jason Kernstock, we couldn't be prouder of you!

Therefore encourage one another and
build each other up, just as in fact you are doing.
—*1 Thessalonians* 5:11

Chapter One

Ice cream fixed a lot of problems, but it wasn't going to fix this.

Drew Gannon passed a chocolate-brownie sundae to Wyatt. The tiny ice-cream shop had two tables inside and a patio full of picnic tables out front. Not much had changed in the fourteen years he'd been gone. If his best friend, Chase McGill, hadn't insisted, Drew never would have moved back to Lake Endwell, Michigan. But Wyatt, Chase's ten-year-old son, deserved a stable life away from the public eye. Drew had promised Chase he'd give Wyatt that life. He just needed to convince Lauren Pierce to help him.

Drew handed a twenty to the teen behind the counter, turned to Wyatt and pointed to the glass door leading to the patio. "Why don't you head outside and save us a picnic table—the one with the striped umbrella."

Wyatt nodded. He was far too grim for a little boy. *Poor kid.* The past nine months had traumatized him, and Drew was doing the best he could to make his life normal again. Well, as normal as it could be given the circumstances. A murdered mom. His dad in jail for trying to avenge her death. What a horrible situation.

Drew tried to spot Lauren. Would he recognize her after all these years? The only women he could see were either too old or not old enough. What if she'd changed her mind about meeting him? He wouldn't blame her. If their situations were reversed, he'd probably never want to speak to her again.

"Here you go." The girl shoved the change in his hand. "Napkins are over there."

He thanked her, inserted a straw into his orange slushie and strolled to the door, pushing it open with his shoulder. An early-May breeze guaranteed sweatshirt weather. The sunshine highlighted Wyatt's scrawny, slumped shoulders. His gaze seemed glued to the wooden table. Drew doubted he'd touched the ice cream.

Maybe he should call Lauren. Grovel if necessary.

"What's wrong with your sundae?" He playfully punched Wyatt's arm. "Don't tell me you suddenly hate chocolate."

His hazel eyes opened wide, as if he'd been lost in his own little world, which, Drew guessed, was exactly where he'd been for the past several months.

"I'm not hungry." Wyatt slowly swirled the spoon in the gooey mixture, but he didn't eat any of it.

Drew took a drink of slushie to ease the helplessness lining his throat. Would the kid ever enjoy simple pleasures again?

He checked his phone to see if Lauren had texted or left a message. Nothing. He needed someone to stay with Wyatt when he worked overnight at the fire station, and not just anyone would do. According to Drew's mom, Lauren had the credentials—years of working with neglected children and a degree as a social worker—as well as the time. Apparently, she'd quit her job in Chicago and moved back to Lake Endwell a few months ago.

When he'd called Lauren last week, her clipped words had made it as clear as a freshly cleaned window she wanted nothing to do with him. She hadn't relented after he'd tried to explain Wyatt's situation, either. He'd finally resorted to pleading with her to just meet him in person before saying no. His words could never convince her the way one look at Wyatt could.

Except he hadn't mentioned Wyatt joining them.

Manipulative? Yes.

Necessary? Absolutely.

The thud of a car door jolted him from his thoughts. He glanced ahead and his mouth dropped open.

Lauren Pierce.

Still had that long, wavy blond hair. She didn't head to the door of the ice-cream shop—no, she strode directly to the patio. A baby blue hoodie was zipped halfway up over her white tank top. Her enormous light gray eyes captured him. A film reel of memories flashed through his mind so quickly he couldn't keep up.

Breathtaking. A woman who stopped men in their tracks.

Why had he been such an idiot back then?

Something had changed, though. Her nothing-gets-me-down smile had been replaced with something else. Something familiar.

Drew darted a glance at Wyatt.

If he hadn't lived with Wyatt's diminished personality for months, he might not have recognized it. Lauren had been traumatized, too. And he wanted to know why. The captain of the cheerleading squad had had everything going for her. She'd never let anything shake her optimistic spirit.

"Glad to see you again. You're looking good." He rose and held his hand out. She ignored it, arching her eyebrows instead. Why had he said that? It was something the old him would have rolled out. Heat climbed up his neck. The last impression he wanted to give her was that he was the same old Drew.

"So when did you get back?" Lauren asked as she sat opposite them.

"Yesterday. Wyatt and I are renting a cabin on the lake. Used to be Claire Sheffield's—well, Claire Hamilton now. Remember her? Her brother, Sam, was living next door, but Claire said Sam, his wife and their little boy moved to a house just outside town, leaving both cottages empty. Anyway, we've made a dent in the unpacking." Drew's knee bounced rapidly. He was babbling, and Lauren gave no indication she was up for small talk. He'd better get right to it. "This is Wyatt. Chase's son."

A flicker of kindness lightened her eyes. "Nice to meet you."

Drew elbowed Wyatt, who belatedly said, "Hi," and dropped his attention back to the table. This was going great.

"Thanks for coming." He didn't blame her if she left, but to his surprise, she stayed. She looked weary—but stunning all the same. "Mom told me you moved back in January. You're a social worker?"

"I did move back, but no." She shook her head, her demeanor icy. "I used to be a social worker. I don't do that anymore."

Hmm... He hadn't considered she no longer wanted to work in her field. "Mom said you had a temp job."

"I do. It's great." She nodded, and her smile appeared forced. She addressed Wyatt. "What do you think of Lake Endwell so far?"

One shoulder lifted in a shrug.

Drew's knee bounced double time. "We'll have to rent a boat or borrow a canoe or something soon. Wyatt here—"

"I don't want to canoe," Wyatt said.

He put his arm around Wyatt. "You'll change your mind. Summer is the best season to enjoy the lake."

"I know a little bit about your situation, Wyatt." Her voice was low, soothing. Wyatt's gaze locked with hers. "It's okay."

"Everyone knows." Wyatt hung his head. "I guess you saw the pictures. Those guys were always sneaking around with their cameras. The whole world knows."

"After a while, no one will care." Compassion glowed from her eyes.

Drew squeezed Wyatt's arm. "No reporters will take your picture here. That's why we moved. We're going to have a nice, quiet, normal life until...you move back in with your dad."

Wyatt didn't say anything, but he studied Lauren, which Drew took as a good sign. In high school, she had always seemed to be an open book. Straight-A student, prom queen, crusader against teen drinking and, of course, the captain of the cheerleading squad. And since he'd been the star quarterback, everyone had assumed they would make the perfect couple.

Not even close. They'd never dated. Not once.

Drew cleared his throat and leaned in. "So why did you move back?"

"I didn't want to move, but I needed a change. And my family is here."

"I didn't want to move here, either. I want to go home," Wyatt said. "Can't we go back to Detroit?"

That made three of them not wanting to move back to Lake Endwell. Drew would have cracked a joke if the atmosphere wasn't so tense.

"What's in Detroit?" A trio of emotions sped across Lauren's face—sympathy, sadness and wariness.

Wyatt hauled in a breath, his face full of animation for the first time in forever; then the joy slid away and he sighed, defeated. "Nothing, I guess."

"There must be something." Her voice lilted, coaxing Wyatt to talk, but silence won. "Never mind. You don't have to answer. We all have things we'd prefer no one knew about."

"My dad," Wyatt whispered. "But he's in jail."

"My dad was in jail most of my life," Lauren said. "He died a few years ago."

Drew straightened. Why was she lying? Her dad had never been in jail. Bill Pierce was one of the most upstanding men the community had ever seen, and he was definitely still alive.

"Really?" Wyatt sounded skeptical and hopeful at the same time. "What did he do?"

"He murdered two men." She rubbed her arm, not looking him in the eye.

"Oh." He dropped his attention to the uneaten sundae melting into a puddle of brown and white. "But you're so pretty."

She laughed. "Thank you. I'm not sure that what I look like has anything to do with it, though."

"Sorry." Wyatt blushed. "I just meant… I guess I don't know what I meant."

"I think I do." She scrunched her nose. "People who look like they have it all together have problems, too. Big problems. Like yours."

He seemed to chew on the thought. Drew dug his nails into his jeans. Maybe he'd been all wrong about Lauren. Was she fabricating a sob story to make Wyatt trust her?

"Would you do me a favor, Wyatt?" Lauren asked. "Go inside and buy me a chocolate ice cream. In a cup, please." She handed him a five-dollar bill. "If you don't mind?"

He took the money. "You want sprinkles?"

"No, thanks."

Drew waited until Wyatt was safely indoors before he turned back to Lauren. "Why did you lie to him?"

"I didn't." Those clear gray eyes held nothing but truth. "But Bill—"

"Bill isn't my real dad. I was adopted."

"What do you mean, you were adopted?"

She shrugged. "Adopted. As in my parents adopted me."

Of course she hadn't lied. Relief spread through his chest, releasing the tension building inside. "Look, I need a babysitter. An adult to stay with him when I'm working at the fire station. Mom moved to Arizona last year or I'd ask her. I'll be on twenty-four hours and off forty-eight, so it's not every day. And I think we both know that not anyone will do in this situation."

She was already shaking her head. "I don't think so."

"Why not?"

"I'm not the right person." She pushed her hands against the table as if preparing to leave.

"You're exactly the right person." Her brittle expression reminded him to be gentle. "Look, I'm sorry. I don't blame you if you hold a grudge, but I'm not the same guy I was. I've changed. And you don't owe me anything except maybe a slap in the head or a kick in the rear, but I'm not asking this for me."

He let her see the sincerity in his eyes. Didn't move. And he prayed. *Lord, please don't hold my foolishness and arrogance against me. Wyatt needs her. I feel it deep down in my gut.*

She shook her head, and he clenched his jaw, trying to come up with something that would convince her. She'd been the most honest, upright person he'd ever met. Someone who would be a good influence on Wyatt.

He didn't deserve someone like that. But Wyatt did.

"I can't be there for him every hour," Drew said. "I need to rely on someone I can trust. Someone with experience dealing with the kind of trauma he's lived through. I wish my mom could help out, but she's on the other side of the country. She told me you're the one for Wyatt, and, frankly, Mom's always right."

"I'll give you the number of a nice college student I know. He'd probably stay with Wyatt."

"Or you could keep the guy's number and make this easy on everyone."

She tilted her chin up. "I don't think you understand. My life is on hold."

"What?" He tried to figure out what she was talking about but came up blank.

"I'm not the person for the job."

* * *

Lauren watched as Drew processed her words. He was even better-looking now than he'd been in high school, if such a thing was possible. And a firefighter? Forget putting out the fires. More like igniting them. He could be the cover model for any fireman calendar.

Stupid hormones. Must be playing tricks on her. She'd never been attracted to him before. Not much, anyway.

Maybe a tad.

A person's soul should match their appearance, and he didn't have the integrity to round out the package.

She probably wasn't being fair. The man in front of her seemed the polar opposite of the boy she'd gone to high school with. Back then he'd been a cocky jerk. It hadn't been enough he'd been the most popular guy at Lake Endwell High—oh, no—he'd been the most popular guy in the whole town. Everyone had loved him. As the big-time quarterback, he'd taken the football team to two state championships. College coaches had scouted him for months. Parents had adored him. The town had revered him.

And she'd loathed him.

He and his friends had made it their mission to mock her. She had never been Lauren Pierce to them. She was "the prude," "Miss Perfect," "do-gooder" and, her personal favorite, "Prim Pierce." They'd invited her to parties where there was beer, knowing full well she didn't drink. Their girlfriends—always the most inappropriately dressed girls in school—looked down on her. The guys teased her for her modest clothes and made lewd comments about her bare legs when she wore her cheerleading uniform.

They'd made her feel like a leper the first two years of high school. By the time junior year had rolled around, her confidence had kicked in. She'd prayed for them, and their taunts might as well have bounced off a shield, because they'd no longer bothered her. In fact, she'd felt sorry for Drew and his crew.

"Are you getting married or something?"

She barked out a laugh. "No, nothing like that."

"Then I think you *are* the person." He tapped the table twice with his knuckles.

"You don't know anything about me." *Oops.* She'd let bitterness creep into her tone. *Oh, well.* Bitterness had crept into every cell of her body since last December. She'd failed Treyvon and Jay. Would she ever fall asleep at night without seeing their trusting faces?

"You're right." He ran his hand through his short, almost black hair. "But I know you have integrity and devoted your life to helping others. Back in school, I had an ego as long as the Mississippi and as deep as the Grand Canyon. I never thought about anyone but myself. I apologize for that. And I apologize for—"

"Look, we don't have time for unnecessary apologies. Wyatt will be back soon. I want to help you out, but I can't. I *was* a social worker, but I don't work with troubled kids anymore."

"What will it take for you to say yes?"

"Nothing." She lifted her hands, palms up. "I give you credit for using your best weapon—Wyatt—to try to seal the deal, but no."

His nostrils flared. "Do you have another job?"

"Yes."

"Permanent?"

Ugh. He knew. Always knew people's weak spots.

"I'm filling in at LE Fitness for Laney Mills. Maternity leave. She'll be back next week."

"There you go. The timing's perfect. You need a job. I need help. I'll pay you whatever you're making there, plus ten percent."

She fought irritation. This relentlessness was part of Drew's personality, part of what had made him a winning football player. But, for real, the man needed to accept the word *no.* She didn't owe him anything. "You can find someone else."

"He needs *you.*"

That threw her off. Drew didn't know her, not really. "How can you say that with a straight face?"

"Look, he's been through a nightmare I wouldn't wish on anyone, and he's hurting. Withdrawn. I'm worried he'll never be the same fun kid I've spent so much time with over the past ten years. I'm all he has."

A nightmare... For eight years she'd worked with kids embroiled in nightmares. Chicago's inner city had supplied a lifetime of them. She'd thought she could help. She'd been wrong. But Wyatt's face when he'd admitted there was nothing for him in Detroit scratched at her heart. She knew exactly how he felt.

There'd been nothing for her anywhere the first seven years of her life.

Drew squared his shoulders. "I could find a babysitter or someone else with children where he can stay on my overnights, but he's been through too much. You know how to handle kids like him. Know what he needs. I want someone who will come to our house. I want him to sleep in the same bed every night. Feel safe. Grow up as normal as possible."

Kind of like the normal life her adoptive parents

gave her. *Uh-oh.* He'd twisted the screw into her vulnerable spot.

"Even you have to admit he needs special care right now. He lost his mom. His dad's in jail. He's scared of photographers jumping out of the bushes. Please, Lauren."

Yes was on the tip of her tongue, but the memory of last December's phone call haunted her. "I can't help. When I say I can't, I mean I really can't. Even if I agreed, I'd only be giving you false hope he'll be okay. He's not an easy fix, Drew."

He opened his mouth to counter, but Wyatt came back, setting the ice cream and the change in front of Lauren.

"Thank you, Wyatt." She smiled at him. Skinny with light brown hair and one of those cute faces destined to grow up handsome. She couldn't halt the longing in her heart to help him. To take him under her wing and just let him be a kid. Help him adjust to life without his parents.

She'd had the same longing every day since she was sixteen years old. She'd thought she was meant to help kids like Wyatt—kids like her—ones with broken wings and matching spirits. But her efforts were for nothing. Worse than nothing. She'd given those two boys hope, and look where they'd ended up.

How had she been so wrong about her life? Her calling?

Her neck felt as though a noose was tightening around it. "Well, I'd better get going."

"But you didn't eat your ice cream," Wyatt said.

She tried to smile, but his hazel eyes held a glimmer she recognized. It was a sliver of need, asking her if he was worth anything. *Yes, Wyatt. You're worth every-thing, but I'm not the one who can help you.*

"I guess we're even, then." She pointed to his bowl. He blinked, and the glimmer vanished. Guilt compressed her chest until she could barely breathe. She darted a glance at Drew and wished she hadn't. He looked unhappy.

Without a word, Wyatt pivoted and jogged away. Drew followed him.

The guilt squeezing her chest so tightly exploded. She'd made the sweet kid feel unwanted, and she *did* want to help him. Wanted to get to know him, to hear all about his little-boy day. She wanted him to know his parents had made bad choices, and none of it was his fault. She wanted to be part of his recovery.

But she wasn't recovered herself.

One broken soul couldn't fix another.

Lauren watched Drew draw near the boy. He crouched to his level and put his hand on his shoulder. The picture they presented radiated love. It didn't take a degree in psychology to see Drew would do whatever was necessary to keep the boy safe and make him happy.

For the briefest moment, she wanted the same. For Drew to chase her and do whatever it took to keep her safe and make her happy.

Which proved how messed up she was.

She'd had her life planned out since she was sixteen. Devote her life to neglected kids, eventually get married, have a family of her own. That was the funny thing about life. Plans changed. Not always for the better.

Now what? She had no plan. Temporary jobs didn't fulfill her. She wanted a new life purpose. Something to dig into. Something to make her feel alive again.

In the distance Drew rose and kept his arm around Wyatt. He pointed to a black truck. While Wyatt trudged to the passenger door, Drew marched back to her.

"That was my fault," he said, head high. "I took a chance bringing you two together, and it blew up in my face. I'm sorry. But I'm still asking you to consider it. Don't decide now. Give it a few days. I'll call you."

Please don't.

He strode, tall and confident, back to the truck.

She grabbed the ice-cream containers and threw them in the trash. Drew didn't need her. He thought he did, but Wyatt would be better off with someone else.

Anyone else.

For months she'd avoided thinking about her next move, but this meeting drove home the fact that she needed a long-term plan. A new career. A way to get out of this nothingness she'd been in. But what?

Drew Gannon was dangerous. He tempted her with the one forbidden fruit she'd promised herself she'd never take a bite out of again. Her purpose no longer included helping kids with hard lives. Not even ones who wiggled into her heart and made her want to feel again. Not even Wyatt.

"See how I'm holding the rod? You want to bring it back like this, then flick it forward while you hold the reel's button." At the end of the dock in front of their cabin, Drew demonstrated a perfect cast.

After leaving JJ's Ice Cream, he'd driven to the elementary school to sign papers for Wyatt's enrollment. The kid hadn't said a word since they'd gotten home an hour ago. Wyatt held a fishing rod in his hand, but he'd yet to attempt to cast a line. "Try it."

With a loud sigh, Wyatt laid the pole on the dock and slouched in one of the camping chairs Drew had brought down. He stuffed his hands into his sweatshirt pockets and stared out at the sparkling blue water.

Drew was ready to pull his hair out. Today had been bad. Really bad. What had made him think springing Wyatt on Lauren would help his cause with her? He shouldn't have badgered her. Shouldn't have expected her to help him out, not after the way he'd treated her years ago. Not only had it backfired big-time, but he was no closer to finding a babysitter than before. Unless the college kid she mentioned... No. He didn't want anyone but her.

Did Lauren still have the same impression of him from way back when?

What did it matter?

If he could just figure out how to get through to Wyatt. He'd always been a big part of the kid's life. Chase's career as a wide receiver kept him training and traveling nine months of the year, so Drew had helped take care of Wyatt off and on during football season. Wyatt's drug-addicted mom had never been around. Even if she had been, she certainly couldn't have taken care of him.

"Don't you want to show off your fishing skills when your dad gets out?" Drew kept his tone light. Chase made mistakes—big mistakes—but Drew believed in him and hoped Wyatt would, too.

"Six years from now." Wyatt kicked at the dock with his sneaker.

"His lawyer said he'll get out in three if he models good behavior."

Wyatt looked up at Drew. "Do you think he'll do it? Get out early?"

Drew lowered himself into the chair next to him, ruffling Wyatt's hair with his free hand. "Yeah, I do. He'll do anything to be back with you. He loves you."

Wyatt's face fell again.

"What did you think of Lauren?" Drew asked.

He shrugged.

"We went to high school together. I wasn't very nice to her."

"Is that why she left without eating her ice cream?"

"Maybe she wasn't hungry." Drew cranked his line in a little ways. "I don't think she left because she held a grudge. Like I said, I was mean to her in high school, but she was probably the nicest person I knew. Very genuine."

"Why were you mean?"

Drew kept one eye on the bobber out in the lake. "I was stupid. When I was fourteen, I had a crush on her. One of my friends told me she'd never go out with me. He said she was too perfect. I asked one of the other cheerleaders if she thought I had a chance with Lauren, and she laughed. She told me Lauren would never date me, that she thought she was better than everyone. I took their word for it. And my pride made me say things and treat Lauren in ways I regret."

"She deserved it if she thought she was better than you."

"No, she didn't. No one does." Drew shook his head. "I trusted people who didn't have my best interest at heart. I should have asked Lauren myself, instead of listening to my so-called friends."

"What do you mean?" Wyatt's face twisted in confusion.

"Looking back, I think every guy in my class had a crush on Lauren."

"She's pretty."

"Yeah, and some of the cheerleaders were jealous of her."

"Oh."

"They had their own reasons for not wanting me to ask her out. Lauren kept to herself, but it didn't mean she was stuck-up. I hope you think about that as you get older. Don't believe everything you hear."

"Like about my mom." Wyatt got a lost look on his face again.

Whenever Drew tried to talk to him about his mother, Wyatt's mouth shut tighter than a vacuum-packed seal. Maybe this was the opening he needed. "What about your mom?"

"Forget it."

"Why don't you tell me?"

"People said things."

"People say a lot of things."

Wyatt's sad eyes met his. "They said she was on drugs and owed that Len guy money, and that's why he killed her."

Drew reeled in the rest of his line as he tried to figure out the best way to respond. Missy and Chase had never married. They were together for only a few years before Missy left and got mixed up with drugs. "You and I both know she went to rehab last year and was trying hard to live a healthy lifestyle."

"Yeah. I was glad when she moved by us. We'd play games with Dad and go to movies."

"Your dad cared about her. They were even talking about getting back together."

Wyatt nodded, the corners of his mouth drooping. "Do you think she was in a lot of pain before she died?"

While he was glad Wyatt was finally talking, it hurt to think he had to have his conversation. No kid should have to deal with this. A murdered mom? A dad in jail? Wyatt deserved an intact family—didn't every kid?

"No. The police said she died quickly."

"Do you think she's in heaven?"

He squirmed. This was another one of those tricky areas. Drew had no idea what Missy had believed. "The Bible says as long as you trust in Jesus as your savior, you go to heaven."

"But what if she didn't?"

"I wish I could tell you your mom is in heaven. I hope she is, but I don't really know. What do you think?"

"I want her to be."

"Me, too."

Wyatt grabbed his fishing rod and stood at the end of the dock. "How do I do this again?"

Drew showed him the steps. Wyatt's first attempts didn't get the line far, but after a few more tries, he cast it out several feet. Drew gave him a high five.

"Hey, Wyatt, we're going to be all right." He put his arm around him. "I hope you know that."

"Do you think Lauren would stay with me while you're at work?"

Drew's chest expanded. The kid liked her. Wyatt had already opened up more in the last ten minutes than he had since Chase went to jail three months ago. But Lauren didn't work with troubled kids anymore. She'd made that clear. What had happened in Chicago to make her quit?

"I don't know." This conversation alone hammered

it home—Wyatt was dealing with much more than the average kid. He didn't need a college student around to watch TV and heat up chicken nuggets. He needed to make sense of his shattered family. He needed Lauren. She might not believe she could help him, but Drew knew she could.

And maybe in the process, he could help her, too. Her sunny smile had grown cloudy since he'd last seen her, and he wanted to bring her joy back.

He'd just have to figure out how to get her to say yes.

Chapter Two

"I've been talking to Stan, and we think you should offer a class."

Lauren looked up from her computer screen at the reception desk of LE Fitness the following afternoon. Megan Fellows, one of the Zumba instructors, stood in front of her. Since moving back in January, Lauren had reconnected with Megan, two years her junior, and they'd become good friends, partly because Megan was so upbeat and made it her mission to not let Lauren dissolve into a puddle of depression. What would she think of Drew's offer?

It didn't matter. Lauren had made her decision. She needed to stay strong and say *no* when Drew called. If he called…

He would call. His take-charge personality assured her he would not let this matter fade away.

"What kind of class?" Lauren typed in a new client's information.

"A tumbling class for cheerleaders."

A tumbling class? The idea didn't horrify her. "I don't know."

"You keep saying you're figuring things out, but you don't have a plan." Megan's brown ponytail bounced as she drummed her fingernails on the counter. "And Laney will be back on Monday. What are you going to do?"

The million-dollar question. She had no idea. Megan was right about her not having a plan—every time she tried to figure out her next step, she froze. It was difficult letting go of the dream she'd had for most of her life. She couldn't handle the heartbreak of social work, but she still liked kids. Tumbling classes might be something to consider.

"I don't want you to go all hermit-like in your apartment again." Megan rested her elbows on the counter. Her face had the concerned look that poked at Lauren's conscience.

"Well, I *have* been offered a babysitting job."

"Babysitting?" Megan grimaced. "What ages are we talking? Three? Five?"

"Ten. Do you remember Drew Gannon?"

"Do I remember Drew Gannon?" Megan rounded the counter in a flash and took a seat next to Lauren. "Tall, built and studly? Oh, I remember."

"That's him." Lauren had probably been the only girl in school who hadn't drooled all over Drew.

"I've had a crush on him since I was in second grade. I know he's a little older than me, but how could a girl *not* like him?"

"Every girl in this town liked him at one point or another." Lauren straightened the papers on the desk. "He's back. Hired in at the fire station. He's taking care of his best friend's son."

"Why?" Megan's screwed-up face almost made Lauren laugh.

"I'm not getting into all the gory details, but Wyatt will be living with him for several years."

"A single dad. Maybe he needs some help…from yours truly."

Lauren swatted at her arm and laughed. "I'm sure once word gets out he's back in town, there will be plenty of willing female bodies at his door."

"He's single, then?"

"Seems to be."

"So how do you fit into all this?"

"His schedule," Lauren said. "Twenty-four hours on. Forty-eight off. He needs someone to stay with Wyatt while he's at work."

Megan pressed her index finger to her lips. "Why you?"

"My degree. Experience. His mom recommended me."

"Please tell me you jumped at the chance?"

She shook her head. "I can't, Megan. You know I can't."

"I know no such thing. You can. And you should."

"Uh, no. I'm not putting myself through it. No more emotionally damaged kids. My heart can't take it. I'm finally getting back to normal." If normal included not sleeping well, avoiding any public event and refusing to date any of the men brave enough to ask her out since she'd moved back…

Her new normal sounded sad. Add a few more felines, and she could be a reclusive cat lady.

"You love kids. And this is only one kid. It would be perfect. You wouldn't be trying to find him a foster home or visiting him at a crack house. You'd be heating SpaghettiOs and helping with math problems. Easy." Megan snapped her fingers.

Megan always made things sound easy. Unfortunately, Lauren knew better. There were so many factors making the situation impossible. Like the fact that Drew had been a complete jerk to her for years. Sure, he'd seemed caring with Wyatt and had apologized yesterday, but it didn't guarantee he was a stand-up guy.

And then there was Wyatt. Withdrawn, emotionally shattered—it was written all over him. She couldn't be simply a babysitter. She didn't have it in her. No matter how much she told herself not to grow attached, not to fall in love with the kids, she did. She'd love him. And she'd get hurt. If she took care of Wyatt and made a bad decision, it could send him back to square one.

"You want to say yes," Megan said. "I can see it in your eyes."

"He was so skinny and small and withdrawn. He was sweet, too. I felt an instant connection."

Megan smiled slyly. "And did you feel the connection with his temporary dad?"

Oh, yeah. When she agreed to meet Drew, she'd been sure she wouldn't find him attractive at all. His personality in high school had made him unattractive to her. But watching him interact with Wyatt? Seeing the way he pushed and pushed for Wyatt's sake?

Made him enticing.

"Um, I guess a little bit. I mean, I have a pulse, and he looks like…"

"A hot fireman."

"Yeah." Lauren glanced up as someone headed her way. *Phew.* Saved by the shift change. "I'm out of here."

"I think you should go for it," Megan said. Lauren grabbed her purse out of the drawer, ignoring her. "If not, consider the tumbling class."

She gave Megan a backward wave and walked out, soaking in the afternoon sunshine. Why was she still thinking about Drew's offer? She wasn't changing her mind. She'd made her choice.

She drove to her apartment over the hardware store on Main Street. Maybe Megan was on to something with the tumbling class. Lake Endwell High used to have an elite cheerleading program, but it had been several years since they had won any competitions. Tumbling classes would help, but not enough to get the program back on top.

What Lake Endwell needed was a boost to its cheerleading program.

Cheer academies had popped up all over Chicago while she lived there. One of the foster moms she knew owned one, and Lauren had visited it several times. The students came from surrounding school districts, and they traveled all over the country for competitions. Most of them went on to cheer in high school.

She parked in the lot behind her building. Years of gymnastics and cheerleading qualified her, but she hadn't choreographed in a long time. And own a business? She wouldn't know where to begin. While making her way to the back door, she checked her phone for messages.

Drew stood near the entrance. "I called the fitness place, and Megan Fellows told me you just left. She said I could find you here."

I'll get you back for this, Megan. She plastered a

smile on, ignoring the way her heartbeat stampeded at the sight of him. "What can I do for you?"

"I feel bad about yesterday. Let me buy you a cup of coffee."

"No need to feel bad or buy me coffee. We're good. Your conscience can be clear." She tried to push past him, but his broad shoulders blocked the door. He wore loose-fitting jeans and a dark gray pullover. By the strained look on his face, she'd say she annoyed him. *Good.*

"Will you please hear me out?" The words were soft, low. She let out a loud sigh.

"This isn't necessary. I hold no ill will against you. I hope you have a wonderful life." *Without me in it.*

"You were never good at lying." The side of his mouth quirked up, and challenge glinted from his brown eyes.

"You're right. I'm not." Hiking her purse over her shoulder, she tipped her chin up. "I like Wyatt. I'm tempted to help you because of him. But I never worshipped you like the rest of this town did, and I don't plan on it now. So go ahead and demand your way, but you won't get it—not from me. All you have to do is walk three steps and you'll find someone else who's more than willing to do whatever you ask."

He scowled. Maybe she'd gone too far. She hadn't seen him in years, and it wasn't his fault her life fell apart, so why was she taking her anger out on him?

And why was she so angry, anyhow? She'd been keeping it together reasonably well for months.

"I don't want anyone to worship me. I'm just a guy. Someone who messed up most of my life." Drew crossed his arms over his chest. "I admire you for being straight with me. Don't worry—I'll leave you alone."

"Wait." She caught his arm. His muscle flexed under her hand. She swiftly pulled back. "I guess one cup of coffee wouldn't kill me. I know you're trying to help Wyatt."

"The Daily Donut?"

She shook her head. "Closes at two. Have you been out and about yet since moving back?"

"No, why?"

Tapping her chin, she realized he had no idea what was about to hit him. "Then let's skip the coffee and go to City Park."

"Isn't there another coffeehouse in town?"

"You're missing the point. When word hits around here you moved back, you're going to be bombarded."

He grimaced. Had he paled? "City Park it is."

Drew Gannon, scared? She'd never thought he could surprise her, but never was a long time. Why wouldn't Mr. Hometown Hero have made the rounds when he arrived?

"Give me a minute to drop off my purse." Maybe a little chat in City Park wasn't such a bad idea after all.

Drew strode next to Lauren along the sidewalk. If he was going to have any chance at getting her to help Wyatt, he needed to show her he'd changed. This would probably be his only shot. She smelled fresh, the exact same way she looked. He'd always thought she belonged on a California beach. All-American, pure sunshine.

But the sunshine had sharpened to lightning over the years—she certainly hadn't held back with her opinion a minute ago. The way she'd put him in his place had shocked him at first. But, oddly enough, he liked her even more because of it.

He'd dated too many women who had their own agendas. He couldn't remember any of them saying exactly what was on their minds.

How long had it been since he'd been on a date?

Five years? Six?

"Where's Wyatt, by the way?" She easily kept pace with him.

"School. His first day. I'm picking him up at three thirty."

"School already? You don't waste time, do you?"

"I wasted enough time when I was younger. I don't see the point in waiting when something has to be done."

"What do you mean?" They reached the last store on the street. A quarter mile and they'd be at the park.

"You know how I was in high school?" He didn't glance at her, not wanting to see how she viewed him. He could guess well enough. "I thought I was some-body. Didn't work hard at anything but football, and by senior year I wasn't even giving that my all. I believed my hype. Thought I was special."

"Well, everyone around here agreed, so you probably were." Her dry tone made his lips twitch.

Keep it serious. Show her you mean this.

"I was unprepared for college. I actually thought the coaches were going to fawn over me the way it was here, not that you would know what I mean..."

"I know what you mean."

"Yeah. I guess you would, but I had no clue. I got to college and was a nobody. Third-string quarterback. For the first time in my life, everyone around me was as talented—more talented—than I was."

"I hope you don't expect me to feel sorry for you."

He shot her a look. There was the megawatt smile he'd missed. He chuckled.

"I had it coming. I struggled at practices, and instead of working harder and giving it my all, I complained about the coaches. Told everyone they didn't like me. That I deserved to be a starter." He gestured to the park entrance, and they headed toward the gazebo. "Do you know how many snaps I took in games?"

She made a face and shrugged. "None?"

"Two." He almost shuddered. "None would have been better. I threw two interceptions. The sum total of my freshman year stats. Two plays. Two interceptions. I gained weight, lost muscle, didn't attend a team meeting. And I was so dumb, I was actually shocked—and I mean shocked—when I was cut from the team. No more scholarship. No more college."

"I'm sorry, Drew. I didn't know all that."

"Well, you're the only one from this town who didn't. I have my doubts about moving back."

She hopped up on a picnic table and perched on the top, facing the water. Seagulls landed in the distance, and two ladies power walked on the bike trail. The unmistakable smell of the lake filled the air.

"Why did you come back?" Lauren pushed her hair to the side of her neck. The LE Fitness lime-green T-shirt she wore under a black formfitting warm-up jacket hugged her slender body. He liked the way it looked on her.

"Chase asked me to. He wanted Wyatt to grow up in a healthier environment, away from the reporters and the private school full of kids with wealthy parents. He always joked I was the most normal person he knew. He wanted normalcy for Wyatt."

"You? Normal? Debatable." She leaned back, resting her hands on the table, and grinned. Understanding knitted between them. The peace of the lapping waves nearby mellowed his senses.

"You gave me the ten-second version on the phone, but what really happened to Wyatt's mom? And how did you become his guardian?" Lauren crossed one leg over the other and faced him.

"It's kind of a long story."

She propped her elbow on her knee. "I've got all afternoon."

"Don't say I didn't warn you." *Where to start?* "Chase and I met in college. We were roommates. We had a lot in common, liked the football lifestyle. The girls, the parties, the accolades."

She snorted. He opened his hands as if to say, *This is what you get.*

"Chase was more grounded than I was. The guy was pure talent. And he worked his tail off to be the best. I can't tell you how many times I wished I would have followed his example."

"Yet he's in jail, and here you are." The words were barely audible.

"True. Anyway, he's my best friend. I refused to come back to Lake Endwell after getting kicked out of college. And even if I could have afforded out-of-state tuition, I had no desire to continue. I was bitter. Worked at a gas station, shared an apartment with a group of potheads. I couldn't face life without football. Couldn't face my parents. Certainly couldn't face my old buddies from home."

"Some of them would have been supportive. There are some good people here."

"You're probably right, but I couldn't handle it. I'd gone from being the hero to a nobody. Chase was the one who kept me going for two years. He told me I was better than that. Helped me realize I could do something with my life besides football. He fronted the money for me to take classes to be a firefighter and an EMT. A few years later I decided to continue my training and become a paramedic. It was brutal. I almost quit. Chase didn't let me."

"Sounds like a great guy."

"He is." Drew leaned forward, his clasped hands dangling between his knees. "He met Missy while I was working at the gas station. She was gorgeous, and she liked to party. That was all Chase looked for in a girl. At the time it was all I looked for, too. They fought a lot, but they'd make up just as quickly. She got pregnant his junior year. Moved to Chicago with him when he got drafted. They never married. She left when Wyatt was two, taking him with her, and the next year Chase was traded and moved to Detroit."

"Did she move, too?"

"No. Not then, anyway. If she would have, things might not have spiraled out of control the way they did. She found a new boyfriend, Len, who also became her drug supplier. When Chase realized how addicted she'd become, he fought for full custody of Wyatt—and he won. From that point on, I was a big part of Wyatt's life."

"How so?"

"I'd gotten a job in Dearborn the year before. When Chase gained custody of Wyatt, I transferred to a fire station closer to them. He was on the road or training for over half the year. He hired a part-time babysitter, but I stayed at his house whenever he was traveling. I had my own apartment the rest of the time. Wyatt has no living grandparents. That's why the courts appointed me to be Wyatt's guardian."

"So you've been helping take care of Wyatt for years?" She tilted her head.

"When Chase couldn't."

"That's actually a good situation for Wyatt. He's comfortable with you and doesn't have to learn a new routine."

"Living here will be a new routine for us both. I hope his first day is going okay."

"I do, too. Kids make friends easy at his age. I'm sure he'll fit right in."

Drew gazed out at the water. "I don't know. He's too quiet. And he never used to be shy."

"Losing your parents will do that to you." She rubbed her upper arms although it wasn't cold. "You still haven't told me what happened."

He hated discussing it. It wasn't as if he hadn't memorized the details. Once he opened his mouth, he knew he'd be able to tell her the facts in a detached voice. If only his insides wouldn't twist and cry out at the senselessness of it all. Missy hadn't deserved to die, and his best friend shouldn't be in jail.

"Over a year ago, Missy went to rehab and, once out, decided a change of scene would help her stay clean. She moved to Detroit to be in Wyatt's life. She and Chase reconnected, were even dating again. On a hot day in August, Len showed up at her apartment. They fought. He choked her to death." He cleared his throat to dislodge the lump forming. "It changed Chase. He became obsessed when Len skipped bail. He hired a private investigator, and when they located Len, he went there to confront him. No one knows exactly what happened, but Chase drove over Len with his truck."

"He didn't kill him, though?"

"Broke his leg." He rubbed his chin. "Chase was found guilty of second-degree attempted murder. Len is serving a life sentence in prison for first-degree murder."

Drew glanced at Lauren to see her reaction. "Is that the saddest story you've ever heard?"

She shook her head. "No. It's not."

"That's pretty heartless."

"Is it?" She stood, shaking her legs out. "Work in the inner city of Chicago for eight years. You'll see worse."

He rose, too, shoving his hands in his pockets. Logically he knew awful things happened every day all over the world, but they hadn't touched him the way Chase and Missy did. His own line of work put him face-to-face with horror on an ongoing basis. While he cared about the people he helped who had been in accidents and fires, he didn't love them the way he did his friends, so their tragedies didn't feel as devastating. He probably should feel guilty about that, but he didn't.

"Let's go walk along the lake." He took her by the elbow, directing her to the lakeside path. "Tell me about Chicago."

She strolled beside him. "I'm trying to forget."

"What do you want to forget?"

"It's kind of hard to forget if I talk about it." She acted lighthearted, but the tiny furrow in her forehead revealed the truth. Whatever had happened must have affected her deeply.

"You got me there." He wouldn't push her.

"Yeah, well my do-gooding days are over."

He cringed, remembering the way he and his friends had taunted her. How she'd walk down the school halls with her spine so straight it looked like it would snap. They'd thought she was stuck-up, but he knew better now. She'd been protecting herself from them.

Why had he been so clueless? So thoughtless? So mean?

"I hope that's not true," he said. "The world needs more people like you."

She snorted. "Not even close. I was so naive. Thought I could make a difference. I tried. I really did try."

"I'm sure you made a big difference in a lot of people's lives."

She quickened her pace, and he sped to keep up with her. "I'd get kids placed in a foster home, and the next month they'd be removed at the foster parents' request. They needed stability, but did they get it? Or I'd try to get kids out of an unhealthy, neglect-filled home, but the parent would find a way to work the system."

"Some of the cases you worked on must have turned out well."

"Some did. The last one, though… I couldn't do it anymore. Those kids meant too much to me. I always got in too deep emotionally."

"It's better to be emotionally invested than to be apathetic. When you don't care about other people, you only really care about yourself. Trust me. I know."

"What if you don't care about yourself, either?" The breeze blew the hair around her face, and she tucked it back behind her ear.

"Then you end up living with a bunch of potheads

and working at a gas station because you're so mad at the world, you can't handle living in it." He checked his watch. "I didn't realize the time. I hate to cut this short, but I've got to pick up Wyatt."

"No problem." They turned around and started walking back to her apartment. "Do you ever miss playing football?"

"Miss it? I still play."

"When?" Skepticism laced her tone.

"Me and the guys throw the ball around whenever possible. You should see us when football season starts. We watch all the college and NFL games, and we split into teams to play outside, too. Well, we did back in Detroit, anyway."

Her smile lit her face. "So I assume you'll be coaching a rec team for Wyatt this August, huh?"

"Unfortunately, no. Chase made me promise I wouldn't let Wyatt play."

"Why not? Isn't he the big football star?"

"That's part of the problem. He blames the celebrity lifestyle for coloring his decisions. Like I said, he wants Wyatt—"

"To have a normal life."

"Yep."

They crossed the street at a traffic light.

"Hmm…" She appeared deep in thought.

"What's the 'hmm' for?"

"I guess I was thinking no one really has a normal life."

Drew opened his mouth to refute it, but she had a point. What was normal?

His job was normal. He loved being a firefighter.

Craved the adrenaline rush of his duties. Didn't mind the danger.

Lauren's complexity intrigued him. What about that last case had made her lose her faith in herself? What had her life been like in Chicago? Why did this golden girl, who seemed to have it all together, not view herself the way he—and everyone else—did?

The questions would have to wait. They reached the parking lot, and he stopped in front of her building's back door. "Thanks."

"For what?"

"For giving me the time of day. For letting me talk to you."

A blush spread across her cheeks. *Whoa.* He couldn't help staring at her and wishing things were different.

"Listen, I'm taking Wyatt to the fish fry at Uncle Joe's Restaurant Friday night. Why don't you join us? Say, six thirty?"

She bit the corner of her lower lip and averted her gaze. "I'll think about it."

At least she hadn't said no. It would have to be enough. "You know where the restaurant is?"

"Everyone knows where Uncle Joe's is."

He nodded and jogged to his truck. As he started it up, he looked back, but she'd disappeared inside.

For a firefighter, he wasn't being smart. He knew better than to light matches near a dry forest. What was he doing, thinking about beautiful Lauren Pierce? He ran his palm over his cheek. Just because he'd made peace with his past didn't change the fact that he'd made big mistakes.

She'd been too good for him then, and she was too good for him now.

One thing had changed, though. She'd grown sassy enough to tell him off.

Maybe this was life's funny way of getting back at him. Because that sass only made him like her even more.

Lauren didn't bother changing out of her work clothes after Drew drove away. Instead, she poured a glass of sun tea, selected an adult alternative radio station to play over the wireless speaker on her shelf and stretched out on the couch. What was she going to do now? Babysitting Wyatt no longer felt like an absolute no. But what about the tumbling class or researching a cheerleading academy? Wouldn't either be the smarter move?

Zingo, her Maine coon cat, jumped on her stomach. "Oof. Watch it, big guy." He circled on top of her legs three times before curling into a purring ball. She reached down to pet him. "Love you, too."

Staring at the ceiling, she tried to empty her mind, but it churned with all the things Drew had told her. About Wyatt. About himself.

Hearing about Wyatt's parents hadn't shocked her, and she sniffed at how Drew thought it was the saddest story. Yes, it was sad, but so was the destruction she'd witnessed over and over in her life.

Physical abuse, parents giving drugs to their small children, molestation, death—it horrified her. She'd dealt with it all, seen it all, and she wished Wyatt could have been spared. At least he had been able to rely on Drew all this time.

A laugh escaped her lips, and she clapped her hand over her mouth. Where had that thought come from? In one day she'd flipped from thinking Drew a complete waste of time to an upstanding guy?

He'd been honest. Open. Bared his soul, not knowing if she'd retaliate or not.

She was surprised she hadn't. Well, she kind of had. Her angry outburst earlier had come out of nowhere. The venom still puzzled her.

What had Drew said about being mad at the world? She closed her eyes, trying to remember. They'd been discussing her getting too close to the kids, and he'd said something—something important.

Being so mad at the world you couldn't handle living in it. That was what it was.

She sat up. Zingo glared at her in protest, then resettled on her lap. Mindlessly, she stroked his fur.

Was that why she couldn't move forward?

Was she so mad at the world she couldn't handle living in it?

No. She shook her head. *Of course not.* She wasn't angry. She was protecting herself from a job that wasn't good for her anymore.

She could move forward. She *would* move forward. The idea of helping the local cheerleaders had sparked something inside that had been dormant since high school. "Sorry, baby, but I have to get up." She cradled the huge gray tiger-striped cat and kissed his head before setting him back on the couch.

She'd call Angela Duke, the foster mom who owned the cheerleading academy in Chicago, and find out what was involved with starting her own. She hoped she still had Angela's number. Where had she put the files with her Chicago contacts?

Rummaging through her bedroom closet, she found

a box of old purses, a bag stuffed with receipts from the past five years, stacks of books, a jar full of change and two suitcases. Three boxes sat on the top shelf, so she located her step stool and dragged them down.

One looked like the box where she'd thrown the file with her personal contacts. She pawed through it. Appliance manuals. Why did she keep them? She tossed one over her shoulder, unearthed an old trophy and kept digging.

The purple duffel bag.

She dropped it like it was covered in battery acid. Taking two steps back, she fell to her knees.

A home movie of her earliest memories played through her mind, stealing her breath, stinging the backs of her eyes.

She'd kept the dirty, ripped purple duffel bag packed with every one of her belongings from the time she was three years old until she was eight. She'd been living with the Pierces for more than a year before she finally believed they were her forever family.

Creeping forward, she took it in her hands and held it to her chest. Emotions rushed through her. Remembering the fear of being placed in a new foster home. Five different homes in four years. Some had been good, others not so good, but none had lasted.

She'd been unwanted.

The purple duffel bag had been the only thing she'd owned. Every night before she went to bed, she'd fold her clothes and zip them into it.

Always ready. Always prepared to move.

One of the boys at the third home tried to steal it from her, and she'd grown blind with rage. Six years old. Already too street-smart for the world. That night she'd snuck into the kitchen, grabbed a paring knife, went into his room and waved the knife, demanding he give it back.

He had.

And she had been placed in a different home two weeks later.

The look in Wyatt's eyes yesterday, the one questioning if he was worth anything, roared back. Wyatt hadn't lost all his hope yet. Not the way she had so early on. And he wasn't living in a hovel with his meth-addicted mom on a notorious gang's street like Treyvon and Jay had been.

Drew thought she'd be good for Wyatt.

She clutched the bag tightly and almost laughed. He had no idea that six-year-old Lauren had threatened a kid with a knife to get this bag back. Her nicknames had been "Prude" and "Do-Gooder" and "Prim Pierce," and they were so far from the truth, it was laughable.

She wasn't a wild, angry little girl anymore. Her adoptive parents had given her more than a home. They'd given her faith in a loving God. They'd given her a baptism, a new person to replace the old, rotten, unwanted one.

And she'd promised herself she would be worthy of their love, and she'd help kids like her, the way they had.

She uncurled her legs, set the duffel bag on top of the box and sat on the edge of her bed.

Lord, I've been avoiding the hard prayers lately, the ones where I ask You to show me Your will. I was afraid—I am afraid—You'll ask me to do something I can't handle.

Could she babysit Wyatt and not have her heart broken?

Who would help Wyatt if she didn't?

At least he had Drew.

The longing she'd sensed in Drew before he left earlier had drawn her heart, unbidden, to him. He'd given her a peek of who he'd become, and she had to admit, time and experience had turned his drive into something less selfish than it had been in high school.

Could she say the same about herself?

She'd consider meeting him and Wyatt at Uncle Joe's Restaurant Friday night. In the meantime, she'd find the Chicago file.

Chapter Three

"Hope you're ready for the tastiest fish fry you've ever eaten." Drew glanced over at Wyatt next to him in the truck Friday night. Daylight was sticking around longer—a nice change from the short winter days behind them. He wondered if Lauren would join them tonight.

"I hate fish."

"Well, you're going to love this fish. It's covered in batter and deep-fried. Ask for double the tartar sauce. Just a tip from me to you."

Was that an eye roll? Drew grinned. An eye roll was better than dead silence. At least the kid was showing signs of life. He'd been subdued, shrugging and grunting yesterday when Drew asked him about school. Drew had met with his teacher earlier, and she'd assured him Wyatt, though quiet, was settling in fine.

He wasn't so sure.

If Lauren didn't show up tonight, he would take it as a sign he needed to find another babysitter. In fact, he should find someone else, no matter what. After she'd told him about leaving Chicago and not being able to handle the emotional pain of her cases anymore, he understood. It would be unfair to ask her to help, knowing she was still upset about whatever had made her quit her job.

What *had* made her quit her job?

The parking lot was ahead. The building must have been remodeled. It looked bigger, newer than it had when he was in high school. One thing that hadn't changed? It was packed.

All his peppiness about the fish fry wasn't fooling his roiling stomach. This was the first time Drew would be out in public, and he dreaded what was coming. How did people greet a fallen hometown hero? He supposed he was about to find out.

Parking the truck, he studied the entrance. Did any of his old friends still live around here? Would they treat him the same? He hoped not. He wasn't the same. Didn't ever want to be that guy again.

"Aren't we going in?" Wyatt asked.

"Yeah. Let's go."

Drew said a silent prayer as they crossed the lot. *Lord, whatever happens, help me take it like a man in there.*

"Hey, Uncle Drew, isn't that Lauren?" Wyatt tugged on the sleeve of his shirt.

Just hearing her name flooded him with relief. There she was—long blond hair waving down her back. Her jeans, bubblegum-pink T-shirt and athletic shoes made him smile. She couldn't have been prettier in a ball gown.

"Lauren," Drew called. She turned, a smile spreading across her face when she spotted them. She waited near the door until they joined her.

"So, Wyatt, is it okay if I sit with you two?" Her eyes twinkled.

Wyatt's tongue must have frozen because all he seemed able to do was nod.

"Good to see you." Drew opened the door for her.

She entered the restaurant. "Let's find a table."

Drew stopped at the hostess station. The girl behind the stand held a stack of menus. "It's a thirty-minute wait inside, but we have a few tables open on the deck."

He looked at Lauren. "Do you want to eat outside, or is it too cold for you?"

"Outside is fine. It's a beautiful night. What do you think, Wyatt?"

Wyatt was eyeing the fish and deer heads mounted on the pine walls.

"Wyatt," Drew said.

He flushed. "Huh?"

"Do you want to eat outside?"

He peered at the crowd. Large windows displayed views of the lake. "Yeah, sure."

They weaved through the tables on their way to the patio doors. Drew didn't look left or right. He concentrated on following Lauren's graceful movements.

"Gannon?" A voice boomed over the lively conversation. "Gannon the Cannon?" The man leaped out of his chair and stood between Drew and Lauren. Wyatt instinctively huddled closer to Drew. He kept his arm around the kid's shoulders.

"It's me, Mike Schneider. Man, I haven't seen you in ages. How've you been?" Mike clapped him on the back, his face beaming.

Drew's inner serenity crumbled faster than a week-old cookie. Mike Schneider had been a linebacker on the team, one of the guys he ran around with. Someone who had thought he was above getting in trouble. The same way Drew had been.

"Good to see you, Mike." He nodded, hoping to bypass the reunion and get to the deck ASAP.

"So what brings you to town? You visiting?"

"I'm actually moving back. I start at the fire station next week. You still live here?"

"Just visiting my folks with my wife—you remember Tori?" He pointed to the corner of the table, where Tori waved above several empty beer glasses. Another vaguely familiar couple sat across from her. "My sister, Paige, joined us. This is her husband, Brent."

"Good to see you, Drew. You're looking good." Tori winked. He gave her a tight nod. Tori James had flirted with Drew throughout high school and, if his memory served him correctly, had never had a nice thing to say about Lauren. The same way he hadn't.

The ladies began to whisper as Mike continued. "Hey, remember sneaking out to the Flats with Brittany? Man, did we have fun. Late-night swimming has never been the same."

Shame lit a bonfire in his gut. Drew stepped forward. "Yeah, well, we're holding up traffic."

Mike ran a calculating gaze across Drew over to Lauren, and his eyes about bugged out. "Am I seeing things or what? Is that Prim—"

"It's Lauren Pierce." Drew frowned. Lauren's face was a polite mask—nothing was getting through it.

"What? Are you two together?" Mike chortled as if it was the funniest thing he'd ever heard. "Is this your kid?"

"This is my godson, Wyatt. Good to see you." Drew clenched his jaw and propelled Wyatt forward. His veins felt like they were going to explode. Every table they passed seemed to be staring, pointing and whispering, but maybe it was his imagination. The patio doors were merely a few yards away.

"What's wrong, Uncle Drew?" Wyatt rubbed his biceps as soon as Drew let go when they made it to the deck.

"Nothing."

"Are you mad?" Wyatt sounded worried.

"I'm fine." Drew studied the people seated outside but thankfully didn't see anyone familiar.

Lauren led them to the most secluded table. She patted the chair next to hers and smiled at Wyatt. "Drew hasn't been home in years."

Wyatt didn't look convinced. He began to nervously chew his fingernail. "Let's go home."

What was bothering him? He'd been okay when they had arrived.

"Do you want to go home?" Lauren asked, her voice calm and reassuring.

"I don't know."

His face looked pale. Drew ticked through possible reasons Wyatt had gone from excited to jittery so quickly. Was he getting sick?

"Are you sure you're not mad, Uncle Drew?"

"I'm not mad," Drew said. "Like Lauren said, it's been a long time since I've been here, and I guess I'm nervous."

Lauren tapped Wyatt's arm and pointed to the lake. "The water is so shimmery tonight, and, look, there's a duck and her babies." Slowly Wyatt's color returned, and he seemed to relax. A waitress stopped by for their orders, and a family came outside with a young girl and a boy about Wyatt's age.

"Hey, Wyatt." The boy waved and sped over to their table. "I didn't know you were coming tonight. Want to go try to win a prize with the claw?"

Yearning and fear collided in Wyatt's expression. Drew hitched his chin. "Go ahead. I thought I saw the claw machine inside those doors. You can see us from there."

"I'd better stay here." Wyatt shrank into himself.

Lauren smiled at the other boy. "Why don't you pull up a seat? You two can talk a bit and play on the claw machine a little later if you feel like it."

"Okay, let me tell Mom and Dad." The boy ran off.

Wyatt straightened, clearly happy with her solution. A round of Cokes arrived, and the kid returned, taking the seat next to Wyatt.

"I'm Wyatt's uncle Drew, by the way. What's your name?"

"Hunter."

"Nice to meet you, Hunter."

The kid had already turned away and was asking Wyatt about a video game. His enthusiasm must have been contagious because soon Wyatt couldn't stop talking about the world he was building, whatever that meant. Drew guessed it had something to do with his new video game.

Now that Wyatt was occupied, Drew could focus on Lauren. He'd been waiting all day, wondering if their conversation Wednesday had changed her mind about him. She'd been less prickly when he'd told her about life after football, but she'd had time to process it all since then. He wouldn't blame her if she didn't want to be around him. Especially not when Mike had just reminded her Drew had been such a jerk before.

He'd just have to show her he'd changed. For good.
"I'm glad you came tonight."

"Me, too." The low sun at her back made her hair
glow.

"I want you to know I'm not—"

"Drew! We thought that was you!" Two attractive
women squealed, prancing to their table. His stomach
plummeted. Shelby Lattimer and Beth Jones. They'd
been on the dance squad in high school, and he'd dated
both. Not at the same time, of course.

"Well, look who's here." Beth narrowed her eyes at
Lauren. Beth wore painted-on dark jeans, a tiny black
shirt and sky-high heels. Drew raised his eyebrows at
the too-revealing outfit. "Haven't seen you anywhere
but the fitness center since you moved back, Lauren.
You're finally hitting the town, huh?"

"Hey, Drew." Shelby's long brown hair was pulled
into a low ponytail, and she twirled a section in her fingers. Her outfit, a tight red dress and stiletto boots, also
left little to the imagination.

"Beth, Shelby." The glint in Lauren's eyes was the
only crack in her composure. "Didn't see you at spin
class Monday night."

"Yeah, I had a date." Beth's gaze flitted to Drew, and
she smiled suggestively. "Just casual, though."

Drew almost choked at the way Lauren's lips pursed.

More people joined Beth and Shelby, all talking at
once to Drew and Lauren. There were a lot of shoulder
slaps and references to football. There were a few veiled
sneers. He couldn't make sense of most of it, just kept
nodding and repeating, "Yeah, it's good to see you,"
and keeping an eye on Lauren, who handled the questions thrown her way with ease.

The waitress arrived with hot platters of food, and the crowd dispersed. His mind tumbled with impressions. The night had just begun, and dealing with all these people from his past already exhausted him. What could Lauren possibly think about this? She probably thought he loved all the attention. High school Drew would have loved it.

"Well, Wyatt, dig in." Drew waved his fork at Wyatt's plate. He craved the anonymity of the previous years, wanted nothing more than to go home, sit on the couch and watch TV the rest of the night, but tonight wasn't about him. "Best fish you'll ever eat."

"I ordered chicken tenders," Wyatt replied in a deadpan voice. Hunter, still sitting next to him, snickered. Wyatt offered a piece of chicken to Hunter, who happily accepted it.

Lauren lifted her Coke to the boys. "To the best chicken tenders you'll ever eat."

They exchanged curious glances.

"You're supposed to clink your glasses with mine," she whispered. They brightened with understanding and lifted their Cokes. "Cheers."

Drew sighed. Lauren was so good with Wyatt. But she'd already told him she wasn't babysitting. This entire night hammered home why he'd been delusional. His past was messy, and he didn't want to drag her back to those hurtful days.

He might as well forget the whole thing. He'd find another babysitter and wouldn't force his way into her life.

"Can I have some quarters?" Wyatt and Hunter stood next to Drew with their palms cupped. "You're right. I can see the claw machine through the window."

Lauren wanted to pull both boys into a hug and kiss their foreheads and assure Wyatt Drew wasn't going anywhere. He'd be right there, where Wyatt could see him. She set her napkin on her plate and watched in amusement as Drew unfolded his wallet and handed Wyatt a five-dollar bill.

"Go up to the front desk and they'll give you change," Drew said. "Come back if you need anything."

The boys ran off. Lauren noted that Wyatt looked back three times as if he were certain Drew would vanish at any moment.

"He's scared for you." Lauren turned back to Drew. "Afraid you'll be gone like his mom and dad."

The stunned expression on Drew's face cleared. "That's crazy. I'll never leave him."

"He probably thought the same about his parents." Lauren pushed her plate away. "I think that's why he wanted to go home earlier. He sensed the tension when you were talking to Mike."

"Tension is normal." Drew shifted back in his seat. She didn't recognize the expression in his eyes, and she was good at reading people. If she had to guess, she'd say it was regret.

"He's on high alert. Dealing with a lot of new developments in his life. Tension isn't normal for him, not now, anyway."

"I'll have to hide it then." He wiped his hand down his cheek. He had the look of a man in way over his head. The actions she'd witnessed the few times they'd been together said otherwise. He was good at this—good at handling Wyatt. He just didn't know it.

"I didn't mean to imply… You don't have to hide anything." Lauren bit her lower lip to keep from saying too much. She'd been close to a decision about babysitting, and everything she'd seen tonight—from Drew's obvious discomfort with Mike and Tori to the kind way he'd greeted everyone who stopped by the table without encouraging them to reminisce about the good old days—showed her he'd changed.

He'd told her football had been the only thing he'd cared about in high school. Well, his single-mindedness had shifted. The man would do anything to protect Wyatt and give him a good life.

She would help them. Who else would take care of Wyatt when Drew was at the station?

Beth? Shelby?

Over her dead body. No, Drew was right. Wyatt needed someone who understood what he was going through.

Wyatt needed her. At least until he started feeling at home here. The summer should give her plenty of time to make him comfortable in this town. Then he'd be equipped to get through his days like other children. And when Angela Duke called her back, she'd research the cheer academy. If it seemed to be way over her head, she'd teach a tumbling class and find another office job this fall.

Lauren folded her hands and straightened her shoulders. "I'll babysit."

"What?" His jaw dropped; then he closed his mouth and swallowed. "I thought you said—"

"I changed my mind."

He steepled his long fingers. "I don't know. After what you told me about getting hurt and leaving Chicago, I'm not sure it's best for you."

"Are you saying you don't want me to babysit anymore?" She had never considered she'd actually convinced him she wasn't a good fit for Wyatt.

"Lauren, I would like nothing more than for you to take care of Wyatt. You're way more in touch with his emotions… I feel like a dummy compared to you."

Could her heart smile? Drew looked adorable when he was complimenting her and unsure of himself.

But he wasn't unsure of himself. He'd been born sure of himself.

He also had this idea she was perfect, and she'd be the easy solution to making Wyatt's life all better. She couldn't even figure out her own. And perfect? What a laughable concept. When Drew realized she was a mess, would he send her packing?

The purple duffel bag flashed in her mind.

"Are you sure you want to?" Drew tilted his neck to the side, and his expression—so raw, so apologetic—tossed cold water on her doubts. She was being silly. They were grown-ups. And this was about Wyatt.

"Yes." She nodded decisively. "But only until the end of the summer. He'll have made enough friends by then you'll have no problem finding someplace he can stay when you're at work. And, please, keep your expectations realistic about him. He's not going to bounce back overnight. It might take years."

His face fell, but he nodded. "Fair enough. Don't hold it against me if I badger you to continue when September comes around, though. Can you start Monday?"

"I can."

"Good. Stop by tomorrow, and we'll go over everything."

Nervous excitement swirled in her stomach. Or maybe it was the greasy fish. Either way, she hoped she'd made the right decision. Chicago was behind her. She couldn't help the boys she'd left behind. But she could help Wyatt.

She just prayed she really was what Wyatt needed. She'd never forgive herself if she let him down, too.

Chapter Four

Drew knocked on the fire station door Monday morning at 6:30 a.m. Boxes containing two dozen doughnuts teetered, but he tightened his hold on them. Every station he'd worked at welcomed food, especially the sweet stuff. He had a feeling he'd need every ounce of help to fit in with his new coworkers. What was the Bible passage about prophets not being accepted in their hometowns? Not a great analogy, considering he wasn't a prophet. His soul was too tarnished to even contemplate that thought.

"Gannon. You're late," Chief Reynolds barked as he let Drew in. He was in his midfifties with receding salt-and-pepper hair and a powerful upper body. He reminded Drew of a bulldog, except bulldogs were friendlier. "Follow me."

"Yes, sir." Drew kept his head high and his feet moving through the corridor. He was thirty minutes early since his shift started at seven, but hey, he understood this was Rookie Mind Games 101. He'd been through it at both his previous fire stations. Each station had its own unique way of welcoming new hires, and by welcome, he meant harass, intimidate, make fun of and generally try to wean out the ones who could handle the job from the ones who couldn't.

He could handle the job.

His coworkers just didn't know it yet.

"Listen up." The chief stopped in the kitchen, where two men and one woman stood near the coffeemaker. "This is Drew Gannon." He sent Drew a sideways glance without a hint of pleasure and nodded to the man in front of the stove. "Ben Santos. Gary Walters. Amanda Delassio." He addressed the three. "Don't bother remembering this one's name. He won't be around long enough for it to matter."

Drew shook their hands, making mental notes to keep their names straight since he didn't recognize them.

"Are you done lollygagging?" The chief marched ahead and disappeared through the first door on the left. Drew followed. "Check in at station dispatch. Sign-in's over there. We keep a daily log. Think you can handle that?"

"Yes, sir." Drew scratched his name on the list, but the chief was already out the door.

"Secretary is on duty eight until four Monday through Friday. Locker rooms are to your right. Classroom is up ahead. You'll get a key code for the supply room. We don't use radios. Every room is wired into the speaker system. I expect you to keep your ears open at all times."

Drew practically raced to keep up with him. The chief continued upstairs, filling him in on the workout room, living area and basic rules. They completed a brief tour of the garage, trucks and the equipment.

"Got all that, hotshot?"

"Yes, sir."

"You're getting off easy with a six-month probation period and only because I'm trusting the letters of recommendation from your previous supervisors. Personally, I don't see you lasting two weeks, let alone six months." The chief circled back to his office with Drew at his heels. "Be ready at seven for assignments. And let's make one thing clear—I've got no use for quitters, whiners or superstars. You're the bottom of the barrel in my station, and don't forget it."

If Drew had already been working there for a couple of years, he would have said something like, "I love you, too, Chief," and winked at the man, but he'd learned the hard way to keep his mouth shut, ears open and attitude humble until they accepted him.

If they accepted him...

They would. Eventually.

"Well, if it isn't the NFL wannabe." Tony Ludlow, a former classmate of Drew's, blocked the hallway. His beefy arms were crossed over an equally muscular chest. Drew's stomach dropped to his toes. Of all his possible coworkers, how had he ended up with Tony? They'd graduated from the same class and enjoyed a healthy competition on the football team and off, particularly with girls. Drew cringed, remembering how he'd tried to steal Tony's prom date. It was probably too late to wish he hadn't succeeded. What was that girl's name, anyhow?

"Tony." Drew stuck his hand out, but Tony didn't shake it. Surely almost fifteen years had been long enough to douse Tony's anger about the whole prom thing.

"Aren't we fortunate? The pretty boy is back," Tony

said to the group in the kitchen. "I wouldn't trust him near a corpse, let alone your wives or girlfriends."

Apparently fifteen years hadn't dampened Tony's fury. *Great.*

"What about my husband?" Amanda said, smirking. "Should I be worried about this guy hitting on Jack?"

Good one, Amanda. Drew had a feeling she'd be fun to work with…someday.

"I would be, Mandy." Tony sized Drew up. "You might as well quit now. No one's going to hold your hand here."

"I'm giving him three weeks," Ben said.

Hey, it was a step up. The chief had given him only two weeks, so he must have impressed Ben more than he'd thought. A call came over the speakers, and everyone got to work.

The next several hours were spent checking equipment, learning procedures, cleaning toilets, prepping gear and responding to emergencies—two 911 calls and one fire call, which turned out to be a false alarm.

After dinner he finally had a break and managed to call Wyatt. He'd tried not to worry, but he couldn't help wondering if Lauren and Wyatt were doing okay.

"Hey, buddy, how was your day?"

"Oh, hey, Uncle Drew. It was fine." It sounded like music played in the background, but that might have been the television.

"How's it going with Lauren?"

"Okay."

The kid was a real conversationalist. Drew tried not to sigh. "Have a lot of homework?"

"No."

"What did you have for dinner?"

"Um…" Wyatt must have pulled the phone away

because Drew heard Lauren's muffled voice say something. "Some noodles. Lingreeny."

"Linguine?"

"Yeah, that's it."

Drew asked a few more questions and got monosyllabic answers. "Don't watch too much TV."

"I can't. She won't let me. We're listening to music. Lauren likes *weird* stuff."

"What's weird about it?"

"I don't know. She called it jazz."

He chuckled. "Jazz, huh?"

"Yeah. If I could figure out her phone's pass code, I'd change it to something good."

"Keep your hands off her phone."

"Uncle Drew," he whined.

"I mean it. Jazz is…educational." He grimaced, thinking of the torture the poor kid was experiencing.

"Whatever."

"I love you, Wyatt."

"You, too, Uncle Drew."

They hung up.

"Hey, Gannon," Tony yelled as he entered the living room. "Locker-room floor needs mopping."

"Yes, sir," Drew said softly.

He was living the dream, all right. As much as he loved his job, he found himself eager for the shift to end. He'd forgotten how miserable the early probation period could be, and it was that much worse with Tony poisoning the rest of the crew's impressions of him.

It would be nice if they could see the man he'd become instead of the boy he used to be, but time would take care of that. If not, he'd have to majorly suck up and apologize to Tony.

Who else in town needed an apology from him?

He groaned, heading to the closet for the cleaning supplies. Maybe if he scrubbed the floor hard enough, he could erase all the damage he'd done in his teen years.

At least he didn't have to worry about Wyatt on top of everything else. The kid was in good hands. And if Lauren could see past his mistakes, the rest of the crew could, too. He hoped so, at least. He'd have to be patient and work at it.

Were frozen waffles a proper breakfast for a ten-year-old boy? Lauren plucked two out of the toaster and dropped them onto a plate. Opening the refrigerator, she scanned the shelves for fruit. A carton of orange juice stood next to a gallon of milk. Strawberries hid behind a brick of cheese. They would have to do.

She was out of her element here. Last night had been awkward. Since Wyatt had said he didn't have any homework, he'd fired up his video games as soon as he'd gotten home from school. Then, when she turned them off after an hour, he'd wanted to watch television shows she found entirely inappropriate. Dinner had been quiet. She'd turned on soothing music, but it hadn't helped.

Drew would be home in thirty minutes. Should she tell him she was having second thoughts about their arrangement?

She rinsed and sliced a few strawberries, fanning them out across the waffles. She set the plate in front of Wyatt.

"Here you go." After wiping her hands on a paper

towel, she checked her watch. "What time did you say the bus picks you up?"

"Why are these things—" he grimaced, holding a strawberry slice in the air "—on my waffles?"

She propped up a smile. "They're strawberries. Full of vitamin C."

His shoulders drooped as he pushed all the strawberries to the side. His hair was sticking up in the back, but at least he'd changed into his school clothes.

"They're good. You should try them." This morning wasn't going much better than last night. She'd spent her life helping kids, but she had no experience taking care of them. "At least eat the waffles. You need some food in your stomach. It will help you learn."

Wyatt wolfed down the waffles, ignoring the berries. Lauren heard the telltale screech of brakes in the distance.

"Grab your backpack. The bus is almost here."

He trudged to the hall and slung his backpack over his shoulder. "Will you be here when I get home?"

"No, I won't. Your uncle will." She opened the front door. "Have a good day."

His eyebrows rose in worry, but he nodded and walked to the end of the drive right as the bus pulled up. Lauren waited in the doorway until he was safely on, and then she shut the door and tidied up the kitchen and living room. She was getting ready to take her first sip of coffee when Drew walked in.

"How did it go?" he asked, his eyes roaming over the room. He draped his jacket on the back of a chair and set a stack of papers on the table.

Lauren debated how to answer. The weariness in Drew's posture and the bags under his eyes set her in motion. She poured him a cup of coffee. "Do you want cream and sugar?"

He wiped both hands down his face. "No, thanks. I like it black."

She returned and set the mug on the coffee table in front of Drew before taking a seat on the couch. "Sit."

He lifted a brow, smiled and kicked back in the recliner. "Yes, sir."

"Sir?"

"Sorry." He chuckled. "Habit. I've repeated those words more times in the past twenty-four hours than I care to admit. It's going to take a long time and a lot of effort to get them to accept me."

"What do you mean?" Lauren hadn't considered he wouldn't be instantly accepted at the fire station.

He took a drink, shaking his head. "It doesn't matter. The new guy always needs to prove himself. Unfortunately, I have more to prove, given my past."

She sipped her coffee. "Is there bad blood or something?"

"Tony Ludlow is one of the crew."

"I always liked Tony," she said. He'd treated her with respect in high school. Never teased her. He'd pitched in to help with homecoming floats and fund-raisers for Students Against Teen Drinking on many occasions.

Drew's expression darkened. "Figures."

He sounded jealous. She bit back a smile.

"How was your first night with Wyatt?"

First night…and possibly only night? How honest should she be?

"Well, I slept good. Thanks for setting the room up for me." She'd been surprised to find a pullout sofa made up with a pretty butter-yellow comforter in the office.

"Of course. Do you need anything? Say the word, and we'll get it for you."

"It's perfect."

He nodded. "And Wyatt? How did it go?"

"Um, I don't know."

Drew sat up straight. "What happened? Is he okay? Did he get on the bus? Was he worried?"

"Whoa, there, tiger." She held both palms out. "Wyatt is fine. It's me. How can I put this? Um… I don't have much experience taking care of kids."

He collapsed back into the recliner. "Is that all? No problem. You'll get the hang of it in no time. Wyatt's pretty easy. It's not like you have to change diapers or anything."

"True." She avoided eye contact. "But I don't really know what to do with him."

Drew slapped his thigh. "Easy. Homework. Video games. TV. Bed."

"Well, he said he didn't have homework. I did let him play video games for an hour, but I don't think he should be playing them all night. And the television show he wanted to watch was entirely inappropriate for a boy his age."

"What show was it?"

"*Monsters Inside Me.*"

"Oh, that's a good one." Drew grinned. "Last week a man had worms in his intestines and didn't know it. It was disgusting."

She gagged a little bit. "It sounds disgusting. And traumatizing. I turned off the TV and put on music. I suggest you do the same."

"Yeah, I heard you were playing jazz last night."

"Oh, did Wyatt like it?" She took another sip.

"He called it weird and told me he would change the channel if he knew your pass code."

Lauren was taken aback. Then she laughed. Drew joined in. A comfortable feeling spread through her, sitting here in Drew's living room, drinking coffee, chatting about Wyatt.

"Thanks again, Lauren." His voice lowered, and she had to look away from the sincerity in his eyes. "With you watching Wyatt, well…everything else isn't so bad."

She swallowed the doubts she'd been tallying. "I don't know what I'm doing, though."

"Just be here for him. Physically be here. That's what he needs."

Exactly. She'd been overthinking it. She just needed to show up and make sure he had dinner and went to bed on time. That was it.

But maybe a few of her rules wouldn't hurt him. Less video games, no scary shows and more creative time. Couldn't hurt.

"You look beat." She got up and took her mug to the kitchen. After rinsing it out, she grabbed her purse and returned to the living room.

His eyes were already closed. Should she tell him to go to bed? She stood there and watched him a minute. Dark lashes splayed across high cheekbones. His hair was tousled. He looked vulnerable. So handsome.

She pushed the recliner's button for the footrest to extend and covered him with a soft gray throw that had been slung over the couch.

It had been a long time since she'd felt maternal. Strange, Drew brought out her nurturing side. She'd thought it had died back in Chicago.

Maybe it would have been better for them all if it had.

Nonsense. If last night proved anything, she didn't have to worry about growing too attached to Wyatt. Or Drew. She was the babysitter. That was all.

"What do you mean he's behind in school?" Drew held his phone to his ear and listened to Wyatt's teacher explain the benchmark results. "Those are just tests. They don't mean anything."

"Tests tend to reflect basic skill levels, and he hasn't been turning in his homework. I'm not trying to get Wyatt into trouble, but I wanted you to be aware of the situation."

Wyatt wasn't turning in his homework? Drew sighed. It was much easier being the fun uncle than the responsible father. "Thank you. I'll take care of it."

The past two weeks had been hectic. Work had not improved. He'd tried to apologize to Tony, but Tony wouldn't hear him out. Since then, Drew had met all the firefighters, and two had played football with him in high school, although they were younger than him. They kept bringing up old games, and he couldn't take another sentence beginning with, "Hey, remember the time you…" He wasn't sure what was worse—Tony's snide remarks or their hero worship. The chief still hated him, too.

And now this.

Wyatt wouldn't be home for almost an hour. Drew didn't know what to do or say. Should he confront him? He had a vision of himself waving papers in front of Wyatt's face, demanding to know why he wasn't doing his homework. Then it would move to ranting about how important school was, how Wyatt didn't want to have poor study habits like Drew or he'd get kicked out of college and end up working at a gas station.

Probably not the lecture Wyatt needed at this point in his life.

Lauren would know what to do. He tied his running shoes, snatched his keys off the hook and let the front door slam behind him.

Five minutes later he parked behind the hardware store and jogged to the back entrance. Shifting his weight from one foot to the other, he pressed the intercom.

"Who is it?"

"Drew."

"Drew who?"

"Very funny." He rolled his eyes and smiled. "Do you have a minute?"

She buzzed him in. He took the steps two at a time and found himself face-to-face with a wooden door. Lauren opened it. "What's up?"

He followed her inside. Now that he was here, he was curious to see how she lived. Galley kitchen to the right. Small table and chairs in the dining area. A cream couch and matching love seat took up most of the living room. Neither would stand a chance at staying clean with him or Wyatt. They merely had to look at something that light in color for it to get dirty. She'd placed a fluffy peach rug under the coffee table, and matching pillows adorned the couches. What stood out most of all, though, were the plants. Two tall potted trees stood in opposite corners, flanking a picture window with a view of Main Street. A fern hung from the ceiling, and three other plants—one appeared to be tall grass—were placed in various spots.

"Have a seat." She waved to the couch. He admired

her casual style. Jeans rolled up at the ankles and an oversize Kelly green sweatshirt. She looked natural. Fresh. "What's going on?"

He sat on the edge of the couch, knees wide, elbows resting on them. "I got a call from Wyatt's teacher, and I'm hoping you can tell me what to do."

Her hand flew to her throat. "Oh, no. What is it? He fell. He's hurt. He's missing. He's not missing, is he?"

"No, of course not. Nothing like that." The way she'd rapid-fired off the worst scenarios poked his conscience. He hadn't put any more thought into what had made her quit her job in Chicago, but from the way she reacted, he could imagine only the worst. "He's behind in school."

Her upper body seemed to dissolve as she melted into the love seat. "Oh. You had me worried."

"Well, I *am* worried. He's not turning in his assignments. And his benchmarks were low."

A huge gray tiger-striped cat appeared out of nowhere, weaving in between his legs.

"What in the world?" He hopped to his feet, glaring at the cat. "Where did that thing come from?"

Lauren rolled her eyes. "The bedroom. This is Zingo. He's the best kitty in the world, so I'd tread carefully if I were you."

He pursed his lips and, keeping his eyes glued to the cat—who continued to rub his body around Drew's leg—sat back down. The beast jumped on the couch and onto his lap. He froze. "What. Do. I. Do?"

"Well, for one, you can stop acting like a big baby. He's a cat, not a poisonous snake."

"I can see that," he snapped.

"Pet him." She widened her eyes in emphasis and pointed at the feline.

He'd never been around cats. Didn't they carry diseases? Or kill babies? He'd heard rumors…

Gingerly, he touched Zingo's back. "Hey, he's soft."

"Duh."

Zingo curled up on his lap. "Is this normal?" When she nodded, he shrugged. "Okay, then. Back to the problem. What am I going to do about Wyatt?"

Lauren crossed one leg over the other and lifted her finger to her chin. "Hmm…"

He patted the cat's head. It started purring. He decided to ignore it.

"Did the teacher say he's behind in all his subjects or certain ones?"

"Math. Doesn't know how to multiply. He does okay in reading, but his writing needs work."

Lauren bridged her fingers. "Are you going over his homework with him at night?"

"He never has any."

"Yeah, he tells me the same. Obviously, he does have homework and is choosing not to deal with it."

"And lying about it." Drew clenched his jaw. He hated lies. "Unacceptable."

"You look mad. Are you going to say something to him?"

"Of course. I can't let him get away with lying."

"Right. You're right, but…" She frowned. "Maybe I should be there, too."

"Why?"

"To keep it peaceful."

"I'm not going to coddle him about this. He needs to be responsible."

"This isn't about coddling. It's about your approach. He needs to feel it's safe to make mistakes."

Exactly why Drew had come here in the first place—to get her opinion. He sat back, mindlessly stroking the cat's fur. "All right. What do you suggest?"

"Let's go back to your place, and when he gets home, we'll talk to him. Together."

He almost closed his eyes in relief. *Together.* The best word he'd heard since taking custody of Wyatt. "I'll drive."

Forty-five minutes later, after Wyatt had gotten off the bus, they all sat around the kitchen table, munching on a plate of grapes and cheese Lauren had thrown together. Wyatt popped one grape in after another. Drew glanced at her, and she nodded.

"Your teacher called today. Seems she's missing some of your homework."

Wyatt stopped chewing and stared at the table. "She must have lost it."

"Wyatt—" His voice rose. Lauren touched his arm.

"I don't recall you bringing any home." Lauren gestured to Wyatt.

He swallowed. "I do it at school."

"All of it?" she asked.

He nodded. Drew regained his composure. "Listen, buddy, homework is important."

"Dad didn't make me do it." Scowling, Wyatt crossed his arms over his chest.

"Since when?" Drew asked. "You can't pull that one on me. We've been together for years. School's always been important."

"I don't need it. I'm going to be a football player like Dad when I grow up."

Drew wasn't touching this topic. He hadn't talked

to Wyatt about Chase's no-football decree because it hadn't come up. He did *not* want to get into it now.

"Your dad had to get into college to play football," Lauren said. "He was required to get good grades."

"Really?" Wyatt tilted his head slightly.

Saved by Lauren. Again.

"He worked hard at school." Drew leaned back in his chair. "You know we were roommates. He pulled plenty of all-nighters studying for tests. Did you know he has a degree in marketing?"

"I didn't know that."

"Yep."

"If it's okay with you, Drew," Lauren said, "let's make a new rule. The first thing Wyatt does after school is homework. Drew will help you with it when he's home, and I'll help when he's at work."

"First thing?" Wyatt whined. "Can't I have a snack first?"

"Of course you can have a snack." Drew grew serious. "But, Wyatt, I don't want you lying to me. If you're going to grow up to be a man of integrity, you have to tell the truth."

Wyatt nodded. "I'm sorry, Uncle Drew."

He held his arms out, and Wyatt fell into them. Drew met Lauren's eyes and mouthed, "Thank you." She'd taken a potentially volatile situation and made it okay. It felt good to have someone in his corner for once.

At least one person in this town was on his side.

Chapter Five

"**S**nack time is over. Haul out the books." Lauren clapped her hands the next afternoon. Wyatt looked like he'd just brushed his teeth with vinegar. Drew had said Wyatt just needed her to be present, and that was what she'd been for the handful of times she'd stayed with him so far. But now she had a mission to help Wyatt improve his grades—whether he wanted help or not. "I printed out worksheets to help you with multiplication."

"Those are for babies. I already know how to multiply." Wyatt pressed the tips of his fingers against the cracker crumbs and licked them. "We learned it last year."

"Good. Then you'll get through these really quick."

He let out the most pitiful sigh she'd ever heard. How did one motivate a ten-year-old boy to want to learn? Math was important. School was important.

"C'mon," she said. "The sooner you get these done, the sooner we can get out of here."

His eyes lit up, almost gold in color. "Where are we going?"

"I'm taking you to my parents' house." She gestured

to his backpack, and he grunted but took folders and books out of it. "Mom and Dad are cooking us lasagna."

"I thought your dad died."

"My birth father died. My birth mother, too. I'm taking you to meet my parents, the ones who raised me. They adopted me when I was seven. I think you'll like them. They live on the other side of the lake."

Wyatt clicked through a short piece of lead in his mechanical pencil until a new one worked its way down. As he opened a blue folder, Lauren took the seat next to him at the table.

"How did your mom die?" His freckles emphasized his innocent face. She wanted to kiss his forehead, which was ridiculous. He wasn't her son. But this was the first time he'd asked anything of her beyond, "Why can't I play another hour of 'Minecraft'?" and "Please, can I have another brownie?" The urge to share her past with him pressed on her heart.

She didn't want to burden him. Would talking about her messed-up past confuse him more?

She remembered when a girl in her third-grade class announced to everyone her parents had adopted a new brother for her. Part of Lauren had rejoiced the girl was so excited to have an adopted sibling, but the other part wanted to blend in with her classmates and hide the fact that she was adopted. Since the Pierces had moved to Lake Endwell when Lauren was in second grade, it wasn't common knowledge she wasn't their natural-born child. That day had made her feel less alone, knowing other kids got adopted, too. In fact, the other girl's attitude had changed her view of herself, paving the way for her to accept the fact that her parents wanted her the same way her classmate wanted her new brother.

Telling Wyatt about her past might help him feel less alone, too.

With her elbow on the table, Lauren rested her cheek against her palm. "My mother died when I was two. She was a drug addict, and she died of an overdose."

"Really?" Wyatt turned to face her, his feet dangling and kicking as if they couldn't take being immobile on the floor. "My mom did drugs. But she didn't die from them. She quit. It was Len who killed her."

"Yeah, well, in a way drugs did kill your mom."

"No, they didn't." His voice rose. "She went to rehab."

"I know." She gave him a tender smile. "I guess I meant when you get mixed up in drugs, you put yourself in a dangerous situation. If she wouldn't have hung around people who liked that lifestyle, she wouldn't have met Len."

"I wish she'd never met him. It's all his fault. I'm glad Dad tried to kill him. I wish he would have!" Two red spots blared from his cheeks. The outburst seemed to deflate him, though, and he laid his forehead against his arm on the table.

Her throat knotted. She lightly touched Wyatt's hunched back, and when his slender frame shook with silent tears, she scooted closer, rubbing small circles between his shoulders. "I know. I know."

She put her arm around him and pressed her cheek to his hair. He sat up with wet eyes and wiped the back of his sleeve across his face.

"You probably think I'm a big baby for crying." His face couldn't look more miserable.

"Why would I think that?"

"Men aren't supposed to cry."

"Says who? Jesus cried. When we're sad, we cry. It's

healthy. Relieves the tension building up inside. If you don't cry, the tension comes out in a bad way."

"Like how?" He sniffed again.

"Well." She looked at the ceiling briefly. "Some people get mad and yell at whoever is there for no reason. That's not good. Or what about this? Sometimes when I'm sad, I don't want to cry or feel bad, so I eat a bunch of cookies. Then I feel even worse!"

"I'd rather eat cookies than cry."

She laughed. "I would, too. But even if you eat half a bag of cookies, the sadness is still there. You just have a stomachache, too."

"Don't tell Uncle Drew I cried." His eyebrows dipped in a pleading manner.

She pretended to zip her lips and throw away the key.

"Why'd you do that?"

"It's like zipping your lips and locking it."

"That's weird."

"Yeah, well, that's how we kept promises back in my day."

Wyatt pulled out a homework paper and stared at it a minute. Then he turned to her. "Did Jesus really cry?"

Lauren nodded, swiping her phone. She opened her favorite Bible app and typed in 'Lazarus.' When the passage came up, she showed it to him. "Right here. *John* 11:35, 'Jesus wept.'"

"Why?"

She filled him in on how Jesus's friend Lazarus had died, and Jesus went to comfort the man's sisters, Mary and Martha. "Then Jesus raised Lazarus from the dead."

"That's pretty cool." Wyatt flicked his pencil against the edge of the table.

"Listen, Wyatt." She needed to proceed with caution

here. What she wanted to say was important, but Wyatt might not take it very well. "I totally get why you hate Len and wish he was dead. But the anger inside you doesn't hurt Len. It only hurts you."

"I hate him," he said through gritted teeth. "I'll always hate him."

"When you're ready, when hating him feels too heavy, pray for him. That's all. Give your anger to God."

"I'm not praying for him. Ever."

She held her hands up near her chest. "Okay. That's your choice. Forgiveness has a way of giving a person peace, though."

"He killed my mom." It sounded less adamant than his previous declaration.

"Yep, he did, and he's being punished for it."

"Forgiving him is like saying what he did doesn't matter, like it was okay for him to kill her. It's not okay."

Oh, how well she understood his thinking. Life would be so much easier if the people she'd needed to forgive had acknowledged they'd hurt her. The thought of forgiving them had felt like it would be giving them a free pass to treat her terribly.

"Forgiveness is a tricky thing. It's not about acting as if the person didn't hurt you. It's about moving on with your life and letting God be their judge. Some of the people you'll forgive won't even feel sorry for the things they've done to you."

"That's why I'm not forgiving. They have to at least say they're sorry."

"Forgiving someone who never apologizes is one of the most difficult things you'll ever do."

Wyatt blew out a breath. "I don't think I can."

"I understand. It's hard. But it's also the best thing

you can do for yourself. Forgiving someone doesn't erase the hurt, but it helps you move forward." Lauren drew him into a half embrace. He didn't pull away.

"Do I have to right now?"

She chuckled. "No, silly. When you're ready, pray for God to help you with it."

"What if I'm never ready?"

She'd thought the same thing many times. She'd forgiven a lot in her life, given her anger and pain to God the way she'd just advised Wyatt to, but... She frowned. She hadn't gotten around to forgiving the people responsible for destroying Treyvon's and Jay's lives. How did one forgive nameless faces?

What about me? How can I sit here and preach to this kid when I haven't spent two minutes in prayer about those boys other than to blame God for letting it happen?

"You will be ready." *And I will be, too.* She patted his back. "Now, let's get this homework figured out."

A few hours later, Wyatt had finished his spelling homework, written a sloppy paragraph about insects and failed more than half the multiplication problems on the worksheet before they called it quits and drove to her folks' house. Lauren sighed. She didn't know how parents did it. How did they keep up with the emotional ups and downs, as well as schoolwork, activities and making sure the kids were fed, dressed and healthy? It was exhausting.

She sat with her mom on the deck overlooking the backyard. Wyatt and Lauren's dad were attempting to fly a kite on the spacious lawn. So far it hadn't flown more than four feet in the air, and they were currently untangling the line. Again.

"What time is it?" she asked her mom. Mom had turned sixty a month ago, but she didn't look her age. Tonya Pierce had short brown hair and the kindest eyes Lauren had ever seen. She described herself as "fluffy," but her cute turquoise capris and T-shirt hid her extra pounds.

"Almost seven, why?"

"I need to have Wyatt back to his house by eight. His dad, Chase, is calling him." Lauren had to hand it to Chase; he called Wyatt two or three times a week. Drew kept a log of each phone call, too, for Chase's lawyer. The log would help Chase reestablish his parental rights when he was released. Lauren wasn't sure how she felt about that. The guy hadn't put Wyatt's needs first when he went on his revenge spree. Would he be the dad Wyatt needed when he was released?

"What do you think of him?" Mom crossed one ankle over the other.

"Chase? I don't know. I haven't met him. He's good about calling Wyatt." She hoped Chase was worthy of being Wyatt's father. The boy had been through too much. He needed someone he could count on. A rock who wouldn't budge.

Drew came to mind. For a rock, he was surprisingly flexible about many things. She'd been impressed he actually came to her for advice about the homework situation.

"Did you hear back from the woman in Chicago?"

"I talked to her this morning." Lauren swirled the straw in her glass of iced tea. "I spent a few hours researching everything she told me, and honestly, Mom,

I'm not sure if I should bother looking into it more. I don't think it's going to work out."

"Why not?"

"I would need a large building, permits, insurance and equipment. Add the uniforms, tournament fees and teachers' salaries, and I don't think it makes financial sense."

"But she's successful at running one, right?"

"Yes, but hers is in a suburb of Chicago. Lake Endwell isn't big, and it's a thirty-minute drive to Kalamazoo. I doubt I'd get enough students to make it worthwhile."

Mom made a clucking sound with her tongue. "I see what you're saying."

Her dad let out a whoop as Wyatt jogged by holding the string, making the bird-shaped kite soar higher. She snapped a photo of him and texted it to Drew.

"Nice job, Wyatt," Lauren yelled. He gave her a thumbs-up.

"He's a cute kid."

"He is."

"I'm glad you're taking care of him."

"Yeah, well, it's just for the summer. I need to figure out my long-term plans."

"Oh, that reminds me. I found out some interesting news. The varsity cheer coach, Joanna Mills, is quitting."

Lauren sipped her drink. "So?"

"So, you'd be perfect for the job."

"I don't think they pay much to cheerleading coaches." Lauren pulled her hair to the side.

"I've got Joanna's number. Give her a call. Find out what's involved. It couldn't hurt."

It probably couldn't. The cheer academy looked like

a no go, and Lauren trusted her mom. She gave great advice and usually didn't stick her nose into Lauren's personal affairs.

"Give me the number. I'll call." Maybe this fit the old saying about one door closing and another opening. She doubted a cheerleading coach earned enough to support herself, but she could combine it with another part-time job if needed.

What about my future? Retirement? Fulfillment?

"You seem a little better lately, honey." Mom had a knack for seeing right into her soul.

"I feel a little better."

"Taking care of Wyatt is good for you."

"For now. Hopefully I'm helping him."

"You are. Look at him." She hitched her chin toward the lawn. The kite had fallen, and Wyatt and Dad were winding the string again. "Resilient, considering all he's been through. But you would know, too, wouldn't you? You went through a lot of the same things."

"Not everything. His dad loves him and wants a relationship with him."

"You're not jealous, are you?"

Lauren laughed. "Of course not! Why would you think such a thing? I'm happy for him."

"Good."

They stared out at the pretty green lawn. The woods' edge cast shadows in the distance, but the evening sunshine warmed Lauren's arms.

"Haven't seen you in church in a while."

Lauren's good mood darkened. "No, you haven't."

"Why don't you join us Sunday? We'll pick you up."

"I'll think about it."

Mom raised her eyebrows. "You've been saying that for five months."

"And you've been saying *that* for five months."

"I care, Lauren. I care about you. I care about your soul. Don't shut God out."

Lauren sat up, rubbing her arms. "I'm not."

"Then come with us."

"Mom, I need to do this on my own terms. I'm not going to be guilted into going back to church. I don't think God wants that. Doesn't He want a cheerful giver?"

"Oh, Lauren…"

Thankfully, Mom dropped the topic. How could Lauren explain something she didn't understand herself? Of all the cases she'd worked on, all the kids born into negligent, dangerous homes, Treyvon and Jay had affected her the most. And right when she'd been close to helping them, tragedy had struck. God could have stepped in, but He didn't. And she still loved God, but she couldn't quite trust Him.

Trust and love. Faith and hope.

All intertwined.

Without one, could she have the others?

And how could she keep talking to Wyatt about faith and forgiveness and God's love when she'd been shutting God out for months? No matter how many sips of tea she took, Lauren was left with the taste of ashes.

Shaking the raindrops off his jacket, Drew hung his keys on the hook and nudged the front door shut behind him. Yawning, he tried to erase last night's scene. The car wreck had been fatal. Gruesome. He went straight to the bathroom to wash his hands before hunting for Lauren. First stop, the kitchen.

"You didn't have to make breakfast, Lauren." He paused in the doorway at the welcome sight. A stack of French toast steamed from a plate, the coffeemaker gurgled and bacon sizzled from the frying pan.

"I know." She smiled sweetly, spatula in hand. "But I made Wyatt French toast, so I figured you might want some, too."

"I do." Was his exhaustion playing tricks on him, or was she even more beautiful than before? Her hair flowed behind her, sending his previously comatose pulse into high gear. The house smelled delicious, all sugar and spice and everything nice.

Rain streamed down the windows. Lauren switched the light on over the table and set a platter loaded with bacon in the center. Drew poured two mugs of coffee as she took a seat.

"Mind if I say grace?" he asked. She bowed her head and folded her hands. He said the prayer, then sliced into his stack of French toast. He savored the light texture and maple syrup. "Mmm…delicious."

"Glad you like them." She beamed. "Did you put out any fires?"

"No, but Tony and I were sent on a nasty call last night." A shudder rippled down his spine. The only good thing about the night? It had opened a crack in Tony's granite-hard attitude about him. Tony had actually told him he'd done nice work out there. It was a start.

"That bad, huh?" Worry lines creased between her eyes.

"Yeah, it was." Outside the station, he never discussed the fires, 911 calls or accidents he responded to, but that might be because he had no one to discuss them with. A glance at Lauren had him biting his tongue. He wouldn't ruin her day with tales of twisted limbs and death.

"Was it the accident out on Ridge Road?" She took a drink of coffee, staring at him over the rim of her cup.

"Yeah, how did you know?"

"I get local news updates on Facebook. I was hoping you weren't called to that one. It looked horrible."

"It was." He set his fork down for a moment, trying to push away the visions in his head, but they kept coming, making his blood pressure climb.

"Tell me about it."

"I don't think so. You don't want to hear it."

"I can handle it."

Could she? He doubted it. She obviously couldn't handle all the bad things she'd witnessed in Chicago or she wouldn't have quit to hide away here.

That must be his exhaustion talking. He didn't think less of her for moving.

"It might help to talk about it." Her gray eyes probed, saw too much.

"You first." He bit into a piece of bacon, too tired to think straight. "What happened in Chicago?"

She suddenly grew very absorbed in the half-eaten food on her plate. With her fork, she pushed a bite deeper into the syrup pooling around her French toast. Seconds ticked by with only the sound of the rain coming down.

"See?" he said. "Talking about it doesn't help."

Her fork dropped with a clatter. "You're wrong. I... I just wish..."

"What?" He lowered his tone, smoothing out the edge to it. "What do you wish?"

She pushed her chair back and turned away from him to look out the window. *Nice going, Gannon.* The woman had made him bacon—bacon!—so why was he picking on her? She was doing *him* the favor by taking care of Wyatt, and here he was, asking questions he knew she didn't want to discuss.

He admired the graceful line of her neck as she continued to stare at the rivulets of water streaming down the glass. When the silence had stretched too long, he opened his mouth to apologize, but she started to speak.

"I worked for child welfare services in some of the rougher neighborhoods of Chicago, and I was used to hard cases. I mean, eight years of being surrounded by poverty coats you with Teflon. Sometimes I'd go home and wonder if I was getting burned-out. But then I'd remember why I got into the field, and I would keep going."

He wanted to ask why she got into the field, but she continued. "Treyvon and Jay were brothers. Treyvon was fifteen. Jay was twelve. They lived in Englewood. I always dreaded cases from that part of town."

When she didn't say anything, he cleared his throat. "What's wrong with Englewood?"

She jerked, meeting his eyes. "Poverty. Gangs. Drugs. Way back when I first moved to Chicago, I was assigned a case that brought me in contact with an elderly Englewood resident. From that point on, Mr. Bell watched out for me whenever I had to make home visits, which wasn't very often. Regardless, I never went alone, always had a coworker go with me."

Drew stopped chewing as her words sunk in. *Home visits. Rough areas.* She'd willingly put herself in dangerous situations. His chest felt tight. He hated that she'd been around criminals.

"In Jay's situation, a teacher filed a report, and I was

assigned his case. He'd been a model student, and one of the few kids in the class who showed up regularly. The teacher noticed he was absent more often and was distracted at school. She called his mother and realized his home situation had deteriorated. I conducted the routine interviews. He was a nice kid. Smart and polite. Treyvon was, too."

Drew reached for his coffee, frowning as he processed more of the words. Like her use of the word *was*.

"Didn't take long to find out his grandmother had been living with them and their drug-addicted mom. A few months prior to the teacher filing the report, the grandma had a stroke and was moved to a nursing home to recover. Jay's life—and Treyvon's—had dissolved into chaos. I'll spare you the details of their situation, but neither had the clothing, food or supervision necessary. I was doing my best to work with their mother to create a healthy home situation until the grandmother could return home."

"Wait." He raised his hand. "They still lived with their mom even though she was on drugs? For how long?"

"I'd been working with them for about a month. I convinced her to get a family friend to live with them until the grandmother was released. The doctor's reports were promising. Although her speech was slurred, her right side had regained enough mobility for her to walk with a walker. Their grandma was expected to be home within a few weeks."

"But why let those boys stay there at all?" He couldn't wrap his head around it.

"We work with the children's family to fix problems first as long as the kids aren't in danger. Their mom agreed to ask her friend to stay, and that alone solved several of the issues. She also agreed to a treatment program."

"I see." He didn't, though. Not really. Kids shouldn't live around drugs.

"It's next to impossible to place two adolescent boys into a foster home. Treyvon flat out told me he'd run away with Jay if they couldn't stay together. They'd been well taken care of by their grandmother. My hope was when she returned, they would go back to their normal life."

He took a drink of lukewarm coffee, dreading the way the story was heading.

"Long story short, the grandmother got pneumonia and died unexpectedly. The family friend moved out. I had two weeks to place both kids in foster homes. I tried so hard to keep them together. I called everyone on my list."

"You couldn't help it if they had to be separated."

Her eyes, silver with unshed tears, met his. "They didn't have time to be separated. Jay was shot in a drive-by. Gunned down on a sidewalk. Twelve. A boy his age shouldn't be outside at one in the morning, and especially not in that neighborhood. I know he was looking for Treyvon."

Drew pushed his plate back, no longer hungry. "Where was Treyvon?"

"Robbing a mini-mart. One of the local gangs recruited him. That's exactly what I worried about when he told me he would run away. The odds of escaping gang life when you have nowhere to go and aren't old enough to have a job aren't good."

Drew sucked in a breath. He felt bad about the kids,

but Lauren worked in gang areas? How much danger had she been in all those years? Unwanted scenarios, all bad, popped up in his head, but he shook them away.

"So Jay—did he make it?" He reached over, covering her hand on the table with his. She didn't pull it away, which he took as a good sign.

"He died near a vacant lot two blocks from his house." Her flat tone worried him. "And Treyvon's in a juvenile detention center until he's of age."

"I'm sorry, Lauren." He stood and pulled her into his arms, inhaling the coconut smell of her shampoo as her head leaned against his shoulder. She wrapped her arms around his waist. Having her in his arms felt right even if it was only to comfort her.

She took a slight step back, but he kept his arms around her.

"I should have gotten them out of there sooner. I failed them, Drew. They were good kids. They tried hard to rise above their situation, and I was their liaison. I was supposed to help them, and both their lives are ruined because of me."

Tipping her chin up with his finger, he looked her in the eyes. "Hey, it's not your fault. How were you supposed to know their grandmother would die? Or Treyvon would join a gang?"

"I knew the signs. Kids in that neighborhood were always being pressured to join one of the local gangs. All the gang members had to do was threaten to hurt one of their loved ones…" She shivered. "Jay and Treyvon were acting secretive when I met with them those final two weeks. I told myself they were sad about their grandmother. That they were worried about what would happen to them. I should have put two and two together."

"Don't do this to yourself, Lauren."

She slipped out of his grasp, rubbing her biceps, and faced the window. "It's hard. I saw so much potential in Jay. When I think of him shot down—he was just a boy. I made him promises I didn't keep."

"Didn't or couldn't? There's a difference, you know." Drew put his hand on her shoulder. She glanced up at him, her expression pleading for something—redemption maybe—but she turned, picked up her mug and padded to the kitchen. He followed her. She shut the microwave door and jabbed the buttons until the machine whirred to life.

"What does it matter now? He's dead. Another bright light in this world snuffed out. I thought I could make a difference..." She leaned against the counter.

"You did make a difference."

"Now who's lying?" She let out a brittle laugh and ran her fingers through her hair. "Never mind. I should get going."

"Your coffee hasn't finished warming up."

"I'm not thirsty anymore."

She grabbed her purse, but Drew held on to her arm. He should let her leave, but everything inside him screamed to make her stay. "Wait. Don't you want to hear about the accident last night?"

She shook her head. "You were right. I can't handle it."

And she left.

Drew stared at the closed door. She'd handled far worse than he did. He was a first responder, detached from the personal lives of the victims he helped. He didn't blame her for quitting, but why had she stayed with it for all those years to begin with?

Was it selfish to be relieved she was no longer a social worker? Too dangerous. When he thought of her walking through gang areas, making visits to drug addicts' homes…he wanted to lock her up and keep her from ever being in danger again. She was sunshine, a bright light to protect and cherish.

But she wasn't his.

At least she wasn't in Chicago anymore. He liked her right here in sleepy Lake Endwell.

He just hoped he hadn't pushed her too far.

Lauren's windshield wipers swiped angrily as she drove away from Drew's. Gripping the steering wheel, her hands trembled.

Don't think. Just go.

When life got to be too much, she would drive to a secluded area several miles out of town. On warm days, she'd stroll along the path next to the river. On rainy days like today, she'd sit in her car and soak in the view of the trees and river for as long as possible. The place soothed her in a way she couldn't explain. She'd missed this spot when she lived in Chicago.

As soon as she drove into the deserted parking lot, her tension lowered a bit. She flexed her hands open and shut a few times and forced her jaw to relax. Even through the rain, the bright green leaves on the trees looked supple and new.

Drew was right. She should have found Treyvon and Jay foster homes from the start.

But their situation had been so tricky. She'd been sure their grandmother would come home. Treyvon had been adamant about not getting separated from Jay. And their mother had agreed to drug counseling. Lauren had convinced her to get another responsible adult in the household. The woman had complied.

How had it gone so wrong?

Why, Lord? Why did it have to happen that way? Why did You let it happen?

The ping of rain against the roof was the only answer.

Her chest felt as if it were being squeezed by a giant clamp. She choked back threatening tears, refusing to give in to the hopelessness that wouldn't subside.

Her phone dinged. She glanced at it. Drew texted, Are you okay?

No, she was not okay. She might never be okay.

Jesus wept. She could hear her voice saying those words to Wyatt.

She was the world's biggest hypocrite. Always had an answer for everyone else but didn't take her own advice.

Okay, God. I told Wyatt to give his anger to You. But I haven't given mine up. I'm clinging to it, and I don't know why.

Because like Wyatt had said, forgiveness seemed like a free pass. Like what happened didn't matter.

Lord, help me release my anger. I want to stop being angry with You. With me. Even with Treyvon. I don't know how. I can't make any sense of why Jay died. Why? Why did it have to end so badly?

An old Bible verse came to mind, something about God working all things out for the good of those who loved Him.

She typed in her Bible app. But before the results showed up, she closed her eyes. Could she really believe God worked *all* things out for good? Even the horrible, sinful, evil things?

She didn't want bad things worked out for good.

She wanted them good to begin with. Shouldn't Wyatt be living with his father? Shouldn't Jay and Treyvon's grandmother have lived? Shouldn't both boys still be going to school?

She closed the app and tossed her phone in her purse.

The anger she'd work on, but she wasn't ready to forgive. Not God, not the shooters, not the gang members, not Treyvon. Not even herself.

She might never be ready.

Chapter Six

Two weeks later, Lauren tapped her foot and checked the clock above Joanna Mills's desk in the art room at the elementary school. She had exactly fourteen minutes before Wyatt got out of school. Once she signed him out, they planned on surprising Drew with treats at the fire station for his one-month anniversary. After she told Drew everything about Chicago, they had fallen back into their routine. He didn't ask probing questions, and she kept her focus on Wyatt, where it belonged. And now two dozen chocolate cupcakes fresh from the Daily Donut were nestled in her backseat, but Joanna still hadn't returned to the art room.

"Sorry about that. I found it." Joanna licked her finger and rifled through a folder before selecting a paper. "Here it is. Everything you need to know about getting certified to be a cheerleading coach. The program goes over a lot of stuff like keeping the cheerleaders healthy and preventing injuries. It's worth the time."

Lauren scanned the paper. "Thank you."

"No problem." Joanna smiled, setting the folder on top of a teetering stack of papers. "Did you know they need another high school counselor? Great hours. Typical pay. You really should apply for the position. You'll have a much better chance at getting hired as the coach if you're employed by the school."

School counselor? Lauren didn't realize a position was open. The very words sent dread from her head to her toes. "I'm not interested."

"No? I thought you used to be a social worker. Seems like a great fit. But, then, it's pretty tame around here. I don't blame you if sending transcripts to colleges and changing kids' schedules isn't your dream job."

Sending transcripts and fixing schedules actually sounded quite nice.

"Tell me more about the position."

Joanna filled her in on what she knew. Lauren had to admit it appealed to her, but she didn't have time to think about it. She needed to sign Wyatt out. He would worry if she wasn't waiting for him. "Thank you. I'll think about it, but I have to run."

Joanna followed her to the door. "Go online and fill out the application. There will be about a million hoops to jump through, but don't let that stop you."

"Thanks, Joanna. I appreciate it."

Twenty minutes later, Lauren and Wyatt rolled down the car windows on the way to the fire station.

"Can you believe it's June already?" Lauren grinned. "How many days left of school?"

"Four." Wyatt tipped his head back as the wind blasted his face. "I can't wait! Jackson and Levi told me they're playing football this summer. It starts in August. I have a sign-up form. It's going to be awesome!"

Lauren frowned. *Football.* Hadn't Drew told her

Wyatt wasn't allowed to play? She made a mental note to ask him about it later. "What about Hunter?"

Wyatt's face fell. "I don't know. I think he plays soccer. But all the cool kids are playing football. Levi's dad is coaching. I hope I get on his team."

"The cool kids, huh?" She waited for the traffic light to turn green. "Isn't Hunter a cool kid?"

Wyatt mumbled something.

"What was that? I couldn't hear you?"

"Hunter's nice, but Jackson and Levi..."

When he didn't elaborate, she prodded. "Are cool?" There was his smile. He nodded happily.

She parked the car and figured she'd talk to Drew about the football situation later. "Here. You take a box, and I'll take a box. Together we might get all twenty-four of these yum-yums into the station without dropping any."

"Yum-yums?" Wyatt shook his head, acting disgusted. But he held his hands out for her to set one of the boxes in them. "You have the weirdest sayings, Lauren."

"Weird? *Moi?* You should be glad you have me around to enlighten you." Grinning, she held the other box and shut the door with her backside. Wyatt fell in beside her. Tony Ludlow let them into the station, and they followed him to the kitchen.

"What's this?" Tony tried to lift the cover of her cupcake box.

"No peeking." She gave him a fake frown. "Is Drew around?"

His smile faltered, but he hitched his chin. "Sure. I'll get him."

Drew appeared. "Why are you guys here?" The twinkle in his eyes contained more than simple happiness.

He looked genuinely surprised. Hadn't he ever been the recipient of a nice gesture before?

"It's your one-month anniversary. We thought we should celebrate it." Lauren winked at Wyatt, who lifted the lid off the boxes. The cupcakes spelled out, "Thank You, Drew and Station 4."

"You did this for me?" Drew gazed at her intently, then pulled Wyatt into a hug. "Wow, thank you."

"Well, go on." Lauren waved at the box. "Try one."

Two guys joined them. "What's this? Oh, hey, Wyatt, how's it going?"

Wyatt fist-bumped the men, clearly familiar with them, and Lauren watched in amusement as they interacted. Like wolves catching a whiff of a fresh kill, the rest of the crew filled the kitchen. Drew introduced Lauren to the people she didn't know. Tony strolled back in and read the lettering on the cupcakes.

"Drew, huh?" Tony sniffed, grinning at her. "Be honest. You did this to thank *me*—didn't you Lauren?"

She laughed, glancing at Drew. He'd frozen with half a cupcake in his hand, the other half in his mouth.

"You think so?" Lauren punched Tony's arm lightly. "And I suppose you're the king of the station around here."

"I get the job done." His smug expression made her chuckle. "Unlike your boyfriend here."

Boyfriend? She sputtered. Tony thought she and Drew were…dating? *Absurd!*

But…the idea wasn't horrible. She darted a peek at Drew's lips. Chocolate-frosted lips.

"Who's dating Gannon?" one of the guys yelled out.

"Well, there goes my chance with her," another one muttered.

Wyatt looked excited, doubtful and a tad confused.

"Hold on there." Drew held his palms out. "We're not dating."

Lauren blinked, oddly disappointed Drew sounded so adamant about it. They chatted with everyone, and within minutes, the cupcakes were gone. Drew walked Lauren and Wyatt to the door. "Thanks for doing this. It means a lot to me."

"You're welcome."

"Hey, can you stick around for a while when I get home tomorrow?"

"Why?" Her stomach started twirling.

The intensity in his stare didn't help her tummy. "I have something I want to talk to you about. I'll bring breakfast."

Lauren nodded and nudged Wyatt to the parking lot. Drew was bringing her breakfast. She liked the sound of that. But what did he want to talk to her about?

She guessed she'd find out in the morning.

Drew juggled the paper bag filled with carryout containers from Pat's Diner in his hand as he fumbled with his keys to unlock the front door the next morning. Ever since that idiot Tony had said the word *boyfriend* about him and Lauren, Drew had been hammered with endless comments about how hot Lauren was, and how she was a legend in high school, and why hadn't she gotten married, and maybe Miggs or Dan had a chance. At least Tony was married, so Drew hadn't had to listen to him go on and on about Lauren.

He'd wanted to smash cupcakes in the other guys' faces. But that wasn't acceptable behavior, and the cupcakes had been long gone at that point, so he'd had to grit his teeth and not say a word. Not one word. Or they would tease him mercilessly the rest of his working days.

He was still on extremely thin ice where his coworkers were concerned. Sure, he and Tony had been getting along slightly better. But the chief continued to harass him. Drew always got the worst cleanup jobs, and he wouldn't be assigned driving duty until the probation period was over. He was the backup, the *probie*, and it bugged him.

But not as much as the thought of Lauren dating one of the guys from work.

Or anyone.

Except him.

Like she would ever go out with him. Not a chance. It would be a bad idea, anyhow. If they dated and it didn't work out, she'd quit watching Wyatt. And speaking of Wyatt, Drew needed some advice. He opened the front door.

"Hey," she said. "You survived another day at work."

His mouth went dry at the sight of Lauren standing in the living room with no makeup on, her hair flowing around her shoulders. She wore a white short-sleeved button-down shirt with ankle-length fitted jeans.

"Why don't we eat outside?" Lauren slipped a pair of sandals on and strode to the patio door. "Leave the bag out there, and I'll get plates and coffee."

Drew crossed the room. After setting the bag on the table, he held his hand up to the bright sun. *June already.* Man, he loved summer. Maybe he could take Wyatt out canoeing later.

"Give me a minute to change," he called on his way to his bedroom. He shrugged into a T-shirt and khaki shorts, then joined her on the back deck. She'd already transferred the omelets and hash browns to plates and sat with a satisfied grin under the maroon umbrella.

"You look happy," he said.

"I am. Isn't it a beautiful day?"

The day wasn't the only thing that was beautiful. He lunged for his coffee cup, scalding his tongue when he took a drink. "Yeah, it's nice out."

Soon they dug into the food on their plates. A trickling sound from the waterfall flowing into the ornamental pond punctuated the peace of the day. The yard wasn't overly large, but it was encased by a privacy fence and had mature trees around it. He liked it. Not too much to mow but big enough to host a barbecue.

"Thanks for bringing Wyatt over yesterday and for the cupcakes. Everyone loved them."

"You're welcome. He was very excited. He thinks the fire station is one of the best places on earth."

"Well, he's not alone." Drew grinned, unsure of how to broach what was on his mind. "Can I ask you something?"

"Sure."

"Chase wants me to bring Wyatt to visit him. Do you think it's a good idea?"

She finished chewing before replying. "It depends. Have you asked Wyatt what he wants?"

"Not yet. I wanted to run it by you first." He blew across the top of his mug, hoping the coffee would be cool enough to drink without becoming a burn victim.

"Do you know what's involved?"

He'd talked to Chase about it. "Yeah. For the most part."

"Does the correctional facility have a children's room or a comfortable area for Wyatt to be with Chase?"

"They have a visitor's room with a children's area. I'm already on the approved list, but we'd have to schedule the visit." He leaned back in his chair. It didn't seem too complicated. Apply for a visit, adhere to the dress code and flash some identification.

"Good. But don't rush into a decision." She twisted her lips as if trying to decide what to say. "Prisons are pretty intimidating. The property itself might stress Wyatt out with the fences and barbed wire. Plus he'll have to go through a metal detector and be around other inmates. I don't know if it's wise at this time."

He stared out at the green lawn, where a few dandelions had poked through. His present view was the opposite of what Lauren had just described—fencing, barbed wire, metal detectors and other inmates. Did he want Wyatt to have those images in his mind?

"That being said, in my professional opinion, kids need relationships with their parents, and the courts will be more likely to reinstate Chase's parental rights if he maintains contact with Wyatt."

"Chase told me that, too. Plus he really misses the kid. Wyatt was his life."

She dusted crumbs from her hands. "If that were true, Chase wouldn't be in jail. He should have thought about Wyatt before he went on his revenge trip."

He opened his mouth to defend Chase, but he couldn't. "Well, he's paying dearly for it. His career is over, he's stuck in prison and he wants to see his kid."

He could just make out her eyebrows arching over the rim of her cup as she sipped her coffee.

"His wants are not as important as Wyatt's needs

right now. Ask Wyatt if he wants to visit his dad. If he does, thoroughly prepare him on what to expect."

She made good points. Wyatt's needs were important. And he was starting to act like a normal ten-year-old again. Drew didn't want to set back his progress by traumatizing him with a prison visit. But he also didn't want to prevent his best friend from seeing his son. Lauren might think Chase was a loser, but Drew knew how much the man loved Wyatt.

"Thanks," he said. "I'll do that."

"Oh, and before I forget again, I think you should know Wyatt is determined to play football this summer."

"What?" His voice hardened. Couldn't one week go by without a new complication?

"Yep." She flourished her wrist. "Seems there are some *cool* kids playing, and one of their dads is coaching a team."

"Must be rec ball." He'd played at that age, too. It had been fun. A sport tailor-made for him. Sure, he'd made bad plays at times, but football had been his life. "I don't think the school district sponsors teams until seventh or eighth grade."

"Are you going to let him play?"

"I can't." He propped his elbows on the table. "If it was up to me, I'd sign him up. Let him learn about life himself. But Chase couldn't have been more clear on the topic."

"Could you ask him again?"

He shook his head. "I don't think so. I mean, I can try, but when he gets something in his head, watch out."

"Maybe you could sign Wyatt up for soccer or something else instead."

"Good idea." Chase hadn't said anything about soccer. "I'll check online later." He yawned. Overnights were exhausting. The middle-of-the-night calls had done him in.

"I'd better get out of here so you can have your beauty sleep." Lauren stacked the plates and stood.

"Leave them. I'll clean up."

Her lopsided smile sent a surge of energy through his body.

"I've got it," Lauren said. "Go to bed. I'll see you in a few days."

"Wait." He didn't want her to leave. Wanted to prolong each minute with her. But she was opening the patio door to go inside. "Won't I see you tomorrow?"

Turning back, she narrowed her eyes. "Why?"

"The pancake breakfast." She must have seen the signs around town or the ones plastered to the fire station door. "Aren't you coming?"

"Pancake breakfast? What are you talking about?"

"Our annual fund-raiser. It's at the station. Tickets are cheap. We've got fun and games. I'm sure you want to hop around in the bounce house." He plucked the plates out of her hand and slid the patio door open wider for her. "You should come."

"What time?"

"Seven to eleven."

"Can I bring a friend?"

A guy friend or a girl friend? He sighed. He had no right to ask. "Sure."

"I never miss the annual pancake breakfast." Megan adjusted her sundress straps.

"I always miss it." Lauren sidestepped two young

boys chasing each other. What a silly thing to say. Of course she did—she'd lived in another state.

It felt good to go to a public event. The few times she'd ventured from her apartment outside of work or errands since moving back had been the Friday dinner with Drew and Wyatt at Uncle Joe's Restaurant and the visit to the station with Wyatt. For the first time in months, she actually wanted to be out and about. She couldn't deny she'd been smiling more now that Drew and Wyatt were in her life. She wondered if Drew had discussed visiting Chase with Wyatt.

"Something tells me you're here for more than the pancakes." Lauren followed Megan to the back of the line. The entire town must have shown up. An enormous white tent was set up on the lawn behind the station. Rows of tables and folding chairs were already full of families dining on sausage links and pancakes, and out on the lawn, two bounce houses jiggled in the light breeze. Tables with activities were set up beside them, and a playground and baseball diamond were a short distance away. "Do you think we'll find a spot to sit?"

"Oh, yeah. No problem. I've got this." Megan waved dismissively and leaned in. "I've had my eye on Ben Santos for a while now. See? Over there. The cutie serving sausages."

Lauren squinted. The line moved surprisingly fast. "Black hair? Tall?"

"That's him." Megan tipped her chin up and plastered her brightest smile on as they approached the food station. A female firefighter handed them both plates. "How's it going, Amanda?"

"Can't complain." The woman didn't seem overly thrilled to be there. "Ben and Stan will get you set up with hotcakes and sausages. Juice and coffee are on the table at the end."

They shuffled down the line, but Megan dug her heels in at the sausage station. "Hey, Ben."

"Well, hello, Megan." The man looked happier than a five-year-old skipping to an ice-cream truck. "It's good to see you."

"I always show up for a good cause." Megan twirled a section of hair around her finger.

Talk about obvious. The line behind Lauren was getting restless, but Ben seemed oblivious.

He set the tongs down, leaning over the warming tray. "I'm sure glad you did. Where you sitting?"

"It's pretty full." Megan shrugged, somehow making the gesture seem helpless. "I guess we could stand and eat, huh, Lauren?"

Lauren choked down a chortle at the overly disappointed tone in her voice. Megan should have been an actress. Was this Ben guy actually buying this?

"You can't eat standing up." All business, he straightened and gestured to another firefighter standing behind him. "Miggs, take over for me. Come with me, ladies." A minute later he escorted them to a side table where a few of the fire crew were taking a break. "Scoot over."

One of them grumbled, but at the sight of Megan and Lauren, they all quickly scooted down.

"Plenty of room. Right here." A man patted the bench and grinned at Lauren.

She was going to strangle Megan later. Ben and Megan had squished in at the other end of the table. Neither had eyes for anyone but each other.

"Actually, Lauren, there's a free spot next to me."

How had she not noticed Drew sitting at the end?

"Thanks, Drew." She sat next to him and spread a paper napkin across her lap. "Good turnout."

"Yeah, it is."

"Where's Wyatt?" A smear of butter and a hefty dose of syrup completed her hotcakes. She cut them and took a bite.

Drew straightened, turning his head to check the bounce house area. "He's off playing games with a few friends. I think one was named Levi."

"I'm glad he's comfortable enough to do that now. This will be fun for him." The name Levi rang bells in her brain. Wasn't he one of the cool kids Wyatt mentioned?

"He stuck by me real close the first half hour. Boredom must have loosened him up enough to go with the boys."

"Did you have a chance to talk to him about playing football?"

He took a drink from a foam cup. "No, I had enough to deal with just discussing the possibility of visiting Chase."

She lowered her voice, not wanting everyone around them to hear. "So you talked about it then?"

"Yeah. He wants to go."

"Don't sound so excited."

"You made me think about it more. I'm worried it will be a lot to take in. Like you said, it might be scary for a young kid. Barbed wire, metal detectors. Is that good for him? I did a little research, though. One article said visiting an incarcerated parent helps a child maintain attachment and can get rid of some of the kid's fears about how the parent is doing in prison. What do you think?"

"Chase wants a relationship with Wyatt, and vice versa, so I say yes. Try a visit." She sopped up another bite with syrup. "Did you go over what to expect?"

Drew gazed off in the distance. "I did."

"And?"

"He still wants to go," Drew said. "He asked if you'd go with us."

She finished chewing. "Me?"

"I told him not to count on it." He averted his eyes.

"Why not? I'd be happy to drive with you. What facility is Chase in?" She'd been to prisons before. It didn't bother her any more than home visits in dangerous neighborhoods did. Not her favorite, but it was part of the job. She'd taken self-defense classes in her early twenties, always carried pepper spray and kept a pocketknife in her purse at all times. More important, she prayed for protection. She didn't live in an invincibility bubble, but she forged ahead anyhow.

"I didn't know how you'd feel about it, and I don't want you to feel obligated. You're already helping so much."

She waved her hand, scoffing. "I'm not doing much. Hanging out with a sweet kid like Wyatt isn't difficult. Tell me the date of the visit, and I'll come with you."

Drew filled her in on the specifics.

"I won't be allowed to go into the actual visitation room with him." Lauren set the used plastic silverware on her empty plate. "You guys can drop me off somewhere nearby while you visit. But let Wyatt know I'll be there for him before and after."

"The prison is two hours away. Are you sure you're up for it?"

"I'm up for it."

"Thank you." His eyes shone with gratitude. And something else.

A woman approached. She had a professional air about her, and unlike the rest of the people eating breakfast who wore casual clothes, she wore dress pants and a blouse.

"Excuse me. I'm sorry to interrupt, but are you Lauren Pierce?" She stood behind her and Drew. Lauren shifted in her seat to stare up at the woman while Drew excused himself to get another cup of coffee.

"I am."

"Susanne Gilbert, principal of Lake Endwell High. I talked to Joanna Mills yesterday."

That was quick. Lauren hadn't yet decided if she was going to apply for the counselor job. When she'd opened the online application file, icy tendrils had wrapped around her heart. She wasn't dumb. The job was more than transcripts and schedules. It was teen suicide, bullying and drug abuse. It was high school dropouts and cliques.

It was troubled kids desperately in need of help all over again.

She stood and shook the woman's hand. "Nice to meet you."

"I'd love to set up an interview with you. Joanna mentioned you'd be interested in coaching our cheerleaders."

"I am interested in coaching. I used to be a cheerleader here, and I really enjoyed it. I'm not sure about the counseling job, though."

"Why not apply? We can discuss the details over an interview. I have several other applicants, but given your background in Lake Endwell and your experience as a social worker... Well, let's just say I did some research and was impressed."

"Thank you." She wouldn't be so impressed if she knew Lauren's mistakes.

Principal Gilbert handed her a business card. "The link to the online application is on the back. Hope to hear from you soon."

Drew stood nearby. He held their empty paper plates in his hand. She couldn't read his face.

"So you're applying for a job?" He took a few steps in the direction of a large trash can. She joined him.

"I'm considering it. Cheerleading coach."

"And the counselor job Mrs. Gilbert mentioned?"

She shook her head. She couldn't go there. Not yet. Maybe not ever.

He tossed the plates in the can. "You'd be great at it."

"I don't know about that."

"You're good with Wyatt. Helping kids is in your blood." He strolled toward the bounce houses. In her blood? Her blood came from a drug addict and a murderer. Anything good inside her came from the Pierces and God. "For what it's worth, you're a natural. I think you should go for it."

"I'm researching a few other things." Like the cheer academy idea she'd all but abandoned. Or getting a safe and boring desk job. She grimaced.

He craned his neck to peer into the bounce houses. "Do you see Wyatt?"

She tried to look inside them but didn't recognize the kids. Slowly spinning in a circle, she checked the nearby park. "Isn't that him on the swings?"

"It sure is." Drew's eyes darkened as his jaw clenched.

"I told him to tell me before going to the park. I'm going to have a word with him."

He strode in the park's direction. Lauren stayed and watched. A woman with a camera stood to the side of the playground, snapping several photos. What was she doing? Drew had told Lauren he hadn't had any issues with aggressive reporters since moving here.

He stopped to talk to the woman. By his posture, Lauren assumed he knew her. Probably a mom of one of the kids.

Overreacting. She'd been overreacting to her fears for months.

Lauren turned back to find Megan. The sun warmed her face, but her insides were chilled. She was glad Drew took Wyatt's safety serious. A ten-year-old boy had no business running around without telling an adult where he was. On one hand, she wanted Drew to come down hard on him so he wouldn't do it again. But the other hand sympathized with Wyatt and wondered if she was making a big deal out of nothing.

Running off to a playground without telling Drew wasn't that big of a deal. But if it led to worse mistakes, like sneaking out in the middle of the night...

Discipline was worth the pain. If Jay would have gotten an ounce of discipline from his mother that week in December, he might have lived. And what about Treyvon? By the time she was assigned his and Jay's case, Treyvon had been fifteen with eyes wide-open about life. She had cared about him. Her heart squeezed at the thought of him in juvenile hall. Since quitting her job, she'd made no contact with him. He was no longer her case.

He might not be her case, but did that make him nothing to her?

Her conscience prodded. Maybe he *was* her case. Not as a social worker but as a human being who cared about him. Maybe it was time to contact him. Find out how he was doing.

Ask him to forgive her.

She dropped to a picnic table bench.

How could she ask him to forgive her when she hadn't really forgiven him?

She blamed him for Jay's death.

More than she blamed herself.

Oh, God, I'm sorry. I try not to think about it, but I'm so mad at that kid. Why did he join that awful gang and give in to their demands?

The day no longer seemed as bright. She needed to go home and sit with Zingo until the urge to help Treyvon or apply for the counseling position passed.

Her heart wasn't ready for either.

Maybe a boring desk job was the way to go.

Chapter Seven

Bringing Wyatt to visit Chase was the right decision, wasn't it?

Drew studied the visitation room at the correctional facility. One wall was painted bright blue with a mural of fish. A bookcase with picture books and several tiny chairs were under it for small children. The rest of the room was filled with round tables with seating for two or three people. He, Wyatt and Chase sat at one of the tables. After the two-hour drive, they'd dropped Lauren off at a nearby mall before traveling the last few miles here.

"You doing better in school?" Chase had teared up initially at seeing Wyatt, but after a few sniffs and a quick wipe of his eyes, he'd gotten down to business. "Are you keeping up with math? Reading books?"

"School's done." Wyatt hugged his arms tightly around his body. "I don't need to read."

"You have to keep up with reading over the summer." Chase's eye twitched. "Drew will take you to the bookstore. Pick out some good books for you."

Wyatt glared, then averted his gaze.

"What was that look for?"

"Reading is boring. I'm playing football."

Drew could practically hear Wyatt completing the thought, *Just like you, Dad.*

"No. Absolutely not." Chase shook his head.

"That's not fair." Wyatt brought his hands, balled into fists, on the table. "Levi wants me on his team. His dad is the coach. It's flag football. I won't get hurt."

Drew exchanged a charged look with Chase and gave his head a slight shake.

"We can talk about it more later, Wyatt," Drew said. "Why don't you tell your dad about yesterday's end-of-school-year picnic?"

Wyatt sighed, answering Chase's questions in monosyllables. Maybe coming here was a mistake. Drew would do about anything to talk to Lauren right now. He needed advice. Or reassurance. Maybe both. But he'd had to check in his phone at the front desk when they arrived. He and Wyatt had signed in and gone through the security procedure with the other visitors. Wyatt had grown quieter with each passing minute, and his discomfort seeped around him like a bubble full of jelly. Drew could have reached out and touched it.

"Lauren and I are going to play tennis next week. I've never tried it before, but I'm pretty sure I'll beat her…"

Drew raised his eyebrows at that one. At least Wyatt was talking without the huge chip on his shoulder.

"So this Lauren, you like spending time with her?" Chase's smile was tender as he listened to Wyatt.

"Yeah. She's awesome. But she listens to awful music."

"You'll have to introduce her to George Strait."

Chase grinned at Wyatt, who grinned right back. "Show her some good music, right?"

"Yeah." Wyatt grew serious. "Are you doing okay here, Dad?" His forehead creased in worry.

Chase blinked. "Well, uh, it's not bad. I have a schedule, kind of like with football. I do things at certain times, and I work out. I have time to read, too."

"You're reading on purpose?" Wyatt grimaced. "Why?"

"I'm filling my mind with good stuff. All those years playing football were busy. I never took the time to slow down. I've got time on my hands now, and I've got questions."

Wyatt looked confused.

"The books I'm reading are helping me answer some of those questions."

Wyatt chewed on his bottom lip.

"Wyatt, will you do one thing for me while we're apart?"

He stared expectantly at Chase.

"Fill your mind with good stuff." Chase's chest expanded, and he leaned back in his chair. "I'm praying for you. Keep going to church. Listen to Drew. And put in some George Strait for Lauren."

"I wish you were coming home with us, Dad." Wyatt's face fell. "Then I could play football and—"

"You're not playing football. Period. End of story."

The guard announced the visit was over. Chase looked emotional as they left. Wyatt didn't make a peep until they finished their paperwork and were halfway to the mall to meet Lauren.

"It's not fair," Wyatt said.

"What isn't fair?" Drew ached to pull over and hold

Wyatt, but the boy's stiff-as-a-steel-rod posture probably wasn't ready to accept a hug. He didn't blame the kid. Visiting the prison had been difficult for him, too, and he was a grown man. Between the guards stopping them on their way into the parking lot, the metal detectors, pat down, sign-in process, limited contact and strict rules throughout the visit, Drew felt completely and utterly exhausted.

"Why does Dad have to be in jail? He didn't do anything wrong."

"He did do something wrong, Wyatt."

"I would have done the same thing."

"I hope not."

Wyatt stuck his bottom lip out and turned away to face the window.

"Look, that wasn't easy, going to see him. It will be easier next time."

"I'm not going back."

Drew's stomach dropped. "Why not?"

"He wouldn't even listen. He doesn't care. I wish I could live with you forever, Uncle Drew." The last words were practically spat out.

Drew scratched his head. Why would Wyatt feel that way? Drew thought the visit had gone pretty well, all things considered.

"He cares about you." Drew kept his tone low. "He loves you."

When Wyatt didn't respond, he tried to figure out what to say to get through to him. He couldn't shake the feeling his quest to make life normal for Wyatt had just taken two enormous steps back. Thankfully, the mall entrance was up ahead. Maybe Lauren would have some insight in how to fix this. Whatever it was.

* * *

Lauren tapped her fingernails against her empty smoothie cup and stretched to see if Drew and Wyatt had arrived. Drew had texted her ten minutes earlier to say they were on their way. The sitting area in the center of the mall had comfortable faux leather chairs and was filled with busy shoppers.

She had a bad feeling about the visit. The first time was always hard on kids. As much as she didn't want the inconvenient feelings of caring about Wyatt, she had them. She cared deeply about him. And she knew he was hurting. She just knew it.

As soon as she spotted Drew's dark cropped hair above the crowd, she weaved through the shoppers on her way to them. Even fifteen feet away Wyatt looked pale and miserable. Her chest tightened. How she wanted to take his pain from him.

Not caring about the people trying to get through the aisles, she stopped directly in front of Drew and took Wyatt in her arms. She held him tightly, kissing the top of his head. He melted into her arms, his small shoulders shaking as he began to cry.

She met Drew's eyes over Wyatt's head. She mouthed, "Give him a minute." He nodded. Drew's face was taut, his easygoing manner nowhere to be found. The visit must have done a number on both of them.

Chase, you stupid jerk. If you only knew what you did to these two. I want to wring your neck.

"It's okay, Wyatt," she whispered, holding him tightly. She'd never let him go. "It's okay."

He sniffled and, keeping his head down, tried to wipe his eyes. *Poor baby.* Probably was afraid to let

Drew see his tears. Tears of her own sprang up. Why did kids have to have parents in jail? *Why?*

"Come on, honey. Let's go somewhere private." She straightened, keeping her arm around him, and led him toward the entrance of an upscale store. She'd scoped it out earlier. They rode the escalator in silence with Drew behind them, and she took them to the corner, where a nice restroom and lounge were tucked away. She kept Wyatt close to her on a sofa, and Drew sat in a chair across from them.

"You were brave today, Wyatt." She took his hand in hers and squeezed. He leaned his head against her upper arm. "I mean it. It takes a strong person to visit a prison."

Drew cleared his throat. "You would have been proud of him, Lauren. He didn't flinch when the guards patted us down."

"Well, that wasn't a big deal." Wyatt sat up. Lauren wanted to tuck his head back on her arm, but she was glad he seemed to be recovering. Instrumental music played softly around them, and the scent of lilac from the nearby candle section filled the air.

"It is a big deal," she said. "I'm guessing Drew begged them not to touch him. He probably swatted their hands away."

"Guilty." He grinned, but it didn't quite reach his eyes. "I don't like people patting me down."

"I don't, either." Wyatt folded his hands in his lap. "I wish…"

Drew's mouth tightened into a thin line.

"What?" Lauren prodded.

"I wish he wasn't in jail."

"I wish he wasn't, either," she said.

"He doesn't even care."

Drew opened his mouth, but she shook her head as nicely as possible to cut him off.

"About what?" She kept her voice quiet, soothing.

"About me. He won't let me play football. He doesn't care I only got to see him for a little bit and twenty billion people were in the room. He doesn't care we don't play video games. I miss our old house."

Wyatt's body throbbed with pent-up anger. She feared touching him would make him snap, sending him into a million pieces.

"He cares," Drew said. "Trust me when I say he would do anything to live with you and play video games and hang out with you again. He just can't."

"Drew's right, Wyatt, but you still have every right to be angry about it."

Wyatt dropped his face in his hands, and his body shook with quiet sobs. Lauren wrapped her arms around him. "It's okay. Let it out."

As she held him, Drew stalked to the archway. If Wyatt's demeanor screamed "shattered," Drew's shouted "in over my head and angry about it." He thrust his hands in the pockets of his jeans and rocked back on his heels, a grim expression on his face.

Lauren reached into her purse and grabbed a tissue. She handed it to Wyatt, and he wiped his eyes and blew his nose. When he seemed like he had himself together, she tipped his chin up with her hand and looked into his eyes.

"I'm glad you're not holding it in."

He nodded.

"Remember, it's good to cry when you're sad. When you're ready, why don't we go somewhere fun to eat?"

She tilted her head to see what Drew thought about her proposition. His lips parted and he nodded.

"Your choice, Wyatt."

Wyatt wiped his nose one last time and threw the tissue away.

Lauren took a deep breath. *Thank You, Lord, for letting me be here today. Thank You for letting me be part of his life, even if it's only for a few months.*

"Do they have a Dave & Buster's here?" Wyatt asked.

"Dave & Buster's it is."

Three hours later Drew checked the rearview mirror. Wyatt had fallen asleep. After pizza and more games than Drew could count, they'd hit the road to drive home. The sun descended bright and beautiful in the sky, a welcome reminder of God's daily blessings.

"I can't begin to thank you." He glanced at Lauren. "Thank you. Thank you."

"I should be thanking you. I was glad I could be there for him." Her sweet smile landed right in his heart. Even across the seats he could smell her tropical perfume.

"I'm so far in your debt it's not even funny." He shook his head, feeling lighter than he had all day. "How did you know how to handle him? I had no idea what to say. He was so mad when we left the prison, and I thought the visit went pretty well. Shows you how much I know."

"I'm sure the visit did go fine." She shifted to face him. "Seeing your parent in jail brings out emotions you have no control over. It's not something most people have to do. It's confusing."

He hadn't really thought of it that way. He turned the volume of the country station down to hear her better. "Well, he claims he's not going back to visit again."

Traffic on I-94 hedged them in, forcing Drew to slow until a semi passed. What if Wyatt refused to visit Chase? The caseworker might not let Chase have custody when he was released. It would be a crime for Wyatt and his dad to be separated longer than necessary.

Lauren faced him. "Was it awkward between Chase and Wyatt? Did they seem uncomfortable? What was their conversation like?"

Impressions of the visitation room came to mind. Unspoken emotions had bounced off every person in there, including him. "We all sat at a table. Chase wants Wyatt to read more."

She chuckled. "I'm sure he took that well."

"Yeah, right. He doesn't see the point in reading." He grinned, glancing her way. Man, she was pretty. *Eyes on the road, Gannon.* "He mentioned football, and Chase barely let him finish. It was just no, and that was it."

"Wyatt probably didn't like that."

"Nope."

"Anything else?"

"Not really. We talked about normal stuff. Nothing newsworthy."

She brightened. "I'm guessing Wyatt's reaction was pure nerves. Maybe some anger mixed in. He'll change his mind about visiting Chase. It might take time, though. Are you willing to wait?"

"I'll wait as long as I need to. Wyatt and Chase were always close. I don't want that to change." The vehicles were driving at a normal speed again, allowing him to relax his grip on the steering wheel. "You know a lot about this. Did you visit your dad in jail?"

"No. I have no memories of him."

No memories of her father? He frowned. "So I'm assuming when he went to jail your parents adopted you?"

"Not quite." Her gaze remained level. "Apparently, my birth mother raised me until she died—I was three at the time—and then I went to foster homes."

Homes. Plural. The conversation was starting to bother him, but he needed to know more.

"How many are we talking about?"

She drew her knee up and rested her chin on it, tilting her head slightly. "Five."

"Five?" He hadn't meant to bark. "Why so many?"

Her smile faded. "The first was temporary because I had nowhere to go when my mom died of an overdose. I think I was there a few months. I don't remember. The next one I lived in for two years, but they had twins and another baby on the way, and I guess it was too much. I didn't live at number three for long. And number four wasn't a good fit, but they were friends with the Pierces, so it worked out for the best."

"When did they adopt you?"

"I was seven." Her face grew pensive. "Do you remember the day we walked to City Park? You told me about college."

He nodded.

"That afternoon I went to my closet to look for a file. I found my old duffel bag. It's stained, ripped and purple."

Where was she going with this? Who cared about an old purple bag?

She continued, "My earliest memories are of shoving all my clothes, every tiny thing I owned—and I didn't own much—into that bag each night."

"Why did you do that?"

"I never knew when a social worker would show up and take me to a new home. It took me over a year of living with the Pierces before I trusted them enough to unpack it."

It was as if someone had shot staples into his chest. Hard to imagine the amazing woman next to him as a child so prepared to move constantly she'd kept a packed bag. "That's terrible, Lauren."

"It's why I am who I am. I wanted to help kids like me. But…" She shrugged. "Guess that didn't work out so great, either. I think I'll always be the little girl with a packed bag, waiting to be shuffled off to another home."

If an exit or rest stop had been nearby, he would have taken it. This wasn't a conversation for his truck. He wanted to comfort her, hold her. But the cars whizzing past kept his hands planted on the wheel.

"You're so much more than a little girl getting shuffled off. You see that, don't you?"

She stared out the front windshield, her shoulder lifting slightly.

"You understood what Wyatt needed today."

"Anyone would have done the same."

"That's not true. I wish you'd stop doing that," he said. "Wyatt needed you today—I needed you today—and you came through for us. That matters. It matters to me."

"Don't count on me, Drew. I might not be there next time."

He ignored her words, catching the fear clouding her gray eyes. He'd asked a lot of her ever since moving back to Lake Endwell, and he hadn't given much back in return.

What did he have to give? He'd admired his memories of her, but the adult Lauren next to him was more—so much more—than he'd imagined.

He didn't have anything she needed, but he could give her his friendship. With no strings attached. Good for life. No matter what, he would be there for her if she needed him.

"Lauren, I will never forget what you've done—what you're doing—for Wyatt." *And for me.* "I care about you, and I never want you to feel like that little girl with the duffel bag again. I'm here for you. Whatever you need, I'll be here."

Her throat moved as she swallowed.

"I don't need—"

"I know what you're doing." He glanced over at her. "You can push me away all you want, but I'm here for you. Always. That's a promise, and I'm not budging."

He was falling for her. He knew it. He wasn't stupid enough to think he had a chance with her, but her friendship meant a lot to him. And he *would* do everything in his power to make sure she never felt unwanted again.

Chapter Eight

"I never expected Drew Gannon to be so..." Lauren searched for the right word and set a plate in front of Megan before sitting across from her the next evening. The windows in her apartment were open to let the breeze inside. Zingo looked up at her and meowed. The cat thought he wanted people food, but every time she offered, he turned up his nose and stalked away, tail high. *Picky thing.*

"Sooo...what?" Megan rubbed her hands together and eyed the chicken Caesar salad Lauren had thrown together.

"So understanding. And patient." Lauren fluffed the salad with tongs. She kept seeing his kind eyes. The way he'd tried so hard to make Wyatt feel better playing games at the restaurant. Then there was his profile—handsome, strong—in the truck last night. And his words... Her heartbeat sped up. "He really surprises me."

"Ben said he's great to work with. Humble but not afraid to take charge. A lot of the guys look up to him, not that they'll stop ribbing him anytime soon."

"I could see why they would think that." She chewed a bite of the salad.

"Am I sensing a romance?" Megan waggled her eyebrows.

"No. I'm helping Wyatt. Just for the summer." But Drew's promise had replayed in her mind roughly a thousand times since he'd said it last night. Could someone make a promise like that? No matter how much she pushed him away, he'd always be there for her? As much as the thought filled her with hope, she was realistic. She pushed people away for their own good. Including Drew.

"Mmm-hmm." Megan bit into a crouton. "Yum. This is so good."

"Thanks. I made the croutons myself." Lauren enjoyed playing around with recipes. She hadn't had the time or energy to cook much in Chicago. "How is it going with Ben?"

"We went to a movie yesterday. He invited me to dinner next week."

"Sounds promising."

"Yeah, I like him." Megan grinned. "We should double date sometime. You and Drew and me and Ben."

Lauren lifted her gaze to the ceiling. "I'm not dating Drew."

"Why not? He's supercute, seems to like you and he's available."

And he'd unwittingly gotten her to tell him things she'd never told anyone before. Things he could use against her. Scary things. He might say she couldn't push him away, but he was wrong. At some point he'd add up everything she'd revealed, and she wouldn't have to push him away. He'd leave on his own, and then where would she be?

Not heartbroken—not if she could help it.

She needed to get Megan off this topic, pronto. "What do you think about me as the varsity cheerleading coach?"

Megan dropped her fork. "I think it would be fabulous! Did you apply for the job or something?"

"No, not yet. Joanna told me I'd have a better shot at it if I worked for the school. And I chatted with Principal Gilbert at the pancake breakfast while you were making googly-eyes at Ben. She's interested in interviewing me for a guidance counselor position."

"Well, there you go." Megan threw her hands up as if the solution was obvious. "You'd be an amazing counselor, and you'd be an awesome cheer coach. Isn't it great how this worked out?"

"Whoa there, lady." Lauren stabbed a forkful of lettuce. "I haven't applied for either job, and who knows if I would get them?"

"*I* know. This is ideal. Please tell me you're considering. After dinner, we should go through the application."

Lauren had to admit both jobs appealed to her. Lake Endwell was safe and tame compared with Chicago. The teenagers she'd be working with wouldn't be recruited to gangs or shot dead on the sidewalk two blocks from their homes.

"I guess it couldn't hurt to apply. It's not as if I have to take the job. And she might hire someone else."

"Right." Megan's knowing smile made her chuckle.

"I know you think it's a done deal, but my life usually doesn't work that way."

"We'll see about that."

Lauren had discussed the position with her mom earlier in the afternoon. Mom and Dad thought she'd be smart to apply and that the job would suit her. But she hadn't confided all her fears to them. They knew she'd left Chicago because of the boys, but she hadn't told them everything. How guilty she felt about it.

Megan pointed her fork at Lauren. "You have all these credentials, and you're great at knowing what to do or say when anyone is going through a rough time. I'd love to see you using your talents—all of them— right here in Lake Endwell."

The backs of Lauren's eyes prickled. Megan thought all that? "I have no plans to leave Lake Endwell. When I moved back it felt like I was taking the easy way out, trying to escape my mistakes, but I knew being close to Mom and Dad would help me recover, and I was right. Now I can't imagine not living near them. And I have to admit while I'm enjoying my time off when I'm not with Wyatt, it's getting boring. I definitely need a new career."

"Good." Megan reached over and squeezed her hand. "Let's get a résumé together and fill out the application."

How many years had she longed for good friends like Megan and Drew? And now she had them.

If Drew meant what he said…

He might have good intentions, but he could turn out to be a seasonal friend.

She hoped not. She'd have to wait and see.

"Gannon. You're riding with Ludlow on the LSV today." Chief Reynolds barked out everyone's duties Tuesday morning, and they dispersed.

Drew wished his probation period was over so he could drive the ambulance again. He and Tony usually

didn't talk much, but he could sense a grudging accep-
tance from him. As for the other firefighters, Drew still
heard a lot of stupid comments about failing at college
football or someone droning on about the good old days
playing for Lake Endwell High. He'd conditioned himself not to respond.

Sometimes he felt as though the only people who really knew him were Chase and Lauren.

"I'll be in the supply room if you need me." Tony
hitched his chin toward the door at the end of the hall.

"Sounds good. I'm going to knock out a few things
on my list." Drew went upstairs to the weight room.

He'd talked to Chase last night. Wyatt had refused
to come out of his room for the phone call. Drew had
to break it to Chase that Wyatt was upset after the visit.
The silence on the other line had stabbed at him, but
eventually Chase had begun talking. He'd told Drew
he'd been thinking about his life a lot and all the mistakes he'd made. He was studying the Bible, and he'd
broken his silence with the press to talk to a reporter
from *People* magazine. He wanted other people to learn
from his mistakes.

That was good and all, but it didn't exactly help
Wyatt out now. The kid had barely talked or eaten the
past two days. It was as if Wyatt had reverted back to
the withdrawn boy Drew had driven into town.

Drew stretched his neck from side to side to loosen
the building tension. He'd better call Lauren and find
out if she was faring any better with Wyatt.

He could still see her big smile in his truck the other
day. She'd revealed so much—more than he ever expected—and he meant what he'd told her. He owed her
and not in a let's-get-this-over-with-and-let-me-pay-you

way. He owed her for trusting him when she had no reason to. For giving Wyatt the comfort Drew hadn't realized he needed. For being generous with her time and emotions even though it cost her.

He now knew how much caring about other people cost her.

And he was falling for her because of it.

Alarms beeped through the speakers. Listening to the call, he ran down the stairs to the ambulance. Pulled on his gear as Tony joined him. They both listened to the directions and prepared to leave. Chest pains, possible heart attack. Didn't sound good.

"I know that address." Tony's voice hardened. "My uncle lives there."

"Then we'd better get there quickly." Drew mentally prepared as Tony drove the fastest route available. "Can you handle this?"

"I'm on this call for a reason."

"We'll take care of him. Is he married?"

"Yeah, Aunt Luann is probably a wreck."

"Are you sure you're okay? I know this is your uncle, and you're probably tempted to take the lead."

"It's my uncle. I should take the lead." His face reddened.

"No. We stick to the plan. You're going to have to trust me. If anything goes wrong, you can blame me forever, but I've been doing this for almost ten years. I'm just saying I'm detached." Drew raised his eyebrows. The address was a few miles away.

"Okay. Gannon, so help me—"

"You can kill me. I get it." Drew nodded grimly. This was about more than being accepted in Fire Station 4, although Tony's feelings toward him teetered on the edge of a cliff. The next hour would determine the fate of Tony's uncle's life. *God, I need Your help. Help us save this man.*

"What interests you?" Lauren dragged her finger along the spines of the middle-grade books at Lake Endwell Library. The scent of magazine pages and old books filled the air. She hadn't seen Wyatt since the prison visit. So far the day had been full of monosyllables, shrugs and mopey looks. Everything in her yelled to ask him how he was feeling now that it had been a few days since visiting Chase, but she knew better than to push. At least not yet.

"Nothing here." Wyatt scuffed his toe on the carpet, his face as sullen as his voice.

"Nothing interests you? Not one thing?" She straightened, crossing her arms over her chest and tapping her foot. "That is just sad."

Nothing really interested her here, either. She wasn't much of a reader, but she wasn't about to tell Wyatt that.

Her thoughts kept returning to her future. She and Megan had spent a few hours last night working on the online application for the high school counselor position. But she hadn't pressed Send. Couldn't. Not yet.

Maybe not ever.

She didn't know if working with teens and all their complexities would be wise. Every time she told herself Lake Endwell was different, the reality of teen problems—bullying and suicide and broken families—filled her mind.

"What about an adventure novel?" She selected a book about pirates. "This seems interesting."

He refused to look at it.

"Oh, I've got it. Perfect for you." She held up a pink book with a princess on the cover. Wyatt's glare could have frozen a fiery comet. "Okay. Maybe not. Do you like comics? They have graphic novels. Or magazines?"

"I'm not reading. Just because *he* wants me to doesn't mean I have to."

Ahh... That *he* was as loaded as the baked potato she'd piled high with toppings for lunch. Chase.

"You don't want to read because your dad wants you to?"

"I don't have to listen to him. He's not here."

Lauren weighed her options. Wyatt wasn't in the right mental state to get books, and he clearly needed to discuss his feelings about his dad. "Come on—let's get out of here and get ice cream."

"Finally." He zoomed straight to the entrance.

Out in the warm sun, robins flew back and forth between the lawn and trees along the sidewalk. She strolled in the direction of JJ's Ice Cream three blocks away. Green grass lined the sidewalks. It felt good to be wearing shorts and walking outside on a beautiful summer Michigan day. If only the conflicted boy next to her could catch some of that feeling, too...but that would be doubtful considering the conversation she needed to have with him.

"Why don't you think you should have to listen to your dad?" She kept her tone even and her gaze straight ahead.

"He's not here." His legs marched next to hers, and she inwardly sighed at the pent-up anger punctuating each step.

"No, he's not. He still loves you, though. He's your dad."

"Some dad," he said under his breath. It went straight to her heart. She knew. She'd been on the merry-go-round of emotions about her biological parents countless times growing up. They reached a small public area with a shaded lawn, benches and a fountain surrounded by pink-and-purple flowers.

"Let's sit here a minute." She took a seat on the bench facing the fountain.

"I thought we were getting ice cream."

"We will." Lauren patted the spot next to her. The water gurgled, and tall oaks towered over the area. Wyatt dropped onto the bench. She tipped her head and smiled at him. "You're mad at him, huh?"

"No, I don't care." He made it sound as if his dad being incarcerated made no difference to him.

"I think you do. It's okay to be mad. He let you down."

"He did not!" Wyatt glared up at her with a glint of vulnerability in his eyes. "He had to do it."

"What did he have to do?" She knew what he was alluding to, but she wanted him to verbalize it.

He reached down and picked a blade of grass, smashing it in his fingers.

"Wyatt, I want to hear you say it."

The grass dropped from his hand. "He had to get even with that guy."

Lauren weighed her options. Wyatt's one-track mind made sense to her, but his actions conflicted with what he said. If she pointed it out to him, he'd get defensive. Maybe she could guide him to the truth without stating it.

"What if he hadn't gone after him?" She watched his reaction. His legs were bent so the toes of his athletic shoes just touched the sidewalk under the bench.

"He had to."

"What if he hadn't?" Should she keep pushing?

His skinny knees bounced under his basketball shorts. "Len would have gotten away with it."

"What if Chase had contacted the police with Len's whereabouts instead of going after him?"

His little jaw shifted. "Then we'd still be in Detroit, and we'd live together, and I wouldn't have to visit him in prison. I'd see him every day. I'd be playing with my friends and going to my old school."

"You miss all that. I don't blame you," she said. "Your dad made a choice, and you got hurt by it."

"He did it for my mom."

"And what about you?" she asked quietly.

"I would have gone after him, too." Wyatt turned away from her. For a minute she thought she'd gotten through to him, but he wasn't ready. Maybe it gave him comfort to cling to the idea his dad *had* to take the law into his own hands.

Lord, please open Wyatt's heart to the truth. Let him see and accept his dad made a mistake.

"Well, we all make choices. Sometimes we make the right ones, and sometimes we make the wrong ones."

"He made the right one."

"Did he? Making the right choice isn't always easy."

"How do we know what's right and what isn't?"

Lauren hesitated. "Does Drew take you to church?"

"Yes." His stomach gurgled.

"Let's talk while we walk." She stood again, and they strolled in the direction of the ice-cream shop. "Tell me what you know from going to church."

"Dad and Uncle Drew always say your heart knows

the right thing to do. Your conscience tells you when you're doing the wrong thing."

"That's true. Your conscience guides you."

"And Dad and Uncle Drew told me being loyal is important."

"Yes, it is. But being loyal and blindly agreeing with someone's actions aren't the same things. You know it's normal to be mad at your dad, right? I was mad a lot before my parents adopted me."

"I'm not mad."

"Are you sure about that?" She stepped over a raised crack in the sidewalk. "I'd be mad if I couldn't see my dad every day. Or if I had to go to a correctional facility to see him."

"I thought you didn't get to see your dad every day. He was in prison. Did you visit him, too?"

"I was talking about my adoptive dad. My real dad— no, I never met him." They stopped at a crosswalk until the traffic light changed. "Your dad loves you, Wyatt. My real dad never wanted me. Your dad does. He loves you."

Wyatt stared across the street, and the color drained from his face.

"What's wrong?" She kneeled and put her hands on his shoulders. "Wyatt, are you okay?"

He blinked, his mouth opening and shutting. She checked back over her shoulder and saw a man with a camera jogging around the corner of the dentist office, where bushes swayed. Had that man just taken their picture? She thought back to what Wyatt and Drew had said about reporters.

Fury boiled her blood. How dare they? How could anyone sneak around and hide to take an innocent little kid's picture? Weren't there laws about this?

If there weren't, there should be.

"Come on." She held his hand tightly. "You do not have to worry about some jerk taking your picture. Not if I have anything to say about it."

"Wh-what are you going to do?" His voice shook, and his fingers seemed so small in hers.

"First, we're going to the police. Then we're telling your uncle Drew."

Wyatt wrapped his arms around her waist and hugged her as if he never wanted to let her go. She stroked his hair, her heart hurting that some insensitive photographer would prey on a wounded child to make a buck.

"It's okay, Wyatt. You're safe with me."

He looked up at her through scared eyes and whispered, "Thanks."

She leaned down and kissed the top of his head. How could she make a statement like that? *You're safe with me?* What if he wasn't?

She'd have to do everything in her power to back that statement up.

I don't have to do this alone.

For months her prayers had been sporadic. Sure, she'd prayed for Wyatt a few minutes ago, but how long had it been since she'd opened her Bible? Attended church? She might pray now and then, but she wanted more.

And right now she needed power. God's power.

This was for Wyatt, and she refused to let him down.

Lord, please protect Wyatt from predators and give me the strength and wisdom to protect him, too.

Drew leaned his forehead against his forearm propped against the wall in the locker room. This morning felt an eternity away. When they'd arrived at Tony's uncle's house, the man had shown clear signs of a heart attack, but he was alive. Drew immediately went to work. They followed protocol, stabilizing him and getting him to the emergency room in record time. Last they'd heard he was recovering from an emergency angioplasty. Tony had stayed at the hospital with his aunt, and the station had called Amanda to fill in for him.

He wanted to drop on the couch and forget today had ever happened.

It had been packed with one call after the other, including a minor car accident and an interior fire, where he'd treated an elderly woman for smoke inhalation. The firefighters had gotten her out quickly, but she'd been unconscious. He and Amanda had done everything in their power to clear her airways and get her breathing, but she'd been pronounced dead at the hospital.

An electrical short. A seventy-eight-year-old woman.

He couldn't make sense of it. The fire department had gotten to the scene within minutes. The search-and-rescue unit made it in and out with no problems. Her 1940s bungalow had survived with minor damage.

Why had she died?

Why hadn't he and Amanda been able to save her?

"Drew, there's someone here to see you." One of the guys stood in the doorway of the locker room.

"Be right there." He rubbed his face with both hands, straightened and took a deep breath. He tried to clear his head as he strode down the hall, but the woman's sunken cheeks, closed eyes and frail body hooked up to oxygen kept invading his thoughts.

He'd failed that woman.

Lauren stood in the kitchen, a lighthouse against a stormy sea. Without a thought, he closed the distance between them and took her in his arms. He held her tightly, pressing his cheek against her soft golden hair.

"What happened, Drew?" Her concern drove through his muddled brain, forcing him to step back. Reluctantly he let her go.

"It was a hard day." Pressing his finger and thumb into the bridge of his nose, he scrambled to get his emotions in line. *Get it together, Gannon.* "Why are you here?"

"You look awful." Lauren ran her hand down his arm. "I wouldn't bother you, but… Is this a good time to talk? Or is that allowed?"

He looked at his watch. Almost five. "Now's a good time." Only then did he realize Wyatt wasn't there. "Where's Wyatt?"

"He's at my parents' house."

Drew gently took her arm and led her down the hall and outside to a nearby bench. "What's going on?"

"Wyatt and I were walking from the library, and we saw a man with a camera across the street." She sat and shifted to face him.

Her words filled his gut with dread. "I take it he wasn't a tourist?"

She shook her head and tendrils of hair escaped her ponytail, framing her face. "Tourists don't usually creep around the bushes of the dentist office."

Things clicked into place. Chase hadn't talked to the press in months, but the fact that he was speaking to *People* magazine had probably gotten leaked, bringing out the bottom-of-the-pond suckers who made their living taking pictures to sell to tabloids. He brought both hands to the back of his head and leaned back, trying not to freak out. "And Wyatt? He saw the guy?"

She nodded.

"Then what?"

"He was shaken up. We marched to the police station, and I talked to an officer." Her gray eyes grew darker than storm clouds, and her pretty chin tipped up. "If you think I'm going to let some scumbag prey on Wyatt, you are wrong. You should have seen his face, Drew. He was terrified. I can't stop fantasizing about finding that guy and slapping him upside the head and telling him exactly how I feel—" Her eyes widened, and she frowned. She lowered her voice. "Sorry. Got carried away there. I'm just not putting up with anyone scaring Wyatt. He has enough to deal with."

All Lauren's righteous indignation drove out the defeat he'd been feeling earlier. He not only liked this warrior side of her; he needed it. Needed her strength right now. With her flushed cheeks and flashing eyes, he could picture her confronting a photographer. He could almost feel sorry for the guy if it ever happened.

"*You* are terrifying." He dragged his gaze from her lips.

Chin high, she sniffed. "Are you making fun of me?"

His lips curved upward. Her nervous glance his way only made his grin grow. "I'm not. I'm admiring you."

"Well, don't." Her back stiffened all prim and proper. One little tug and she'd be in his arms. What a mistake that would be. He had to stop thinking about her in a more-than-a-babysitter way.

"What did the police say?" His voice sounded husky, and he didn't care. He knew what she was going to say—he'd been to the police many times on Wyatt's behalf.

She folded her leg so the knee was on the bench between them. Her face grew animated. "Get this. They told me there isn't anything they can technically do. It's legal for anyone to take Wyatt's picture when we're out in public. I told the officer that was the stupidest thing I'd ever heard. I asked about stalking laws and privacy and you name it." She rolled her eyes.

"Thank you." Her hand was on her knee, and he took it in his, tracing her thumb.

"For what? I'm so frustrated. I mean, what are you supposed to do? Keep him chained in the house? At least the police were willing to help a little bit."

He frowned, confused. The police hadn't been willing to help him back in Detroit.

"The sheriff is friends with my dad. He'll let us know if anyone sees any suspicious people hanging around town."

Ahh...that makes sense. Drew patted her hand. "It's the tourist season. There will be a lot of people hanging around town."

Lauren sighed. "I know. But it's something."

"You did good." He wanted to close the inches between them and hold her. Not in a brotherly or thankful way. No, her maternal-lioness instincts attracted him, made him want to be in her protective circle. Not that he needed protecting—it just was great having someone care enough to fight on Wyatt's behalf, too. "You are the strongest woman I've ever met."

His words were out before he thought them through. They were true. But was it wise to put them out there?

Lauren's lips opened slightly as she mulled over them. To his disappointment, she withdrew her hand.

"I'd better get over to my parents'." She uncurled her legs, and he rose with her.

More than air stood between them. Awkwardness. Attraction.

He wasn't ready for it. He doubted she even felt it.

It was time to reclaim his role. To be strong. "Thanks, Lauren, for telling me and for going to the police. Don't worry. I'll take care of it. Nothing's going to happen to Wyatt."

Her shy smile warmed him. She turned, strolling to the sidewalk leading to the parking lot. Once she was safely in her car, he went back inside. A group of guys, including Ben, stood around in the kitchen.

"I wish Lauren Pierce would drop by to see me sometime."

"Like she'd ever look twice at you, Miggs."

This was usually where Drew buried his irritation and pasted on a grin to show them all he was a good sport. Not today. He just couldn't do it today.

"A photographer was snooping around town taking pictures of Wyatt." His voice sounded loud and harsh even to his ears.

A hush fell over the kitchen.

"What are you going to do about it?" Ben asked, widening his stance.

"There's not much I can do. It's not illegal for them to take his picture if he's out in public. We had to deal with this in Detroit, too. It's one of the reasons I moved back here."

Ben pushed his chest out, cracked his knuckles and looked dead serious. "Taking pictures might not be illegal, but that doesn't mean we have to roll out the welcome mat for anyone bothering the kid."

"That's right," Miggs said. "I'll ask my cousin Marie

to let me know if anyone starts nosing around the Daily Donut."

"And we'll put the word out to our friends and families," Ben said. "I have two sisters. They know everything around here. If they hear about someone snapping pictures of him, we'll know within three seconds."

Drew fought back emotion. All of these guys who'd given him such a hard time since his first day had his back. They were his brothers. He could depend on them.

"I won't forget this." He made eye contact with each of them.

"You'd do the same for us."

"I would. Anything."

An ordinary day had gone from bad to worse, but the past ten minutes had blessed him unexpectedly.

Thank You, God, for sending me help. Lauren. My coworkers. I don't deserve it, but I'm thankful for them.

Chapter Nine

Sunday morning Lauren arrived early at church to gather her thoughts. She found a seat and soaked in the quiet peace. The space was bright and smelled of flowers and wood polish. Welcoming. Comforting. Exactly what she needed.

The past four days had been quiet. No one had seen any photographers around town, and for that she was glad. She'd finally pressed Send on the online application to be a high school counselor. Every time she thought about it, her stomach got upset, though. She'd purposely put it out of her mind as much as possible. But there were two things she couldn't get out of her mind no matter how hard she tried.

Drew. And Treyvon.

She had no idea why she couldn't get Treyvon off her mind. She'd been drawn more to Jay. Hadn't known Treyvon all that well. But he pressed against her heart more and more...

Then there was Drew. Why her brain fixated on him wasn't a mystery. He devoted his life to helping others. He loved Wyatt. He was spectacularly gorgeous.

He'd told her about how his coworkers at the station had rallied around him to protect Wyatt. What a blessing to have a community to rely on in times like this. And Drew made her feel special, like she was better than she believed. It was a heady feeling.

Lauren crossed one leg over the other. She didn't trust feelings like that. Oh, she trusted Drew. How could she not? But the way he made her feel special, their closeness—she couldn't deny it—those were the things she didn't trust. Drew was seeing her good side. What would happen when he saw the bad side? The one who unintentionally hurt kids in her care?

He'd be done with her. He wouldn't look at her like she was special anymore. That's why she couldn't succumb to the lure of him. He probably didn't know he was alluring.

Families and older couples filed into the pews around her. She flipped through her bulletin but couldn't focus. Which brought her thoughts back to Treyvon.

Fifteen. So young. And he'd tried hard to stay out of the gang life before his grandmother fell ill. Lauren had studied the reports from school. He'd gotten good grades. Was never tardy. Had excellent attendance.

Yet he was in juvenile detention until he turned eighteen.

And then what?

Where would he go? What would he do? Who was counseling him? How had Jay's death affected him? She didn't want to think about these things, but there they were. Whispering. Shouting.

He'd made a terrible mistake, but didn't he deserve a chance at a good life?

Would he have that chance?

Her chest tightened at his reality. No support system. No money. Nowhere to go after his sentence was served.

Organ music began to play, and her parents shuffled in beside her.

"You're here." Mom beamed, sitting next to her. "I'm so glad you came."

Dad sat next to Mom and leaned over to wink. "Good to see you, sweetheart."

"How's Wyatt been?" Mom whispered. "When you brought him over the other night, my heart broke at how pale he was. Dad and I want to help in any way we can. Maybe we could all go to a water park or take the boat out or something. Get his mind on fun stuff again."

"Thanks, Mom. That's a good idea. I stayed with him Friday. He's still not himself. He barely talked and seemed withdrawn." Lauren frowned. He wasn't just withdrawn. He'd been spending a lot of time by himself, and it bothered her.

Mom patted her hand. "That's understandable. The poor dear."

"Tell him I've got the telescope out," Dad said. "He can come over and look at the stars any night he wants."

"He'll like that. You busy tomorrow night?"

"We're not busy, but it's supposed to be cloudy. He wouldn't be able to see much."

"We'll figure out another time later this week."

The pastor opened the service, and Lauren sank back, ready to worship. The opening hymn was a favorite of hers.

"Have you ever had someone say the exact thing you needed to hear?" The pastor stood at the pulpit. "Maybe you were nervous about a child or a perfor-mance review, and, randomly, you ran into someone who unwittingly calmed your fears with their words. In *First Thessalonians*, chapter five, we're told to 'encourage each other and build each other up, just as in fact you are doing.'"

Is that why Treyvon had been on her mind? She'd thought not being his caseworker was the end of her season with him. But maybe she'd been wrong. Could she help him, not as a social worker but as a friend?

Did she even want to?

The service continued, and the sense of not having closure about Treyvon grew. Was it too late to make an impact on his life?

She clutched her hands together until the knuckles turned white. Would he want to hear from her? How would she go about it? It wasn't like she could show up at the detention center and demand he speak to her. She didn't want to demand anything. She wanted...

She wanted his forgiveness.

His forgiveness?

She loosened the grip on her hands. She'd told herself Treyvon was to blame for Jay's death, but she'd blamed herself, too. And she'd blamed God for letting it happen. And Jay for sneaking out late at night in a dangerous neighborhood. And his mother for being a drug addict. And his grandmother for dying.

Lord, I've blamed everyone except the garbageman, and I could probably find a way to blame him, too. None of them shot Jay, though. I want to let go of this.

The strains of another hymn flowed, and she grabbed the hymnal to join in. She didn't let her thoughts wander the remainder of the service.

Soon she followed her parents out of the church to join everyone on the lawn. Her breathing hitched when she caught sight of the back of Drew's dark head. She craned her neck—yep, Wyatt was with him. She hadn't realized they attended her church.

"Oh, there are Drew and Wyatt. Let's go say hi." Mom bustled in their direction.

"Lauren and I were just talking about you," Dad said, addressing Wyatt. "You know the telescope I mentioned? I found it in the shed and set it up. Lauren will bring you around sometime this week if you want to see the moon and stars up closer."

Wyatt's face lit with a smile. "Really? That would be cool."

Lauren met Drew's eyes. Appreciation glittered within.

"Well, I have an idea." Mom tapped her chin with her finger. "Why don't you all come to dinner at our house Wednesday night? Drew, are you working that night?"

"I have Wednesday off." Drew smiled. "We'd love to come over. If it's not too much trouble…"

"No trouble at all. Bill will grill some burgers, and we can have a bonfire. How does that sound, Wyatt?"

Wyatt nodded happily. "And we can look through the telescope then. Lauren, can we go to the library and get books out about constellations?"

She was taken aback by his animation. "Of course. We'll go tomorrow."

"Awesome!"

"Okay, let's plan on seven. See you kids then." Mom took Dad's arm. They waved and headed to the parking lot. Her parents had always gone out of their way to include people, to help others. What would they do in her situation with Treyvon?

If she had to guess, she'd say they would offer an invitation. Like the one they'd just offered to Drew and Wyatt.

Drew raised his eyebrows. "Big plans this afternoon? Wyatt and I are taking the boat out to go fishing. You're welcome to join us."

She smiled and shook her head. "Sorry. Maybe next time. I have something I need to do."

No sense in wasting time. She was writing Treyvon a letter. Today.

She just wanted the kid to know he wasn't alone. He had someone who cared about him. After that, well, it was up to God to work on Treyvon's heart.

"He hasn't stopped poring over those books you got him the other day." Drew gathered the ketchup and mustard and followed Lauren through the sliding door into her parents' house Wednesday night. They'd eaten cheeseburgers and pasta salad on the deck, and Wyatt and Bill were carrying the telescope to a clear area on the lawn. Bill claimed it was the best spot to see the stars. Lauren's mom had gone upstairs to put a load of laundry in the dryer, leaving Drew and Lauren alone to clean up. He didn't mind.

His thoughts about Chase had been troubling him lately. Part of him wanted to discuss them with Lauren, but the other part wasn't so sure.

"Wyatt? Poring over a book?" Juggling the pasta salad and an empty platter in her hands, she glanced back over her shoulder and grinned. "Better take a picture of that."

"Already did." He opened the refrigerator and found room on the shelves for the condiments. Lauren turned on the faucet and squirted dish soap in the sink. The window poured light on her features. *Beautiful.* He leaned against the counter, crossing one ankle over the other, and watched her slide plates into the soapy water.

"Well, his interest in the solar system has taken his mind off photographers." Lauren washed and rinsed the dishes and set them on the dish rack. Drew crossed over to help.

"I didn't tell him, but one of the guys at work said his sister—she works at Quick Cuts—was trimming a guy's hair, and he asked about Chase McGill and if it was true his son lived here. She didn't reveal anything to the guy, but she wanted me to know."

Lauren rinsed another dish, her bouncy demeanor sober. "I don't understand people like that. Doesn't he see what he's doing?"

"Those reporters consider celebrities fair game." Drew took the dish from her hand, their fingers touching.

"Fine. Celebrities choose their career. But their kids?" With her lips drawn together, she shook her head. "Unbelievable."

"I know. Eventually they'll realize there's no story here and leave him alone."

"They'd better."

"And we'll do everything we can to make them feel unwelcome if they do show up." Drew dried the silverware. For the past week, his coworkers had treated him like one of them. They'd been concerned about Wyatt, and they'd gone out of their way to help him protect the kid. What a change from when he'd started. "In the meantime, I was hoping Wyatt's interest in the solar system would have gotten him off this football obsession, but it hasn't."

Lauren finished the few dishes and wiped the counter. "I take it Wyatt hasn't given up on his football dreams?"

"No. He keeps bringing it up. Whining about it. Getting mad. I don't know what to do."

She folded the dishcloth over the sink. "Come on—let's talk out on the deck."

They went back outside and sat on lawn chairs. In the distance Wyatt bent to adjust the telescope and Bill crouched next to him. The green lawn spread out for almost an acre before disappearing into a tree line. What a perfect summer night. Not too hot. No mosquitoes. The sun still shining for another hour at least.

"So what did you mean about not knowing what to do? I thought you were respecting Chase's wishes." Lauren extended her legs on the chair.

Drew mimicked her, stretching his legs out on the cushion. Before moving to Lake Endwell, he'd followed Chase's instructions to the letter. But something about the move had changed him—was still changing him—and he didn't know what to do about it.

"I was. I am." He rubbed his hand over his cheek. "But lately I've been thinking Chase is wrong. I get he thinks he's protecting him, but shouldn't Wyatt have some say in his life?"

And shouldn't I?

"Do you think football will be good for him?" Lauren asked.

"I don't know. But good or bad, we learn from experience. He's just going to resent me and nurture some unrealistic fantasy about football if I don't let him try it."

"So you're worried about him resenting you?"

That's why he liked talking to her. She figured out the heart of what he was saying before he even did.

"Kind of."

"He probably will at times no matter what you do. You're his parent now. Kids don't like being disciplined." She smiled. "He'll appreciate it when he's older."

"And in the meantime he'll hate me."

Lauren swung her legs over and faced him. "This football thing. Is it about not wanting Wyatt mad at you or you wanting what's best for him?"

He swatted a fly away from his shorts. He could handle Wyatt being mad at him. The kid hadn't wanted to move here, and they'd worked through it. Homework? Same thing. This was different.

"I want what's best for him."

Lauren nodded. "I know you do."

"I just don't get why I can't make some of these decisions. I'm the one raising him for the next several years. Shouldn't I have some say?" As soon as the words were out of his mouth, he wanted to take them back. Who was he to question Chase's desires for Wyatt? It wasn't as if Drew had kids or any parenting experience. And Chase was a great dad.

"Have you talked to Chase about it?"

"Yeah, and he's as stubborn as Wyatt. I'm getting nowhere with either of them."

"Puts you in a tough spot."

It sure did. He didn't like having people mad at him. Part of him had been trying to avoid disappointing anyone ever since his college fiasco.

"Technically you're Wyatt's guardian. You can override Chase about this."

"But should I?"

"I don't know. Will it kill Wyatt not to play football? Plenty of kids get through life fine without it."

"And plenty of kids get through life fine *with* it."

"Sounds like you've made your mind up."

He sighed. "Not really."

"Have you prayed about it?"

"No." Why hadn't he prayed about it? His prayers tended to revolve around keeping Wyatt safe and helping people he loved. He rarely prayed for himself.

Why didn't he pray for himself?

Because I don't deserve anything more than I already have.

Lauren's mom slid the patio door open. "Lauren, Drew? Would you mind driving to the Bradley Farm and getting some firewood? I'll have Bill start a bonfire later. Oh, and pick up graham crackers, marshmallows and Hershey's bars. I'm hungry for s'mores."

"Okay, Mom."

Drew stood and offered his hand to Lauren. She placed her soft hand in his, and he hauled her to her feet. He caught his breath at her nearness. Tanned face, sun-kissed hair and pink lips—tempting. Too tempting.

Her eyes flickered from his eyes to his mouth, and her cheeks flushed.

Maybe she felt it, too. He stood taller, his pulse racing. How could he fight this attraction when she looked at him that way?

I don't deserve—

Wait.

Why not?

Why didn't he deserve her? Why was he so sure he was bad for her?

Because if he started believing he deserved her, he'd

give his whole heart away. And if she didn't want it, it would be worse than getting kicked out of college. And just like then, he'd have no one to blame but himself.

Lauren climbed out of Drew's truck at the farm outside town. They'd enjoyed an easy silence driving here with the windows down. It had given her time to think. About Drew's situation and how pleased she was he confided in her. She hadn't told anyone about writing Treyvon. She wasn't sure why. She'd considered telling her parents and Megan, but what if they thought it was a dumb move? Or said something she didn't want to hear? But Drew…she could tell him. He never seemed to think less of her when she confessed her secrets. Would he now?

Her sandals flapped against the gravel drive, and Drew strolled by her side as they approached a stand full of logs. A small box with a padlock and a slot for cash was attached to the side.

"One bundle or two?" Drew stopped, legs wide, before the logs stacked into dividers. Each section was considered a bundle. His muscles strained under his faded navy T-shirt, and she let out a tiny sigh at all the male strength standing in front of her. How had Megan described him? *Tall, built and studly. Yep.* That about summed it up.

"Two." She yanked a log out and carried it in both arms back to his truck.

"You don't have to do that. I can carry them." He jogged to catch up with her, motioning to take the log out of her arms.

"I've carried them a hundred times with my dad."

She kept moving until she reached the bed of the truck, dropping it in with a thunk. "It's no big deal."

He took her hand. Her heartbeat hammered. What was he doing? Gently, he flipped her hand over and trailed his finger up her forearm. She shivered.

"The wood scratched you." His fingers lingered on the tender skin. And the look in his eyes? Her heart was going to beat right out of her chest. This was the second time in less than an hour she'd thought about kissing him.

Kissing him? No way. Not smart.

"It's just a little mark. No big deal." She dropped her arms by her side. Turning, she headed back to the stand. "Did I tell you I finally applied for the counselor position at the high school?"

"That's great." His smile grew. "You still thinking about being the cheerleading coach, too?"

"I sure am." She hauled another log into her arms. He did the same. "I know I can handle being a cheer coach. And I'm feeling a little better about the counselor position. I talked with Megan about it and researched the job a bit. I know I'd be dealing with teenagers with emotional problems, but I'd also be interacting with a lot of teens who don't have those problems. From what I can tell, I'd be helping upperclassmen with college decisions and adjusting students' schedules. I think I can handle that."

"I know you can handle it." He hoisted three logs as easily as if they were rolled-up newspapers.

"Well, I still have to be interviewed. It's not a sure thing." She dropped her log in the back of the truck. "Can I tell you something?"

"Of course."

"Remember how I told you about the boys in Chicago?"

"How could I forget?" He stacked the wood in the truck bed, and they went back to the stand for another round.

"I've been thinking about Treyvon a lot."

"You still mad at him?"

"No. I'm…well, I'm worried about him. I tried to put him out of my mind, but he kept coming back. I wrote him a letter."

Drew grabbed three more logs but didn't say anything.

"I got to thinking about a few years from now. What will happen to him? He'll be out of juvenile detention, but where's he going to go? Back to his mom? Back to the gang? His brother's dead, his grandmother's dead and he has nothing to fall back on."

Drew's jaw clenched. He took big strides to the truck. She fought to keep up with him. After he stacked the remaining logs, he wiped his forehead with the back of his hand. "So what did you put in the letter?"

She brushed her hands on her shorts. "I apologized. For not getting him and Jay out of the house sooner. For not finding them a safe environment. I told him I blamed myself for failing him and Jay, and I told him about my childhood. I checked with the detention center. They won't let him call me, but he can write. I sent writing supplies and stamps. Told him to write back if he wanted to."

"That's all?" They stood behind the truck. He cocked his head to the side.

"Isn't it enough?"

"For a minute there I thought you were going to say you invited him to live with you when he gets out."

She hadn't thought about it. "And if I had?"

"I'd worry." He stepped closer to her.

"Yeah?" Her pulse took off in a sprint.

"Because he might have gone into juvie a scared kid, but he could come out a hardened man."

"I don't know what will happen to him, but I want him to know I care. I hope he writes me." She lowered her gaze to the ground.

Drew brushed the back of his hand down her hair. The touch startled her, and she stared into his eyes. Got lost in their rich brown depths.

He leaned in, his lips grazing hers. And she met him, pressing hers to his.

The kiss was the definition of Drew. Strong yet gentle. Confident and generous. All man. All Drew.

She put her palms against his chest, and without thought, slid them up around the back of his neck, getting closer to him, kissing him back. Instantly, his hands wrapped around her lower back, holding her tightly.

She was lost in a sea of sensation. The scent of his cologne, the warmth of his skin, the taste of his lips, the sound of her heartbeat thudding in her ears.

They pulled away at the same time, remaining in each other's arms.

"We shouldn't—" Lauren turned her head to the side. Kissing him, standing in his embrace felt so good. But her head shouted, *No, no, it's all wrong! Protect yourself!*

He cleared his throat. "Uh, yeah. Complicates things too much."

Her heart dropped to the gravel under her sandals.

The words were right. So why did they sound so wrong? She was falling for him. And she had no idea how to make it stop.

Drew clutched a coffee mug and watched the sun rise over the lake the next morning. He stood on the dock in front of his cottage. Pink-and-purple clouds spread into blue. Steam wreathed above his mug, reminding him to enjoy his coffee while it was hot. Speaking of heat... What had possessed him to kiss Lauren yesterday? When she'd said they shouldn't, he'd snapped back to reality. Of course they shouldn't. They were in a complicated relationship, and Wyatt was at the center. What would it do to the kid if he and Lauren started dating only to break up? Wyatt needed stability. And Drew needed...

His mind flashed to her soft lips. How magnificent she felt in his arms. He'd wanted to keep her there forever. To hold. To protect. To love.

Love. He'd never really been in love. There were a few times in his past when he'd thought he'd been, but back then the only one he'd loved was himself.

Could he say the grown him was any different?

Yes.

Where had that yes come from?

He took a tentative drink of coffee. Hot but not scorching.

I've changed. Lauren had helped him see it. He could almost believe he was worthy of loving her.

Almost.

She'd surprised him yesterday when she'd talked about writing Treyvon. He'd never thought about the kid's future. It wouldn't occur to him.

But caring was in her DNA.

He hoped the kid wouldn't disappoint her.

God, please don't let this kid be another negative in her life. Help her see her life matters. Show her she didn't fail anyone. I'm not asking for me—

He frowned. Did he always end his prayers with "I'm not asking for me"?

Yes, his prayers usually had a stipulation he wasn't praying for himself.

Okay, Lord, I am asking for me. What in the world do I do about Lauren? I care about her. A lot. It's veering toward love, and I know that's not wise. But what am I supposed to do? I'm drawn to her. I can tell her things I don't tell anyone else. And I want to spend time with her. When we're together, I feel right. Good. At peace.

He gazed out over the lake glistening under the rising sun. Calm. If he wanted to be at peace, he could feel it here. Without Lauren.

He didn't want to mess up her life. She'd said they shouldn't, and he had agreed. Better to preserve their friendship than to throw it away for a risky shot at more.

Chapter Ten

Where had Wyatt gone?

Lauren stretched her neck to see beyond the massive playground to the swings and tennis courts nearby. She and Drew had resumed their nonkissing relationship. They hadn't been talking as much, either, but it was for the best. Had it only been a week since he kissed her? She'd never be able to buy firewood from that farm again without remembering his lips pressed against hers.

Principal Gilbert had called two days ago to set up a phone interview next week about the counseling position. Apparently the school had a process, starting with a phone interview. Lauren had also signed up for a cheerleading certification course. The certification manual had arrived, so while Wyatt had been running around the play structure with a pack of boys his age, she'd studied it to prepare for the timed exam.

But now it was getting late. She needed to find Wyatt and stop at the grocery store for a few dinner items. She ambled around the perimeter of the large park. Children of all ages laughed and chased one another across the wooden bridges and slides. But she didn't see Wyatt or his friends.

An uneasy feeling came over her, but she shushed it. No need to panic. He had probably run to the bathroom without telling her.

Wyatt still wasn't talking to her as much lately. Between the prison visit and the photographer incident, she'd figured he was working through complicated issues and needed some space. He didn't have a cell phone, but he did have an iPod with an app to text his friends. Had she been wrong to let him have his space?

She broke into a light jog, looking for his light brown hair and skinny legs and black basketball shorts. Around the corner, she spotted him and the other boys lined up at the water fountain.

Relief made her stand still a moment. Of course he was there. Just getting a drink with his friends the way any ten-year-old would.

She waved to him. "Wyatt, we need to leave."

He held a finger up. The boys gathered closer to him, discussing something. She narrowed her eyes. It was so hard to know if they were good kids or schemers.

Wyatt trudged her way, flushed but not smiling.

"Did you have fun?"

"Yeah."

"Don't sound so excited." She strode across the lawn to the parking lot. He didn't crack a smile or say a word. They buckled up and drove to Lake Endwell Grocery.

"You grab a cart, while I try to remember what I need." Lauren gestured to the carts. She needed to know more about those kids he was hanging around, but his quiet, closed-off wall wasn't giving her much to work with. Maybe they could do something fun tonight, and she could figure out how to approach him later. Wyatt pushed a cart, and they weaved through the produce aisle. "So what do you want to do after dinner? We can fish on the end of the dock, play some beach volleyball or rent a movie."

He shrugged, turning away.

Okay, then. She tossed a prebagged salad mix into the cart and moved to the meat department. After selecting a package of chicken breasts and a bottle of Italian dressing, they stopped at the ice-cream aisle.

"Moose Tracks or Oreo Explosion." She pointed to the glass door.

Wyatt sighed. "Oreo Explosion, I guess."

She added a carton to the other items and continued to the checkout lanes. Wyatt walked ahead of her to the magazines, pulled one off the shelf and held it in both hands, not moving.

The headline read, "My Life in Jail." She didn't recognize the man on the cover, but the name hit her like a bucket of ice water. Chase McGill.

Wyatt dropped the magazine and covered his face with his hands. She gathered him to her, but every muscle in his little body had tensed. A tap on the arm might shatter him. Her heart filled with indignation and pity. How much more could this kid take?

"Come on—let's go outside." Lauren left the cart and looked at the checkout girl. "I'm sorry. We have an emergency. I can't buy these now."

"Did you want us to hold them?"

Lauren shook her head and hustled Wyatt out the door to her car. Her apartment was nearby, and she didn't debate it—just drove to her place, helped him up the steps and made him stretch out on the couch. Then she wet a washcloth and set it on his forehead. She sat on the other end of the couch, unlaced his sneakers and put his feet in her lap.

He hadn't said a word. Wasn't crying. He looked devastated.

Zingo strutted to the couch and hopped right onto Wyatt's stomach.

"No, Zingo. Now's not a good time." But the cat sat on Wyatt's chest, staring at his face. Wyatt reached up to pet him, and the kitty got comfortable, folded his legs and started purring.

"Can I get you anything? Do you want to talk?"

Wyatt didn't move, didn't respond. Just kept stroking Zingo's fur.

Lauren didn't know what to do. How did moms handle things like this? Well, most moms didn't have to worry about their son seeing a big photograph of his father on a magazine with a caption about life in jail. And it wasn't as if Lauren was Wyatt's mom. He didn't have one. She'd have to do for now.

Of all the selfish things to do, why had Chase chosen this? Didn't he realize how difficult life was for Wyatt? Shouldn't he know Wyatt wouldn't want everyone reading about his dad's life in jail?

What should she say? What did Wyatt need?

Lord, I don't know what to do. What do I do?

She slipped into her bedroom, shut the door and leaned against it, blowing out a breath. As the air released, she curled her hands into fists. Anger wouldn't help this situation. She massaged the back of her neck with both hands. No wonder the photographer had just happened to show up when he did. Probably knew the article was coming out and wanted to capitalize on it by selling pics to the tabloids. *Scumbag.*

She cracked the door open to peek out at Wyatt. His hands rested on Zingo, who'd fallen asleep. She tiptoed out there. Wyatt's eyes were closed, too. Probably exhausted from the playground and the shock.

Padding to the kitchen, she picked up her phone and debated her first move. Drew needed to know. She'd better call him. And she'd text Megan to pick her up a copy of the magazine. It would be better for Wyatt if they knew exactly what was in the article.

She cringed as it hit her that his friends could read it. Would they tease him? Bully him? Stop hanging out with him? She peeked at Wyatt's sweet face, her heart cracking. None of this had been easy on him, and it wouldn't get any easier if Chase didn't start putting his son first.

She returned to her bedroom, shutting the door behind her. She pressed Drew's number. If Chase were here, she'd give him a piece of her mind. But he wasn't. As usual, Drew would be left picking up the pieces of Chase's mistakes. Lauren would do anything necessary to help Drew and to protect Wyatt from his father's careless decisions.

Even if each passing day left her heart unguarded and more vulnerable where Drew was concerned.

Wyatt didn't have anyone but Drew and her. She'd be there for both of them, for as long as it took. At some point they wouldn't need her anymore, and she'd have to move on without them. But for now she was part of their lives. And she was going to let Drew know exactly what she thought of Chase's actions.

* * *

Drew sprayed the side of the fire truck one final time. He liked this part of the job, cleaning the equipment, making sure it was ready for the next call. The warm summer sun bounced off the stream of water, causing a miniature rainbow to appear. He grinned. A little reminder God was watching.

His cell phone buzzed. He turned off the hose and wiped his hands on a towel before answering. "Drew here."

"We have a problem."

Dread knotted his stomach at Lauren's tone. What could this be about? "What's going on?"

"Well, it seems your best friend thought it would be wise to have *People* magazine interview him. He obviously had no consideration for Wyatt or his feelings. I can't believe Wyatt had to see his dad's face on the cover with the headline, 'My Life in Jail.' Doesn't he have any clue how this affects his son?"

He blinked. Fury poured out of her words, but it took a moment before their impact hit him.

The *People* interview. He smacked his forehead. He'd forgotten…hadn't really given it much thought. When Chase wanted to do something, he did it. Drew never interfered. Figured he was a grown man and could make his own decisions.

"Chase told me he was doing it." Drew used his free hand to pick up the rags next to the truck.

"What?" That was a loaded word if he'd ever heard one. He'd be smart to tread carefully with Lauren in an angry mood. She continued, "And you didn't talk him out of it?"

Looking back, he should have talked him out of it.

He hadn't thought it was a big deal. Hadn't considered how it would affect Wyatt.

Why hadn't it occurred to him Wyatt would be hurt?

Because he wasn't like Lauren, who instantly recognized how events would affect others. He was always two steps behind in the consideration department, and Wyatt always seemed to be the one who paid for it.

"You're right," Drew said, throwing the rags into an empty bucket with more force than necessary. "I should have talked him out of it. I didn't think. It's my fault." And now he'd have to do damage control to a kid who'd had enough damage for a lifetime.

"Are you kidding me?" Her voice rose to new decibel levels. "Don't you dare take the blame for this. I know Chase is your friend, but come on. You weren't the one who agreed to the interview. He did. He needs to take responsibility for this. For going after that guy. For ending up in jail. For all of it!"

He held the phone an inch from his ear. Wow, she was really worked up. "Calm down—"

"Don't tell me to calm down."

"Okay." He pinched the bridge of his nose. "What do I do? I can't come over right now. I'm on duty. Do you want to bring Wyatt over here? I can talk to him. If you give me an hour, I should be able to find a replacement."

"Don't bother." Her tone softened. "He's resting. I asked Megan to buy me a copy of the magazine so we can read it and figure out the best way forward. If you want to do something, call Chase and tell him he just ruined his son's life all over again."

"Hey now. It's not like he set out to hurt Wyatt."

"I don't care what he set out to do. The result's the same."

He clutched the phone, fantasizing about throwing it a hundred yards downfield, getting the perfect spiral on it while he was at it. Man, he hated this helpless feeling.

"What's done is done," he said. "How do we move forward?"

"Megan is renting movies and bringing a pizza over to my apartment. We're going to distract Wyatt tonight. When you get home in the morning, we'll figure out our next move. Come to my apartment when your shift ends."

"I can try to get someone to cover for me tonight."

"No. We can handle him. We'll talk in the morning." She sounded as if she was going to hang up.

"Wait, Lauren?"

"What?"

"What are you going to say to him tonight?" He didn't want her bad-mouthing Chase in front of Wyatt, but how could he ask her not to? This situation grew more complicated each second.

"I don't know."

"I know you're upset with Chase, but can I ask you not to talk bad about him?"

"I'm not stupid, Drew. Chase is Wyatt's dad. Of course I'm not going to trash-talk him. I *will* be discussing choices and how they affect the ones close to us, though. Wyatt has every right to be upset with his dad."

"Fair enough."

"I'll call if anything comes up."

The phone went dead, and with a heavy step, he put the rest of the cleaning supplies away. His heart was torn. Should he ignore Lauren's advice and call someone in for him?

She could handle it. Megan could, too. Wyatt had

never had a real mother figure in his life. It would probably do the kid good to have two women fussing over
him. Besides, he had a feeling if he showed up, he'd
get a verbal lashing he would *not* enjoy. He was in the
doghouse, and he deserved it.

After he'd parked the truck back in the garage, he
went up to the living quarters and sank into a couch.
Why hadn't he thought about Wyatt when Chase mentioned the interview? Did he have to be hit over the
head with a two-by-four to realize the article would be
a bad move for Wyatt? He should have asked Chase
not to do it.

Don't you dare take the blame for this.

Drew covered his face with his hands.

Lauren was right. He'd been picking up the pieces
left from Chase's mistakes for too long. In a few
months, it would be a year since Missy had died. The
previous ten months unfolded in Drew's memory, and
anger shot through his veins. He'd nipped this rage in
the bud countless times since Chase was arrested, but
right now he had no energy left to fight it.

When Chase drove off to confront Len, Chase hadn't
thought about anyone but himself. And he continued to
make decisions based solely on his emotions. His needs.

*Oh, you wanted to be the big guy about Missy. You
didn't care about her when she lived in Chicago and
was spiraling out of control from the drugs. You never
married her, but you had to go off and avenge her
death, huh? What about us? What about me? I miss
you. You're my best friend. And Wyatt? You are everything to him, and I'm a sloppy substitute. If it wasn't
for Lauren, who knows what kind of emotional shape
Wyatt would be in right now?*

And this article—this stupid article. You feel guilty, do you, buddy? So you want the media and all your fans to see you've learned your lesson? Well, what about Wyatt? Lauren is right. What kid wants his friends to see his dad's face on the cover of a magazine with that headline?

Drew jumped to his feet and paced the room. Wanted to punch the wall.

He strode to the weight room and pummeled the punching bag until his energy drained.

"What crawled down your shorts? That bag isn't the enemy, you know." Tony stood in the doorway, his arms crossed over his chest.

Drew wiped the sweat from his forehead. "Everything."

"Drama queen." He crossed the room and gestured for Drew to follow him into the living area. "What's really going on?"

"Lauren just called—".

"Are you two dating or what?"

"Forget it." Drew glared.

Tony threw his hands up in defense. "What? You two have *couple* written all over you, but whatever. Live in denial, brother. Continue."

Drew didn't have the energy to contemplate Tony's words. "Chase is on the cover of *People* magazine."

"And you're jealous?"

"Are you kidding me? Of course not." Drew stood up so quickly his head spun. "I'm thinking about Wyatt. How would you like it if your dad was on the cover of a national magazine with a headline about being in jail?"

"Oh. That kind of cover." Tony grimaced, waving him to sit back down. "Hey, I know I give you a hard time, but I give you a lot of credit for moving back and taking care of Wyatt. It can't be easy."

"Wyatt is easy. Even if he was the worst kid in the world, he'd be easy. I love him. And, well, Chase is my best friend."

"But you're mad at him."

Drew swallowed. *Yeah.* He was. "I shouldn't be."

Tony scoffed. "Why not? I'd be mad. You went from single to legal guardian overnight. If it was me, I wouldn't want to move and leave my fire station."

"I didn't want to move. They were my brothers."

"You've got new brothers."

Drew met Tony's eyes and nodded. "I appreciate it, man."

"When you started, I was sure you were going to be the superstar quarterback who left town after high school. You've changed. You've got a lot to complain about, but you never do. The guys look up to you. I was wrong about you."

He didn't know how to respond. He'd never expected to hear those words from Tony, of all people.

"I appreciate it, Tony. But I don't have anything to complain about. I'm doing what I love with good people. I've been blessed."

"That's where we differ. I'd complain." Tony grinned. "So what's the deal with you and Lauren?"

"Nothing. She's Wyatt's babysitter."

"You don't look at her like she's just a babysitter."

"Does any guy look at her like she's just a babysitter?"

"Point taken."

Drew rubbed his chin. "She chewed me out. Big-time."

Tony chuckled. "If she's chewing you out, that's a good sign."

He shook his head. "It's not like that."

"You going to be a bachelor forever? A girl like Lauren Pierce doesn't come around that often. She's single, but for how long? You should make your move."

"I've got enough to think about without dealing with a relationship."

"Have it your way, but don't come crying to me when she starts dating someone else."

Was Tony trying to give him a stroke? Drew wanted to date her. But…if she wasn't helping with Wyatt, he'd be lost. He couldn't jeopardize their working relationship to explore a personal one. And today had driven home what he'd known all along: Lauren would never be interested in someone as selfish as him. She put other people's needs before her own. He didn't even know what other people's needs were.

If he couldn't rely on her to babysit Wyatt, he'd be back to where he started. And Wyatt would be the casualty. They both needed her. He'd lock up his attraction to Lauren and bury the key.

"How is he?"

"Sleeping." Lauren followed Drew into her living room the next morning. He held a take-out tray with three cups in one hand and a paper bakery bag in the other. She'd woken this morning calm. Life was too short to cling to anger, even if it was justified. Ultimately, her hot emotions wouldn't help Wyatt. A cooler head would.

After Wyatt woke from his nap yesterday, she and Megan had plied him with pizza and silly movies until it had grown late. They'd waited until he was asleep before reading the magazine article. She had to hand it to Chase; he sounded contrite in it.

"Where is he sleeping?" Drew tossed the bag on the table and set the drink tray down.

"He's in my office. I set up my sleeper sofa for him."

"Thank you." He put the tray down and turned to her. "I feel like such a jerk."

She craved his embrace. Hadn't realized how draining the night had been, how much she yearned for his physical support right now. But just because they acted as Wyatt's parents didn't make them anything more than a guardian and a babysitter. She had no right to step into the role of parent. And she had no right to step into Drew's arms and ask him to hold her, either. So she didn't.

"You're not a jerk. We'll handle this, and Wyatt will, too. It's probably not going to be easy for him, though. You know how awful some kids can be. They smell weakness and pounce."

"Yeah, I do. I was one of those kids. You should know." The muscle in his cheek jumped.

"And you changed." She pressed her palm to his face, meeting his eyes. "I forgave you a long time ago. Isn't it time to let it go?"

"If you say so." He passed her a coffee. "Full of cream and sugar. Just the way you like it."

He remembered how she liked her coffee? Her throat tightened. She'd been taking care of herself for years. She'd forgotten what it was like to have someone care enough to remember the little details.

She'd closed herself off for a long time. Hadn't dated. Had devoted all her energy to her job. But maybe she'd been wrong. Maybe having someone who knew the little details—someone who cared—wasn't a bad thing. Maybe this closeness—this taking care of Wyatt's needs together—was what she needed, even if it scared her.

She was getting tired of living life on her own.

Drew sat at the table and opened the bag, sliding a doughnut her way. She sat across from him.

His cheeks puffed out as he exhaled. "Before we get into this, I think you'd better know there's a chance more reporters and photographers will show up here. Articles tend to trigger something in them. The tabloids, especially. When Chase was on trial, every time an article was published, a bunch of photographers would try to get Wyatt's picture." He took a big bite of his doughnut, and when he'd finished chewing, he sipped his coffee.

Zingo trotted up to Drew and jumped on his lap. Drew stared wide-eyed at Lauren as if to say, "What do I do about this?"

"Relax. We've been through this already. It's a cat, not a bomb."

"Sure," he mumbled, petting Zingo. "So what's the plan?"

"Have you seen the article yet?"

"No."

She went to her room, found the magazine and brought it back to him.

He flipped to the article. She watched him as he read it. His eyebrows dipped; then he grunted, and the final paragraph seemed to hit him. He appeared reflective.

"I didn't realize I was mad at him until last night," Drew said softly. "I've rationalized his behavior with excuses, but I haven't admitted how angry I am that he went after Len and landed in jail."

Lauren nodded, not sure what to say. This was a huge step for him. She thought back on all the times Drew blamed himself for Chase's decisions. He'd probably never realized he had a right to be mad.

"I miss him," Drew said softly. "I miss my best friend."

"I know. And you don't have to stay mad at him." She covered his hand with hers. "What do you think of the article?"

"I think his intentions were good. I think it accurately reflects his sincere regret at taking the law into his hands and messing up his life. But I'm tired of him doing things like this without considering the effects on Wyatt. And, honestly, Lauren, if you weren't here, I think Wyatt would be a mess. It hadn't occurred to me the article would affect him. You get him in a way I don't."

He thought too highly of her. She had no idea what she was doing, and Wyatt could end up a mess in her care. She'd made bad decisions before. This job—trying to anticipate Wyatt's needs—was hard. But she wanted to do it. If she could just be sure she wouldn't fail him...

She shook her head. "He wouldn't be a mess. You're exactly what he needs. As far as the article, I agree. I think Chase had good intentions, too." She sipped her coffee and tore off a small bite of a doughnut. "I think we should let Wyatt read it."

"Okay. I have a feeling his friends are going to have a lot to say about it, too. He might lose a few of them."

The food soured in her stomach. "I know."

They sat in silence, sipping coffee. Wyatt shuffled

to the table. He rubbed his eyes and yawned. His hair stuck up in back. As soon as he saw Drew, he fell into his arms.

"Hey, buddy. How'd you sleep?"

"Good. Zingo slept with me. He's soft."

Drew kept his arm around Wyatt's shoulders. "I heard about the magazine."

"Oh." Wyatt dropped onto the chair next to him.

"Here, I bought you a hot chocolate. There's a doughnut with chocolate frosting and sprinkles in there, too."

Wyatt plowed into the pastry but stopped midchew when he noticed the magazine on the table.

"We think you should read it." Lauren slid it his way.

"I don't want to."

"Your friends might read it. It's good for you to know what you're dealing with."

"Why did he have to go and be on the cover?" His pitiful eyes tightened Lauren's chest like a screw. "I hate that he's in jail."

"We all do, buddy." Drew clapped his hand on his shoulder. "But I think Chase wants to let other people learn from his mistakes."

Lauren drank her coffee, trying not to stare at Wyatt as he turned the pages and read. When he finished, he closed the magazine and pushed it away from him.

Drew rapped on the table with his knuckles. "I have a feeling we might see more photographers and reporters over the next couple of weeks. So we're all going to be extra careful."

Wyatt slumped, but he nodded his agreement.

"And if your friends talk about the article, be honest with them." Lauren wiped crumbs from her hands.

"You don't have to answer any questions, but you don't have to pretend it didn't happen, either."

"I'm not telling them Dad's in jail."

"They all know."

"Well, I don't want to talk about it to them. I don't want any of this!" He lurched to his feet and ran to the office. Drew followed. Lauren almost did, too, but she sighed, knowing he needed to take care of it. She wasn't Wyatt's mother or guardian. If she was going to adjust to not being Wyatt's babysitter this fall, she needed to remember that.

The trouble was she didn't want to adjust to life without them. She wanted to be there for Wyatt every day. Wanted to rely on Drew in a way she'd never relied on a man.

But how could she?

He thought she was good for Wyatt, but what would happen if he realized she wasn't? If she made a poor judgment call that hurt him? He'd move on to someone else. Someone better.

She was better off alone.

Chapter Eleven

References: check. Phone charged: check. Notebook and pen: check.

Lauren's nerves were twitching like sparks from a bonfire. Her interview with Principal Gilbert was in ten minutes. They'd originally scheduled it for yesterday, but a staff meeting had forced the principal to cancel. Lauren had tried to avoid having it while she watched Wyatt; however, the principal's schedule was full. No other time would work.

"Wyatt?" He'd disappeared into his bedroom after lunch. All day he'd been secretive. Or was it her imagination? Drew told her Wyatt had met up with friends at the park the other day. Had they said something to upset him? Taunted him about the article?

If not, what was bothering him?

She straightened her papers on the kitchen counter for the tenth time. Wasn't his dad being in jail and on the cover of a national magazine enough to bother anyone? Two reporters had nosed around town over the weekend, but the people of Lake Endwell had discouraged their questions and politely suggested they leave Wyatt alone.

After knocking on his bedroom door, she peeked inside. He lay on his bed with his knees up, earbuds in and his thumbs moving overtime on his iPod. She didn't like that device. He spent entirely too much time playing video games and texting other kids. The open window allowed a breeze to ripple through the curtain.

"Hey." She stood in the doorway, arms crossed. "I'm going to be on the phone for about thirty minutes. Do you need anything now?"

He shook his head, not looking up from the small screen.

"Okay, I'll be in the kitchen if you need me. We'll do something when I'm done. We could get the inner tubes out and go swimming. How does that sound?"

He didn't bother responding. Tempted to rip the earbuds out and toss the iPod into the trash, she sighed, closing his door behind her. She missed his sweet nature. Wished the kid who'd been so excited to see the stars from her dad's telescope would come back.

Her phone rang, and she hustled to the kitchen where she'd left everything.

"Lauren, it's Principal Gilbert. Thank you for accommodating my schedule change."

She chatted with the principal about Lake Endwell High and answered questions about her degree and the type of work she'd done in Chicago.

"I'm reassured about your experience with troubled teens. Your supervisor raved about the work you did. Our community, while quiet, isn't immune to modern teen issues. We have our share of students dealing with typical problems, big and small."

"What kind of problems?" Lauren pressed her hand to her stomach.

"Suicide. Depression. Bullying. Drugs. Alcohol. The usual."

The list triggered anxieties she'd set aside for months. "Would you say you have a high percentage of troubled kids?"

"No, I wouldn't. But we do have students facing challenges, and they need an adult who will guide them appropriately. Someone they can trust."

Trust. Could teens trust her? The way Treyvon and Jay had? She still hadn't heard from Treyvon. He must blame her. She would if she were him.

She'd been a fool to think she could handle this job. What if she counseled someone and they ended up committing suicide? Could she have that on her conscience, too? Her gut churned.

"Of course, if a student seems suicidal or is caught with drugs or alcohol, you would advise the parents to seek appropriate help like therapy or a treatment program. The support you'd provide would be limited. As for the cheerleading coach position, Lake Endwell High would be blessed to have you. You're aware of what's involved?"

After taking a shaky breath, Lauren described her experience and mentioned she was in the process of getting certified. Much easier to talk about cheerleading than the other position.

"If you have any questions, please call. I'll be in touch with you soon," Principal Gilbert said. "Thanks again for your time."

She liked the principal but still wasn't sure she could see herself working at the school. Although the principal's assurance she'd be providing limited support helped. Lauren peeked at her watch. They'd talked almost an hour. She'd better check on Wyatt and get the poor kid out of here.

"Wyatt?" She knocked on his door. No answer. *Big surprise.* His earbuds might be permanently glued to his ears at this point. She cracked the door open.

The bedroom looked the same as it had an hour ago, except Wyatt wasn't there. Video games were piled next to the nightstand. A bin of LEGOS sat on the floor. Shorts and a shirt were thrown without thought next to the hamper. The window was open, and his iPod was on his bed. Maybe he'd gone to the backyard while she was on the phone.

She padded on bare feet to the sliding door and stepped onto the deck. The small backyard was fenced, and there was no sign of Wyatt. She went back inside. He could be in the bathroom.

"Wyatt?" She stilled, listening for him. "Wyatt?"

Okay, now she was getting worried. Where was he? She rushed out the front door, hoping he'd slipped out to the dock or something, but she didn't see him there, either.

Where had he gone?

Panic climbed her throat. He could have been kidnapped. Who knew what kind of crazy person had read that magazine article? Had they hatched a plan to hold Wyatt for ransom, knowing Chase was a multimillionaire athlete?

Calm down. Don't rush into worst-case scenarios.

Wouldn't a more likely reason be he'd left on his own?

She ran back inside, shoved her feet into sandals and

grabbed her purse. She paused to check his iPod, but she didn't know his pass code. Before she flipped out completely, she'd better cover any ground she could think of.

He could be at the park. Or the ice-cream shop. Or…

He wasn't allowed to go to any of those places by himself. And he'd never wandered off on his own before. She scratched a quick note telling Wyatt to call her on her cell phone if he came back. Fighting down a choking sensation, she got in her car and backed out of the driveway.

She couldn't prevent the fears drilling through her head. She stopped at the park, slamming the door shut behind her. Running through the play structure, she yelled Wyatt's name. Didn't see him or any sign of his friends, either. She went to the men's bathroom, opened the door. "Wyatt? Are you in there?" But no one answered.

He wasn't at the park.

Covering her eyes, she fought for breath. What could she do? Where could she go?

Get it together. You've got to find him.

She drove to the library, the ice-cream shop and finally ended up right back at Drew's cottage. She hunted through each room and the yard one more time before panic consumed her.

She could barely breathe.

There was one thing left to do. She had to call Drew.

"I can't find him. I don't know where he is and I've looked everywhere. The house, yard, park, library, dock—it's like he vanished!"

Drew froze, the skin at the back of his neck prickling as he held the phone. "Slow down. Start from the beginning."

Lauren's breathing sounded choppy. "I told him to get me if he needed anything. That the interview would only be thirty minutes."

"Did you leave him alone at the house?" Drew tried to make sense of what she was saying, but she sounded distraught. If only he was home and could take her in his arms and calm her enough to understand what she was saying...

"No! Of course not. I was on the phone, and I lost track of time."

"I'll text him."

"He left his iPod at home. What if he's been kidnapped? Or was hit by a car? Or he could have wandered into the woods. Oh, no—the lake! Could he have gone swimming? What if he drowned? I'm going out there right now!"

The phone went dead. He dialed her number, but she didn't answer. He fired into action, rushing down the hall to the chief's office.

The chief looked up from his desk. "What's wrong?"

"Lauren just called. She can't find Wyatt. I'm sorry, but I have to leave. I have to go look for him."

"Go." Chief Reynolds frowned, picking up his phone. "I'll get someone to cover for you. Take the rest of the day off and let me know when you find him."

Relief flooded Drew. He nodded. "Thank you."

"Get out of here. I'll make a few calls. Maybe someone has seen him."

Drew raced to his truck and called Lauren's number again. No answer. He texted, Stay put. I'm looking for Wyatt. The chief is calling around. Call me if you find him.

He peeled out of the lot and tried to think where

Wyatt would go. Lauren had said she'd gone to the park, but which one? Wyatt could easily ride his bike to three different parks within two miles. Drew gripped the steering wheel and pressed the accelerator.

He searched City Park first. No sign of the kid. Got back in his truck and drove to the big playground where most of Lake Endwell's youth hung out. The sun blasted his face as he strode around the play structure. He shielded his eyes with his hand, but none of the kids even resembled Wyatt.

Fear clutched his chest, but he inhaled and shook his head. *Keep your head on straight. You have plenty of places to look.*

What about Wyatt's friends? Drew had Hunter's parents' contact information. He gave Hunter's mom a quick call, but she hadn't seen Wyatt, and Hunter was camping up north with his grandparents all week.

Drew drove to the other park, but only a few young children were there. He sat in his truck, deciding his next move. What now?

Wyatt wouldn't try to see his dad, would he? The kid knew better. What about trying to get back to Detroit? *Doubtful.* But he couldn't take that possibility off the table yet.

Lauren had mentioned kidnapping. While the reporters and photographers were nuisances, they were hardly kidnappers. But with the magazine article recently published, who knew what kind of wacko might concoct a get-rich-quick idea?

Pressure built in his temples, and he dropped his forehead to his hands on the steering wheel.

God, I need You. Where is Wyatt? Help me find him. Please keep him safe wherever he is.

All Lauren's scenarios roared back. Kidnapping. Hit by a car. Lost in the woods. Drowning…

He pounded the steering wheel. *No.* He wouldn't let any of it happen. He was going to find Wyatt.

His cell phone rang. He hoped it was Lauren. The screen showed Tony Ludlow.

"Yeah."

"Check the football field behind the middle school," Tony said. "A bunch of kids Wyatt's age go over there for informal practices this time of year to get ready for the rec season next month. I don't know if he's there, but it can't hurt to look."

"It's worth a shot." Drew stared at the trees ahead of him. "Thanks, man. I'll go right now."

"Let me know when you find him."

"Will do."

Drew hung up and drove over the speed limit the short distance to Lake Endwell Middle School. He parked and jogged around the building to the back where a baseball diamond and a large field used for football and soccer sprawled. A dozen or so kids in shorts were running around in the distance. He could hear calls of "Blue 52." One threw a football. As he neared, he recognized Wyatt. Relief almost dropped him to his knees. *Thank You, Lord.*

As soon as the gratitude washed over him, fury erupted from his chest.

Wyatt might be all right, but that kid had a lot of explaining to do.

Drew strode, shoulders back, head high, out onto the field. The air had been full of shouting and laughing, but silence landed as the boys saw him. They parted like the Red Sea. Wyatt met Drew's eyes, and Drew recognized the fear in them.

Good. He should be afraid. Very afraid.

He gripped Wyatt's shoulder. "Come on. We're going home."

Wyatt had to jog to keep up with him on the way back to the parking lot. Drew didn't care. Kept a tight hold on his shoulder until they reached the truck. Wyatt was the first one inside. The windows were down, but the sticky heat remained. Drew knew better than to drive with this much anger boiling inside his body, so he took a moment to get his breathing back to normal.

He faced Wyatt. "Do you have any idea how worried we were?"

"Sorry," he mumbled, his chin dropping to his chest.

"Sorry isn't going to cut it, Wyatt. What were you thinking? You know we've been worried about all the photographers and reporters coming into town. We thought you might have been kidnapped. Lauren's scared out of her mind." He needed to call her. He pointed at Wyatt. "Don't move."

After hopping out of the truck, he walked a short distance away and called her. This time she picked up.

"What? Do you have news? There's no sign of him—"

His heart ached at how upset she sounded. "Lauren, I found him."

"Is he okay?"

"Perfectly fine. For the moment. Tony tipped me off. Some of the kids play football behind the middle school, and that's where I found him."

"The middle school?"

"Don't worry. I'm handling it. The chief gave me the

rest of the night off, so why don't you go home and I'll stop by your apartment later."

"I'm sorry," she whispered.

"I am, too." He hung up and texted Tony to let the guys at the station know he'd found Wyatt. He slipped the phone in his pocket and marched back to the truck. Slammed the door behind him.

"Start from the beginning." His jaw felt wired shut it was so tight.

"I didn't think—"

"You got that right. You didn't think. Didn't think about anyone but yourself. Lauren has been frantic with worry. I've been all over town, trying not to picture you lying in a ditch or being held against your will."

Wyatt shrank into himself. "I'm sorry." His tone shifted to a whine.

"Well, I hope you mean it, because you're going to be sorry before the day is over. Now tell me what happened." His words chopped like a knife, and he made no effort to soften them. He'd been too easy on Wyatt and look what had happened.

"Levi texted me that he wanted me to be on his team today."

"And what did you tell him?"

Wyatt glanced over. "I told him I couldn't."

"That's funny. Here you are. What changed?" He waved his hand toward the field.

He shrugged.

"Tell. Me. How. You. Got. Here."

"It wasn't a big deal." His voice rose. "He kept saying it would be fun. Lauren was busy with her interview, so I didn't think you'd care."

Drew clasped his hands so tightly his fingernails almost drew blood. "You didn't think I'd care, did you? What gave you that impression? Your dad doesn't want you playing football."

"He's not here!"

"But I am." Drew jabbed his thumb into his chest. "Don't you think I care about you?"

"Well, yeah, but…"

"But what? Look, Wyatt, I'm sorry your dad is in jail. You're not the only one who misses him. But it doesn't change facts. He's still your dad, and I'm your fill-in dad until he gets out. You might not like my rules, but you will obey them. Do you understand?"

"Yes, sir," he whispered.

"I love you, and you scared me. You scared Lauren, too. We aren't keeping you from having friends. If you want to spend time with Levi, we'll have him over."

"You won't let me hang out with him," he muttered.

"Is that right?" Drew clenched his jaw. "I don't recall you asking me to."

"That's because you won't let me play football!"

Drew counted to three. His temper had already surged to nuclear levels, and he needed to bring it down. "Let me get this straight. The only way you can hang out with him is if you play football?"

"Pretty much."

"So he doesn't want to ride bikes, go to the beach, get ice cream? He will only hang out with you on the football field?"

Wyatt shrugged again.

"I think you're making excuses. If it's true this kid won't be friends with you unless you're playing football, than he's not a very good friend." Drew started the truck up. "When we get home, you're going to your room. I have a lot to think about, and you *will* be punished. How did you get here, anyhow?"

"I climbed out the window and rode my bike."

"Well, you'd better go get it. I'll put it in the back of the truck." Drew waited for Wyatt to wheel his bike over, and, after putting it in the truck, Drew drove home.

As they passed houses and fields, he thought about his childhood. How he'd yell to his mom he was playing with his friends. She'd yell out, "Be back before dinner." And he would. He'd grown up in a subdivision outside town. He and his buddies would ride around and shoot hoops in one another's driveways. Just like Wyatt, they'd ride over to the football fields and throw the ball around. His mom never cared.

Maybe he'd come down too hard on Wyatt.

But Drew's childhood had taken place in different times. His father hadn't been a celebrity. Plus, Drew had never snuck out.

Drew stole a peek at Wyatt. The kid had that lost look again, the one he'd worn for months before moving here.

Had he been too hard on Wyatt? Not hard enough? Who knew? He needed a crash course in raising a ten-year-old who happened to be the son of an incarcerated football player. He had no idea how to parent this kid.

Had he given him the impression he could do whatever he wanted? He didn't want Wyatt to become the same entitled jerk he'd been in high school. Or was Wyatt lashing out at his dad's rule? He seemed to be trying to fit in with kids his age. But that didn't mean he could sneak out and play football when it had been forbidden.

Drew drove down Main Street. He'd have to figure out how to deal with Wyatt, but he also needed to check on Lauren. She'd been an emotional wreck on the phone. Drew turned into the parking lot behind her building.

"Don't make me see Lauren now." Wyatt cowered under his seat belt.

"You owe her an apology."

Wyatt looked ready to cry. "I'll tell her I'm sorry, Uncle Drew. But…but please let me do it tomorrow." Tears slipped down his pale cheeks.

Drew almost refused, but he couldn't. Wyatt seemed to be teetering on the same emotional edge as Lauren had earlier. Maybe it would be better for all of them if Drew smoothed things out with Lauren before bringing Wyatt over. With a loud sigh, he nodded. "First thing tomorrow. But I need to make sure she's okay. She was very upset earlier."

He didn't trust Wyatt to leave him alone in the truck right now. If Lauren's parents were home, they might not mind watching the kid for him while he checked on her. Unlike Wyatt, he couldn't wait until tomorrow.

Lauren swiped the hair from her eyes and slid another shirt off the hanger. With jerky hands, she folded it and shoved it into the suitcase on her bed. Zingo found a seat on top of the jeans she'd stacked inside the suitcase.

She'd messed up. Always messing up. And it had taken another bad phone call to acknowledge what she'd known for months.

She wasn't cut out for helping kids.

Not Wyatt.

Not Treyvon.

Not Jay.

And not any of the high school kids, either. She'd been

stupid to even consider it. And Principal Gilbert would regret it if she hired her.

She'd put herself and her needs first today, and Wyatt had paid the price. Her throat constricted for the fiftieth time since discovering Wyatt was missing. Her fault.

All her fault.

It wouldn't happen again.

And what about Drew? He'd depended on her, and she'd let him down. Visions of him smiling over coffee, eating breakfast together, the way he'd looked at her before kissing her—he deserved someone better. Not an imposter like her.

She'd known she was falling for him, but it wasn't until she'd called him to tell him about Wyatt missing that she knew she'd gone and done it.

She'd fallen in love with him.

And she'd broken his trust and not guarded Wyatt.

The fact that Wyatt was okay had made her collapse in the chair and thank the good Lord, but what if he had been kidnapped? Or drowned? Or any other awful thing? She would never have been able to forgive herself.

She had to get out of Drew's life. She loved him too much to disappoint him again. When he'd called her to let her know Wyatt was safe, she'd told him she was sorry. His reply had thrust a knife in her gut. *"I am, too."*

Of course he was. Sorry he hadn't listened to her all those weeks ago when she'd told him point-blank she wasn't the person for the job. She crushed a blouse between her hands. She'd been trying to overcome her failures her entire life. She'd learned at a young age she had to be good. Or else.

Look at what it had gotten her. No stability in her early years, made fun of constantly during high school, head in the clouds with visions of saving people in college and years and years of heartache in Chicago.

Now this.

A knock sounded at her front door. She wadded up the blouse and scurried down the hall. Drew stood in the doorway.

Fall into his arms. Let him hold you. Let him tell you everything will be all right.

She did none of those things. Instead she pivoted and strode back to the bedroom with him at her heels. Carefully folding the blouse, she braced herself for what he was about to tell her.

"What in the world is going on?" He skewered her with his brown eyes.

"What does it look like?"

"It looks like you're leaving."

"Ding, ding. You win the prize."

"Why?"

"I think we both know I can't do this anymore."

His eyes darkened to almost black. He looked like the warrior he was born to be. A rescuer. A leader. A hero.

But heroes saved the good guys, and she couldn't bear to keep up this charade another minute. She'd been trying to be good for almost thirty years. It was time to throw in the towel.

She'd never be good enough for Drew.

Chapter Twelve

Drew took in the half-filled suitcase on the bed, the cat sitting inside it, hangers on the floor and dresser drawers open. The room looked ransacked. She sure was in a hurry to get out of there. Out of his life.

Pain stabbed his heart, and in that instant he knew. He loved her.

He loved this woman who brought sunshine to his days, who'd coaxed Wyatt out of his protective shell, who cared about everyone more than she did herself.

He loved her, and she was leaving.

"Where are you going?" He knew whatever she was about to say was going to make him bleed. His mind sped to the morning his college football coach had called him into the office and told him he'd been cut from the team. It had been the worst day of his life.

Until today.

Didn't Lauren know this would destroy him?

He needed her. Wyatt needed her.

He shouldn't have let himself fall in love with her. She'd always been too good for him. He didn't deserve her, and he knew it. She must have finally realized it, too.

"I don't know where. Away." She set the blouse next to Zingo and returned to the closet.

She didn't know where she was going? Sounded like she was escaping.

Escaping him. He didn't blame her. He'd pushed and pushed her to help him with Wyatt, even after he knew it would be hard on her. Always thinking of himself.

"Wyatt's with your parents," he said, his voice surprisingly calm. "I hope that's okay. I thought I'd better talk to you before bringing him over."

She didn't meet his eyes. "Mom and Dad are good in situations like this."

He took the sweatshirt out of her hands. "Can we talk?"

"What is there to say?"

Was she being serious? His heart was thumping about a thousand beats per minute. "Let's go to the living room. I can't think with you packing."

She nodded, leading the way, sitting on the edge of the couch, ready to spring up at any moment.

She looked fragile. His agitation subsided, replaced with calm. "Lauren, what's going on?"

"I messed up." Her words tumbled out quickly, nervously. She sounded about ready to cry. "The interview took too long, and I knew something was going on with Wyatt. I knew it. Ever since visiting Chase, he's been acting secretive. I should have kept an eye on him. I should have rescheduled the interview for another time. I failed you. I failed him."

"What? That's crazy. This wasn't your fault." Drew moved to sit next to her, putting his arm around her shoulders.

She jerked away, standing. "It is. I can't do this anymore. You're going to have to find another babysitter. I'm calling the principal and withdrawing my application. I'm not cut out for working with kids."

His heart was already black and blue, and she'd only said a few words. How could he convince her to stay?

"Go back in there and unpack your suitcase. Wyatt is fine. He snuck out and rode his bike to the middle school because…well, I don't entirely know why, but I do know it had nothing to do with you."

She whirled to him, eyes stricken. "It has everything to do with me. I've been trained to look for signs, and all the signs were there, Drew. Sullen, scared, secretive. Spending too much time on that stupid iPod. I knew he was up to something, but I didn't want to believe it. I can't help anyone until I get my head out of the clouds. You think a parent is going to forgive me when I miss the signs their daughter was suicidal? No. It doesn't work that way." She hugged her arms around her waist.

He wanted to cup her face in his hands and make her look in his eyes and tell her he loved her and how much she meant to him. But she was ready to shatter. So he stayed put.

"There is nothing to forgive, Lauren. You give people hope. I don't want you to be anyone but exactly who you are."

"You say that, but you don't know me, Drew. You don't." Her eyes flashed silver. "I've never been who everyone thought I was. I'm the daughter of a drug addict and a murderer."

"You're the daughter of the King. God Himself."

She shook her head as if she didn't want to hear it. "Remember that duffel bag I told you about? What I didn't tell you is that I pulled a knife on a kid to get it back when I was six years old. Six! What six-year-old threatens someone with a knife? That foster home knew enough to get rid of me."

Each word landed like lead in his gut. He could picture her, a beautiful little girl. His entire being revolted at what she'd been through. He closed the distance between them.

"No six-year-old should have to defend her property herself. You should have had a mom and dad to protect you."

"I did. Later." The anguish gripping her face sent waves of pain through his chest. "They made me feel like I was good enough, but I'm not. I'm just not. I'm never going to be." Her shoulders sagged. She looked drained.

Drew gently took her in his arms. He kissed the hair next to her ear and held her, but she didn't hold him back.

"You're too good, Lauren. You want to help everyone. I don't know why you think you're such a failure. You're everything to me."

She stepped back. "Don't say that. I'm not. You can't depend on me. I'll let you down the same way I let everyone down."

"You wouldn't. You don't." How could he break through this crust of guilt encased around her heart? "I told you a while back I'm here for you. No matter what. That hasn't changed. I… I promise." He almost said the words *I love you*, but he couldn't. Not yet.

"I don't want your promise. I want to be alone." The finality in her tone and the tremors in her arms concerned him. He was getting nowhere with her. He didn't want to make it worse.

"I'll let you be alone for now, Lauren, but I keep my promises. Wyatt had a choice today. He chose to do the wrong thing. Those kids you're so upset about in Chicago? They had a choice, too. The older one could have said no to the gang. The younger could have stayed in his house where he belonged."

"I should have—"

He raised his hand to cut her off. "You know what? You have a choice, too. You can give up on all that's good about you, all that you bring to the world to make it better, or you can accept that life stinks sometimes, and you can keep trying. But I can't force you."

"Please go," she whispered.

Did his promise mean nothing to her? Did *he* mean nothing to her?

What had he expected? He'd known he wasn't good enough for her. Told himself over and over he'd get hurt if he let himself fall in love. He'd been living a dream—just like when he'd been on the college football team—and now the dream was over. Except this was worse. Much worse.

He wished he would have taken his own advice when he'd moved back and never let himself fall for Lauren Pierce.

He walked down the hall and left her apartment.

Lauren dropped onto the couch. Everything Drew said swirled, conflicted, collided in her brain. She didn't even know where to begin to make sense of today. The only thing she knew? He was wrong about her.

She couldn't get her head straight in this matchbox of an apartment. It suffocated her. She shoved her feet into athletic shoes, grabbed her keys and phone and ran out the door. When she got to the sidewalk, she didn't think, just jogged in the direction of the lake.

The truth of Drew's words nailed themselves into her soul, but she couldn't quite believe them.

You're the daughter of the King.

The park entrance loomed ahead, and she sped up. Could she outrun his voice? Could she outrun herself?

She sprinted along the trail next to the lake until she hunched over, gasping for breath. Why had she been packing her suitcase? It wasn't as if she had anywhere to go.

I'm still that little girl packing her bag, aren't I?

Exhaustion clawed through her body, and she collapsed on a park bench facing the lake. Seagulls swooped down to the water, calling to each other noisily.

"I am a mess." The words escaped without thought. She turned her head from side to side to see if anyone was around. No one lurked. She sighed in relief. Didn't want to add losing her mind to her list of shortcomings.

She leaned back. The sun warmed her face, and the scent in the air held the tang of the freshwater lake.

God, what am I doing? What do You want me to do?

A squirrel chattered a few yards away. He stood on his hind legs with a nut between his paws. Then he bit into the nut and ran away.

Being a squirrel seemed to be a lot less complicated than being a human.

Why am I making it so complicated?

Drew said they all had choices. She agreed with that. But—

How did she know the right choice? How could she trust herself to make the right decision?

She had a strong urge to go to her parents' house. To talk to her mom.

Had Wyatt and Drew left yet?

She texted her mom. Are you busy? Is Wyatt still there?

Almost instantly her mom replied. Drew picked him up a few minutes ago. Why?

She felt terrible for not seeing Wyatt since Drew found him, but she wasn't ready. She texted Mom back. I'm coming over.

Ten minutes later she found Mom in the kitchen.

"Wyatt upset you today, didn't he?" Mom's loving eyes crashed through the chaos inside her. Lauren drifted into her arms. "It's okay. He's okay. No harm done."

No harm done? She let that one slide and hugged her for a long time. Finally, she broke away.

"Come on," Mom said. "Let's go out to the living room. You can tell me all about it."

She didn't want to tell her all about it, but she followed her, anyway. A vase of daisies brightened the coffee table, and the faint smell of vanilla was in the air from one of her mother's candles. "Mom?"

"Hmm?"

"I'm a mess."

She smiled. "We're all a mess, honey."

"No, I'm truly a mess." Her mom never really got it that some people were more messed up than others. She acted like anything Lauren said or did could be washed clean with one of her dishcloths. "I've always been one."

"That's funny because when I look at you I see a beautiful, caring woman."

I've duped her, too. It's time she saw the real me.

"You see a fake. I've been fooling you and my teachers and everyone for years."

Her mom made a tsking sound. "Lauren, you've never fooled me. You're not a fake."

Would the woman not wake up?

"Look, Mom." Lauren leaned forward. "I was a rotten little girl. Got kicked out of four foster homes. I threatened a kid with a knife at one point. As an adult, I've made bad choices with some of my cases, and one boy is dead because of it. Another is in juvie. I didn't do my job today. Instead of babysitting Wyatt, I was on the phone getting interviewed for a job I'm not qualified for."

"Is that what you think?" Mom slowly shook her head. "You weren't kicked out of any foster homes. The first one was always meant as a temporary solution. The second one's parents had life circumstances they couldn't control, and they wanted better for you. The third family was prosecuted for abusing the kids. The fourth led us to you. You were no more rotten than any other kid out there. I don't care if you threatened anyone with a knife. Because I know you. Deep down, I know you. And that girl must have had a good reason to do it."

Emotion swelled in her chest. "But, Mom—"

"No, you're not going to convince me, Lauren. Nice try. You weren't responsible for that boy's death any more than you were responsible for Wyatt running off today. Look, these kids are doing things out of desperation, the same way you must have done."

Lauren knew that desperation. Had known it as a little girl. Still knew it now.

"Your dad and I are proud of you for wanting to help children, but don't ever think you're required to. If it's too hard, get into another field. God didn't put you on earth to save every soul you come into contact with. He's the one in the saving business. Let Him do His job."

Is that what she'd been trying to do? Save everyone? *Yes.*

Her mom was right. She almost laughed at her arrogance. Who did she think she was?

Mom took her by the shoulders and stared into her eyes. "Lauren, you do understand God loves you as is, right? You can't earn His love. It's a grace thing."

That sobered her up. *A grace thing.*

"I've never let anyone get too close," Lauren said softly. "I don't even think I've let God get too close."

"It's never too late." Mom held her arms open. Lauren embraced her, inhaling the rose scent of her mother's favorite soap.

"I think I'm in love with Drew Gannon."

Mom stepped back, her mouth dropping open. "It's about time."

Lauren did a double take. "What do you mean by that?"

"I've waited years and years for you to get serious with someone. I'm ready for grandbabies to spoil."

Grandbabies?

"Don't get your hopes up. I was pretty awful to him this afternoon."

"You're a strong woman. Go there and apologize."

"I can't."

"You can."

"No, I mean, it's over. An apology isn't going to cut it." She'd burned her bridges. She was good at it. Had kept herself an island most of her life.

"He's a good man. He stares at you like you're a princess. He's strong, kind, and he works hard. Go after him."

That was the problem. He was good and kind and stared at her like she was something more than she could claim.

"If God loves you exactly the way you are, and your dad and I certainly do, don't you think Drew does, too?"

Lauren squeezed her eyes shut. It had taken time, but she'd grown to accept and cherish her parents' unconditional love. But Drew? He had feelings for her, sure. But he didn't love her.

If God loved her exactly as she was and her parents did the same, why didn't she love herself, flaws and all? Was it even possible?

She had enough to think about right now, and all she wanted to do was go home, crawl into bed and pretend today had never happened.

Chapter Thirteen

Drew held a paper plate with two slices of pepperoni pizza. Wyatt held an identical plate. They sat side by side in chairs on the backyard deck. Neither had touched their food or said a word since Drew picked him up from the Pierces'. He didn't know what to say. His anger had dissipated. Confusion had taken its place.

He was used to running these situations by Lauren to find out what to do. But this time he was on his own. He couldn't ask her how to handle the aftermath of Wyatt sneaking out. Not now. Not after all he'd said to her earlier.

He'd pushed her too far.

Right when he'd needed her the most.

He loved her, and this was his punishment for all the things he'd done wrong over the years. He'd fallen in love with beautiful-inside-and-out Lauren Pierce, and she was leaving.

And his promise?

Might be the one promise he shouldn't or couldn't keep. He'd told her he'd always be there for her, that nothing she did could ever push him away, but he wasn't what she needed. He took and took, and what did he give back?

He'd pressed her into a babysitting job she didn't want to take. Today, he'd saddled her with a tense situation beyond her control. Why hadn't he taken a leave of absence after the *People* magazine article came out? He'd seen the signs in Wyatt, too. The secrets. The attitude. And he'd ignored them, carrying on as if nothing was wrong. It had been easier than facing the truth.

"Uncle Drew?" Wyatt still hadn't touched his pizza. His eyes darted back and forth like a scared rabbit's.

"What, Wyatt?"

"What's going to happen now? Are you going to send me away?"

Send him away? Why would the kid ever think that?

"No. I would never send you away."

"You promise?"

Drew waved his fingers between Wyatt's eyes and his own. "You and I are family. There's nothing you can do to make me send you away. Got it?"

"It's just—"

"I know. You feel bad. You should feel bad. That's your conscience telling you that you messed up. But God forgives all sins—so pray for forgiveness and move on. Don't think it means you aren't going to have consequences, though."

"I'm sorry. I'm really sorry, Uncle Drew." He hiccupped, and sobs shook his slim body.

"Hey, it's okay." Drew put his arm around his shoulders. "I forgive you. I did a lot of dumb stuff when I was your age."

Wyatt wiped his eyes, and Drew gestured for him to stand. He set Wyatt on his lap, not caring if he was too old. "The important thing is you learn from your mistakes."

"You made mistakes?"

"I did. Still do." He held Wyatt tightly.

"Like what?"

"Oh, all kinds of things. Mostly little things I knew better than to do. You know, like cutting in line, cheating on a test, being mean to the captain of the cheerleading squad. I learned the hard way to do the right thing, though, and you will, too. Later on, we're going to sit down and hash out some rules."

"Okay."

"But first I want you to tell me why you snuck around to go play football. Do you want to play that badly?"

Wyatt stiffened, then exhaled. "Some of my friends think it's cool Dad played football. They told me they wanted me to be on their football team. I told them no, but they kept asking, and when I didn't say yes, they stopped talking to me."

"It is cool your dad played pro football. But you're cool, too. You don't need a superstar father to be someone worth hanging out with."

"After the magazine came out, one of them said I couldn't play because my dad was a jailbird."

Drew shifted his jaw. Why were kids so cruel?

"And I told him I could do whatever I wanted."

"So you did." Wyatt's actions made more sense now that Drew knew the backstory.

Wyatt nodded. "I miss Dad."

"I do, too."

"Uncle Drew, can I tell you something, and will you promise not to get mad?"

He hated promises like that, but he nodded.

"I used to think Dad had to go after Len, but I don't think he had to at all. What about me? Why didn't he think about me?" He covered his face with his hands and cried. Drew rubbed his back, emotions pressing against his chest. This was one promise easy to keep.

"That's normal, buddy. I'm mad at him, too. I kept excusing him, telling myself what a great friend he's been—and he is a good friend, my best friend—but I didn't want to admit how much I miss him. How I wish he would have thought about you and me before he did it."

"Me, too."

"I think we need to forgive him. Both of us. He's a good man. He's still your dad. Still my best friend. He made a mistake, and he knows it. We're going to be okay until he gets out."

He lifted his head, his eyes swimming in tears. "I want to visit him again."

"It will be a little easier next time. We'll be ready for the pat down." Drew grinned and pretended to pat Wyatt's sides. He laughed. "And, listen, if you really, truly want to play football, I will talk to your dad about it."

Wyatt twisted his lips, considering. "I think I want to try soccer with Hunter."

"I'll sign you up tomorrow."

Wyatt hopped off his lap and returned to his seat. He took a big bite of his slice. After he'd chewed it, he said, "I shouldn't have gone today. I'm sorry. Think Lauren will forgive me?"

"She's just glad you're okay. But you still need to apologize to her. No bike riding unless it's with me, and I'm taking your iPod for two weeks."

"Two weeks?" he wailed.

"Want to make it three?"

Wyatt's lips lifted into a shy smile. "Two's fair."

They ate their pizza in the peace of the summer night. Maybe he wasn't so bad at raising Wyatt. Maybe he didn't need anyone's help.

He might not need it, but he wanted it. Lauren made everything easier. She was the part of him that had been missing his whole life.

And he'd blown it.

Lauren unlocked her apartment after leaving her parents' house and switched on the lights. She felt like she'd been hit by a truck. She idly browsed the stack of mail in her hands as she kicked the door shut behind her. Catalog, bill, advertising postcard. Tempted to dump it all in the trash, she moved the bill to the top of the pile and almost missed the letter underneath.

Treyvon.

Her breathing hitched. She stared at the plain white envelope for a long time. Then she went to the couch, curled her legs underneath her body and opened it. Unfolding the sheet, she paused. *Lord, whatever this letter contains, help me. Just help me read it.*

Neat handwriting and meticulous margins greeted her. Treyvon's teacher hadn't been kidding when she said he was a good student.

Miss Pierce,

I got your letter. If I would have gotten it a week earlier, I would have wadded it up and thrown it in the trash, but things happened I can't explain. You say you believe in God. I did, too, but after Jay died, I stopped believing. I had nothing left to live for.

Two days before your letter came, a pastor made his weekly visit. I ignored that guy. God ignored me all my life. But something happened this time. The words the pastor said broke through. I finally understood the difference between believing there was a God and trusting in Jesus as my Savior. You probably think I'm crazy. Maybe I am. Anyway, after talking to the pastor, I prayed for a reason not to give up. When I opened your letter, I was sure you were going to tell me I was stupid and killed Jay. I know I'm the reason he died. He was trying to stop me. They told me they'd kill him if I didn't rob the store, but they killed him anyhow. I'll always live with that.

I was scared to open your letter, but hearing about the stuff you went through gave me hope. Thank you for writing. I hope you do it again.
Treyvon Smith

She folded the letter and slipped it back inside the envelope, pondering his words.

She'd poured her heart into the one she'd sent him. Told him about feeling unwanted. Shuffled off from home to home. Pulling the knife on that kid. How she still struggled to know her place in the world. She'd told him she wanted him to know he wasn't alone. That she cared about him. She'd asked him for forgiveness, for not helping them in time.

There were no coincidences. Three weeks ago she wouldn't have written the letter. She would have clung to her guilt, her need to blame Treyvon to assuage that guilt and her self-pity about the situation. She would not have reached out to him.

Three weeks ago, if she *would* have reached out to him, he would have thrown her letter in the trash, and she would have assumed he blamed her, never to write him again.

God, You worked in my heart at just the right time. And You worked in Treyvon's heart at the right time. You sent the pastor when Treyvon was ready to hear the words. Oh, God, You truly are awesome! How did You take a preppy girl from sleepy Lake Endwell and an impoverished teen from a gang area and unite us in spirit? How did You change my heart? How did You change his?

The pastor. The Bible. Prayer. Her parents. Drew. All worked together to begin healing them.

Her mom had said something she'd been trying to ignore, but it grew louder in her mind until it drowned out her other thoughts.

God didn't put you on earth to save every soul you come into contact with. He's in the saving business. Let Him do His job.

It really *was* a grace thing.

Tears sprung to her eyes, falling down her cheeks in little rivers. *Thank You, Jesus!*

The burden she'd been carrying vanished. She felt free. Free! She smiled through her tears. Wanted to jump in the air. Why not? She got to her feet, pumped her hands in the air and did a tuck. Laughed as she landed. Boy, she needed to stretch before she attempted that again.

She didn't deserve forgiveness, this apartment, her health, her parents, Wyatt, Drew—anything! She never had deserved them. Never would! But God gave them to her because He loved her.

He loves me.

She sobered up at the word *love*. She loved Drew. And she'd thrown him out. Literally kicked him out of her apartment. She'd driven him away.

Out of fear.

Out of shame.

Out of guilt.

He'd made her a promise, and she'd told him she was letting him out of it. Had she driven him away for good?

She would have to apologize. Beg. Get on her knees if necessary. But she had to tell him how she felt—how she really felt.

Drew had to be mad at her. She didn't want to tell him she loved him in front of Wyatt if things got heated. The kid didn't need more drama in his overly dramatic life. And, frankly, she'd been so awful earlier, a simple apology and "By the way, I love you," weren't going to cut it.

How could she get Drew alone?

An idea formed. A wonderful, scary idea.

God, give me the courage.

Drew dangled his legs off the edge of the dock and into the warm lake. Stars blinked overhead, and a crescent moon reflected off the water. He'd tucked Wyatt in an hour ago, and after tidying the living room and trying to avoid the tangled web of thoughts in his head, he gave up and came out here. What was he going to do about Lauren?

He'd told Wyatt earlier he'd done a lot of dumb things as a kid. He'd done them as an adult, too. And God had forgiven every stupid thing he'd done.

Had Drew really done anything that dumb with Lauren? So he'd pushed her. He'd probably do the same again. It drove him nuts she was missing all the great parts of herself by focusing on what she perceived as her failures.

Kind of like I've done since I moved back here.

Lauren was kind, generous, strong, courageous and compassionate. She had a lot of great parts to focus on. Unlike him.

Says who?

Why was he still defining himself by his past?

He was doing a decent job raising Wyatt. His coworkers were accepting him. So he'd acted like a jerk in high school. He'd outgrown that. And big deal he'd gotten kicked out of college. He'd been blessed with a career doing something he loved.

Were he and Lauren doing the same thing? Clinging to regrets for no reason?

Her early years had done a number on her. He frowned, thinking of the things she'd told him. She probably hadn't felt worth loving.

Did she still not feel worth loving?

Didn't he feel the same? Was *he* worth loving?

Leaning back, he rested his hands on the deck. If he'd learned anything from his mistakes, he'd learned not to give up on himself.

He didn't want to give up on this. On her, on them, on what they could be.

If he was really the man he thought he was, he wouldn't give up because she told him to leave during an emotional meltdown. That would be like not showing up to those team meetings in college. Or getting halfway into a burning building and calling it quits.

He'd been trained to see things through.

She was worth fighting for. He wasn't giving up on her. Not now. Not tomorrow. Not next year.

Whatever it took, however long it took, he would fight for her.

Chapter Fourteen

"What would I do without you, Megan?" Lauren lugged the stack of doughnut boxes from the trunk of her car. Closing it, she took a deep breath. "Thank you. Thank you so much."

"Are you kidding me? I feel like we're on a secret mission. For love! Aah!" Megan clapped her hands, her eyes shining. "Don't worry. Ben and Tony will get Drew and Wyatt to the station. And then you can whisk Drew away, and we'll take care of Wyatt." Megan gave her a knowing stare. "For as long as it takes."

Lauren walked toward the station door. "It might not take long. I was obnoxious yesterday. I can't believe how rude I was."

Megan waved her hand as if her words meant nothing. "We all say stupid stuff when we're upset. He'll get over it. He probably already has."

Maybe. Maybe not. "Thanks for all your help with this. You're brilliant."

"I'm glad you asked me! Oh, look at the time—we'd better get in there."

"I'm nervous. He's going to reject me. I can feel it."

"That's your nerves talking."

"But what if—"

Megan placed her hand on Lauren's arm. "Calm down. If it doesn't work out, I have the whole day off, and we'll get through it. Together. But you don't have to worry. He likes you."

Likes? Or loves? There was a big difference.

They arrived at the doorway too soon. Maybe she should leave. She hadn't had time to talk herself out of this, and the more she thought about it, the more she felt like she was going to throw up.

Telling Drew she loved him? Asking his forgiveness? *Bad idea.*

Bad.

But Megan had already gone inside, and Tony was holding the door open.

Lord, I can't do this. I'm a coward! My parents chose me, but I've never chosen anyone. I've been too afraid all this time. How can I do it now?

Tony frowned, letting the door close behind him. "You okay?"

"I don't know." She shook her head.

"I'm impressed you've helped Drew out with Wyatt all this time. And, hey, it's nice of you to bring all these doughnuts. Don't worry, I called him this morning. Three times. They're on their way."

Her nerves settled the tiniest bit. She didn't make a habit of sharing her feelings with anyone, but she was desperate. "Tony?"

"What?"

"He's pretty great, isn't he?"

Tony grinned and patted her shoulder. "He is. Why

don't you collect your thoughts out here, and I'll make sure Ben and Megan aren't getting too cozy inside."

She let out a nervous laugh and sat on the bench near the door. Chewed on a fingernail as she crossed one leg over the other, kicking nervously. Her stomach couldn't be any more rowdy. It was as if the national cheerleading competition was taking place in there.

What if this didn't work? What if he never wanted to see her again? What if...

"Lauren?" Drew approached her with Wyatt next to him. "What are you doing here?"

"I had to talk to you. To both of you." She rose, holding her arms open to Wyatt, hugging him tightly for a long time.

"I'm sorry, Lauren," Wyatt said. "I didn't mean to scare you yesterday. I feel really bad."

She pressed her lips to his soft hair. "I forgive you. I'm so thankful you're safe." She stepped back, peering into his eyes. "You scared me to death, though. Don't you know how important you are to me?"

Wyatt blinked rapidly. "I guess I do now."

"Well, don't forget it. I love you, Wyatt. Don't ever scare me like that again."

He grinned. "I won't."

"Come on—let's go inside. Megan and I brought doughnuts for everyone. We wanted to thank them for helping us find you." Wyatt opened the door, and Lauren put her hand on Drew's arm. "Can we talk in a little bit?"

His face was unreadable. "Sure."

She wished she could decipher his tone. They went inside to the kitchen. Everyone was munching on doughnuts, laughing and sipping juice or coffee. Ben put his arm around Wyatt's neck and was pretending to rub his head. Wyatt laughed.

"Thanks for helping us out yesterday." Drew pulled Tony into a half embrace.

She couldn't help thinking Tony and Drew had more in common than they realized. Now if she could just get Drew to view *her* differently...

"No problem, man. Um, I think someone wants to talk to you." Tony widened his eyes, nodding at Lauren.

Drew rubbed the back of his neck. "Will you guys watch Wyatt for a minute?"

Megan scooted to his side. "Ben and I want to take Wyatt for a pontoon ride later. Would that be okay with you?"

"Let me ask Wyatt."

While Drew discussed the plan with Wyatt, Lauren pulled Megan to her side and whispered, "I can't do this. I'm going to hurl."

"You can do it," she whispered back. "You walked the streets of Chicago. You're tough."

"But that was just drug dealers and gangs. This is Drew."

"Go." Megan took her by the shoulders, turned her and marched her down the hall to the garage, where the fire trucks and ambulances were parked. "I'll send him out there."

The garage doors were open, letting in the brilliant sunlight. Lauren walked on shaky legs to the ladder truck and sat on the front bumper.

And when she looked up, Drew stood in front of her, legs wide, arms crossed over his buff chest. The man was dangerously good-looking. And his personality clinched the deal. Her heart did a double back handspring. She rose. Swallowed.

"I'm sorry." She forced herself to look into his eyes. They didn't seem to hate her. "I'm sorry I threw you out. I'm sorry I acted like your promise meant nothing to me. It wasn't nothing. It's not nothing. Besides the day my parents told me they were adopting me, it was the best thing I've ever heard."

Drew's mouth had opened while she spoke, but she didn't give him a chance to respond.

"I kind of flipped out yesterday. Like everything that had been building inside me my entire life snapped. I never realized I was trying to make up for my early childhood by being perfect. Mom told me some stuff that hit home with me. And I wanted to believe it, but I couldn't let myself."

Drew inched closer. The muscle in his cheek flexed.

"I got a letter from Treyvon. It helped open my eyes to reality. I've thought I had to be in control all this time, making the right choices, helping anyone I could, but I had it all wrong. God is in control. He's led me to situations where I could help, but ultimately, it wasn't up to me."

Drew moved closer. So close she could smell his aftershave and see the pulse in his throat. "Lauren—"

"I'm not done." She looked up into his eyes, took a deep breath. "You're right. We have choices. And I chose to push you away, but I don't want to anymore. I'm grateful for you. You don't let anything stop you from achieving your goals. I'm amazed at how good you are with Wyatt. I'm dumbfounded you're so good to me. I don't deserve it."

Drew hauled her to him, the warmth of his chest

seeping into hers, and claimed her lips. She had more to say, but his arms surrounded her, protecting her, cherishing her, and she forgot the rest of her speech. None of it mattered, anyhow. She kissed him back.

"Drew, thank you for believing in me, for allowing me to get close to you and Wyatt. You made me a promise, and now I'm making one of my own. No matter how messy or difficult life gets, I won't run away. Because I love you."

"Are you about done, woman?" With his forehead against hers, Drew stared into her eyes, keeping his arms locked around her waist.

Lauren Pierce had just told him she loved him.

It seemed inconceivable. For years, he'd had to fight for everything he wanted. He'd fully expected to wake up and fight for her today. Two dozen pink roses sat in his truck. When Tony had called this morning, he'd refused to come to the station, but by the third call, he'd given up. Decided when he got here, he'd ask someone to watch Wyatt for an hour while he tried to convince Lauren they were right for each other.

The magnitude of God's blessing filled him with wonder.

He held her hands. "There is nothing to forgive. I knew you were upset yesterday, and I shouldn't have pushed you."

"Yes, you should have. I needed it. You were right about all of us having choices."

"I went home last night and had a long talk with Wyatt. He knows he made the wrong one. I think part of him did it to get back at Chase, if that makes sense. And the other part wanted to impress some kids."

"It does make sense. Those bruised and bloody parts inside us make us do things we know aren't smart. I should know."

"I know, too. I've been stuck in regrets. You helped me see I've changed. Before I moved here, I'd been hiding from my past. Let's face it—I avoided Lake Endwell for more than a decade. But you didn't see me the way I saw myself. And if anyone should have, it was you. Lauren Pierce, I love you."

"You do? But I—"

"Yes, I love you. I couldn't love you more than I do right here, right now. I'll get on the speaker system and announce it to the entire fire station if I have to, but I want you to be one hundred percent certain of this—I love you, and I'm never giving up on you."

Tears slipped down her cheeks. "You really love me? I didn't think you could—"

He silenced her with his lips. He couldn't believe his dream girl was in his arms. Genuine—Lauren was genuine.

With a contented sigh, she pulled away. "If you change your mind—"

"Will you be quiet for one minute?" he asked. She blinked. "I've loved you for a while, but I didn't want to admit it."

She grinned, tracing his cheek with her finger. "Same here. So you're not mad? I don't have to get on my knees and beg?"

The only way to get her to stop talking seemed to be kissing her. He pressed his lips to hers again. She tasted like forever.

Reluctantly, he ended the kiss. "You made me see I'm capable of more than I thought. I was clueless about raising Wyatt through all this drama before you had mercy on us. You've given me confidence. Not just in being Wyatt's father, but in myself in general. I don't know how I got so blessed to have you, but I'm not letting you go. Ever."

"Good. I don't want you to let me go. Ever."

He got lost in her eyes, smiling in understanding.

"So yesterday you said you were withdrawing your application to be the high school counselor."

She shook her head. "Not anymore. I think for the first time in my life I'm truly prepared to help emotionally damaged kids. It's not all on my shoulders anymore. It's on God's."

"Smart woman." He loved the way she felt in his arms. "Do you still want to babysit Wyatt? You don't have to. I can find someone else if it's too much."

"I want to. I've always wanted to. I love Wyatt, and the thought of losing him scared me so much." She stood on her tiptoes and kissed him, then added, "Do you still want me to babysit?"

"I clearly haven't convinced you." He claimed her lips, but the sound of applause made him lift his head. *What in the world?*

Everyone who'd been in the kitchen stood in the garage and whooped and hollered.

Wyatt ran to Drew, and he scooped the kid into his arms. "So, buddy, I kind of fell in love with your babysitter."

"She's really pretty, Uncle Drew." He smiled, all teeth, up at Lauren. She laughed.

"She sure is."

"I have a confession, too, Wyatt. I kind of fell in love with your uncle."

"Well, he is a firefighter." Wyatt made it sound as if that explained everything.

"He sure is."

"Are you two going to get married?"

A hush fell over everyone.

Drew glanced at Lauren, her eyes shining bright, and he smiled. "Let's take it one day at a time, okay?"

"Hey, Wyatt," Megan said. "Let's let the two love-birds have some privacy. We'll go out on the lake."

"Yes!" Wyatt pumped his fist in the air. "Can I drive the pontoon?"

"You're way too young." Ben put his arm around Wyatt's shoulders, leading him away.

Drew took Lauren's hand and dragged her out of there to where his truck was parked. He pulled the bouquet out of the backseat and handed it to her. "I was on my way over to convince you to give us a chance."

"Too late. I'm convinced." She lifted the pink roses to her nose, beaming, and inhaled their scent. "All these beautiful flowers for me?"

He wrapped her up in his arms. "Everything for you. That's a promise."

Epilogue

"Stop fidgeting."

"I can't help it." Drew clasped his hands as he stood next to Tony at the front of the church. Today was the day. Lauren Pierce would soon be Lauren Gannon. *Thank You, Lord.*

They'd dated all summer, and he'd asked her to marry him at halftime during the homecoming football game at Lake Endwell High. Her cheerleading squad had helped him plan it. All he'd known was she'd said yes. And now here it was, almost Christmas, and he couldn't be happier. Or more nervous.

He glanced over at Wyatt at the end of the line of his groomsmen. Wyatt gave him a thumbs-up. Drew winked back. He wished Chase could be there, but it would be a few more years before he'd be out of prison. Surprisingly, Chase had started writing Treyvon after Drew had mentioned the kid's situation. Chase had become Treyvon's mentor and planned on working with at-risk youth when he was released.

The prewedding music stopped, and everyone stood. Drew's breath caught at the sight of Lauren. The organ began playing as Lauren walked up the aisle on her father's arm. Drew hadn't thought she could be more beautiful, but today she positively glowed. Her white gown had short cap sleeves, lace overlays and intricate beading. It showed off her slim waist, and her hair was piled on top of her head. She carried a bouquet of pink roses. After handing the bouquet to Megan, her maid of honor, she hugged her dad, and he placed her arm on Drew's.

Sweat broke out on his forehead, but he didn't dare wipe it away. He glanced her way, and she smiled. That smile did something to him. His nerves fled. Joy filled his heart. He tucked her hand more closely under his arm. His to protect. To cherish.

"Do you take this man to be your husband?"

"I do."

He slid the ring on her finger, meeting her gaze, promising her forever with his eyes.

She was really his.

The service went by in a flash. Drew and Lauren strolled down the aisle together, and before the bridesmaids and groomsmen joined them, he dragged her to the side.

"Lauren?"

"Yes?" Her teeth sparkled she was smiling so wide.

"We're married."

"I know." She scrunched her nose, sounding awed.

He claimed her lips, holding her close. He couldn't believe he was privileged enough to spend the rest of his life with this amazing woman.

"Okay, okay, break it up, you two." Tony clapped him on the shoulder. The bridesmaids and groomsmen formed a circle around them. "We have a little surprise for you. It's a tradition."

Chief Reynolds popped his head into the group. "For the record, I know nothing about this." He waved and left.

"You're coming with us." Tony grinned.

Lauren elbowed Drew. "Do you know anything about this?"

"Not a clue." But he could guess.

"Everybody to the station."

A gentle snow fell as they stepped outside, and Lauren laughed, still carrying her bouquet.

"Are you cold? Take my jacket." He shrugged off his tuxedo jacket and draped it over her shoulders. He slipped his arm around her waist and lifted her off her feet, carrying her the short distance to his truck, which had been decorated with balloons and a "Just Married" sign.

"Did you do this?" Lauren asked.

"Nope."

They stared at each other a minute in the truck and burst out laughing.

"This is fun," she said. "No one told me getting married was fun."

"It is. Getting married to *you* is fun." He leaned across the seat and kissed her.

A few minutes later they pulled up to the fire station. The garage doors stood open, and the bridal party and everyone on duty had lined up by one of the trucks.

"Do I even want to know?" Lauren asked. Drew grabbed her hand and they ran inside.

"Attention, everyone." Tony raised his hands. "Our own Gannon the Cannon got married today. You know what this means."

They all solemnly nodded.

"Drew, if you want the marriage to last, you need to kiss her on the fire truck."

One of the guys whooped.

"I'll kiss her for you, Drew," another hollered.

"Not on your life, Miggs," Drew shot back. Laughter erupted.

Tony brought Drew's helmet over and handed it to Lauren. "Sorry, sweetheart, but this might mess up your hair."

"So it guarantees a lasting marriage?" She pretended to consider it. "I'll take messed-up hair."

She set the helmet on her head, and Drew climbed onto the side of the truck. He held his hand out and hauled her up. Her body brushed his.

"Go on already, Gannon. Kiss the girl!"

He grinned, not taking his eyes off Lauren.

And he kissed her.

"How was that?" he asked.

She glanced up sideways and bit her lip. "Umm…"

His kiss wasn't up to her standards? He'd show her. This time he captured her lips, luxuriating in her touch, and he didn't let up.

"Whoa, there. Get a room, you two!"

He stepped down and held his arms wide. She jumped into them.

"I have everything I'll ever need right here in my arms," he whispered into her ear.

"You're all I'll ever need. I love you, Drew."

"I love you, too, Mrs. Gannon. Forever. I will never let you go."

* * * * *